Alone

Anna Michelle Page

 Lunebrook Publishing

Copyright © 2025 by Anna Michelle Page

Cover Design by Melissa Williams Design

Cover copyright © 2025

Lunebrook Publishing
PO Box 146 West State Road 56 West Baden Springs, Indiana 47469
lunebrook.com

Originally published in U.S. Trade Paperback Edition and ebook:
September 2025

The Lunebrook name and logo is a trademark of Lunebrook Publishing.

The publisher is not responsible for websites (or their content) that are not owned by the publisher.

Lunebrook provides authors for speaking events. To find out more, go to lunebrook.com or email dee@lunebrook.com

Library of Congress Cataloging-in-Publication Data has been applied for.

ISBNs: 979-8-9992919-1-2 (trade paperback), 979-8-9992919-0-5 (ebook)

This book is dedicated to my mother
for teaching me the love of words.

1

Shuddered at the Image

The windowpane captured the reflection of London's back in the evening sun as she dressed for work. Grabbing a shirt off the dresser, she shuddered at the image. The sight horrified and tormented London since Blake had inflicted the lesions that crisscrossed her skin.

Flicking the calendar by her bedside, she bent over to pull on a slant heel Ariat bootie. *Eight years, eleven months, and twenty-two days. I'm still alive, asshole.*

Without mirrors, London rarely saw the scars. Raised earthworm-shaped scars marked her, a constant reminder of Blake's claim on her life and the blade he'd used to brand his girls. Not seeing them didn't keep her from calculating the days as a reminder.

A deep breath, a glance at the clock, and she shoved her nightmare into the past. "I am alone. Alone is safe."

With one foot thrust into a bootie, she ran out the door of her rooftop apartment, down two flights of stairs, hobbling into the Whiskey River Saloon below, before pulling on the second boot. She passed through the doors as the Whiskey Boys, the bar's only band, covered George Strait's "I Hate Everything."

A deep breath, a glance at the clock, and she shoved her nightmare into the past. "I am alone. Alone is safe."

Late, again.

Foul-faced Claire Paczynski glared at London with a Jekyll-to-Hyde transformation. The head chef and overseer of the saloon, Claire, hated London's lackadaisical attitude. Her scowl grew more intense, creating deep lines around her eyes, as London skittered past into Joe's office. Joe Park managed the paperwork, and London catered drinks to thirsty American soldiers stationed at the Harry S. Truman Marine Base in Cheondochon, South Korea.

This month was her sixth working at the saloon, a cover-up to the trio's true purpose in Asia to rid the world of a super engine or die trying. She hated the job, serving drinks to sloppy soldiers who'd left their manners in the States. Men who would die for one another yet still considered women entertainment.

Around ten, London noticed six Korean soldiers arrive, easy targets since few locals showed up at the Whiskey River. They sat in Claire's section between the entrance and the bar.

London studied the men while she set a round of beers on a nearby table, watching for any clue her cover had been compromised. With the last Michelob placed, a callused hand covered hers, drawing her attention back to the soldier at her side.

She gave the man a playful smile and bent close. "Do you like me, sergeant?" Her long fingers, tendrils of affection, caressed his jutted bristly jawline. The cocky gunnery sergeant's pronounced dimples deepened, then vanished as London's finger pressed into a point between his jaw and neck. "You're new here, aren't you?"

Unable to release the hold he'd taken on her wrist and his body paralyzed by pain, he grunted.

London bent closer, eyes a hurricane of sea-green, and whispered, "Death by honor is found on the battlefield." *Learn it, creep.*

The confrontation went unnoticed by the noisy crowd. London straightened and carried the tray back to the bar, having reduced the proud soldier to a shriveled version of himself.

That's how her evening, every evening, went. A night of lascivious gestures, her nostrils clogging with the pungent stench of yeast and bourbon. The work-worn hands of men that touched her, their greedy eyes hidden behind fake smiles, while country songs urged the customers towards a night of frenzy and ill-repute.

Claire pulled London's tray across the bar and removed the empty mugs. "What happened over there?"

London leaned against the bar. With her back to Claire and her attention drawn toward the Korean soldiers, she asked, "What?"

"That soldier looks pale."

After a quick glance at the pale sergeant, London said, "Perhaps," and tossed a handful of bills on the counter. "He's new here. So," she hung onto the 'o,' "I introduced myself."

Claire unkinked the money. "Stupid bitch. We need happy customers to keep this dump hole going."

London swiveled the stool, unfazed by Claire's hatred, and placed bent arms on the bar, pulling the change under with an unmanicured hand. "What's with the local clan?"

Claire's anger dwindled to a mild disgust as she bent forward. "I'm wondering the same thing. You think they're watching us?"

London shrugged.

The lead mustang sat straight in his chair, a hand on

his beer. She enjoyed referring to all men as mustangs, not just this one.

When they arrived, London noticed he wasn't the loftiest of the bunch but displayed an air of command with ease and confidence. The tallest, a burly soldier with arms the size of a 1966 Lamborghini Miura's headlights, stood around six-foot-three.

Lifting the tray of shot glasses and a bottle of Wild Turkey, London took mental notes of each man around the table until she settled on the youngest and found him watching her.

An instant smile warmed his pretty-boy features.

His charm might make other women flush, but her skin crawled with disgust, which bordered on the threshold of hate. With a thud she slammed a whisky bottle on a nearby table. Too busy to give the strangers more thought, she tended to her tables, grateful when she balanced her last tray of empty bottles for the night.

Joe had come out of his office and was busy wiping the bar. "Tips good?"

"Never."

Wiping down the bar was Joe's nightly ritual—a way to study the crowd.

He understood people in a way London couldn't. He saw them as opportunities, while London saw the men as wild horses, clamping their opponent's necks as they drove them to the earth. Injury and death risked for mating rights.

She smelled one of them approaching now, a young colt with an overpowering scent of testosterone, a mixture of vanilla and cheese. The smell overwhelmed her nostrils as he grew closer.

At her side, he drew in a long breath. His exhale reminded her of a stallion's victorious snort. His intended reward? London.

"When does your shift end?"

London tucked her roll back into its pouch and, pushing the tray away, turned. A masculine arm covered in light hair blocked her path, his hand on her waist. Private Nelson leaned in. "Come on, baby. I've been asking for weeks. Let's make tonight unforgettable."

Assessing the situation, London gauged the distance from her knee to the private's groin. She'd killed men more like bull elephants in musth. To subdue this one . . . *Simple.* "If you don't remove your hand from my waist, this night will earn number one on your most embarrassing moments. One . . ."

Private Tony Nelson's arm dropped, and his body stiffened. His face contorted in obvious pain.

Her rescuer? The lead Korean mustang.

London watched Nelson struggle, unable to free himself from the enemy who held him. Satisfaction rose in her throat, a sickening pleasure rushed through her veins.

She delighted in the scene the way she often relished a good comic book. London admitted she admired the lead mustang, who stood six inches shorter than the six-foot-five sergeant, appreciating his unclear style and undisputable technique as she asked, "Do you need help?"

He winked. His dark eyes penetrated her inner thoughts as if he understood her. When he spoke, his soft accent carried a menacing tone as the private's pupils widened. "Koreans respect customs, and customs call for respect. You disrespect lady." His minimal English difficult to decipher but his simple message resonated.

London stared at Nelson, amused by the twist of pain on his face, though unsure what method her rescuer used. *A crippling twist of the private's arm? Hmmm . . . Interesting.* Rather than wait for an apology, she took a second look at those dark irises and turned to wipe tables.

As she moved through the remaining customers, the Boys, as they were affectionately called, performed "Meant to Be," by Bebe Rexha and Florida Georgia Line. She stole a glimpse at the dark-skinned man. He stood at the cash register. When he scanned the room, their eyes locked.

London shivered and questioned for a second time whether he'd been assigned to track her. Flat monolids broke the connection. He handed Joe money and tucked his wallet into a back pocket. As he walked out the door, he turned to look at her again. The look kindled a long-forgotten passion deep in the layers of London's fortified wall.

A customer yelled, "Come on baby, get me a beer!"

Shaken, the trance broke. "Sorry, soldier. My shift is over. If you're thirsty, I hear the Korean bars stay open all night."

Minutes later, she walked past the soft-spoken commander's empty seat. He'd left, but the residue of his presence lingered.

The stallion, without a name, or knowing what he drank, had stepped inside the repressed responses of her subconscious and out again, leaving behind a lingering longing. A visceral uniting that demanded exploration. A blood bonding, perhaps. *Will one, or both of us, perish?*

Mesmerized, she wondered how this man had rattled her. Her. Of all people. She detested men, so how had he stepped into her life like a footprint in the mud and made himself a part of her?

Later, as she lay in bed, thoughts of him ran through her mind. She covered her eyes.

His gaze had held her captive. She wanted to see him. Hoped she'd see him. Even tingled with anticipation at the thought of battling a man she recognized as an equal in skill. If not to kill him . . . *Why? Because he saved me?* She curled on herself with a deep, cynical guffaw.

A hero. Me? Really? What do I need with a hero?

Staring at the ceiling, she imagined him standing there. Humor, not hate, had twinkled in the depth of his whisky-brown eyes. Nor had those eyes roamed to her breasts. His pupils, normal. She jolted upright, heart hammering against her ribs.

He saw me. He knows who I am.

Shaken and vulnerable, London pulled the covers over her head, cocooning herself within its protective shell.

Stupid girl. You're a killer.

She focused, crushing hope. The job mattered. *Not this.* Dead, none of this would matter. Not this place, the job, nor him.

Fingers spread—tips pressed against the blanket, imaginary blood ran across her hands and onto visions of her semen-covered belly.

Screaming, she pulled the blanket tight around her head, cutting off any air that might seep through the fibers.

Can I survive him?

2

Jingle of the Doorbell

The Boys played louder than usual this night, but London's ears prickled with each jingle of the doorbell. She took another peek.

Not him.

She'd worked every night for two weeks in this hellhole, naively thinking he'd return.

Stupid mustang.

Jaw clenched, she stalked into the kitchen. A rack of cups exited the conveyor dishwasher. She pulled one out, dislocating several more, and left them. Hot, she pitched it across the room and grabbed another off the rack. *Waste of time.* A blast of cool air from the refrigerator did nothing to dispel her foul mood as she poured orange juice.

The bell jingled again.

I'm not running this time. Leaning against the counter, she held the cool drink to her cheek.

That bell chiming man is already forgotten.

Pizza dough spun on Claire's hand and landed with

a 'flop' on the large stainless-steel countertop. "Talk to me, girl."

"Talk?"

Red sauce spread with ease over the dough, followed by a handful of pepperonis. London's relationship with Claire had proven to be rocky, despite their years together. Claire loved Joe, while Joe, although he kept his emotions hidden, loved London. Claire pumped London for information. "Why aren't you out workin'?"

"Uh . . ." Plucking an oversized grape, London popped it into her mouth and watched Claire with lackluster eyes. Indifferent to the older woman's hollow concern, she popped another and answered. "Research."

"Spill it. What research?"

"You know, memorizing mountains, rivers. Stuff like that."

"Stuff like that, huh?" Claire scooped the pizza up on a pizza peel and slid it inside a brick oven before she grabbed a fresh wad of dough. "If you got all this memorizing to do, whatcha' doin' in the bar every night?"

London tossed the empty cup into a sink of soapy water. "I got bored." She grabbed an empty tray and went back into the bar.

At the sound of wood grating against wood, London twisted, briefly coming face to face with a careless bar patron as she turned. To stop the tray from tumbling, she tilted right into the arms of the man who kept her ears tuned for the bell.

Staring into his whisky eyes, London's surprise turned to fury as powerful hands held her steady.

"*Aigoo* . . . Okay, you?"

A calm exterior belied the muddled mess she held inside. "Sure." . . . *are you?* She grabbed the tottering tray with her empty hand and straightened. "I'm fine."

His hands slid from her hips. "Fine."

Rigid with unwanted stimuli as one emotion pinged off the next, London stepped aside to let him and his men pass. At the rear of the line, Pretty-boy smiled.

"Excuse me, Miss." His English sounded rehearsed.

The six men in military uniform walked to a corner table and removed their black berets as they sat.

Shit.

Each cap displayed a silver star dead center. *Special forces.* That explained how her hero overcame Private Nelson, a broad and tall man, with a chest comparable to a silver-back gorilla.

She tasted bile as she set the tray on a nearby table. Wobbly knees threatened to buckle as she pulled out an ordering pad and pen. Her eyes glued to the pad, she asked, "What can I get you?"

Unlike other tables, where customers order in quick succession, these men waited for their leader to order first. The lead stallion wore three diamonds on his epaulets. *A commander.*

"Coors Light."

A shaky pen pressed against the pad as London focused. His eyes met hers. "Uh . . . I'm sorry, but could you . . .?"

Lips, plump and pleasing, seized her attention as the commander answered a second time. "Coors Light."

She stood fixed, staring, and wondered if his lips had ever seen the sun. *A paper chaser in the special forces? Impossible. Paper chasers don't charge to save ladies in distress. Ladies in distress?* London giggled and shifted her eyes to the black panther patch stitched into his right sleeve. "I'm sorry. What did you order?"

"Cass."

When the Commander asked for a Korean beer, London's stress level took a momentary reprieve. Irritated with her absentmindedness and his flippant attitude, she cracked, "Sorry, we carry Bud, Bud Light, Coors, Coors Light, Miller, Michelob, and Pabst Blue Ribbon . . . American beers." With a wave of her arm, she hid her discomfort by adding a touch of western sass. "We're an American bar."

The Commander's expression softened as he flashed a toothy grin. *He's teasing. It worked.* Flustered, London broke her stance ready to knock the chair out from under him.

The lead stallion winked. Her knees quavered a second time.

Toying with her, he ordered again. "Coors Light."

The other men chuckled before ordering according to rank.

Raw and angered, London repeated their order. "Okay, two Bud Light, one Pabst Blue Ribbon, and three Coors Light." Without waiting for confirmation, she tucked the notepad in her apron and turned toward the bar. Afraid her legs might falter, she grabbed the back of a chair, glanced over her shoulder to see him watching, and grimaced. Inhaling, her training holding her together, she walked to the bar. After slapping the order on the counter, she left the room.

In the kitchen, London crossed to the sink, with dishes piled high as the new hire managed the spray valve. "Move." She shoved him aside and turned off the hot water.

The boy soaked himself as water sprayed from the valve. "Hey!" Cursing in Korean, he took three steps backwards, his rubber gloves dripping water and soap bubbles on the floor.

"Take a break, kid." London leaned over the sink, one hand clutching her stomach. The tips of her hair immersed in soapy suds, she heard the boy pull off his gloves and slap them against the drying rack.

She splashed cold water against her face, hard and fast, willing an unscratchable itch to settle. Early in her training, she'd used this method to calm her fear when challenging a bigger comrade. Unfortunately, this time, it didn't work.

As a seasoned killer, a similar itch, a mix of pain and excitement, one that defied fear, swelled each time she faced an enemy, but this scratch frightened her. *Maybe, just maybe, the mustang shares destiny with me. A date, of sorts. Maybe a death date.*

Did fate's hand demand the dark stallion's death? Or was she the one to die? Remembering the ease with which he had handled Private Nelson, the way he'd confidently winked, she knew he was formidable. London shivered with fear and anticipation.

A fight with him could prove to be her last.

An ending she'd waited years to embrace.

She splashed her face a second time and pulled a scratchy paper towel off the roll. *Nerves. Yeah, that's right, it's nerves.*

3

Weekend Shift at the Bar

After a week in the field gathering data for one final mission, London hurried back to her apartment for a weekend shift at the bar. She tossed her rucksack against the bedroom wall, ran scalding hot water in the tub, and stripped off her clothes. Before stepping into the tub, she turned the control valve to cold, careful to step where the water ran.

Bronze skin glistened as soap bubbles slid between small breasts. A quick scrub was all she required, although given her time in the field and the toll it took, she would've enjoyed a long soak.

Stepping out of the bath, water rivulets dripped onto the floor, leaving prints across the tile as she entered the bedroom. Instead of air-drying, she tugged clean clothes over damp skin, sure Joe awaited her report. The shirt clung to her well-toned physique.

With her next shift in thirty minutes, the clock clicked over, relentless in its mindless countdown.

Wet shoulder-length hair spun into two braids, gave her a Laura Ingalls appeal. A product of the Tennessee mountains, London, though not stunning, carried a youthful beauty with long lashes and a trim torso. Her legs were her finest feature, long for her height and athletic. Back home, her dad had called her "Grasshopper."

When she burst into Joe's office next to the saloon's kitchen, he looked at the clock and cocked one brow. "You're late."

"Back off." She plopped into the hard-backed chair across from him. "I covered over a hundred miles of terrain this week." She lifted a leg and dropped an agate green Ariat boot on his desk. "Not by air, may I remind you, but by foot. I don't fly. I leave prints." London giggled, the lyrics of old songs ruminating in her head.

She'd listened to old songs hundreds of times back in the Smokies. The woman who'd taken London in after her mom abandoned her, loved music. Betty hadn't talked much, but endless songs kept the silence bearable.

Joe tilted forward, making his chair creak. He glared at London over his glasses. "I don't get it."

"An old joke between me and Lady Green. Dainty women are light on their feet, dancing around the light of the moon, like in the song, Buffalo Gals. Nothin' dainty about me."

"What are Buffalo Gals?"

London unrolled the map she'd drawn from her ruck and stretched it across Joe's desk. "Instead of me detailing old iconic folk songs, let me show you what I found."

An hour passed before Claire stood at the office door, scowling. Angry over having to serve a packed bar, Claire shoved a tray into London's hands when she stood. "Table seven."

London lifted the server tray to her shoulder and scanned the room. Her throat tightened when she saw him.

For the past week, he'd haunted her thoughts, frightening the shit out of her. Field work demanded concentration, and every minute out of the game, death kissed her ass. The subject of her possible annihilation sat in the corner between his minions.

Determined to ignore the special forces unit, London walked to table seven and delivered their beers. Silver-back signaled. London pretended to not notice.

Claire waited on Silver-back's crew, while London ran ragged to tend to a full house.

Private Nelson sat with his buddies at table ten near the band. London delivered the table's third round and felt Tony's hand on her hip. She slapped it away, noticing Nelson's smirk directed toward the stallion.

"Are you lookin' for trouble, Private? Didn't learn anything the last time you touched me, huh?"

Nelson's glassy blue eyes studied the length of her and snickered. "That local boy won't save you tonight, baby." His hand landed back on her hip, where she swiped it a second time. "Last time, he caught me by surprise, but that won't happen again. When tonight ends," his index finger slid beneath London's shirt as he licked his lips, "You're mine."

A Cheshire cat smile crossed her lips as she went in close. "You'll be passed out by then." To finish the creep off early, she added a pocket-sized piece of information to fuel his rage. Closer, so their eyes were even, she whispered, "And the local commander will share my bed tonight."

Tony's eyes changed from a crystal blue to a storm-filled gray.

Rising, London walked over to the corner table.

The stallion's eyes rose to meet hers. He seemed to anticipate her request as he set his beer on the table.

Ignoring the burning hatred mingled with a flutter of anticipation, she said, "I owe you a dance."

He stood.

The breadth of his shoulders up close surprised London, an impenetrable wall that tapered to slim hips and long, sturdy legs. Without speaking, he led the way to the dance floor, his service uniform neat and pressed. Before turning to face her, he nodded to the lead singer.

Every nerve ending a firecracker, London accepted his hand. In close, his warmth and their overt body connection gave her the collywobbles. She squeezed her innards, praying a bathroom break didn't end their dance. Anything less and Nelson might not recognize her utter disrespect for the private.

The singer started strumming the opening bars of a slow tune on his acoustic guitar.

London pulled away. "I don't . . ."

The stallion eased her back, his wide palm covering the small of her back as the band sang, "Me and You," by Kenny Chesney.

It's warm. Comforting. Safe.

Neither spoke. Body to body, London felt his power. Riddled with anxiety and sweet mercy, she moved against him, unable to step away and terrified to stay. One dance turned into two. He sang to her, not with the country twang of the lead singer, but with a pleasing tenor, as lyrical as the *geomungo*, a stringed instrument she'd once enjoyed on the streets of Seoul.

When the music ended, Claire yelled, "London!"

Her trance broken, London glared at Claire, whose expression could pass for Satan's hairless cat, thankful for the woman's intervention.

"You got customers needin' a drink."

London remained frozen, her eyes locked with the stallion's, dazzled by his mustang smile. When his hand slipped from her waist, its disappearing warmth left an emotional slice where his touch lingered. He bowed and turned to his table, stroking her fingers as he passed. The touch, his undeclared words.

Claire grabbed London's hand and pulled her into the kitchen. "You fool girl. What are you thinkin'?"

Air filled London's lungs as she broke Claire's hold. "It was a dance."

"A dance?" Claire snatched a towel and dried her hands. "Humph. From the bar, the signals were electric."

London overheard a minion call the mustang, Commander. "Forget it, Claire. It was a dance. In seven years we've known one another, when have I ever gotten involved?"

Intimidated by the change in London's posture, Claire shrugged, taking two steps back as London continued.

"Are we close?"

Claire didn't answer.

London took a step, her poise alone a physical threat. "I asked you, are we friends?"

Claire shook her head, powerless to argue.

Inches from Claire's face, London said, "No." She allowed the answer to linger on her lips. "So don't try and figure me out. I know my job. You . . .," she pointed a finger at Claire, "are here to assist me. Don't pretend we go deeper than that." Striding into the saloon, London inhaled before twisting back to Claire. Her girlish smile, bright and innocent, masked the hidden malice behind lowered lids. "Lighten up." And she went back to work.

4

Anticipated His Approach

London noticed Private Nelson watching her three aisles back at the local grocery chain and anticipated his approach. She grabbed a bag of brussels sprouts as the clang of their colliding carts arrested her movement.

A shadow loomed.

"I'm off duty, private."

Tony's colossal frame presented an unwelcome wall as he leaned against the front of her cart. She gave him a contemptuous smirk. Oblivious of her disdain, he smiled back, and said, "You knew it was me?"

"Have you seen combat, Private?"

Tony straightened. "Sure."

London furrowed her brow and squinted. "You survived?" Without waiting for a response, she separated their carts and rolled to the check-out.

Tony tagged along like a shadow. As she laid a handful of items on the conveyor belt, he hovered behind. "You shrug me off, yet you'll dance with that Korean local." He leaned in close, his upper chest lightly touching her back. The tone of his voice turned menacing. "He ain't one of us, baby. You and me, we're cut from the same cloth. Red, white, and blue. You get it? You're mine."

London made a slow, deliberate turn, her eyes locked on his. Tony's cocky smile faltered and then faded as she pulled him to eye level, one hand crushing his balls. "I'm not who you think I am." Her tone had a sinister edge. "Shock and pain. Isn't that what they teach you in the military?"

He didn't move. He didn't breathe. His back hunched at an odd angle, hands out to the side like a gunslinger ready to draw. Tears rolled, his frozen face thawing as deep agony set in, the kind of agony that makes a man feel hollow. His face scrunched, as if constipated, begging relief.

"I enjoy hurting people who touch me. Next time you judge my life choices, I suggest you mull that over."

Her release was as instant as her grasp. *Thick-skulled brute.*

Calm, she faced the cashier, her anger morphing into a twinkling smile, exposing a single dimple. "How much?" Her voice with laced charm she didn't feel.

The adolescent girl, mouth agape, stared, eyes wide until London repeated her question. The girl's gaze darted from London to the check-out screen and back. Her voice trembled. "Fifty-five thousand won."

London held out the money and grasped the girl's shaky hands. "It's okay. I can't hurt a big guy like the private here. He put on a show for your sake."

Once outside, ready to walk the two blocks to her apartment carrying four bags, a jeep braked, obstructing her path. The Commander jumped out the side of a doorless 1953 Willy. London eyed it appreciatively. Gliding her fingers along the willow green polly fender, she asked, "Where'd you get this?"

"A hobby."

Placing both hands on the warm hood, she nodded. "She looks good for a World War ll relic."

The Commander looked up. "Who?"

London giggled. "The Willy."

"She?"

"Yes. Willy is a girl. Tell me you haven't ever gendered a vehicle?"

"Why would I?" He took her bags, placing them on the back seat before climbing in. Patting the bucket seat next to him, he said, "Come on, I'm hungry."

Leaning over the side, she retrieved her bags. "I can't." Amused by his surprise, she asked, "You gotta' name?"

"Commander Kim. You?"

London lifted her bags in defense. "Whoa, soldier, don't move too fast."

She stepped away.

The Commander jumped out and ran around to the passenger side. "One meal."

"I can't."

"Why?"

She glanced over her shoulder. "My food will spoil."

"Vegetables?

"How ..." Taking a deep breath, London emptied her lungs. Arguing was a waste of time. She dismissed him with, "Never mind." Her smile held tight. "When I'm home, I prefer the quality stuff."

"When you're not home?"

"I eat whatever I can find. Snake isn't bad."

"You need spicy soup," clasping her free hand.

She felt small and defenseless, but warm before wrenching away.

"Look," he said, pointing to a restaurant across the street. "Soup, quality stuff."

London removed her cap, wiped her brow, and turned

toward home. "It's ninety degrees out here."

A hand on her arm, he gently steered her back to the jeep. "Today is *malbok*."

"*Malbok?*"

He counted. "*Chobok, jungbok,* and *malbok* are hottest days of year. We eat spicy soup, 'fight fire with fire.' Hot soup makes body and stomach same temperature. *Samgyetang* medicine."

"Medicine? Right." Second guessing her skills against the Commander's, London climbed into the passenger seat hoping to discover more about his interest in her. *If needed, I think I can take him.* She felt no immediate threat. At least, not yet. "Okay. One bowl. I can use a little balance between my stomach and body." She looked for the seat belt.

"Old vehicle. No seat belt."

"Right." *I know.* "Do you always speak in so few words?"

The jeep's engine revved. "Yes. Quick explicit commands prevent misunderstandings. Also, English is not much. I learn in quick time."

"How long have you been studying?" she asked.

His brow rose. "One month."

For me? London felt her first true inkling of a threat. The words snagged something deep inside—instincts she couldn't fight. It wasn't physical. It went deeper, threading through parts of her she'd sealed off.

Worse was the urge to welcome it.

That, more than anything, made her want to run.

The raspy engine sounded like an old refrigerator compressor as they left the parking lot and made a U-turn, parking in front of a small dump of a building. A rectangular metal plaque above the door read, "Soup," in bold Korean letters. When he didn't grab his keys, London did.

Inside, the Commander surveyed the room. He called

the server, 'auntie,' and asked for a window seat.

Seated at a small round table in the front corner, the woman handed them menus.

"*Soju?*" she asked.

Auntie's Hangul is different from the commanders, possibly from a distant Province.

The Commander answered, speaking in the same dialect, "*Insam supeu du geuleus.*"

Hungry, London said, "Ginseng soup? Yum."

"You speak Korean?"

In Hangul, the Commander's native tongue, she answered, "I speak several languages. French, German, Arabic, Swahili to name a few. Korean happens to be one of them."

"Why didn't you tell me?"

"You didn't ask."

The 'auntie' placed a bottle of soju with two glasses on the table.

Shoving the glass aside, London asked for water. "I don't drink."

"You work in a bar, but you do not drink? Why?"

London shrugged. "Maybe I don't care for the flavor."

The Commander poured himself a cup, turned his head and swallowed. Setting the cup on the table, he said, "That man, the one who keeps bothering you. I saw."

"In the grocery store?" *Crap.*

"Yes."

"Oh! That explains how you knew ..." Any argument rushing out of her, she said, "Forget it." The image confronting Private Nelson heating her cheeks. "You didn't see ..." London fumbled over her words, "me, uh ..."

He clenched his fist and lowered it. "How do Americans say, squeezing the bollocks?"

She choked. "You mean cracking his nuts."

"Yeah."

"I didn't crack them." She paused, lifting her chin defiantly. "Let's call it a warm-up to the big event."

His laugh was hearty, the kind that burns calories.

The soup arrived, steaming hot. It smelled earthy, like a rotting log in the forest. London raised her spoon, scooped rice, soaked it in the soup and ate, sure the Commander watched. Leaning over her bowl, she peeked from under her lashes. "What?"

"That night," he spoke in Korean. London guessed what night he referred to. "You didn't need my help. What a way to emasculate a guy."

"Then, I guess we're even."

His first spoonful stopped midair. "How?"

"You witnessed me being less of a lady."

He downed another shot of soju and plunked the glass on the table. "Perfect lady you may not be, but you're woman enough for me."

There was that tingle again, the one she'd felt when the Commander grabbed her waist. She hoped this wasn't a grim omen, since experiencing something similar the first time she'd killed a man. "Tell me about yourself, Commander," enjoying his pleasure at her show of respect.

As he talked about his childhood, London watched him. She liked the way his quiet hands moved, like a dancing cobra, yet powerful like a tiger. He'd killed before, maybe more than once, and would kill again. And now, he wanted to defend her, a killer. The thought . . . *Intrigued.*

5

The Mildew-Ridden Window

Leaning against the mildew-ridden window, London propped her feet on an empty chair as she listened to the Commander.

"I was a chubby kid, spending my free time reading military biographies."

"Chubby?" she asked. Her eyes swept across his chest. An exquisite portrait nipped at her mind of a full, muscular chest harmoniously sinking into an aesthetically pleasing torso. The vision caught her breath, leaving her hungry for more. Stunned by her thoughts, London snapped back, keeping her eyes above his neckline.

"Grandfather visited too many street vendors. Seems I have a weakness for *ttoekbokki* and *Bungeo-ppang*."

London's legs dropped to the floor as she leaned on the table. "I tried *ttoekbokki* once. The red chili pepper sauce made my mouth numb." She swallowed a spoonful of soup, biting into tender chicken stuffed with infused rice. The king's nut, the ginkgo, and sweet-smelling red dates enhanced the rich broth. "What's fish bread?"

"*Bungeo-ppang* is a fish-shaped waffle with red-bean paste in the middle. It's a popular street food in the winter."

London admired the Commander's rigid posture, and the way he remained relaxed and engaging, making her unconventional seating an embarrassment.

"We have that in America. Only it's tubular shaped, filled with white cream and called a Twinkie." She took a sip of water. "Did you and your grandfather spend much time together?"

"My grandparents raised me after Mom died of cancer. Her name was Sodam. It means 'a sunny lady.'"

"What happened?"

"Breast cancer. I was still in elementary school and remember little things, like the butterfly embroidery on the sleeve against the white of her hanbok. I remember how its wings began beating as it lifted off the sleeve and flew away as they closed the casket. After her death, Dad chose alcohol for comfort, so my grandparents stepped up."

London felt an odd urge to comfort him but pushed it away. Instead, she feigned indifference. "Too bad. Some people suck at parenting."

The Commander poured himself another cup of soju, the country's rice wine, and took a swallow before he asked, "Did you live with your parents?"

"Nah." She leaned back against the window. "Dad died in Desert Storm." She fiddled with the edge of her glass, surprised by her desire to be truthful. "He was a pilot." She looked up. "A good one too." Her eyes shifted to the window where a family passed by, and back to her water.

"He loved tinkering with old cars and revving up a rebuilt engine."

"Where's your mom?"

Her sea-blue eyes turned dark purple. "My Mom?"

The Commander studied her, like he'd done the first time they'd met. Her stiffened posture hinted at hidden secrets. He hid his grin behind the glass of soju, remembering how her angry purple eyes softened when he'd winked. A sucker for the wounded. Even then, he'd hoped to learn more about the damsel who didn't need him, but clearly wanted him.

Unable to bear his direct gaze, London focused on the server across the room. "Last time I saw Mom, she kicked me out after her prick of a boyfriend came on to me. I guess I'd be round fifteen."

His warm hand covers hers.

She jerked it away. "No big deal, I planned to run away anyhow." She turned her attention back to the server busily waiting on another table. "Mom's a social butterfly. She just prefers a man's attention over her only child. Hell, more than anything. She favors men with money and power and thrives on self-importance and manly indulgence." London lowered her gaze and chuckled. "Sometimes she gets her pants on fire and forgets she's still on the ground. Anyway," she raised her head, her face impassive. "I got in the way."

"Where did you live?"

"The streets frightened me, so I headed into the woods. Bears aren't as scary as people. Trees suit me. It must be because I'm part Cherokee on Dad's side. *Duda*, my grandfather, was the Chief of his tribe."

"Cherokee?"

"Cowboys and Indians?"

"Oh. Indians have black hair. Is the blonde natural?"

"You bet." Their server returned with another bottle of soju and removed their empty bowls.

"Mom is from Denmark. An Island in the Baltic Sea. Duda also married a blonde. So, tell me. Why did you enter the Special Forces?"

"I'm fond of sleeping."

London leaned back, crossing her arms. "Sleeping?"

"Grandma wanted me to become famous and sing. But sleeping is a priority."

The pleasing tenor of his voice had appealed to her. The stage would have suited him. "Don't K-pop singers sleep?"

"A little."

"And Special Forces Commanders sleep often?"

His eyes twinkled when he smiled. "Some." His phone rang. London listened, recognizing the same brief answers and respectful tone her dad had used with his commanding officer. Closing the phone, he placed a cap on his head and stood. "I'm sorry. May I take you home?"

"Nah. I'll get my groceries and walk."

He paid the bill and met her next to the jeep.

London tossed him the keys, earning a questioning glance, and grabbed two bags in each hand. She backed away from the vehicle, hesitation in her step as she watched him climb in and turn the key.

Shoving the gearshift into first, he glanced over at her. "Will you tell me your name now?"

London shifted her position away, then turned back. "London. My name is London."

The name rang true. Her body language told him it was a lie.

The top of his head disappeared as he drove off. *Shoulda' lied. Too late now.* London questioned his attention toward her. Did he have intel on who and what she was? Doubtful, since her mission was top secret. Still, he was suspicious. She'd have to be careful. The thought of taking him out in the line of duty produced an unfamiliar ache. *Regret?*

6

Willy Sat at the Gas Pump

When London stepped out of the 7-Eleven, six miles outside Cheondochon, a week later, Willy sat at the gas pump. The Commander got out and walked toward her. Wearing hiking gear and being this close to the North Korean border, she wondered if she'd heightened his suspicions.

With his hat in hand and sunglasses hiding his eyes, she caught his smile and assumed he intended it for her. As they neared each other, he said, "Hello, London."

She liked the way he emphasized the 'don' pronouncing it as 'dawn.' He slapped the cap between his hands as he spoke. "What brings you this far west?"

"Nothing much . . . I'm searching for tigers."

He grinned. "No tigers around here."

London popped the tab of her soda, took a swallow, and wiped her cheek. She must have looked a mess and wanted to run. "That's what the experts say, but I don't believe it."

"Why tigers?"

"I'm a photographer." She pulled the camera strap from her shoulder, holding a Sony a99 camera out for him.

The Commander studied the camera. "Is that why you are in Korea? To photograph a tiger?"

"You bet." London pulled the strap back onto her shoulder and tucked the camera under her arm. "Serving pays the bills, but my genuine passion is in the button's click. What brings you west?"

"Gas." He pointed to the station. "Cheapest in town."

She giggled. "Of course. How stupid . . ."

"Not stupid. I foolishly spend my savings each time I come. I'm addicted to 7-Eleven cold brew."

"I figured you for hot coffee. Well . . ." She nodded and stepped past him.

His hand stopped her with a light touch to the arm.

She pulled back, questioning his intentions.

"I'll give you a lift," he pointed to Willy. "That is, after I get my brew."

She wanted to accept his offer, although being alone with him terrified her.

He leaned in close and whispered, "I may have information you want."

"What information?" Slender fingers wrapped the handle of a short blade scout knife. The knife hung horizontally against her back, attached to a worn leather belt. As she waited for his answer, her mind raced through the motions of deploying the knife and slashing his throat. *Is this the moment? So soon?*

"Come with me, and I might tell you."

With no threat of a counteroffensive, she released the handle. Conscious of his eyes on her, she turned her back to him. After tossing her ruck in the rear seat, she jumped in. Eyes forward, he was visible in her peripheral. "You won. Now, go get your cold brew." *Better to wait.*

The Commander placed his cap back on his head and strode into the station.

London liked the way he walked. His step, purposeful. He screamed leader.

In the three and a half minutes he was in the store, she found the wallet he must have intentionally left behind. *Why?* Inside, she discovered he was twenty-nine with a level two valid ROK driver's license, giving him authorization to drive any motorized vehicle. A standard issue pistol rested in the glove compartment with the safety on and a small martial arts knife lay under the dash. When she reached under the driver's seat, she found a combat knife.

By the time he climbed into the jeep, she was half asleep. Sleep, a vital part of keeping her strength, came quickly. She'd trained for weeks to catch her zzz's whenever and wherever needed. She'd once slept suspended from the Octavio Frias de Oliveira Bridge. The next morning she'd rescued an agent from the "Crimes of May" murders in Brazil.

Just as her breathing deepened, Willy roared to life, catching the summer breeze as they drove along the two-lane highway. Her head back, she absorbed the sun as the wind whipped through her hair. Later, she'd regret the tangles, but for now, this was her idea of peace.

With an air of indifference, she asked, "So, what have you got that I want?"

"A tiger."

All pretense ended, London squirmed like a child before closing the distance between them, her face inches from his. "You know where there's a tiger?"

He winked. "Not just one."

His devilish grin made her squirm with anticipation.

His eyes on the road, he said, "A den. Mom with two cubs."

London stood, clinging to the windshield, and

'whooped' seeing the Commander's eyes darting from the road to her.

"Sit, please. You will get yourself killed."

London snickered as she contemplated dying from a vehicular accident in her line of work. "If I sit, will you take me?"

"Depends."

She dropped back into the seat. "On what?"

"You off Saturday?" Willy slowed. The Commander glanced at London. "Are you an experienced hiker?"

"Experienced?" She turned toward the windowless door. "I guess I am."

"Good, this Saturday then. I drive. You bring lunch."

The twenty-minute drive back to the saloon gave London the opportunity to ask the Commander a barrage of questions. Like why he preferred cold brew over hot coffee and whether he prefers beer or soju. He answered her questions, asking none of his own, an attribute London appreciated. The past or present didn't hinder their time together, while the two enjoyed the jeep, the wind, and each other. Right before they reached the Whiskey River Saloon, London said, "Drop me off here. I prefer to walk the rest of the way."

"I do not mind driving . . ."

"Joe and Claire are at the saloon by now. Being seen together . . ." She shook her head. "I'd rather not." The Commander's brows rose. "It's nothing personal," she told him. "I prefer to keep to myself. If people saw us together . . ."

He pulled up to the curb and put the jeep in park. "Too late to play that card."

London knew he referred to the dance and winced, uncomfortable that she'd insulted him and regretting her rash decision. When walking a tightrope, she was a pro at halting forward progress. "Right, the dance. That was to piss off Nelson." She smirked. "It worked too." Jumping out of the jeep, she pulled her rucksack and camera from the seat and walked away without a backward glance.

7

Regretted Her Words

The Commander didn't come to the Whiskey River Saloon that night. London worried he might be angry and refused to take her to photograph the tigers. She collapsed on the bed's quilted blanket and regretted her words, knowing she'd repeat the offense if a similar situation arose.

Pushing away the guilt, her hands pressed against the stitching.

I didn't ask him to misunderstand a dance. It was one stupid dance, not a confession. People fight. Big deal. I punched Nelson in the gut. Surely, the Commander can tell the difference. Right?

Even as she spoke, the uneasiness of regret nagged at her, the same sickly gut-twister she got after lying.

She recalled the Commander's hands on her waistline. His touch, the sandalwood fragrance of his hair, the warmth of his body, brought with them sensations she hadn't experienced since . . . *Blake.*

Memories of a different time flooded her mind back to

a time of fear and loneliness, when love had both healed and broken her innocence.

"*Baby, come on.*" *Blake's light kisses ignited butterflies in her belly.*

Desperate for love and safety, Sarah clung to him.

Blake's forehead pressed against hers as he spoke in a low, breathy tone. "We're good together. You don't need that old woman. Come stay with me."

Sarah no longer wished to resist his pleas. The image of the old woman alone, searching the woods, angry . . . scared . . . a painful reminder of the days after Sarah had learned her dad's plane crashed, gave her the strength to back out of Blake's arms.

"*I can't, Blake. She needs me. If I left—*"

Long fingers raked through Blake's thick blond hair; his eyes screwed into narrow slits. "What about me?" He turned his back, then swept back around. His arms thrust to each side, he stepped into her. "I need you!"

His aggression forced Sarah to take a step backwards, the mountain air seeping beneath her clothes as she shivered in the darkness. "I love you . . ."

Eyebrows drawn together, his hands stuffed inside jean pockets that hung low over his hips, Blake said, "If you loved me, you wouldn't give a damn about that old lady. You'd be mine.

Sarah slipped her hands around his waist, hugging him. "I don't give a damn about her. It's you I love." Sarah choked on her lies. The old woman had taken her in, fed her, accepted her as family. "Give me a chance to say 'goodbye.' Please. After that, I promise. I'll pack my things and leave."

Blake's grip on her arms made them throb. "Tonight." His arms dropped. "Or forget it."

Sarah cried, "Not tonight. I can't. Please don't ask."

"*If you love me, prove it. Come with me.*"

Fear of losing Blake had driven her actions that night. Their love had once felt like a full moon, shining its glow on a path that led her from darkness. She'd wanted to trust him. She'd needed his love. After convincing her, the mumbling old woman didn't care. She had agreed to go.

That single damning decision had manifested London into a suicidal stealth killer. To hide her shame, she covered her face with the sleeve of her sweater.

Tormented by the memory of Blake's lifeless face and blood-soaked body, London left the apartment. She didn't cry. She ran. Running blocked memories. The sweat washed away the Commander's warmth. Back then, a year of dwelling in the woods, fending for herself, had left her vulnerable. No longer young or innocent, Blake had turned her into a killer. The Commander could do nothing to change it.

Sprinting down the sidewalk, she tried to focus on her pace, estimating a time of four minutes ten seconds for the previous mile. As she sprinted, her crippled mind envisioned the Commander lying next to her, their bodies connected, skin against skin. It had been so long since she'd felt loved.

Determined to defeat these unwanted urges, she ran harder, challenging her Achilles tendons while focusing on the Commander's expected future betrayal. Wrought with anxiety, she screamed into the night, "You can't fool me!" Her feet slammed hard against the pavement before abruptly stopping. Bent over, hands pressed against her knees, she gulped air as she screamed, "I'm not that . . ." *huh* "pathetic . . ." *phoo* "little girl . . ." *huh* "anymore . . ." *phoo*.

A sudden stitch ripped a muscle beneath her rib cage and forced London to straighten. Sensing someone nearby, she turned. A man of middle age in a black suit, his hair pulled tight in a samurai ponytail, tattoos covered both hands. On the right side of his neck, she saw a black serpent scale with dark purple shading and recognized his connection with the most formidable gang in South Korea, The Black Scales.

The Serpent's gang member. She looked around. *And I'm alone.*

Greed and lust spread across his face the way ink flows from an octopus.

Arms stretching, London leaned to her left. "Give me a second," she told him. "I've got a nasty side-kicker to work out. Then I'll be ready."

"Don't need to wait, Lady." His menacing words slurred. "I'm ready now." His hand caressed the swell of his penis pressing against his jeans.

London inhaled deeply as she stretched. Her hammering heart forced oxygen to her muscles as they recuperated from the run. She stretched left, holding up her index finger, asking for one more minute.

The man's eyes shifted to her tilted face. "What are you? A freak?"

Hands pressed together at chest level; London rotated at the waistline. "I'm the woman of your dreams and soon to be your worst nightmare."

"I don't have nightmares, bitch." He threw a punch. Missed.

London stepped inside his guard and landed a counter punch to his gut. Whisky spittle landed on her lip as she readied herself for another attack. "I assume that miss wasn't your best work. Huh, buddy?"

He swung again.

London sidestepped his attack and jabbed his jaw with a hard left, landing an uppercut to his chin. Ali light on her feet, she smiled, taking a controlled stance for each subsequent strike after. "It's lucky for me you showed up. You're just what I needed."

The gangster's sickening bloody grin broadened, but the telltale signs of doubt belied his eagerness to fight. Wide eyes narrowed. A trickle of perspiration dripped along his hairline.

"Yeah? Well then, let's get busy." Again, he rubbed a hand against his groin. "You're just what I needed too. All this foreplay is fun, but what I've got in store for you is even better."

When he swung, London bounced on the balls of her feet and stepped under his arm, rising to his right.

"Are you ready?" she asked.

The creep flicked open a butterfly knife. "Oh, I am?" He slashed at her.

Both arms crossed, she brought them down on his wrist. The impact sent the weapon skating across the cement.

She kicked him in the kneecap and threw him to the ground. As she dropped with him, she picked up the knife and pressed it against his jugular. Blood dripped from the stranger's neck. "I should save myself some time and slit your throat right here, but I'm in a good mood tonight." She rose and tossed the knife into the weeds.

A look of puzzlement crossed his face. He staggered as he stood, a hand to his neck. "Geez, lady, I'm bleeding."

London spun, landing her boot against his skull.

Staggered by the hit, he wobbled but remained standing.

London cranked her neck to the right and heard the familiar pop before her elbow jabbed him in the throat, dropping him back to his knees.

He gasped, tottered, and fell.

"Tell me when you've had enough, 'cause I can keep going for hours."

Spitting blood, he crawled toward his motorcycle.

"Enough?" she taunted him, kicking his side.

Curled into a fetal position, he continued to inch away

from her.

London dropped to one knee, studying him as he squirmed on the cement. "I thought you had more fight in yah. I'm disappointed. Guess I'll have to finish you to work out my frustration."

"Please." He moaned. "Don't kill me."

"I can't let a scumbag like you go. What about your past and future victims? Someone's got to avenge and protect them from creeps like you."

"I . . . I promise. I won't hurt anyone."

Brushing loose strands from her face, London laughed as she straightened. "That's right. You won't." She lassoed his feet with a rope from her rucksack, and drug him to a nearby telephone pole. "Get up."

A serrated knife at his neck, slobber and snot dripped from his lips and nose as he inched up the pole. Once tied, London cut off his belt.

"No . . . Please . . . I swear . . ."

Her fist sunk into his solar plexus. Air exploded from his lungs in a single gasp. Red-faced, he couldn't defend himself as she delivered an overhand right to his chest. Something cracked. His chin dropped to his chest as he moaned in pain.

With a single slow swipe of her knife along his zipper, the man urinated on himself. "Tutt, Tutt, Tutt." A demonic smile twisted her face. "Ta, Ta."

The night breeze on the walk back home felt refreshing.

Back at the apartment, her energy depleted, London stretched across the bed, unmindful of the night passing. An impenetrable wall of self-preservation erected. She closed her eyes and slept. Here, behind a perceived barrier, Sarah was safe.

8

A Great Smoky Mountain Cap Pulled Low

The sun rose to the third-floor bedroom window of London's apartment as she pulled on burnt olive cargo pants and stuffed the pockets with camera filters, batteries, and memory cards. A long-sleeved cloud gray expedition shirt, with UV protection and waterproof snake gaiters and a Great Smoky Mountain cap pulled low on her brow, completed her guise of a wildlife photographer. She tucked an extra pair of Bombas wool socks in her rucksack around the batteries. *Equipment rattle is my biggest enemy.* After hooking a tape covered metallic water bottle to her belt loop, she left the bedroom.

In the kitchen, she stood, staring into the open refrigerator. Inside, her canvas bag, packed with the food she'd prepared the night before, stood out against the stark, clear water filled bottles that filled the otherwise empty shelves. A sigh escaped her lips as she slipped the sack's strap over her shoulder, opened a bottle, and guzzled the clear liquid. The bag's wide band slid down her arm as she hefted a sixty-pound rucksack and stepped out the door to cool, damp air. It had rained that morning, leaving puddles on the wet cement steps. The *'waaahhh'* of an ambulance siren and barking dogs echoed in the early morning background.

To avoid waking Joe and Claire in the apartment below, she stepped lightly down the steps. She didn't need the hassle of one of Joe's lectures. He's a stickler for protocol, and Claire is a downright nosy and judgmental bitch. Nervous enough over her hike with the Commander, London avoided their questions.

She found the Willy parked on the corner facing east. The Commander had parked where she'd left him the previous night. Now, like then, he sat in the driver's seat as he scanned his cell phone. London loathed the man and shook with excitement at the same time. *I must have left stony brains in the mountains.*

To keep her ruse believable, she grew conscious of her footsteps, making each heavier than normal. When she reached the jeep and jumped in, he'd heard her approach.

The Commander closed his phone, sat upright, and turned on the ignition. "Did you bring your camera?"

London tossed their lunch in the rear, set the backpack on the floor between her legs, and patted it. "I hope we get lucky."

On the drive out of town, she knew the man next to her threatened her mission. Any threat, even familiarity, exposed weaknesses. And weakness brought death. She hated that he'd exposed her, while quelling the desire to punch him. Instead, she leaned back and crossed her arms.

The morning breeze, salty as they neared the ocean, relaxed her as he drove.

The Commander pointed to a white bag between the

seats. "I got coffee and breakfast."

London released the tension in her arms, sitting upright. "I don't usually—"

"You should eat."

London opened the sack, smelling the warm, sweet buttermilk pancakes. She pulled out an individually wrapped cake and bit into it.

The Commander's hand shot out as she spit the morsel into her hand. "That's hot!"

"I tried to warn you." He laughed, handing her a bottled water from behind the seat.

London took a drink and pressed the cold bottle against her lips.

"Burnt your lips?" he asked.

"No, but the cold feels good next to my mouth." She took a sip, ripping off a small chunk of cinnamon filling, popping it into her mouth, chewing with her lips open as she blew air between her teeth. "It's good."

A cicada whisked close to London's face. She smacked the bug. Missing. Cinnamon and sugar stuck to her cheek and nose. One hand holding the bottle, the other out front, she said, "Great. I'm covered in goo. Could you hand me a napkin?"

The Commander parked on the roadside and wrenched the emergency brake. Dousing a napkin with water, he leaned toward her.

London backed away. Instinct warned her to jump out of the seat and surprised herself when she didn't. *What the . . .*

He cupped her chin. "You like Isolde." The napkin cleaned her sugar-coated nose.

A girlfriend? Really? He's comparing me. Her fists balled. "Who?"

"When little didn't you read? Isolde's Curious Compass?"

"Sure. Comic books."

The Commander dabbed her lips as he spoke. "Isolde Wilde is the story of an eight-year-old orphan." He took a fresh napkin, folded it and dried her face. "She lived in Wales. Ummm ..." he stopped a second before continuing, "at Killay House, where she learned needlework."

Close, his cinnamon sweet breath brushing her cheek, London questioned her sanity. *Why sit here? Punch him, you idiot. Then jog back to base camp. Easy peasy.* Baffled, she said, "How?"

To overcome fight instincts, since flight failed her, she absorbed the adrenaline rush and steeled herself against the sudden rise in her heartbeat. Trapped in the midst of a neurochemical typhoon, she fought the urge to act out. When her body remained seated, she listened.

"Isolde's tiny, like you." The Commander seemed unaware of London's internal battle. "The youngest girl at Killay, she always carried her dead father's compass. She'd often be found by the Killay ladies with the compass in hand venturing off from the rest of the girls." Finished cleaning her face, he climbed out of the jeep and walked around to her side.

Like a fool, London twisted to face him, cupping her hands outside the jeep. The Commander poured water over them.

"After my parents passed," the Commander twisted the cap back on the bottle, "I cared for five-year-old cousin. We read all Isolde books Eleri Wyn Morgan wrote. Like you, Isolde stands first in line to see wild animals."

When he blew on London's fingers, an intoxicating blend of neurotransmitters launched shivers up London's arms, her lungs expanding and releasing the mix of cold and hot air that surrounded them. Spellbound by his voice, his words, a mere whisper, flowed like a poem written for her.

Frightened, London yanked a half open bottle of water

from the center console and bolted from the jeep. Water spilled on her shirt when the cap flew off. The icy cold liquid snapped her back to the present. Shuffling from foot-to-foot like a boxer, she laughed nervously, then paused before drinking the remaining water in a single gulp. "I, uh . . . I got thirsty."

The Commander picked the bottle cap off the pavement. His expression curious and bewildered as he dropped the cap into her open palm.

London climbed back in as he rounds the vehicle, stepping back into the driver's seat.

When the brake released, London spoke in a tight voice, "Temps due to reach the nineties today."

"In higher ground, the temperature will cool," he told her. "Cable car easier, but I'm betting you hike. Tough climb. Worth the effort."

"Grade?" She wondered if he'd understand.

"Class system, possible four. Should not be too much. Photographer used to woods?"

"I've trekked a few miles." She hid her smile, wondering if he caught her sarcasm.

"Good, we walk."

He shifted gears as they drove uphill. "How you begin photographing predators?"

"At Dollywood. I worked there after I turned fifteen."

"Dollywood?"

"It's a theme park in the Smoky Mountains. It's where I grew up. Um . . . Picture Lotte World."

"Oh."

"Anyway, I showed my boss pictures of black bears I'd taken in the mountains. They contracted me to take shots for advertisements and brochures."

"Bears? As a teen?"

"Well, yeah, we're known for our black bears. To capture them on film is no sweat if you can find them. I learned I could make decent cash selling shots. That's what I've been doing since."

Eight kilometers further along National Route 44, they passed the Jirisan National Park entrance. "Not long now."

After taking a side road, the Commander pulled over and parked on a roadside lot. He reached into the back seat. "As a child, I am very alone. Grandparents worked long hours to care for me. You, like me, spend hours with no one by your side. I buy you a gift, so you are never alone."

A skinny toy bear hung from his hand. It had long legs, arms, and torso, with a squat bulbous head. "A present."

One brow cocked. She cracked a grin. "You bought me a stuffed doll?"

His eyes twinkling, he lowered the bear behind her seat. When the toy peeked between the seats, the Commander said in a weirdly Yogi voice with an Asian intonation, "Don't you want me?"

London stretched out her arm, her head turned toward the window. Repressing a laugh, she grabbed for the toy.

The stuffed bear retreated.

Surprised, London turned and reached for it. "Give it to me."

"Bear sensitive, like me."

London no longer held the laughter. "You sensitive?" She caught sight of the bear peeking out again. Serious now, she said, "Quit. Just give it to me."

"I don't know. You'll ditch him." The merriment in his expression shown vivid in his eyes. The bear disappeared again.

He's enjoying this. London reached around the seat, took the bear from the Commander's hand. Face to face, London's heart skipped as she jerked back and stuffed the toy into her sack, her fingers fidgeting with the material.

"See." She gave the Commander a hateful glare. "I'll keep him right here. I promise."

"What is his name?"

"Name?"

"Yes. His name."

"Uh . . . yeah, a name. His name is . . . Isolde."

"Cannot name a boy Isolde. He will have an identity crisis." The Commander tugged the teddy from the pack.

As vehicles passed on the country road, London reached for the bear and tried to pull it back.

"You can't take him back." Her last present a blanket from the old lady she'd lived with in the woods had kept her from freezing. This one, to keep her company. A need to own the bear grew. Unsatiable, she'd give him what he wanted.

"I can, and I will, unless you give him a boy's name."

"Okay. Yona." She held up her hand, circling her thumb and index finger to ask if the Commander found the name okay.

The Commander handed her the bear. She studied the toy, stretching long arms out to each side. "He reminds me of my first bear attack with my Duda. My *harabogi*, or grandfather, as most people say in America. He taught me everything."

She looked at the Commander, a distant memory vivid in her mind. "On a day in early October, we walked through the mountains. I was around seven. A thin bear, maybe two hundred pounds, picked through the blackberries ahead." A small smiled touched her lips. "I got excited and yelled, 'Bear!'"

London held her arms up as if drawing a bow. "That bear lifted its black boar head as Duda pulled an arrow from his quiver." Her arms remained stretched, steady on the fake bowstring. "Duda held the call against the bow and that big old bear watched. I remember the branches breaking under the bear's paws when he chuffed and stomped the ground. Duda stood motionless." She sighted down her imaginary arrow. "When it charged, Duda dropped him with an arrow to the heart." She lowered the imaginary bow. "Yona means bear in Cherokee."

"Ready?" he asked.

She absently stroked Yona. "Yeah. We're ready."

9

The Dome-Shaped Rocks

Heat blasted London as she stepped out of a shaded path into the sunlight. A 12-meter lateral canyon of white boulders, that ranged between six to nineteen meters high, vertical joints, stood before her, the dome-shaped rocks made of Proterozoic granite. "You're saying you want me to climb those?" she pointed.

The jerk who'd minutes before had given her the stuffed bear had the audacity to grin. "Too difficult?"

London's nose crinkled. "Yeah!" *Did that sound sincere?*

The Commander patted her shoulder as he side-steps around her. "No worries. I help."

London contemplated the climb. If she showed her true skill level, the Commander might get suspicious. If she showed too little . . . Decision made, she stepped to the first monolithic boulder. It resembled an over-sized recliner, an easy convenience for her first step up the hillside and used her palms as a boost.

The Commander leaped between boulders, checking over his shoulder for London's progress in between, noticing she kept to the smaller ones. He wondered if pretending to struggle carried any truth behind her refusal to climb anything higher than a sixth of a meter. Halfway, he waited above.

Near the top, London removed her cap and sat with her back to the rock, breathing deep and felt the Commander lowering himself overhead.

"Take hand."

His body cast a shadow over her brow as London tilted her head, eyes closed, and brushed the loose hair from her face. "I can do it."

"Sure you can. Long hike ahead. Tigers hunt photographers after dark."

With continued theatrics, London reached out, letting him grasp her hand. His strength, though not a surprise, stunned her. He hoisted her effortlessly more than a meter over her head. She landed next to him. London contemplated shoving him off the boulders when he stroked her head and said, "You did well. From here, the climb is easy. I wait up top." Then, with a light spring she could have duplicated, he disappeared.

"You did well . . ." she mumbled through her teeth. "If we ever meet in battle, the real me will be waiting. I'll slice off your hand before it touches one strand of my hair."

"You okay?" he yelled from above.

London nodded and leaped, a simple one-foot jump

Up top, she found him resting, his legs dangling over the side of a giant ledge. Without thinking, she reached to pull him back. Surprised, her arm dropped. She shook her head. *What do I care if he falls?* Then turned to follow a game trail she'd noticed upon cresting.

"London." The Commander's hand touched hers. "Look."

She turned, following his gaze. The view reminded London of home. Only these mountains were black and craggy. The Smokies were thick with trees and long before you reached the Tennessee mountains, people could see the smoky fog that, like dragon's breath, laid low between mountain tops.

Here, with the mountains behind her, she could see for miles. Unsettled, with a longing for home, she paused. She pulled the camera from her ruck and started taking pictures.

"You like it?" His palm rested against the small of her back. Too homesick to shake him, she let it lie. Lost in the view through the lens, she followed a path that led away from the ledge.

The Commander gave her a gentle tug. As the camera lowered, his fingers circled her wrist, the act as natural as slipping on a well-worn glove. "Deer do not travel the path of a tiger."

Stupid, London chastised herself. *I'm such a fool.* Jerking her hand free, she followed, determined not to allow him to corrupt her thoughts. As she walked, she plucked yellow dandelions stems, surprised the Commander didn't object when the action delayed their forward progress.

In a field of thistle saw-wort, he pulled out a machete and whacked a clear path. The image irresistible, London removed her camera lid and bounded onto a rock, clicking as she spoke. "Don't cut them."

The tip of the machete pierced a pointed spike. "Nasty barbs rip gashes in skin. Snow-worts fruit sticks to clothing."

Her camera clicking, London paused. "Snow-wort? Back home, we call it a saw-wort." Visions of a snow-covered mountain, a fire sparkling with red, orange, and white flames, Christmas music, and pine scented crisp mountain air flooded her mind. She jumped off the rock and landed next to him. She covered his hand with her own and begged, "Can't we walk around them?"

He slid the machete into its D-ring sheath and pointed further up the mountain. "First waterfall ahead. Small, but impressive."

Recapping the camera, London trekked sideways around each snow-wort plant, eager to reach the water. She felt oddly comfortable with this man, girlish even, almost like she had with her father and grandfather, only different. "Let's go."

Pine trees closed in around them. The fresh scent refreshed her. The crunch of needles against bare feet invigorated the soles of her feet once she removed her Norwegian Welt Limmer boots. Expensive, but she never skimped on boots. She stepped on a colony of ants marching in a row across the needles, shaking one from her toe. The ants reminded her of the Commander's team.

Curious, she asked, "Do you enjoy working with your friends?"

"My team?" he asked.

"Yeah," she answered. "They, well, it's obvious you're their leader. The way they wait until you order first. Korean customs are confusing. Respectful."

"Americans do not understand respect?"

She sneered. "Nah, we preach respect, but in truth, we're a bunch of egocentrics."

He looked over his shoulder. "Does that include you?"

She thought for a second. "I suppose it does. Probably, I've spouted 'you have to give respect, to get it,' a few too many times."

"I respect you."

Angry at his advances, London scowled, whacking at a branch, sending a colossal spider web snapping into her hair. She hadn't intended to disturb the web but it gave her the perfect excuse to play the fool. She screamed, frantically brushing it away. Through the tangled strands, she watched the Commander. *Is he falling for this?*

When he came in close and started brushing at the white webbing, genuine panic set in from his touch.

Arms flapping like hummingbird wings, she took shallow breaths, mentally scanning his stance—feet spread, grounded— but not threatening. His downward pressure against her shoulders, controlled. Eyes on her head. His touch lacked any signs of a threat. She calmed herself. And in a moment's madness, shrieked, "Is there a spider on me?"

A finger against her lips, the Commander spoke calmly, "Be still. Maybe it jumped off. If not, I will find it. We don't want spider nesting in your hair." His fingers parted her strands as he searched, plucking out the webbing.

"Did you get it?"

"Not yet. Stay calm." He leaned closer, focusing on a level slightly above hers. "I found it."

His hand brushed at the spider. "There. Gone."

London observed his obvious laughter as he stepped away, continuing along the path, proving he'd fallen for her masquerade. She brushed out her hair with both hands in short, quick strokes and ran after him. When she caught up, she said, "I'm not afraid of spiders, you know. It surprised me."

"Surprise both of us," he said. He pointed at the rocky cliff edges. "Not the place for panic."

Trees hung slanted over precipices, their crooked branches fighting the wind and cold to survive. They walked another mile or more until the Commander broke the silence. "I do like working with my men."

"What?" she asked.

"You asked about my team."

Matching his pace, she said, "Oh. Yeah. I did."

They continue following the pine needle trail, avoiding the roots that protruded above the soil. "Why?" London pulled a handful of needles off a branch and rubbed it against her skin. "I prefer being alone, you know, especially when I'm in the woods and stuff."

"Now?" he asked.

She cuffed him with her shoulder as she walked past. "Not now."

Truth. We are getting somewhere. The Commander thought to himself.

"But I feel safest when I'm alone."

Catching up, he matches her stride. "My Duda," he grinned when she looked over at him. "He once said, 'man's greatest bond is between soldiers. Comradeship, bigger than freedom. Bigger than pride in country. Is trust.'"

London laughed once—sharp, humorless—then shook her head. "No one has my back but me. I prefer it that way." The sweet, fermented scent of rotting figs reached her nostrils. She tore a broad leaf off a camphor tree and ripped it to pieces. The ground littered; a strong menthol odor stuck to her clothes.

The narrow mountain pass hid dangers lurking meters from where they walked.

She scanned the treetops, seeing a sun bear stretched on a branch. The bear opened one eye as they passed. She didn't mention this to the Commander, confident a sleeping bear wasn't a hungry bear.

At the summit, they emerged from the trees into the sun, forcing London to shield her eyes.

Rich fuscia spread like a canopy that mingled with other wildflowers on the hillside. Pink lemonade honeysuckle bud into tiny white blossoms. White clusters of umbrellas rose from bushes and bees gathering nectar from the blood red pistil of hanging flowers.

A ravine opened another pass where the Commander led them toward a crystal-clear bedrock creek gushing from a granite slide. From above, she saw how the creek water wound around gigantic boulders to a basin deep in the gorge. The gorge's waterfall reminded London of Mouse Creek Falls back home, only this was solid rock, not the algae covered sedimentary rocks she'd grown up climbing.

"It's beautiful." She ran down the slope, plopping onto the grass next to the creek. When the Commander joined her, she wanted to push him away, to pretend she'd returned to the solitude of her mountains. She ripped off her boots and socks.

"Water is four degrees Celsius."

London dipped her toes. She yanked them free. "Oooh . . . It's frigid!" Her childish joy, obvious as she rubbed life back into her toes.

"I warned you." He pointed to the waterfall. "Underground cave is two meters above sea level. Makes water icy."

Undeterred, London stood and jumped into the water up to her ankles. "Oh my gosh. I love it." She twirled.

The cold temperature took her breath away. She hopped foot to foot, grabbing at her toes.

"Back home, our highest peak is Clingman's Dome. It's around eighteen hundred meters. On rainy nights, I'd sleep under the dome. I mean, not in the winter, but summer nights were perfect. I had the place to myself."

Her fingers used to emulate the rain, she said, "Rain pinged against the roof like tiny metallic bells. The rhythmic, repetitive sound soothed me into a deep sleep. Those nights, I didn't dream." Giddy, she slapped at the water. "The dome has this long circular ramp. During heavy rainfalls," she laughed inwardly, "I'd stand on the ramp and let the rain wash me clean. It feels good . . . to be clean." More somber, she asked, "Do you like American musicals from the thirties and forties?"

The Commander shook his head. "Never seen one."

"The old lady loved movies. She especially enjoyed those from that era."

The Commander watched her moods volley, astonished when she bounced back and danced. "Who is old lady?"

London twirled without answering and sang. When she fell to the grass, her chest rose and fell at locomotive speed.

At her side when she landed, the Commander pulled a cluster of the abundant wildflowers and tucked it in her hair. When his fingers brushed against her ear, he watched her scramble to her feet, eyes wild like the tiger mama on the mountain. To ease her fear, he pulled a blade of grass, sticking the tender reed in his mouth. The move, done without thought, quieted her.

As he chewed on the end, he studied London. *Who caused these two sides of bravery and fear?* "Why sleep under the dome?"

London removed a flower, sniffing for a scent. It reminded her of springtime and honey.

"For shelter, of course."

"Dome home?"

"Nah, I told you, I lived in the woods. The treetops were my bedroom, you know, because of the bears."

"Bears climb trees," he reminded her.

"Well yeah, if food is hanging, or they get scared. That's why I rub myself with pine needles. Bears ignore the scent." She held out an arm. "Camphor. If a moon bear comes along, it won't be me he's after." She gave him a devious grin and stumbled into a hole when she stepped back into the water.

The Commander lunged to his feet, pulling her close. "Watch for potholes."

London's breathing accelerated from steady and controlled to an irregular and rapid pattern. "I . . ." She pushed herself from his arms, coming close to a second tumble. When his arm closed in around her waist, she rolled out of it.

Unfazed by her countermove, he picked up her boots and scooped her into his arms.

Stunned, London clung to the Commander as he stepped through the stream to the other side. With her feet firmly on the ground, he handed over her Limmer's and set off up the next mountain.

"Tigers over ridge."

10

Feigning a Gasp

The Commander's back grew increasingly more distant as London scrambled to put on seaweed-colored socks and boots. She caught up, feigning a gasp as he continued walking. After a glance back, he said, "If you sleep in Korean trees, you'll be measuring the height of an acorn."

"What do you mean?"

"Korean bears - the sun bear and the moon bear - sleep in the trees. You can't compare the American black bear to the moon bear."

London thought back. She'd seen one in a grove of oak trees an hour or so back. *They both still shit in the woods.* "At home, you're more likely to find cubs in the trees than adults. The adults sleep in dens or caves. Leave them alone, and they'll stop and stare but move on. If you're in a tree and a black bear climbs . . . You are dinner."

They passed a patch of ripe blueberries, full of plump blue goodness, perfect for picking. Gathering berries, London put some in a baggy, tucking them into her ruck before popping a handful in her mouth. She bit into them, the juice popping open in her mouth. All but one unripe berry was sweet with a floral aroma like those back home.

As the hill grew steeper, she made frequent stops to further her facade. "Was ... training ... hard? I mean ... to enter the Special Forces?"

He offered her a hand.

Fuck that. And, accepted. Together, they finished climbing the thirty percent incline.

Tired of the ruse, London wanted to end the charade and strike off on her own but didn't. "I watched a documentary once ..." She wiped her forehead with the back of her arm. "Phew, it's getting warm." Despite it being the truth, the heat didn't bother her. "It showed soldiers ... training for the special forces." At the top, she stopped, placing her hands on her knees. Breathing was an effort, or at least that's what she wanted him to believe.

She glanced up at the Commander and saw him near a pond, breathing normally as if the mountain were a hill. Tall cylindrical spikes rose behind him with brown spongy cylindrical shaped flowers. *Yum. Cattails.*

During an assignment in Ghana, London lived near a pond full of cattail and once used the reeds to make a basket. She staggered to the pond and doused her face in the cool water. Breaking off a few at the base, she shed the outer skin the way she'd peeled a stalk of celery and offered it to the Commander. When he didn't accept, she bit off a chunk. "I don't know how you keep going. I can't keep up."

The Commander pulled two water bottles from his backpack. He loosened both lids and handed her one. "Almost there. Here. Drink this. Maybe next time, you do not bring such a big bag."

London set her ruck next to him and guzzled half the water. *Next time. Humph.* Squinting, she looked up and took another drink. "I need my camera equipment."

The Commander reached for her pack. "I will carry it for you."

"No!" London swept it out of his reach, the way a grizzly swipe at salmon. *Crap.* "Ha-ha. I mean, thanks. I prefer to keep my equipment with me." She stopped rambling. *Stupid.* A rookie response and one she didn't intend to repeat. *Why do I keep making mistakes around him?*

The Commander grabbed his bag and flung it over his shoulder, his face expressionless. "You ready? Tiger den is close."

"How close?"

"Short hike. Fifteen minutes."

Difficult to read, London couldn't decipher his thoughts. She had grown familiar with his short and direct sentences. Whoever trained him created the perfect combat warrior. Today had provided him an opportunity to study her, or had he brought her to photograph tigers? *If tigers are in the vicinity, I'll know at least the half-truth.*

"Ahead." He pointed straight. "Skies at tiger's back."

Okay. Am I supposed to know what that means?

Over the ridge and back in the woods, London set the lunch pack on the ground and looked at her wristwatch. *Ten fifty-five.* They'd been hiking for four-and-a-half hours. "You say the cats are that way?" She pointed toward the thickest part of the forest.

"Blue skies show the way."

She picked up her ruck. "Stay here. I'll be back."

"Safer if we go together."

As he's bending to pick up their *Dosirak*, or lunchbox, London moved into him. "If you go, I'll never get the shot."

He's studying her, tension lining the sharp edges of his jawline, so subtle she barely detected it. *Bingo. There it is. The man's manly attitude alive and well. I've hit his tribal button.*

"Listen, I'll be fine. I go. Take the picture. And come right back." *What am I doing? I should deck him and leave.* "Then we can eat lunch and return to town. Okay?" She noticed the doubt and reluctance in enlarged pupils that turned inky black. "I can take care of myself. I promise."

The Commander's shoulders relaxed as he sat. "You have thirty minutes. After that, I come looking for you."

She set an alarm, muting the sound. "Half-hour. Okay. I'll see you in a few.

Setting off at a slow jog, she headed into the forest, looking back over her shoulder once to make sure he didn't follow.

The deciduous forest, full of rotted and decaying Conifer and black pine branches, had roots rising out of the soil. A seemingly endless cavern of darkness made more so from the jagged granite that dotted the landscape. Dead, yet very alive. Humid, yet scented of nutmeg. Solitary yet full of life. Its existence is everlasting. The Commander had said, *Naejang* meant something sacred, and infinite lie hidden in the mountain. She thought of the Koreans' great pride in their culture, having risen through the ranks from a 'hermit kingdom' to a major industrialized nation.

Her lithe body moved easily over and around the brush, as her eyes and ears stayed attuned to any threat.

Squirrels scattered from her stony unmarked path, holding acorns in their mouths, while others dropped bits of shell on her shoulder and head. A Siberian Rubythroat sat on a slender branch, its head cocked as she passed. Nearby, a small musk deer with pointed fangs stood chewing moss, staring. Noisy animals meant an absent tiger. London hoped the day wouldn't be a waste.

The sky grew larger and the forest noticeably quieter the deeper she entered. Branches splotched with dark leaves penetrated by bluish white open air increased in detail as she drew nearer. Close enough to smell fear, a contagious scent that spread from one animal to another, a chain reaction that triggered an amygdala response in London's brain, stimulating her flight or fight response. She had no immunity to fear. She used fear to survive.

To examine the terrain, she climbed a boulder the size of a house.

The smooth-edged granite had few handholds. London swung from one hold to the next, often hanging from fingertips until she found the next. Up top, she found the tiger's den. The sky to its back as the Commander had said.

There weren't any visible signs of the tiger or her cubs, but London found scat through a set of binoculars.

Photography had become the camouflage of her identity. The prospect of capturing a great shot exhilarated her the way Class IV rapids had on the Ocoee River back home.

A gigantic oak, over thirty meters tall, had a bough large enough to be its own tree. It reached toward the den, making it the perfect observation point. She sat on the granite peak and opened her rucksack, pulling out climbing gloves and carabiners.

11

A Nearby Black Pine

After hanging their food in a nearby black pine, the Commander followed London, curious to see her from a distance. Throughout the day, she'd pretended the hike too difficult while carrying a pack that rivaled his own during special ops missions in size and bulk.

Earlier, she'd bumbled her way over boulders as if a Japanese avatar, like Hello Kitty. Then, excited by the snow wort, she bounded onto a four-foot rock. He knew she'd seen the moon bear they'd passed, having heard her steps slow. Now, as she ran off, the forest under her feet remained silent. She is a skilled woodsman, but how skilled? A question he wanted answered.

Like London, his movements were as soundless as the windless sky. He found her two miles from their picnic site, hanging from the side of a granite rock by one hand with the dexterity of a professional free climber. She swung to her next hold and ascended the rock in minutes.

The Commander stepped out from behind a tree and

circled to the far side of the rock. There, he climbed a jagged fissure large enough to fit his body until he reached an overhang. Dangling from his feet, he lowered his upper body with a tactical flashlight in his mouth and studied the rocky edge. After mapping out his handholds, he swung up, gripped a rocky protrusion with his fingers, and pulled himself upright. Secure, he dropped his leg hold. From there, he maneuvered to a point under the sunless edge, searching for an observation point, fingering each hold.

Near the center, he found a craggy section of rock. He braced himself with his legs. Again, hanging, he opened his pack and pulled out a metal wedge and drove it into a crack in the granite. Then attached a rope. After tying several knots, he fashioned a harness that allowed him to gain purchase as if lying in a hammock. Uncomfortable, but it gave him an unobstructed view of the den and London.

London climbed an oak tree, as though she'd been logging a lifetime. Her actions swift, using both hands and feet without a rope—a leopard in motion. At around six meters, she stopped, walked out onto a limb like a tight-rope walker, and dropped to a straddling position. There, she draped a rope over the edge, secured the camera toward the forest floor, and descended, using both strands to stabilize it and control her movements.

The chattering of monkeys and chirping of birds told him the tiger grew closer.

London's prowess didn't surprise the Commander, but he wondered why she kept it secret. He'd known that first night in the American bar, when she'd defended herself using a pressure point against one of the soldiers that she couldn't be a simple bartender. *An independent agent? CIA?*

Moving along the length of the rope, London wrapped the cord around her waist and under bent knees, pulled herself into a ball. When she uncurled, she hung upside

down and slithered along the rope like two mating cater-
pillars dancing in a glittering slime of passion. Halfway,
she pulled the suspended rope to her and untied the camera
before righting herself. Graceful and agile, she pulled and
twisted the ropes the way you form Jacob's Ladder, and
rolled forward, securing her legs while freeing her hands.

* * *

Out of the silence, the tigress moved through the brush.
The Commander had seen her once prior, but never this
close. He didn't move. Each exhale echoing in the quiet
like wind through a narrow cavern. *Too loud.*

The tigress sleek body passed under the overhang,
casting a shadow, turning the bumblebee coat to butterscotch. Front padded claws jiggling as giant paws landed
soundlessly. Her tail banded like a boa. He gauged the
height between them at seventeen feet, just out of her
range. *Close.*

The cat paused; medallion eyes turned up.

Click.

12

Watching

He's here. Watching.

London had sensed the tiger's presence even before the tall grass quivered. In position, the deathly silence, followed by the stamp of a deer's hoof, was reminiscent of her first night alone in the Great Smoky Mountain National Park where she'd felt isolated, but never alone. Animal chatter, or the lack thereof, had been nature's best signs of impending danger.

A half-eaten deer hung limp between powerful forelegs, its tongue flapping as the cat dragged it through the dense Tuscan sun colored brush. Two amber eyes, twin gemstones, stared at London as she clicked the camera button. The apex predator's padded paws stepped silently as it approached. Both fearful and hypnotic, a perfect symmetry of balancing force.

Her first tiger, London fought the urge to drop lower or bounce the rope enticing the cat to drop the deer and play. A part of her hoped the cat would lunge into the air, its massive paws, claws extended, toward her.

Awe-struck, London paused to appreciate the moment.

The tigress's attention shifted to the den. A low rumble, both soothing and terrifying, vibrated through the forest. A pair of cubs poked orange and white butterfly snouts out from a rock and then bounded over one another to circle their dam's legs as she dropped the deer and licked them.

London estimated their age to be around four months. They were healthy, even daring, as they explored outside the den, pouncing on whatever moved, more interested in playing than eating.

Their mother sprawled outstretched on the cool slab rock, unbothered by the thirty-pound tumbling cubs, budding miniaturized killers.

The feline's muzzle, covered in long, sensitive, white whiskers, curled her upper lip when a cub bit her ear. Both cubs scattered when she growled.

The larger cub approached the deer and began licking the dried blood. The smaller joined him. London captured the scene in her camera lens as the first swiped the second, making it hesitate but not back down. The twins hissed, as canines, the near size and shape of a stiletto acrylic nail, ripped into flesh.

Numb, London twisted the rope, pulling herself into a standing position with one foot braced inside a loop. Another looping spiral and the rope became a makeshift swing. Her legs assumed lotus position as the entwining rope supported her. Comfortable, she resumed taking snapshots.

An hour passed before she captured a close-up of the two kittens, their blue-gray eyes wide boulders in a river. As the cubs slink stealthily toward the suspended rope, their mother opened a single eyelid. A low, throat growl grew louder as it bounced off the nearby mountainside.

The cubs dropped low. London froze. The queen of the jungle raised her mighty head, her eyes locked with

London's. A fierce curl of her lip, the Flehmen Gesture, the tigress's final warning.

No longer welcomed, London capped the lens and strapped the camera to her side before ascending. Once again perched on the branch, she wound the rope, draping it over her shoulder, and rose to her feet, a gymnast walking the balance beam toward the trunk. After one last look to see the cubs nursing, she climbed down, landing with a soft thud on granite.

Her cover blown, clammy sweat coated her skin, the humid air preventing it from drying. *The Commander's no idiot. If he searches my files, he might uncover the truth of who I am and what I'm capable of—it could expose me, my team, or my mission.* Again, she wondered if their blooming relationship might lead to one or both of their deaths.

After today . . . London made a pact with herself. This day, marked the end of their . . . *Friendship?* The imaginary line that's drawn between friend and adversary had overlapped.

She lowered herself to the last safe hold on the granite, dropping three meters and rolling into a standing position. Once under the ledge, she half expected to find the Commander waiting for her.

He's gone.

Caring nothing for the animals that scattered in her presence, she ran. Death, being alone . . . didn't frighten her.

Abandonment racked her with unreasoning fear. The fear one experienced alone on the streets of Pigeon Forge.

Why did I trust him? She ran faster. Her heart hammered. *You stupid idiot. Don't make friends. You can't trust people.* Hatred and fear meshed in her mind. *Everyone leaves* . . . Tears burned as they rolled down her cheeks, swept away as branches smacked against her.

*** *** ***

The Commander listened to London's approach, frantic and messy, as if being chased. He pulled back the lid to a can of abalone porridge and suspected that wouldn't be the case. London wouldn't run from a tiger. She'd fight. The thermos lid popped as London stepped into the clearing. Her cap gone; the twigs had pulled loose strands of hair about her face.

She stopped, wiping away tears with the back of her hand.

"You trying to alert the tiger to easy prey?" He patted the ground. "Sit. It has been over an hour since you left. You must be hungry."

London dropped to the ground, her knees bent as she sat next to him, kicking off her boots on the way down. Her breathing heavy, she used the hem of her shirt to wipe her face. "I'm late."

The Commander handed her a bottled water. "You have field skills. Who is your instructor?"

She passed him a handful of blueberries from a baggy she'd picked earlier, thrilled he'd stayed and terrified of the consequences. She shrugged. "I told you. I lived in the woods. You learn things in the woods, mainly how to survive."

The Commander popped the berries into his mouth. "You were good at surviving."

"I was. I mean, I am." Her heartbeat slowed. "How did you follow me?" She picked up a slice of honey apple from one of the open containers and took a bite, enjoying the crunch while savoring its sweetness.

"I have skills of my own."

"Such as?"

The Commander noticed the way she subtly traced her tongue over her lips when he opened the porridge. "You hungry?" he asked, handing her a steaming bowl of creamy oats. He remembered London's cool, standoffish attitude at the saloon. She'd smile then, but her eyes never crinkled. Now, she ate, relaxed, her infectious grin adding a shine to her angry eyes, her skin glowing. The woods changed her. "Brothers? Sisters?"

London covered her mouth to hide the food she ate. "Just me. Mom could never be described as a baby machine."

"I got that impression. Were you close with your dad?" he asked.

Sadness flashed in her eyes for the briefest moment, then sea-blue turned to gray pearls. "Daddy was my world. We did everything together, at least when he stayed home." Her head sagged, and the next spoonful of porridge didn't reach her mouth. "When Daddy died, he left me with Mom. Duda had already passed a year before the war."

"You miss him, your dad?"

"I used to. I missed him bad, but not so much anymore."

"What changed?"

She sighed. "I needed him, and he left . . . and now . . . well, I guess I got used to people leaving."

Wanting to ask more, he kept his tone neutral. "Now that you photographed the tiger, what is next?"

She sat the bowl on a piece of bark and accepted a slice of mango, as she answered, "When I leave here," *in a body bag,* "I'm going to England."

"Why England?"

"The Air Force stationed my dad there for a time. He'd ride his bike through a seaside town called Ipswich. He once said England felt like home." She dipped another slice of mango into the porridge. "As a girl, I dreamed of living in a small house; a thick patch of tulips in the front lawn. Me and Daddy. I'd roll play in the backyard, pretending it bordered an enormous field with a herd of grazing sheep. In the summer months, I'd ride my bike to the pool, pretending it was the ocean. Someday, that's where I'll live, in England near the ocean."

"And sheep?"

"Daddy had an oversized stuffed sheep he'd brought back from England. He gave it to me. I was around three. Lambchop." She laughed, her eyes twinkling when she looked at him. "A book." She brushed away her response. "It's a long story. Anyway, I like sheep."

"Until I move to England, I'll stick around. I'm enjoying the scenery."

The Commander poured them each another cup of juice. "What about me? Do I add to that scenery?"

London flicked her bare toes in the grass and blew at a wayward strand of hair. "Yeah. Maybe." The smile that followed developed slowly, crested into a beautiful full tooth grin and then disappeared in an instant.

The Commander thought he understood the misleading message she sent him. It divulged half-truths. *What is she hiding?* "There is much to learn about you."

London tossed the unfinished mango into the brush. A flash of anger narrowed her joyful eyes to slits. "Don't."

The enduring quiet added to the tension. When the Commander spoke, his words were playful, but his underlying tone serious. "Why not?"

She glossed over her anger, her shoulders softening, as if she had relaxed but hadn't. "If I actively looked for a man, which I'm not, your four squares are my style. I mean, you didn't use to be, but yeah, I like the way you look." She blushed. "But I'm not looking. You see, even though I'm partial to what's on the outside, I'm not a good judge of what's in between."

The Commander, serious the moment before, laughed hard and stretched out on his side, rolling onto his back. His body sprawled on the ground. This man, admired by his men and feared by his enemies, lay vulnerable. When he rolled back to his side, he propped his head on one hand. A single brow rose. "My in-between is just as good."

13

A Windowless Room

The desktop cleared of distribution bills. London sat with Joe in his office, a windowless room behind the kitchen. An overhead corkboard held a blown-up map of North Korea. Using a retractable pointer, London directed his attention to the fence that separated North and South, the site where both countries met the Sea of Japan.

"The shift change begins at nineteen thirty-five. Two trucks hauling thirty men will enter the demilitarization zone here . . ." She aimed her stick at a dirt road that flanked the beach. "The switch takes roughly sixteen minutes, making the relieved border guards' departure at nineteen fifty-one."

Joe stood. Frown lines etched deep grooves around his mouth. "I don't like it. Any timing errors and you're exposed."

"Won't happen. I've swum up and down this section multiple times. During the last storm, I missed my mark by less than a minute."

Both hands on his hips, Joe shook his head. "Too dangerous. Meteorologists predicted Typhoon Jackie touching the shore in two days. Even if she reduces to a tropical storm, you're still facing surface winds up to sixty-three knots. Get in, you may not get out."

"Let's say I'm off." London straightened and shrugged, doubting the likelihood. "No. What if I don't return?" She crossed her arms and leaned back in the chair. "You find another agent. Simple."

"Nothing is simple. A trained agent costs money."

London stared at Joe and contemplated the real reason for his concern. Mentally, she ran a few scenarios. "I'm good."

"London, listen, I don't need a week's worth of papers—"

"If I say I'm good, I'm good." She sat forward and slammed both hands on the table.

Joe's eyes grew cold and businesslike, but London knew better, and she hated the sentiment written on his face.

The saloon was a CIA cover. She'd been assigned to Joe even before her first mission. He'd made it clear from the beginning he hadn't wanted this assignment, or any attached to London. Nor had he wanted a relationship with Claire. London suspected he'd stayed for her.

Could be time to find a new manager. He's gotten too vulnerable.

Years as an operational officer kept Joe calm. He drained his coffee before setting the Styrofoam cup on the table and sat. "Settle down. Worrying is part of my job. Make this easy and drop the death swagger. Then we can both relax." He tapped the stool, rolling it on rusty wheels and propped his foot on the cushion. "What's your next move?"

London stood and used the pointer to plot out her mission. "I estimate three minutes to climb over the road and drop into this field. With ten soldiers guarding the area, it'll take an hour to enter the woods here . . ." London pointed to the forest and hills, nine hundred meters northwest of the beach. "Once I reach the trees, I'll be in relative safety, until here . . ." The North Korean tunnel sat midway up the side of Mount Kumgang. "My goal is to enter the tunnel at midnight the following night."

Joe, a Humphrey Bogart fan, struck a match and lit a cigarette. With a single flick of his wrist, the flame turned to smoke. "Where you go . . ."

"I know. You can't follow."

Lowering his chin, Joe's eyes peered under heavy lids. He wore a crooked smile. "But the Crindlehurst can." The only time Joe didn't frown was when doing some kind of imitation, especially Bogart.

London rolled her eyes and continued to play along. Back in her newbie days, Joe loved telling stories, especially the ones with a boogeyman. He first mentioned Crindlehurst the night before her first mission. Good timing. Crindlehurst was a spectral figure who signaled his victims with a faint, chilling whisper, one no one else could hear. "Crindlehurst." She checked the shadows and whispered again, "Crindlehurst." Both found the joke hysterical, clearing the tense air.

He took another swig of coffee before adding a splash of whisky from a stainless-steel flask, engraved with a bald eagle. "Incognito is safer."

London pulled a pepperoni from the sole of her boot and tossed it aside. "With soldiers guarding the tunnel's perimeters, going incognito appealed to me at first ... I mean, yeah. It made sense. Take one out and go in disguised. But" she drags out the 'u,' "the scenario had too many snags, so I dropped the idea."

"What snags?" Joe asked.

"A dead body."

"Hide the body in a tree."

She brushed off his idea. "The dead attract predators. Besides, dead bodies don't show up for roll call."

Joe folded the map. "How long?"

"A week. Possibly two."

"We'll be short-staffed," he told her. "I'd better call-in help. Claire gets cranky when you're gone."

"She's always cranky." London took the map and tucked it under her arm before starting for the door. "I'll leave tomorrow."

"Hey, kid."

London turned, cringing at the impersonation. "Yeah."

He smashed the cigarette into the overflowing ashtray. "Come back safe."

"Or die." London closed the door, certain Joe watched through the glass.

She smirked. *Safe isn't a place I've found.*

14

Stood Leaning Against the Saloon

The Commander parked Willy in front of the Whiskey River, resting his arm on the window frame. Three of his men jumped out of the jeep. Two more exited the truck next to him. He watched London, who stood leaning against the saloon wall, one knee bent, her foot against the brick, shadowed by the upper balcony.

Without speaking, she pushed off the wall and started walking toward him.

One of his men yelled, "Commander, are you coming?"

"I'll catch up."

London's hips swayed with confidence as she strode toward the jeep. Seductive. Alluring. The type of walk that made a man's blood boil. His masculinity heightened by desire. Her confidence drew him, a perfume he must follow. He jumped out of the jeep and leaned against the cool metal. "You not working?"

"Naw, I'm . . . uh, heading out in the morning. Hired to photograph a sun bear playing in water. Anyway," she shook off the lie and stepped closer. "I thought you might enjoy a clambake."

"A clambake?" Pleased, he asked, "On the beach?"

"Not the Elvis Presley kind of clam bake. Your neighbors," she pointed north, "cook clams with petroleum. It's more intimate than that singing and dancing stuff, but if you wanna sing to me," her glance lowered, long lashes fluttered, "I'd listen."

"Clambake? Sure. Need clams. Have any?" The Commander wanted to brush a loose strand behind her ear but fought the urge. Despite her seductively aggressive stance, he felt her reserve that issued a warning. Don't *touch*.

"I do. They're behind the saloon. Get your men. We can meet around back."

"My men?"

London glanced over her shoulder as she stepped away. "Why? Hoping we'd eat alone?"

Arms crossed; the Commander stood stoic. "Yes."

While rounding the corner, London yelled, "I'll start a fire flaming. Don't take too long."

The Commander threw up his arms. "A clambake?" He took a step toward the saloon, his voice tight as he muttered, "Bring my men? Why not? They will enjoy a picnic."

Sparks flew as another log landed onto the flame, bright embers illuminating London's face in an orange and yellow glow. The six men rounded the saloon and stepped into the firelight. London stood, unshaken by the frown on the Lieutenant's face. "Welcome."

After a quick but stiff bow, Lieutenant Hyuk, a burly man, sat on a log London had propped up on blocks.

The Commander introduced his men. "Lieutenant Hyuk and I served together since basic training."

The Lieutenant's broad shoulders reminded London of a lumberjack. She pictured him pulling a tree from the ground and dragging it across the landscape to toss on the fire. His scowl, the only warning she needed, showed disapproval even before he sat. She wondered about the cause.

Women in general or that she's American? *Jealousy? Possessiveness?*

"Captain Wonsul is our medic." A man of medium build with sinewy arms and legs. Thin lines around intelligent but weary eyes softened as he smiled, a natural and pleasantly clumsy grin.

"Private Namgi holds the ROK speed record for firing a single fire, Daewoo K5. Ten rounds in under 0.9 seconds. Sounds like a machine gun. We call him *Chongjabi.*"

London said, "Gunslinger?" The private, a short man, had thighs the size of her chest. He pulled his pistol, spun it around his thick trigger finger, and holstered it before sitting.

London resisted the temptation to confiscate the gun and break his finger. She held up her hands in self-defense. "You've convinced me." With a fast draw on his team, the Commander's danger level increased. If forced to do battle with all six, London branded Namgi as her first target. The Lieutenant a fast second.

"Private first class Wonho prefers explosives over bullets." The handsome soldier that often danced with the ladies winked. His even, pearly-white smile, more radiant in the fire's glow. At a different time, she might have fallen for his charm. Now, she considered him the team's weak link, easily distracted by curves.

"Last. Newest member, Corporal Joowon. He is our communications specialist." Joowon was young, maybe nineteen, with a youthful smile. As he straightened and took her hand, he blushed.

Ah ... He's a virgin.

London's heart raced as she surveyed the team. They were a link to the Commander, whose threat to her mission increased fivefold if they discovered her plans. Any person caught passing through the Demilitarized zone, one of the most heavily fortified borders in the world, was detained by force if necessary.

Understanding their devotion to him might reveal clues to why he continued to seek her out. She sought his time as well. *Keep your enemy close . . . Maybe.*

She walked over to the saloon's back door and cracked open a cooler, tossing an ice-cold Golden Lager to each of the men. A pile of three dozen clams stood on a cement pad at her feet. "I took a bus ride this morning taking advantage of low tide. Fresh clams sounded good. Anyone want to help?"

Joowon and Wonho jumped off the logs, both reaching for the petroleum and matches.

Wonho poured the petroleum just before Joowon flicked his nail against the match head and lit the clams in a fury of flame. Proud of his accomplishment, he looked to London for approval and said, "YouTube."

London stepped back as the flames roared and noticed Joowon's youthful features were smooth and eager, eyes wide like a baby seal. A server sized smile hid her distaste. "Yeah." She pointed at the clams. "Me too." How many times had she watched starving North Korean soldiers cook clams this way? *Five or six in the last four months? Too many.*

She grabbed a soda and followed Joowon back over to the Commander, sitting next to him. Joowon sat to her left, scooting closer. His hand shot out toward her. "I'll pop your cap."

Inside, she felt herself jump and hoped no one noticed. Her hand covered the butt of a micro-compact .32 caliber pistol tucked in her waistband, hidden under a navy-blue camisole. *Any closer, and you may not see tomorrow, buddy.*

Before Joowon could grab the bottle, the Commander wrapped a thick hand over the neck and popped the lid with his knife, shaking out his hand when foam spilled over the edge.

London jumped to her feet and slurped the foam. She hoped the icy cold soda would chill her discomfort, surrounded by men eager to please. Her skin became cold and clammy. Dizzy from nerves and standing too fast, she took an extra step.

When Wonho jumped to assist, her chest felt tight as her body tensed for battle. She reminded herself why she'd planned this event. She needed to study the Commander and his team. To know what she might be up against.

As she fended off Wonho, she tried to relax. "No. Please. I'm fine. Just hungry. I guess digging clams makes you forget to eat." *If needed, I can take out five of them. That leaves the Commander.* She didn't want to fight him.

The Commander studied London. He'd noticed her cool, but polite, demeanor in the bar, never staying long at a table. Out here, with his team, she acted like a cornered rabbit. *Why? What prompted this get-together?*

Throughout the evening, London kept the flames alive, using up three bottles of petroleum. The flames flicking upward each time.

The younger men relaxed, shooting the wind. The Commander sat at the far end of the picnic table huddled with the lieutenant. Their heads lowered; the conversation appeared prickly. London watched.

When the clams opened, their shells covered in black soot, she grabbed a set of prongs and a metal tray. "Foods ready."

The Commander walked over and added a log to the fire she'd started before they arrived.

Namgi held the tray as London piled on the clams. Once full, he carried it to the wooden table and placed it on the edge next to where his leader sat.

When everyone got seated, the Commander said, "*Jal meokkessumnida.*"

Each man pulled out a combat knifes and dug out the clams.

London reached for a paper plate, sitting across from the Commander, repeating his praise for the food. "I will eat well."

The Commander sat on the edge of the bench with one leg stretched, a hand relaxed against his thigh. He held back as the other men fingered the hot clams.

London grabbed her camera. Her index finger hovered over the button about the time he must have sensed her watching. Soft, trusting eyes met hers through the lens. His smile warmed her.

Snap.

Watching the men inserting knives into the shells, London glanced at her dirty broken nails and reached for the knife hidden in her boot. She stopped herself when her fingers touched the hilt and scratched her calf instead upon seeing the Commander watching.

The awkward moment went unquestioned when he handed her his utility knife.

She withdrew her hand, accepted the blade, and pried the clam from its shell. Chewing, she watched him. He was quick, as if anticipating her every move.

The heat and flavor of the clams surprised her. A mixture of sun and sea, salty and delicious.

One night, her first time on the seashore of the Sea of Japan, she'd danced with the ocean and, from a distance, watched the North Korean soldiers eat clams. This had been her first time. Her mouth had watered as they broke open the cracked shells and chewed one after another, licking their fingers of salty residue. The Commander's team made the same delectable sounds she'd heard that night in the sea, hidden by gentle waves.

As the men continued to eat, London took pictures, surprised the Commander didn't intervene. She glanced his way. When he smiled, she averted her eyes back to the clams.

Private Namgi placed a clam into his mouth as the camera shutter clicked.

"I smell the gas, but it doesn't taste gassy," he said.

The Commander sucked salt from the tip of his thumb. "The flame burns away poison."

"He's right." London put a clam in her mouth. "They're good."

"Good," the Commander agreed.

"I'm glad you like them." London took a picture of him smacking his lips, then zoomed in closer.

She felt Namgi lean in and resisted the need to react, as he said, "This is the Commander's first time."

To force more distance between them, she raised her camera.

Click.

"First time for what?"

"To introduce us to his lover."

The shutter clicked again as she jumped off the bench. "We're—"

Lieutenant Hyuk snapped, "That's enough, Namgi. The Commander's affairs are private."

The Commander lowered his shell and winked at London. "Slow it up, men. Not official, yet. She's still warming up to me."

"We're not dating," London blurted. She floundered for the right word. "Acquaintances. More like friendly equals." When the men chortled, she chided herself. *Friendly equals. Jeez.*

Captain Wonsul took another clam, his head bent as he whispered into his hand, "Oooh, that burns."

London peeked at the Commander, who swallowed the last of his beer, apparently unaffected by her comments. She mentally defended her remark, though embarrassed and surprised she cared. *I didn't lie.* She marveled at his self-confidence. *L'eau de Cologne des hommes.* Having humored herself, she wondered what fragrance carried the scent of his self-assurance.

Savoring the juice from the last clam, the Commander turned his gaze in her direction. His eyes warmed, his smile grew easy, steady, as if he were sending a subliminal message. *You're safe with me.*

Shaken, London broke the trance. She picked up a stick and used it like a croquet mallet to drive a clam shell into the fire.

When the Commander excused himself and walked away, London moved to the table and sat on the edge next to Wonsul. "Do you guys trust him?"

Like a perch of parrots, they bobbed their heads.

"Why?" she asked.

Captain Wonsol dropped his last clam and raised his second beer can. His eyes burned with respect as he spoke, "Commander received his training in the three teachings of the Buddhist Monk, Won Gwang; self-defense, self-confidence, and self-control."

Private Namgi asked, "Who is Won Gwang?"

Captain Wonsul gave Namgi a stern look. "Haven't you studied the great Hwarang?"

"I have, but I can't see what flower warriors and a monk have to do with our Commander."

Corporal Joowon placed a hand on his cheeks and said, "Our Commander is as pretty as a peach blossom."

The men laughed, except for the Lieutenant who slapped his palm on the table silencing the others. Hyuk ran his hand over the stubble of hair on his head, and said, "Ability, benevolence, and integrity are the strong qualities of our Commander, and the reason we follow him is loyalty."

"Loyalty?" London leaned on one hand, the splintered wood digging into her palm. "I bet each of you have walked into dangerous situations without a sure-fire back-up plan."

With clear reverence exposed in his youthful silhouette, Corporal Joowon answered, "The Commander would give his life for us, and that's the truth. Until six months ago, I served under an officer who didn't give a damn about the men who served under him. On our first mission together, I watched three men die while my commander led from the rear, offering us up for a slaughterhouse victory. Commander Kim doesn't shadow."

Wonho scooted closer to Joowon, his face flushed from emotion and drink. "Winning takes skill and a victory without leadership leaves the battlefield with a pile of dead bodies. I'd rather die fighting beside the Commander, then live having never met a man of his integrity and regard for others. I trust him with my life."

London thought he sounded as if he were quoting from a military book.

Captain Namgi slapped Wonho's shoulder, nodding his head in agreement. "Same here."

"We all would." Hyuk made eye contact with London for the first time. She could see the anger and contempt in his dark eyes. "We follow because the Commander's not the type to let a distraction pull him from his team."

Is that what I am? A distraction?

When the Lieutenant didn't drop his gaze, they exchanged a hard stare, each confident and unrelenting. When the Commander rounded the building, the Lieutenant abandoned the struggle for dominance and smiled.

* * *

The Commander immediately noticed the change in London's posture as she stood, as if the camera had become too heavy. Her face somber, she seemed distant. Had his men upset her? The hostility on the Lieutenant's face suggested his part in London's change. Even the other team members appeared uncomfortable as they fiddled needlessly like school children unwilling to tattle on a classmate.

After brushing her sooty hands against her jeans, London approached him. "It's been a wonderful night, and I've enjoyed meeting your team, but I've an early morning." She jiggled her camera between them. "The woods are calling, so I'd better—"

"May I walk you home?" the Commander asked.

"No, thanks. I don't live far." Weary eyes cast downward; London brushed against him as she passed. "I'm good."

* * *

Inside her apartment, London stretched on her side, propped on one elbow in front of the fireplace. She stared at the flames, mentally recording the sounds of crackling fire. *They trust him.* She recalled the sincerity when they exchanged looks. *Can I? He wants me too.* Too tired to hold herself up, she dropped onto her back. *Trust. It's an easy word to throw around . . .*

15

Coffee, a Habit

On a near moonless Sunday night, London grabbed her ruck from a peg and hiked to the 7-Eleven. The lights above the fuel pumps glowed brightly as she entered the convenience store and pulled out a burner phone, calling a cab. Passing the refrigerated section, she noticed several iced coffees lined in neat rows like the armed men of the China's Terracotta statues. Her thoughts turned to the Commander as she poured a cup of coffee, adding cream.

Coffee, a habit. One she'd picked up in Russia to keep her hands warm.

Unwanted memories of the Commander had become a distraction, though one she wanted to shake. A poor omen, allowing her mind to wander in senseless thinking that had nothing to do with her mission, focusing more on the size of his hands and staggering smile than the job ahead.

She stepped outside; the cooling chill of the night air made her grip the Styrofoam cup tighter. A wolf howled in the distance as she waited, leaning back against the glass windowpane. An international orange cab pulled up, and she climbed in, giving him instructions. "Haean-myeon, please."

"Location?"

It appeared every Korean preferred to talk in one-word responses. Continuous thoughts of the Commander distracted her. Frustrated, London quipped at him, "No!"

"Excuse me? Where I take you?"

Embarrassed, she adjusted her rucksack and said, "Turrets. Sorry. Take me to the Haea*n* Catholic Church."

They pulled into the town at 0100 in the morning, when all but a few drunks were asleep. She handed a thousand won to the driver and heard the familiar creak of wood as Father Wadesworth Halverson opened the church's 13th century style double doors. She smiled to herself, pleased to have someone waiting for her. "Keep the change."

She walked lazily toward her contact, tugging her gear over one shoulder. Kind, aging eyes greeted her. "*Hei, hei,* my child."

London kissed his cheek, feeling his bulbous nose against her skin. His breath smelled of fish oil.

"Father," she greeted him. "It's good to see you."

The old priest, his thin lips smiling, guided her inside the church. Its red stone steeple and bell loomed over the entrance. The massive bell hung silent and resolute. This wasn't the grating jingle of a cheap bar, signaling fleeting annoyance or a casual departure. And it certainly wasn't the dreaded clang of a dinner bell, calling her to the unspeakable. No, this was a sound of immense weight, of steadfastness – a resonance that, unexpectedly, reminded her of the Commander. Like him, it stood solid, a silent promise of sanctuary she hadn't known she craved.

The church's designer had drawn up a smaller replica of Finland's Turku Cathedral. The Father, from Norway, spoke with a light, singsong dialect, "I reckon you mun go out, but I ask you to stay with me instead." His o's were rounded, sounding more like an 'ow,' and w's sounded guttural, spoken as a v.

"The day you return to Troms og Finnmark, I'll go home." She smiled sweetly. "Deal?"

Bright eyes lost their glimmer. "Nay. I will die here for my Lord." He handed her a cup.

London accepted the water and drank.

Offering to take her sack, his hand dropped when she refused. "Settle down, London. *Cletch* a family of your own. Plant a life tree, and grow roots, so your ancestors become intimate with the land."

Since Blake, London hadn't wanted a family or roots. In the priest's tongue, she said, "*Oddsen er ikke* på *min* side."

"Mmm . . ." Calm eyes turned cheery. "You say the odds are not in your favor, but here you stand. Alive! There is hope."

In need of privacy, she twisted the handicapped bathroom door handle and dropped her ruck inside. "Let's hope this mission fixes that error."

"You will survive. I know this."

Yona's head plopped against the floor. London patted the stuffed head mindlessly. "I hope he's wrong." She changed into a black bodysuit, waterproof combat boots and a Helly Hansen rain jacket, and tugged on gloves and a beanie. After tucking straggling blonde hair under the hat, she strapped on a combat belt and inserted a set of stars and throwing knives, then double checked the sleeve's seam, making sure the L-pill, in case of capture, remained protected.

Stuffing her common clothes into the rucksack, she stepped into the hall. Father Wadesworth stood waiting, a baggie of food in hand. Inside, she saw nuts, blueberries, and sesame seeds.

"The bait isn't much, but the food is good for the belly."

She secured the bag in her ruck and moved towards the door. Her hand on the knob, she paused, unsure why, maybe hoping God might give her a sign this mission would be her last but refusing to ask. Casting aside hope, a meaningless distraction, she said, "Goodbye, Father. Pray, we don't meet again."

As she strode away from the sanctuary, the pastor yelled, "*Hey up*, my child. *Ha det.*"

She waved, responding to his call. "Careful is my life slogan," and stepped into the darkness, heading northeast toward the mountains. She ejected the memory card from the burner phone and discarded it in the rest-stop trash before tossing the phone into the bushes.

The fresh scent of lilies hung in the air as she passed the 4th tunnel. The tunnel, dug by the North Koreans, is an infinite reminder of the Korean War and the bloody battle of Heartbreak Ridge.

With night vision goggles in place, she climbed the granite hillside, wishing the passage between the north and south was easier, like spelunking through an under-water cave.

Eight hours passed, having hiked a rugged forty kilo-meters. The wind picked up as she crested a hill overlooking Goseong Unification Observatory Tower. Its tower, nestled along the beach, looked over the Sea of Japan. The sun, expected to crest at 0630 hours, began its ascent.

Exhausted, London approached a nearby tree, gripping the rough bark with fingers accustomed to climbing. A meter up, she tied a nylon hammock from a thick branch and straddled it, eating a cold meal of sardines sprinkled with turmeric, a handful of sesame seeds, and almonds.

The thick, leafy branches made it difficult to view the Sea of Japan, even through binoculars. She needed to plan a route to the beach, one the observatory guard might not properly monitor. With the help of a range calculator, she recalculated her swim north. With her path determined, she slept, swaying to and fro with the branches, nature's rocker.

A loud 'Thwack' of lightning startled London from a deep sleep. She woke grappling for the overhead branch. The thin limb had snapped when a second bolt hit a nearby tree, throwing her off the side.

With the hammock in her grasp, she hung by her fingertips when a second bolt of lightning hit a separate tree, catapulting her against a third. Her body hit with a 'thud.' Great drops of rainwater soaked her skin as scattered leaves clung to her clothes.

Bruised, but otherwise unhurt, she offered a 'thumbs up' to Heaven, winking at God. "Right on cue."

With the storm for her cover, she rushed back to her scuba gear, packed the hammock, and dropped over the hillside. The surge threatened the berm as it ripped tall grasses from the roots. No one expected an illegal entry into the north in tropical storm currents.

I'm feeling all Lady Gaga.

A perfect moonless night. If the barrage of lightning didn't make her visible, she'd enter unseen.

Strapping on a rebreather, a meter and a half tall wave crashed against the shore and warned of her failure. As she entered, she fought the rush of water and wind that skirmished for domination.

For a second, she remembered her last prayer as she left the church and contemplated giving into the sea's embrace. Death pressed against her. Its lure tempting. Resisting, she focused on her mission.

Lightning cracked overhead, a menacing piece of her plan. The drag on her dry suit pushed and pulled her against the shoreline, tripping her steps as she navigated out to calmer water. Face mask on, she dove into a retreating wave, cloaked from the tower's beam.

For everyone-and-a-half meter gained, she lost one. She swam deeper, reaching a leveling off point at seven meters where the sea calmed. Her semi-closed rebreather mixed gases precisely, allowing deeper, long stealth dives without alerting surface radars.

Heading north, into illegal water over ninety meters out, London accepted her fate as the predictor of success.

She avoided the fishing boats anchored to the sea floor, seen only by the bobbing lights hung from the captain's cabin, London relied on an acute understanding of how many strides she took per minute, and minutes per mile, along with calculated measurements to guide her through the inky depths. A fish swam close, the friction from its tailfin warming where she swam.

As calculations continued to drive her forward, her consciousness turned to the Commander. *He's trained in underwater combat. We should go deep sea diving after this.* She envisioned the two of them at Barracuda Point, on Sipadan Island, off the shore of Malaysia.

Once, she'd visited the area, but didn't dive. She heard from the locals that the Barracuda were numerous enough to block out the sun.

She remembered a trip to the Keys several years before her father died. She'd gone snorkeling a few meters off Little Palm Island.

The Atlantic's sandy bottom, calm eight meters below, stretched to a black curtain forty-five meters ahead. A tiger shark glided through the curtain, moving laterally side-to-side in her direction. Too mesmerized to be afraid, she'd snapped pictures, disappointed the shark swam an uneventful circle and returned to deeper water.

Unblemished, enhanced by sunlight, had lit up a flourishing underwater world that teeming with life. A barracuda swam closer, its teeth miniature daggers that rose from a protruding lower jaw.

Blowing air through the tube, she'd crested. The boat had floated five meters south.

After swimming the short distance to the pontoon boat, she tossed the inefficient snorkel onto the deck, sucked in a deep breath, and dove again. Despite the salty seawater that had splashed into her air tube, this moment had begun her underwater obsession.

In the mountains, the creeks surged. She'd learned to swim in the icy-cold, fighting currents strong enough to carry her downstream for miles.

Many times, a bear had forced her to hide under water while it drank a foot away. Never fooled by the teddy bear looks of the predator, London practiced until she could stay submersed for four minutes.

Something solid scraped London's arm, scratching against the rubber. *Shark.* Checking her watch, the time showed she'd been underwater for seventy-two minutes. *Damn.*

After removing the knife from her flipper, she treaded water and waited. Adrenaline kicked in, sharpening her senses, her killer instincts calming her hand. She waited, sure the shark would circle again before attacking. She felt emotionally detached from her own impending doom. On autopilot, she remained clear and fully focused.

When it came, London thrust the knife into flesh three times before it passed. The warm blood clinging to her wetsuit. Convinced that other sharks were lurking, she caught a wave closer to the surface, and rode it in, slamming against the shore.

Unsure of the time, but aware she landed at an unexpected position; she crawled toward a small body of water off the beach and entered.

At pond's edge she listened for the border guards, the soft rumble of wheeled transports on dirt roads, careful to avoid the overhead lights that hung over the road, threatening to reveal her location.

Vibrations tickled her insides, a warning as the trucks approached.

When the first truck drove past, the guttural speech of soldiers made the danger level more personal. She wasn't fast enough to pick up the dialect but caught something about a barbed fence. Sinking deeper, she waited for the last truck to reach the bend. Instead of turning with the others, the heavy vehicle crunched to a stop. Four men jumped off, AK47s ready. *Shit*.

Out of time, London stood hunched over, and ran across the road, throwing herself to the ground where her hip struck a rock. Pain jolted her body as she muffled her shriek.

A mental string of curse words helped her work through the throbbing. *It isn't over yet.* She took a deep breath. *Keep moving.* Nerves burned as the injured hip scrapped against the rocky terrain.

The approaching enemy behind forced her to press on.

Itchy, she compared the sand in her bodysuit to a pumice stone. The added leaves and sticks she picked up, slithering across the muddy field, were like leeches and fire ants. More worried the soldiers might find her trail, than the aggravations that cause irritation, she kept moving toward the forest.

The soldiers walked aimlessly, none of them suspecting what lay centimeters away, their heavy footfalls cracking twigs and scattering birds. One kicked a rock that glanced off London's hand. *Good aim Neanderthal.*

A guard's foot landed where her head rested seconds before, splashing her face with muddy water. She hugged a gathering of briar bushes when the wicked odor of an oozing millipede filled London's nostrils. Desperate to free itself, the millipede's tiny legs worked in unison, making a wave of motion up her arm. The pungent odor reminded London of Seal Island, where the large seal colony poo smelled of rotting flesh and fish. She held her nose.

When the front legs of the tubular body touched her cheek, she fought the urge to slap it away. She bit her lip as the arthropod's rotating legs crawled into her hair, along her back, and, she hoped, onto the ground.

As the soldiers searched further into the field, London swiped her cheek. She could still hear them talking, their low and infrequent voices breaking through the rain, but further away as she hurried toward the tree line.

The hiss of a snake stopped her forward momentum fifteen meters from the trees. As if levitating, its head rose, eyes steady. Watching. Rising. Homing in. *Great!*

16

Poised to Take a Bite

Acquainted with the reptiles of Korea, London focused on the snake poised to take a bite, then decided she'd worry about any poison later. If a Mamushi Pit Viper, it couldn't kill her. At most, the poison might liquefy the skin surrounding the wound.

When a guard mentioned being bitten last summer, his light flashed her direction, allowing her to see the cream-colored saddle on the snake's black scales.

A rat snake. Nothing but a damned rat snake.

When the snake slithered closer, she clamped her fingers behind its head, grabbing the limbless reptile's body with her free hand. The snake coiled around her arm, its smooth muscles gliding along her skin. The knife removed from her boot; she cut off its head and tossed it into the tall grasses.

Dinner.

Concealed in the thick branches of a multi-trunk oak, she checked the time. Back at CIA Headquarters, in

Langley, they'd designed a field watch that used an amber radiance to brighten the watch face at her request. The shimmer could be confused with a firefly twinkling.

Trees with girths of five meters or more, and canopies that plumed the clouds, shielded her until sunrise. From here, she had the perfect spot to watch the sun break the horizon.

Still damp from her swim and the subsiding rain, she stripped, tossing her clothes over a limb. A dry towelette cleaned her face and hands, washing away the sand and dirt from her body.

The tension eased as mountain and sea air collided, swirling through the treetops, fingering her flesh on its way through the branches. Her shoulders wrapped in Mylar, she sliced the three-meter snake into several chunks, placing the meat, mustard seeds, raspberries and wild poke, doused in fish oil, into a cylinder and closed the lid to a stainless-steel solar cooker.

Climbing higher, she hung the meal from a twig as the sun broke and the skies cleared.

Her food roasting, she hung her gear from branches, letting the morning breeze dry her naked body. She pulled a canteen from the rucksack and drank deep and long. Quitting mere swallows before the canister emptied as she dined in the sun's glow.

Biting into the charred meat of an overcooked snake, she chewed, savoring the fruity flavor of the berries, and thinking of the Commander. If he were on a mission, she didn't think he'd be eating in a tree. They'd be on rough terrain chewing beef jerky.

Her thoughts strayed to their meal of abalone pudding, remembering how peaceful she felt with him. Pretending he lay at her side, she licked her fingers, curling into the blanket before drifting to sleep in the oak shade tree.

Weeds snapping and low chatter woke her. Drifting

between wakefulness and sleep, she thought of the mountains back home. Deep inside the Smoky Mountains, off the trails and away from tourists, an American could come close to experiencing the quiet of North Korea. Here, near the *Kumgang* mountains, next to the dividing line, the wildlife ruled.

Near the beach, soldiers were always nearby. But here, midway up the mountain, she sat alone except for the occasional farmer.

She slept through the crazed crusade of gathering nuts from the chattering squirrel family that nested above her. The parents running in and out along the branches, scurrying up and down the tree. They didn't fear the woman who reeked of the wild, often stopping on the branch above her, curious enough to come in close before skittering away again.

She drifted off with the smoke from a Newport floating in the air. *Menthol. Blake's choice.*

* * *

Sarah followed Blake through the house. Discarded clothes were thrown in the corners, empty food plates piled on the end tables.

Nothing I can't clean.

At the basement door, Blake grabbed her arm and pulled her toward him. His grip hurt, but she followed.

"Stay close."

The only light to navigate her way down the steps, the blue glow of an old bulb television and his hand pulling her along. Coughing from the clinging smoke of cigarettes, she hesitated to take the first step. "Who else is here?"

"My buddies. Don't worry. They'll treat you real good."

Downstairs, the large room had one small window on the far wall, the carpet matted and dirty. Behind the steps, two guys sat around a cluttered table. Much like the main floor, trash littered the space. "Whatda' you think, baby?"

Her stomach knotted. She took a tentative step backward. "I . . . I don't wanna' be here."

"Ahhh . . . baby, don't be that way." Blake's hand tightened around her arm as he turned to his buddies.

"Why do they always gotta' be this way?"

The two slumming on the couch shrugged.

Turning back to Sarah, Blake pointed to his friend. "These two shitheads are my men. We run this shithole together." Laughing, he draped a possessive arm across Sarah's shoulder, hugging her close, and said, "Shithead, shithole. You get it. Whatda' they call that in school?"

He studied the ceiling, as if answers were written in the plaster and snapped his fingers. "Vernacular?"

"Yeah. Yeah." The one farthest away flipped the ceiling the 'bird.' "Fuck yeah," and smacked the arm of the guy next to him, smirking.

Blake leaned in, eye level with Sarah. "Now that you're one of my girls, we need your charm." His hand slid across her belly and cupped a breast.

Sarah slapped his hand away. "This isn't right."

Blake laughed and grabbed a fistful of hair, his cold, wet lips against her ear. "You'll need an attitude adjustment, Sweetums, but once you've learned your duties, my guest will pay top dollar." He stroked her cheek and relaxed his hold. "You can do that for me, right?"

Shaking, her hands slid up her arms to cover her breast. "I have a job."

"I'm not goin' on bout pennies, baby. We're talkin' big money. Pussy money." Blake's hand slipped between her legs.

"Stop. I want to go home."

"You are home. Now, to be sure, let's ask the boys." He straightened, his hold relaxing. "What do you say *boys, does she look like money?"*

He released her and shoved her into a ripped corduroy chair.

A tall guy with blond hair and blue eyes stood, kicking a Bud can as he neared. Like Blake, the boy with the broad smile had sinister eyes. He placed a hand on her thigh, running it up the length, his gesture slow and provocative. "Nice."

Blake smacked his hand. "For now, she's mine."

Sarah dared a glance. "For now? This is crazy, Blake." She struggled to stand, and he pinned her shoulders.

"Sorry, Baby. I get bored. Who knows, if you got skills, I might get greedy and keep you for myself."

Sarah pulled her knees to her chest, shrinking into the seat while they watched. She watched their greedy eyes, seeing the way their pupils dilated, knowing this place could never be a home.

I need to get out of here.

When Blake stood, Sarah bolted toward the steps.

Blake's fingers entwined in the loose strands of her hair, her body twisting under him, tripping over her feet as he yanked her back. He leaned in, his cheek pressed against her from behind. "Isn't this why you came, baby? To make me happy. To be my girl?"

"You're hurting me!"

"Umm, are you teasing me?" his hand twisted tighter. "I'm already red hot, baby, so you don't hafta' go extra on me." He placed her hand against the front of his pants, his swollen penis pressing against the zipper. "But I like it."

Sarah's belly emptied.

Angry, Blake shoved her to the floor. Smashing her face in the vomit.

Sarah pleaded, "Please," the word broken in her fear, "let me go home."

"I done told you. This is your home now."

When he let her go, Sarah rose onto her knees, facing the deep blue of his gaze.

Wolf eyes leaned in and sniffed. "You got the fresh scent of a babbling brook. I bet your juices taste earthy." His voice hung in the air, slimy. He leaned in closer, their cheeks touching, and licked her. "Yum."

Sarah scooted away, her hands burning against the brittle carpet, then remembered what happened the last time she moved. Fearing Blake, she lowered her head and squeaked, "I'm sorry." Pain shot through her right side when Blake kicked her. Crumpled, she begged, "Please, can I go home? The old lady needs me. I don't belong here."

Blake lifted her chin with his hand, banging it against the wall. Pinned, he hissed, "Try to leave again and the old lady dies. You got it?"

Sarah nodded in agreement, tears streaming off her cheeks, onto her shirt.

"It's basic, baby. You wrapped your candy in gold, shiny and new, so I bought the wrapper, and now, you belong to me. Remember this, I detest girls who don't listen. It makes me salty. Do you comprehend?"

When she didn't answer, his angry tone turned menacing. "Look at me."

Sarah lifted her chin, eyes on the exit.

"Understand?"

With grit, the kind she'd learned from the Cherokee people, Sarah clawed Blake's face, screaming to leave, her feet flaying erratically to free herself as she sprang to her full height. "Let me go. Let me—"

A punch to the gut silenced her fight.

Blake bent over her. "Only way you leave is dead." He stood, allowing 'wolf eyes' to drag her into the closet, closing and locking the door behind him.

Each breath coming in quick gasps, Sarah shivered on the frigid cement floor. She curled in a fetus position, crying, "Mama," for a mother who never came.

Later, when no one returned, she studied the confined space with trembling fingers inching around. Two broken plastic hangers and a chamber pot were the only items she found in the tiny space. It reeked of urine and feces. Careful not to knock over the pot, Sarah tried unlocking the door with her fingernails.

The fragile nails broke unevenly.

She stretched along the wall she was huddled against and nearly reached her full height. When she tried the wall to her back, she couldn't extend her legs. Helpless, she banged against the wood. "Help me. Somebody, help me."

The door opened, flooding her enlarged pupils with light. Blinded, Sarah leaped forward, clinging to the legs of the person she believed had come to save her. "Please, I'm scared."

A man with long legs squatted next to her. "If you want out, please me."

"How? I'll do whatever you want."

He stood, pulling her onto her knees., her eyes shut against the bright background. Sarah heard the distinct sound of a zipper being unzipped. Clinging to his pant legs, she begged, "No. Please. Don't make—"

He forced the engorged penis into her mouth, moaning.

17

Unwarranted Dislike

London woke with a gasp, covered in sweat, the echo of that forced intimacy still burning on her tongue. *Never.* Never again would she succumb to a man's demands. An unwarranted dislike for the Commander, simply for being a man, boiled in her belly as she fought to quell the memory.

His presence, his kindness, his strength—all now tainted by the raw, irrational fear that surged through her. He was a symbol, a target for a rage born years ago, aimed at an entire gender she had learned to distrust. Even the burgeoning trust and undeniable attraction she felt for him couldn't override this primal, visceral reaction.

Heating a cup of pine needle tea to relieve her stress, calming both body and mind, she sat with her legs draped over the hammock and added pine nuts. Her lower legs swung with the after-storm breeze rustling the leaves, adding to her renewed energy.

She caught sight of a red-headed crane, a mere silhouette at the shoreline even through her high-powered binoculars and then turned her attention to the three guards who sat on a rock near the beach, rifles strapped to their backs. Finished eating their scant meal of rice, cornmeal, soybean paste soup, radish and kimchi, a typical North Korean Army meal, they walked to their guard posts and continued scanning the water.

As the sun set, the birds perched for the night, and the enveloping dark stirred. Two deer ate in the field, and a chipmunk stepped out of its hole, cracking a nut.

London continued watching the guards in case they found any tracks. She'd been careful to walk on patches of grass and other already disturbed areas of sand, but if discovered, they'd hunt her until found, or she killed them.

Messy, but doable.

As dusk settled, she packed her gear, dressed in a clean jumpsuit, and shimmied the length of the tree.

Cloaked by darkness, she pulled on a pair of night goggles. Alone, and saddened by this truth, she pondered this unfamiliar emotion. Here, surrounded by nature, she'd always felt safe. The depraved soldiers were the only people here oppressed and denied individuality. Barely human.

In the past, she'd enjoyed these excursions. What's the difference? Sighing, London pushed away the hollowness, intimidated by its magnitude.

Since meeting the Commander, she'd changed. Now, an unfamiliar curiosity unsettled her. *I wonder what he's doing.*

Three months ago, the emptiness of her spirit seemed normal, but now, a hint of wanting crept in, begging to share her life.

Quit being a fool. I'm dumpster trash, and nobody keeps trash.

The urge to run suppressed, London controlled each footfall forward, slow and silent. Now's not a time for flight, but a time to hunt. She gauged the distance on her watch-compass and turned northwest. Undercover, she enjoyed the freedom the night provided.

The tiger may be the king here, but I am his queen.

In the dark, London became hunter and prey. Every sound ignited her instincts, giving her an advantage as the urge to seek revenge against her tormentor heightened.

A rustling in the underbrush dropped London to her knees, knife in hand, ready to face any potential threat. A jackrabbit's twitching nose peaked out, parting the tall grass. The bunny fell dead when the knife sunk into its neck. She dragged it by the ears across the game trail, dropping it into the bushes. She cut off its head, using a serrated knife, leaving it lie in a puddle of blood. If any soldiers found the rabbit, they'd think a fox made the kill.

The whiff of leopard urine cautioned London's steps. Leopards were mysterious creatures and hard to spot. The sound of metal teeth cutting wood confirmed her suspicions.

It's close.

The forest turned stone quiet except for the sound of a bubbling spring nearby. Thirsty and her canister empty, she closed her eyes and listened. Vulnerable to man and beast, she risked exposure, desperate to drink.

She followed a deer path to a small cave. From inside the cave's deep bowels rose a gushing spring that cascaded over round rocks eroded from tumbling toward the ocean.

London dropped to the ground, burying her face in the icy water and gulped her fill. Breathing deep, she drank more before filling the canteen. The water continued to bubble into the half-submersed container when she stilled. Her ears felt clogged, the hum of nothingness pressing against her eardrums as if filled with a howling wind.

Then, a sound so small, like a pad of butter dropped in a warm pan, forced her to recap the canteen, her body coiled to spring upright and flee.

The throaty pant of a leopard grew nearer. He'd found her.

Her chest swelled. She inhaled long and deep, releasing the breath, a singer controlling a single note. She lowered the rabbit, removing the knife strapped to her calf, and stood to face the cat. To part with her food could leave her vulnerable to a worse fate than the quick death of a leopard's fangs sinking into her jugular.

Weakened from hunger might cause her to make mistakes when facing enemy soldiers. In the hands of her enemy, death would come unhurried and torturous, most likely at the hands of scientists.

Starved or carved, she preferred to die by the jaws of the leopard, but she had a job to complete.

Without hurrying, her arms rose over her head to appear more threatening as she backed away. Huge soft pads never disturbed the underbrush as the leopard stepped closer, his eyes locked with hers.

At the edge of the creek, he sniffed the rabbit and then lapped the cool water. Mesmerized, London fought an urge to snap a picture, resisting, and continued inching away. To stand face-to-face with one of the forest's most fierce creatures and live . . . *perfect*. A rare and stunning moment she hoped to never repeat.

Once a dozen miles stretched between her and the cat, London slowed her pace and checked her coordinates. Instincts warned her guards were near as her destination grew closer.

Back in the trees, she scanned the forest and spotted a soldier eight meters away. Moving through the treetops, she closed the distance.

The soldier stood around one and a half meters. She suspected a female. Some Asian families prized sons, seeing girls as a burden, another mouth to feed in an already starving family. In North Korea, she may be weaker, but still a soldier.

London weighed her options. *A uniform ... Cover. Nobody here cares if she dies.*

But a fight with the wily woman might draw attention, forcing London to escape. Closer, London noticed the girl couldn't be over seventeen by her youthful complexion and acne. Mandatory enlistment meant they conscripted women at seventeen to twenty-three.

London contemplated the Commander's choice. She held out both hands as if a scale. *Make the kill? Or let her live?*

She pictured the Commander and his men closing in, the kill neat and clean. London cringed at the thought of working with a team. *I hope they don't get him killed. Alone, death is on me.*

London's mind trailed back to a time she'd trusted friends.

High on opioids and amphetamines, the concoction for the day, Sarah sat between Cassadie and Shaylon on a long settee. A man walked around the ladies of the night, stopping in front of Jabez, a twelve-year-old from Africa.

The man grabbed her flaying hand. The wide-eyed girl dug in with her feet.

Sarah watched, a chill spreading in her belly. She'd talked to the girl after Blake and his gunnies tired of her. Her name meant 'grief.'

Blake had one of their child thieves pay Jabez's parents fourteen-thousand rand, her perp's promising to give her an education for work. 'Study buddies' were the closest she'd gotten to schooling, a smart drug with her morning coffee.

London leaned into Shaylon and whispered, "You know, I've been thinking. If we pulled together, we could get outta' here."

"What you talkin' bout? If we run, they'll kill us."

Cassadie, a swan next to an ugly duckling, pulled Sarah against her. "How we gonna' do it?" They'd pulled Cassadie off the street after spending a year working for pennies to feed her addiction.

Another man entered the room. A regular, bald, and fat, with a penis the size of a pencil, sidled up to Aria. Preferring Asian women, pencil dick always chose Aria or Reza.

"I stole a paper clip from Kodiak Bear." Kodiak Bear, known in most whore houses as the Bottom Bitch, acted as the registered nurse who ruled over the women, pushing them around with three-hundred pounds of her blubber. Her job required she give each girl all the drugs and alcohol the 'ladies' could swallow before passing out or dying.

Rumor had it Kodiak Bear was Blake's aunt. Sarah feared her as much as Blake.

One wrong move, and Sarah spent the evening sharing in Blake's sadistic delights, which left her bruised and bloody.

Shaylon's eyes were wide with fear. "Are you gonna' unlock the doors?"

Sarah asked, "Don't you wanna' get outta' here?"

Cassadie elbowed Sarah. Sarah turned to see Kodiak Bear leaning against the door in the back corner, a hand on her hip. She frowned. Her eyes glued to the three girls on the couch.

Two weeks later, Sarah had unlocked her door and snuck into the empty hall. Stoned and drunk, no one woke before noon. She drew on the teachings of her grandfather, the Chief of the Cherokee reservation, keeping each footstep light and soundless.

When she rounded the corner to Cassadie's room, a hand clamped on her neck, shoving her against the wall. "I told you, you ain't leavin' unless you're dead."

"I'm not. Promise."

Poker, the guy with wolf eyes, opened the door across

the hall. Cassadie stood in front of him, her face twisted in pain, as she cried out, "I had to, Sarah. I ain't got no place to go. I'm scared." Gasping for air, Cassadie looked up at Poker and pleaded, "I . . . need . . . my inhaler."

Poker's pupils dilated as he backhanded Cassadie. Her head bounced off the door frame. "Die bitch, you ain't good for nothin' but berthing more bitches."

Dragged to the basement by the hair, Sarah screamed when the closet door opened and Shaylon sat huddled in a corner, her eyes black and swollen. "Please, no. You're my best friend."

Hands shaking, Shaylon didn't look at Sarah.

Sarah squeaked, "I trusted you."

Blake laughed, "Stupid bitch. Did yah think I'd let you leave? I own you." He shoved Sarah to the floor. "I own all of you." The door slammed shut and the 'clicking' noise of a lock echoed in Sarah's mind.

Huddled in a corner, Sarah turned from Shaylon to Cassadie. Both girls averted their eyes.

Here, friendship ended with the next dinner bell. Addicted to drugs and alcohol; Cassadie and Shaylon needed Blake and Kodiak Bear to feed their fix as badly as they needed to breathe.

In a hellhole of perversion, Sarah knew leaving meant she'd have to kill the bell ringer.

18

His Feet Propped

Lieutenant Hyuk entered the breakroom carrying two beers. He found the Commander lounging on a low back vinyl couch; his feet propped on a metal coffee table, reading a Chinese book called The Art of War.

Hyuk popped a tab, handed it to the Commander, and sat on the squeaky cushion. "Anything new we can use in the field?" The vinyl squeaked.

"A few interesting tactics and," the Commander tossed the book on the table before adding, 'espionage.'

"You think your lady friend is a spy?"

"Who?"

Hyuk finished the last of his beer and crushed the can flat against his thigh, tossing it into the trash. "The one at the bar." He didn't make eye contact as he spoke.

"Could be."

"She's dangerous. Her eyes are wild. Maybe—"

"I can handle myself." The Commander clamped Hyuk's knee and squeezed. "If she's a threat, it's my job to identify the level of danger."

Hyuk cleared his throat. "Why not turn her over to the ANSP?"

"The Counterintelligence Corps. Why?"

"To stay impartial."

"The beer?" The Commander turned the can, a Cass, as if he studied the contents, then set it next to the book as he stood. "You hoped to soften your approach."

Hyuk leaned forward and sighed. With elbows pressed against his knees, he rested his face against hands large enough to palm a ball and rubbed his face before turning in the Commander's direction. "She's a distraction, sir."

"The other men . . . Do they agree?"

"My thoughts remain mine alone."

The Commander stood and walked to the window. Outside, Captain Wonsul conducted rifle training with a dozen new recruits. "Are you suggesting I have lost my objectivity?"

As Hyuk's legs hit the couch, the metal pegs on the table scraped against the cement. "Sir, I apologize."

The Commander signaled Hyuk to lower his salute. "London . . . is complicated."

Though Hyuk did as his commander instructed; his body remained stiff.

The Commander crossed the small space, placing a hand on his friend's shoulder. "Over the years, we've faced many battles together. It's natural you'd disclose your concerns about my relationship with London." After a single pat, the Commander dropped his arm and stepped away.

Hyuk felt the reserve between them return. A brittle snapping point reinforced.

When the Commander spoke, his words sliced through the air. "London isn't a team mission."

* * *

London swallowed the hate that had settled inside her, suppressing a scream for vengeance.

Memories of her past haunted every aspect of her life. Though far from her deceased enemy, and powerless to harm the girl, her hatred burned. Not for the North Koreans, but for anyone who designated women as disposable, granting power to men. She hated the young soldier's mother just as she despised her own. Loathed weakness. In death, at least, life's miseries ended.

When she'd joined the CIA, she joined to die. In an honorable death, she could keep her dignity. Suicide, a frailty she refused to consider unless caught by the enemy. Her grim determination made her a useful recruit. They'd trained most agents to make connections, to build trust through manipulation and coercion.

London's superiors had tried to teach her diplomacy and teamwork but failed.

"If you send me out to trade false nuggets, I'll take a nosedive. I can lie convincingly, but the gadget guy," she pointed up to the Heavens. *"He fizzled on diplomacy. It isn't in my ruck. Sorry."*

The division head straightened his shoulders, two deep furrows beef-up the downward turn of his smile. "I'm in charge, not you."

"Good." London stepped close, close enough to see the razor edge of his stubble. She stood nose to chest with the Director of Central Intelligence, her killer eyes glaring up into his. *"So, mister dude in-charge, send me on missions those diplomatic guys won't take. Whether I live or die, we both win."*

They'd given London clandestine missions, each a potential death trap.

Unmanageable, with a successful list of completes, the director had given London a free hand. A silent understanding passed between them. If she got caught, no one would come to save her. The mission, their priority.

Her current mission is to map a North Korean tunnel and record hidden weaponry.

Her last mission she had flown to Russia to find hackers, called Pretty Bear.

Pretty Bear had connections with the *Glavnoye Razvedyvatelnoye Upravleinie*, known as GRU. The Russian GRU concentrated on amassing foreign intelligence and had become their primary provider.

Her job: destroy a virus that allowed the GRU to view the U.S. government's online activities.

The mission nearly whistled with 'smooth.' As a trained operative, she'd known better than to confront a babushka when the old woman cut in line for a loaf of bread at the Pekarnya Khleb bakery chain in Moscow. A seventy-two-hour unavoidable fast compounded by a recent kill, London had felt on edge that morning.

Russian grandmothers rule the country. When London refused old lady Ivanova a spot in front, the old woman's indignant shouts escalated. Soon, the Moscow city police stepped in. Rather than risk being captured and her identity exposed, London had apologized and crossed the sidewalk, settling for a cup of coffee and a honey cake.

Most agents had a team of experts, not London. Her team consisted of Joe. He was the only handler smart enough to back off and let her plan the analytics of the mission. Once she devised a plan, Joe suggested loopholes.

Now, snacking on nuts and berries near the top of a twenty-four-meter Ginkgo tree with heavy foliage overlooking the tunnel entrance, she compared her view to that of "It," from the Addams Family.

The twelve-by-six-meter opening, supported by concrete pillars on each end, had a grass-covered mobile pad outside the entrance.

London searched for separate access next to a tattered basketball hoop below the rocket launching pad and found it. The narrow rusty door, her access inside the lair.

At 1600 hours, three hours of daylight remained. In need of calories, she searched for common wartime food.

Rabbits are high in healthy fats and iron, which she needed to maintain at operational capacity. Her stomach tight with hunger, aggravated by a bunny stealing leopard, London scanned the ground with pocket binoculars for signs. She searched for clean angled cuts on stems or leaves, at around a meter high.

Once she spotted hopper indications, she climbed out of the tree and weaved through the undergrowth. A fox on the hunt. She pulled two knives from her belt and froze.

Fooled into complacency, two rabbits jumped from the brush. London missed the first, hitting a patch of old leaves. The second knife sunk into a furry neck.

Perfect kill.

The hare held by its back feet; she made her way toward her lookout. The sun, now reduced to a golden sliver, added to the quiet, a common reaction to death in the wild.

A man's flat voice stopped her. At first, she presumed a couple of soldiers were patrolling the area and strained to hear a handful of words . . . 'Motherland, prosper, great Commander and Party's leadership,' words used in propaganda spoken over a loudspeaker.

To decrease her risk of exposure, she took a detour to a mudhole she'd seen earlier. Once there, she removed her bodysuit and climbed in. The cool mud refreshed her muscles as it covered her suntanned skin. Itchy but safe from peering eyes, the mud was harder to see than flesh against bark and leaves.

She used a thin, squirrel colored rope she'd dyed with coffee beans. London raised the rucksack into the canopy before climbing, huddling the rough bark.

Less than thirteen meters away from the enemy, she perched on a branch, concealed by the dense foliage as soldiers raised telescopes towards the sea.

Her movements were kept minimal. She stripped the rabbit and cooked the meat. Drinking nettle tea, she watched, careful to control the camouflaged hammock's swing to that of the leaves as she ate.

The juicy fat dripped from her fingertips. She licked the juice and nibbled on the rancid butter scented fruit of a bilbo seed.

At 1800 hours, she studied the short-range missile on a mobile pad. After taking pictures, she used the binoculars to search into the underground passage.

A dangling bulb and a flat wooden surface convinced London the tunnel had separate quarters. Hopefully, for the sake of cover, a labyrinth of rooms.

As the mud dried, her skin itched, crawling with whatever microorganisms it carried. The dried chucks littered her hammock, a stark reminder of the nights she'd slept between a cattle barn's loft of straw bales with clumps of dried manure between the fibers. The dry stalks had poked her skin as she'd huddled inside the hollowed center, shielded from the frigid autumn.

Tired, she rolled over, listening to a group of men playing basketball, the metallic 'whomp, whomp, whomp' of the ball lulling her to sleep.

Now, under the canopy of the Ginkgo with the sun at high noon, speckled warmth against her skin, she slept as if on a bed of feathered down.

19

Grinding of a Trolley Grated

The tunnel, lit by powerful beams, went dark. Heavy metal doors closed, leaving fresh soldiers to guard the exterior. Ahead and to the north, the grinding of a trolley grated as two shafts of light rolled out of the hillside. The same spot she'd hunted for rabbits earlier.

The car's engine rumbled to life, the pleasing sound of a V8 igniting before it drove off into the inky night. A number seven on the license plate. A tale-tell sign, who sat in the driver's seat. An important political official, a member of the Korean People's Army, called the KPA.

Dressed, London pulled on her spiked sole caulk boots and shoved her arms through the rucksack straps before slipping on spiked gloves and climbing down the tree, hearing only the hoot of an owl as she headed toward the court door. Unzipping a leather belt pouch, she removed a bump key and an Allen wrench, using both to unlock the door.

Inside, her back pressed against the wall, she switched

on a pin light and surveyed the empty hall.

A gym.

Two handball courts faced a small office with a poster on the door that read, 'According to the Party's Leadership, let's work vigorously to a more prosperous country and homeland.'

A caste system for the prosperity of one.

The office held a simple metal table and chair, with two pictures hanging on the back wall, one of Kim Jong-un, the other, Kim Jong-il. She rifled through the drawers and found nothing of interest, only a log of exercise time for the soldiers.

Further in, she found a shooting range, a weightlifting room, and a larger space with EVA foam flooring, used for martial arts. Cracked plaster webbed the walls, and the equipment, rudimentary and clearly dated, showed signs of constant use and neglect. An overpowering smell of sour socks and sweat clung to her.

Down the hall, narrow shower stalls used plastic shower curtains for privacy—the same waterproof polyester, opaque white kind she'd seen in her grandmother's house. After four days of sea water, dirt, and sand left her smelling rank, a deep, aching longing for a hot shower pulsed through her, but the squeak of rubber boots without socks against cement forced her into the rafters above squat toilets.

Poised for attack, a stream of light entered. A woman dressed in a combat uniform stepped on a squat toilet two over from where London hid. After removing her pants and underwear, she squatted, then used copies of Rodong Sinmun newspaper to wipe herself.

London heard the soldier sniffling, most likely from experiencing one of many encounters with an officer that left her violated. That explained why she'd sought the harsh basement facilities. Once she removed the outer signs of assault, she dressed and left, her posture now rigid, no longer displaying signs of victimization.

When the exterior door closed, the eerie quiet one felt deep in a cave, returned, thicker and more oppressive than before. London dropped to the tile, careful to avoid stepping into a hole meant to relieve herself and emptied her bladder.

A set of steps took her to the primary tunnel. Now vacant, minus a few birds nesting in overhead crevices and the short-range missile she'd seen earlier near the entrance. She studied the area, making a mental map, every detail filed away for future use.

She hugged the darkest corners, her knees and balance centered, ready for an attack. Three offices sat empty and dark. She lit a kerosene lamp, keeping the flame low, and fished for any useful information. In a locked room attached to the office, she found their armory. Mortars, howitzer batteries, 122mm, 130mm and 152mm guns lined the walls, along with enough ammo to last a 90-day attack by her estimation.

As she exited the office, a can of WD-40 sat on a ledge. She grabbed it, adding it to the rucksack. The entrance felt hot and dry despite the hum of a fresh air generator.

Bodies filled several rooms, men sprawled on the floor with only comforters for warmth as they slept. Two bathrooms, a mess hall, and a lounge later, she moved on.

At 0530, London found a storage cache for fruit. Fruit kept best at temperatures between two to eight degrees Celsius. She climbed onto the top shelf of several heavyduty aluminum dunnage racks and slept fitfully, with a combat knife in one hand and a suicide pill in the other. With the lower shelves lined with apples, bananas and other produce, the cooks were unlikely to find London, but one could never be sure.

The clanging of pans, sharp orders yelled by head chefs,

and sounds of rice being pulled from large bags, kernels spilling over the sides of scoops, added to London's poor sleep. In the mist of chaos, her ears remained tuned for the cocking of a pistol.

Her sleep ended with the electricity going off, not just inside the temperature-controlled storage units, but the kitchen itself. She sat on top of a chilled range, pulled a pad of paper from her ruck, and drew a map of what she'd seen the previous night, ate scraps of leftovers and headed back out to continue searching for the super engine.

She set into a slow jog for the next ten miles, passing several hallways, much like the one she'd observed the day before. The occasional distant hum of a truck forced her to hide. Low, palms

spread, she recalled the first time she'd gone hunting with her father and grandfather on the Cherokee Reservation.

At nine, her grandfather handed her a bow and quiver full of arrows. "This is for you, fawn." Duda had been the family inspiration for using nicknames. "I made this Osage Orange wood bow to fit your hands. Notice how your thumb and forefinger form a 'V' around the bow grip? With a balanced grip, you can bring down a deer. But remember, little fawn, even the smallest deer can be a mighty opponent."

Back then, London thought everything her grandfather said sounded corny. Now she cherished her memories of him. More often than she could remember, Duda's lessons had saved her life. "Thank you, Duda. I'll remember."

He taught her to walk toe to heel through the woods, keeping her weight on the back foot until she'd tested the ground ahead. "Feel with your toes. Listen to the ground as you step. Even the smallest sounds are trumpets in the forest." She'd watched her grandfather's every move that day, imitating his open mouth, his calm silence, and short steps. She learned to keep the sun at her back, her weapon waist high, and the wind in her face while hunting. Like then, she hunted.

London followed a single lane, passing a bunker filled with warheads and assorted weaponry.

Ahead, the tunnel brightened. Careful to avoid the harsh lights by moving around parked trucks and equipment, she came to a 'Y' on the road. To her right, two lanes opened into a four-lane highway, lit by Russian-made carbon arc streetlamps.

She estimated the road came out somewhere in, or near, North Korea's capital, Pyongyang.

The tall dual sided streetlights, placed every thirty feet, flooded the tunnel in intense light, reminding her of a naval dockyard.

At the entrance, the people had engraved the cement, 'Long Live the Great Commander Kim Jong-un,' with gigantic murals painted on each side.

One poster showed Kim Jong-il and his father, Kim Il-sung, walking along a snowy lane. The other pictured a group of women and children being brutalized by American soldiers. 'Revenge Against Imperialist Murderers.'

In all things, London had found truth in every lie, and she wondered now what truths the people had witnessed during the Korean War. Not every soldier, no matter the side, carried a badge of honor. Taking a life bestowed no glory, but she'd been ordered to do just that more than once and knew the soldiers had too.

Two heavy trucks, one transporting a bedload of workers and the other carrying what appeared to be a load of steel alloy, drove around the bend.

London ran to the artillery storage unit, a half mile back. Inside the unit she hid under a metal rack weighed with artillery shells, missiles, and torpedoes.

She searched the dark for spiders, hating the creepy

crawlies. Out of extreme hunger, she'd eaten a few, but chewing them hadn't eliminated her fear. The females eating their mates after copulation gave her prey anxiety, something she'd experienced daily in the Smokies.

She'd once awoken ten feet off the forest floor, in a tree, dreaming spiders were crawling on her. She'd rolled out of her hammock, grabbing a branch as she fell.

Absent of spiders, the dark chamber offered comfort and sleep. At least for a person accustomed to napping anywhere. She dozed undisturbed until the click of a key turning woke her.

The door creaked open, and London counted four feet in the dim light. One male, wearing a size nine men's shoe, the other one . . . She couldn't tell. The person stood around one hundred and seventy to one seventy-three centimeters. The taller, who stood around one hundred and seventy-six centimeters, held a clipboard from the sound of flipping paper. Pressing her back against the wall, London froze. Listening.

"Empty these two walls and send the missiles to *Haeju*, then stack what's in the truck in here. Another truck will arrive at four from Pyongyang Air Base. Tomorrow, we'll empty the remaining missiles and restock with ICBMs and the Great Leader's new miniaturized nuclear weapons."

Intercontinental ballistic warheads? One missile carries fourteen warheads. London ran mental calculations. *In a room this size, they could store enough power to fire thirty missiles. If every storage unit had this much fighting power . . .*

The thought broken when a man opened the door. "Yes, sir." Both left, closing the door without flipping the light switch.

London raked through her memories and remembered a newspaper article with a picture of Kim Jong-un standing in front of a round bomb. *A miniaturized nuclear bomb. A stockpile of those weapons could . . .*

The shorter person returned with a metal rolling cart used to transfer warheads.

London heard the roar of a transfer truck's engine outside the door. Exposed, if they removed the missiles overhead, she ran through her options. *Hurling knives. Useless in cramped quarters and bars between us. Even if she aimed well, the weapons would strike metal before reaching the soldier.* Forced to rely upon a gun, she pulled out a Swiss mini gun from a zippered pocket. Illegal in the states, she'd seen one at a weapon show in Switzerland and bought it. London held the thirty-five-millimeter close range revolver at the ready. If exposed, the revolver fires at just under one hundred and twenty-one meters per second, with deadly accuracy. The only negatives were people outside the room hearing the blast, eliminating any surprise attack.

At 0100 hours, London had survived potential exposure, and the warheads were gone.

The unlit room echoed an eerie creak as the door opened a second time. This time, the light flicked off. No one flipped through a report. Two lovers started moaning inside the missile closet, pumping against the remaining warheads.

London huddled in the dark.

The snap of a bra followed by heavy breathing, two people kissing passionately. A female voice asked, *"Igeos-i anjeonhabnikka?"*

London giggled. *Is she safe? She's having sex in a room full of bombs. What an idiot.*

"Shh . . . *The Great Leader keeps us safe and is always listening.*"

Creep. The Great Listening Leader doesn't rank you high enough to care whether you blow up, but if he learns of your poor work habits, you're dead anyway.

The rip of a zipper, heavy breathing, and gyrating hips slammed warheads against the cement wall. London processed and dismissed the possibility of escape. Even if she could reach the door, the creaking hinges would expose her. Trapped, London stuffed a finger in each ear, blocking most of the noise.

Sputtering, the woman groaned, "I . . ." a heavy breath, "want . . ." another sharp intake, this time the guy, "more . . ."

He grunted with effort.

'Phhuur.'

The scent of rotten egg tasted like sewage, growing from a slow whiff and building to a lingering bed of sulfur water in the heat of the outdoors. The smell didn't slow the enamored couple as they continued banging bombs for an unwilling audience of one. Not for a single stroke did the retched eggy taste leave London's mouth, nor did the moans belched by the enamored soldiers.

The promiscuous couple faded from London's mind, replaced by the images of men, called Johns, hammering into her mind.

Sarah broke into a feverish sweat. A man's grubby hands pinched her nipples, tugging on them with his teeth as she wiggled underneath him. His sloppy wet kisses covering her mouth, his tongue cutting off her air supply.

She gasped for air as he grunted, driving his cock deep inside her. Desperate, she clawed out from under him, coughing and choking, his nasty saliva covering her chin and lips. Next to the bed, uncontrolled shaking threatened to buckle her knees. She begged the man, "Please. Don't tell Blake. I . . . I'm sorry. I just can't . . . do this." Blake would kill her for not satisfying the customer.

"Mama, please save me." London vomited, passing out, unaware if the lover's discovered her hiding.

When she came to, she lies sprawled on the floor, her

face covered in puke. She slowed her breathing.

The dangers of her body sprawled defenselessly in a tunnel operated by the authority of a brutal dictator were high. That danger could easily become her demise unless she kept her wits, which she hadn't. She crawled out from under the racks and jumped to her feet, blade in hand.

Alone. *Alone is safe.*

Shaken, she sat against the metal frames and wiped her face clean with the sleeve of her bodysuit.

Flashbacks had left her vulnerable on previous occasions. Her last episode had been in Mexico over a year ago. She'd witnessed a van of men kidnap a young girl off the streets of Chiapas. Unable to abandon the girl, she followed them to a house of ass in Ciudad Obregón, known as a *cacuilchil*. She planned to kill the perp and make it appear as a drug deal gone bad.

After observing the house for days, she knew seven armed men guarded the house. Three more were inside with the girls. The house, more of a mansion than a home, stood three stories with over four-thousand square feet. They kept the younger girls on the top floor.

She entered through the basement and climbed a secret passage the traffickers used for hustling new girls inside.

Once in the hall of favors, she sniffed the bittersweet floral scent of baby powder mixed with kerosene. The recollections of being high, intoxicating. She continued to long for the initial euphoria that hits with a person's first high. The drugs were a perfect freedom, without boundaries. No pain. No sorrow. Pure bliss. Being an addict is continuously chasing that peace, becoming the air needed for living. Like oxygen, the body feels breathless without the drug. Heroin, her drug of choice, removed fear and self-loathing, making her invincible. She became the best at everything, with a focus on pleasuring men.

Caught in the euphoric memories, she'd walked

into a den of sex, booze, and drugs. The scent of semen sent London swirling, as if high. She'd staggered into a closet and closed the door, using both hands to grasp the doorknob between fingers that shook too hard to grip. Once safely inside, she'd huddled against a back wall.

Every footstep sounded like Blake's, his rhythmic cadence as he'd walk the long corridor to her room. She felt the lash of his whip, teeth biting into her flesh, and each slice of his knife. Memories of blood and pain rushed at her, bullets from a semi-automatic.

Covered in a sweat, just as now, London had controlled her breathing and exited the closet, closing her mind to everything but her task. She'd taken three lives that day, and the pubescent girl she'd tried to save, refused to follow, her terrified cries still ringing in London's ears, "I cannot go with you. De will kill my family."

20

Find the Tunnel's End

When the lights went dark outside the room, so did the traffic. The two-lane road heading southwest remained barren. It smelled of stale earth and old metal. London tugged at the top edge of her hoodie in the cold, damp air and set off at a brisk run. She needed to find the tunnel's end, and what they had hidden behind these walls.

Four miles later, the main tunnel exited right and led to double doors. The deafening silence of the hall was eerie, oppressively quiet. She checked her watch. Two hours left to explore the room and hide.

The long corridor led to another set of doors.

She used the WD-40 to prevent any squeaking as she cracked open the door and peered into an unlit room. The flick of a red penlight lit up the large, cavernous factory enough for her to find her bearings.

Inside, the beam cut through a pervasive gloom. The air thrummed with a distant, almost imperceptible hum of unseen ventilation. She walked past conveyor belts, their rubber surfaces cracked, stretching into the darkness. They were lined with the same modified versions of the miniaturized warheads she had seen in the article. Under the red beam, they glittered as decorations in a karaoke bar.

Different stages of assembly lay strung out on moving lines, from raw, dull casings to partially assembled units with exposed wiring. Beyond them, massive, cylindrical missiles, their steel bodies streaked with rust, rested on heavy, rolled platforms.

She scooped up a titanium bar, scanned the room for guards, and crossed to the other side.

A row of computers sat to her left. Most of the them were for syncing and development.

The last computer screen showed the schematics for a "super engine" with propulsion technology. One of these engines sat under development to her right. The information on the computer screen revealed Iran designed the high-thrust engine along with North Korea.

This engine was designed to power a new class of miniaturized nuclear missile, allowing it to achieve unprecedented speeds and maneuverability, much like the hypersonic capabilities of Russia's Avangard, but within a far smaller, more evasive package. This new missile, potentially designated BAHRAN, could be fitted with a low-yield nuclear warhead capable of destroying a ten or twenty-mile radius rather than an entire city. The BAHRAN itself used a hybrid system, with a solid-fueled booster for initial acceleration and a liquid-fueled hypersonic glide engine for terminal phase maneuvering.

Victory over resistance. Fitting.

She read through the file and learned the BAHRAN used liquid propellant, with 48 tons of thrust. *How fast could this engine travel?* She tried calculating the F=ma but only had the thrust, not the acceleration or the mass.

A complex engine, it had experienced many failures,

mainly due to instability and difficulty in controlling the speed. It burned the fuel, and failures to equalize temperature and pressure were common. Their records showed the multiple failures had deformed or melted the walls.

Yet, each minor success showed promise: the BAHRAN, the smaller missile itself, could execute rapid changes in course and fly at high speeds, making it difficult for sensors to track and modern defense systems to counter. *If they get it right . . .*

London didn't understand the dangers behind the engine, but the CIA had tasked her with risking her life to find it, driving her to move with urgency. *If Iran is working in cahoots with Kim Jung Un, who else is helping to fund this engine? China? Russia? Iran-backed militias?*

In the hour before workers clocked in, she examined the files, committing much of the information to memory. The sound of footsteps and mumbled voices alerted her outside the twin doors. She exited the screens and hid in a storage unit filled with cleaning supplies, metal parts, and shells. Earlier, she'd noticed the top shelf held two light boxes. The room was wide enough to hold her and the boxes. Climbing and snuggling between two of them, she watched the people work.

The shelf provided the most comfort she'd gotten since entering the tunnel two nights prior. Later, after all the workers left, she woke to a man's voice outside the storage room. His dialect strong and guttural, firmly rooted in the speech patterns of North Korea, blended with the ancient, more tonal historical version.

"Jung Ji?"

Nothing but the sound of fidgeting followed. London peeked through a crack where the wall and ceiling didn't meet, and saw an insignificant man, too thin for his height, standing at a computer. His caller's face appeared on the screen.

"*Hyung.*" The term she'd heard the Commander's squad call him. She knew it meant brother.

"It is good to see you, Jung Ji." For less than twenty seconds, the two brothers exchanged information on family members. The total video call lasted for one minute and twenty seconds. The thin colorless man gave the cherubic face of the other, known as Jung Ji, a list of wants and needs, from medicine to movies, to skin care products, a laptop and one English dictionary. Then it ended.

The last thing Skinny said, "Go in peace."

Defector signed off with, "Be in peace."

With the call ended, she watched Skinny turn off the computer and darting through the factory. Before exiting, he listened, his ear pressed against the hinged framework, before cracking the door enough to look out. Confident no one stood nearby, he inched his way through the opening.

The factory empty, London climbed out of her make-shift bed, her stomach growling, echoing in the silence. She hadn't eaten more than a few nuts since entering the tunnel. From her bag, she pulled some loose granola, pressing the crumbs into her mouth as she surveyed the room.

She opened several lockers, hoping to find something to restock her food supply, but found nothing. Not surprising. The people, though in the army, were malnourished judging by their sunken faces and stick-like limbs.

At the back, she spotted a separate, smaller exit. This exit dropped off, an unfinished project lacking purpose. She'd found what she came for, her mission complete for now. She jumped from the ledge, rolling on the ground, stopping when she struck a bush. *Shit.*

Low in the brush, she mapped the grounds. Less than a half mile from where she exited, another tunnel entrance remained under heavy guard. It too had a launchpad, but she suspected this pad launched the new miniaturized weapons, using the Super Engine designed by an Iranian technician from the Rashidi Industrial Group, or RIG. She repeated the engineer's name, committing it to memory. *Nazari, Doctor Vahid Nazari.*

At the bottom of the hill, a river ran between the two mountainsides. Able to recognize the land from earlier visits and studying maps, London knew the river flowed into South Korea and on through the town of *Dutayeon-ro*. Fortune at her side, the same storm that had helped her enter the North, now helped her exit, having swollen the river's belly.

21

The Horseshoe-Shaped Bar

Claire, the bartender, stood behind the horseshoe-shaped bar wiping wine glasses as the Commander entered. "How can I help you?"

He walked over and sat on a cut bar stool. "London. She here?"

"Nope." Claire raised a glass and hung it on an overhead hook. "Haven't seen her for more than a week. I suspect she's off in the woods taking pictures of some lizard. Why are you asking?"

"She is a friend."

The Commander deliberated reasons Claire didn't worry about a missing employee. His instincts told him she was lying. *Why is everyone around London trained in secrecy?* To find out, he tested Claire to determine when she lied, to find the truth. He started with simple questions. Once he'd learned her cues, he could read her lies. "The bar open? Can I get a drink?"

"Nope. We don't open the bar until five p.m., but I

can make you a burger and fries, or" she slapped a menu in front of him, "our special is meatloaf. It won't be what you're used to, but it will fill your belly."

He studied her eyes. *Minimal movements.*

He picked up the menu and scanned it, uninterested in the contents. "How long London worked for you?" The Commander wished he'd paid more attention in English classes, but he never expected to have an American lover.

"She doesn't work for me. She works for Joe, but she's been here round six months now."

Steady. The commander watched, hoping for a sign that might reveal London's whereabout. *Hands are calm.* Nothing.

"Joe, not mind . . . she gone?"

Claire leaned on the bar; her hands clasped. "London does what she wants around here. If I had my druthers, I'd kick her ass out on the street, but it isn't up to me."

The truth. Hmmm . . . closer to the story? The Commander ordered a cold coffee and threw a handful of American dollars on the bar. "Where she from?"

Claire grabbed the money and responded. "Who?"

"London."

"Hey, buddy, what is this? An interrogation?"

Calm, the Commander watched her reaction and waited.

Claire's face scrunched and her lower lip protruded somewhat. "Who cares?" The glass in her hand slipped as she shifted to her right leg, resting her weight on one hip. "Do you think I've got time to watch the slut?"

A lie, subtle but still a lie. Claire finished the last two glasses without inspecting for spots, turning away as she hung them. *She knows I am on to her . . .* He lifted the glass to his lips and looked around the bar, removing the threatening vibe in the air.

When Claire returned from the kitchen, the Commander

went in for the kill. "When you expect London?"

Claire set the box on the bar with a bang. *One sign.*

"I don't know. What's she mean to you, anyway?"

Her anger is one more sign. *Another lie.*

"Maybe never," she continued. "I can hope the bitch is dead, but I'm not that lucky. Joe pampers her, leaving me with the work."

The Commander watched as she rambled. *Eyes steady. Hands naturally relaxed. Truth. London is in danger. This woman wants her gone. Maybe even dead.*

He took one last sip of his coffee, stood, thanked Claire, and left.

A staircase alongside the saloon drew his attention.

A head popped above the first level landing.

Despite the slump of her shoulders and slow steps, her feet dragging across the platform nose, he knew. *London.* She wore a pair of jeans and a white cotton shirt, with dirty, ratty hair as if she hadn't bathed in days. *Where has she been?*

When she entered the apartment, he climbed the steps. Outside her door, he fought with himself, wanting to break down the door, and needing to be patient. Pushing away an urge to check on her, he turned to leave.

When he came back from a mission, he wanted a soft bed and twelve hours of sleep. *A mission?* His mind churned. *A terrorist? CIA?* He pushed both out of his mind. He'd done that ever since the incident at the grocery store. It's true, he thought, *London is no ordinary girl.* The way she'd handled herself showed strength and courage. The strength one gets from training. *Still ... photographing wild animals ... She'd have to be strong.* His mind pictured her dangling from the rope on one leg, remembering her quiet footfalls in the forest.

He needed answers. *What happens when I learn the truth? Can I act against her?* He didn't think he could.

Back in his jeep, he headed toward Cheondo-ro Military Base. *She could be smuggling drugs. Helping North Korean defectors escape?* He didn't want to believe London could involve herself in illegal activity, but he couldn't deny his instincts.

At the base barracks, inside a small single room he called home, he opened his laptop and ran a military secure electronic search on the name 'London.' To his surprise, the name Sarah Bennett came up with an aka of 'London.' *Is Sarah her real name?*

Searching further, he learned she came to South Korea in November of the previous year. This coincided with what Claire had told him. London's long-term visa remained valid for another two years. No dependent permit proved she was single. Her Multiple Re-entry Permit is still in effect. She'd traveled outside Korea three times since moving here.

What is this file not telling me?

He loaded an American search engine. One article of hundreds caught his interest for Sarah Bennett.

Betty Jo Parker Green died at her residence, 7 December 2010 of cancer. Betty's death is preceded by her husband, Peter Green, and one daughter, Lindsey Jo Green. She resided at 252 Spring Valley Road, Pigeon Forge, Tennessee, for the past 15 years, as the host for Alpine Hideaway Campground. Mrs. Green is survived by Sarah Bennett, an unregistered guardian.

The obituary continued, but the Commander stopped reading. So far, everything checked out and there weren't any obvious danger signs. Still, his gut told him London needed watching. He'd learn what secrets the Whiskey River and its crew were hiding. He shut down the computer and left.

22

Heard the Shuffling Sound of Slippers

Standing at London's apartment door, the Commander knocked. Fifteen hours had passed.

Sure she'd be awake, he knocked a second time. Through the thin hollow wood, he heard the shuffling sound of slippers dragging across the floor.

The door cracked, exposing a small hand that gripped the edge of the wood, and a thin sliver of checkered flannels clung to a faux fur slipper.

"London."

"What?" Her speech was sluggish, sounding like, *whad*.

"I am on R&R. You challenged me to a kick-boxing match. Weather report says rain. So . . ."

She peeked around the door. Her hair, uncombed. "I challenged you. To a fight?"

The Commander's hat shuffled from one hand to the other. "During our hike, you mentioned showing me your skills. I recall, I accepted that challenge. Today feels right. You cannot take photos in the rain."

Her eye disappeared. He heard a slight thud against the wood. The wish to see the early morning version of London tempted him to give the door a slight nudge, but he resisted. Trained to stand tall with feet planted side-by-side, the Commander's legs begged to shift in nervous anticipation. When she said, "Okay," he let out a long-held breath.

Still sounding drowsy, she asked, "Where do you want to meet?"

"Boxing ring on base. I will pick you up at 1500 hours. We can ride together."

"What time is it?"

He checked his watch. "Eleven hundred." Again, silence. He remembered how thin she'd been the previous afternoon and wondered if she'd eaten. "Breakfast? I can scramble eggs—"

"No!" The eye reappeared. "Uh ... Thanks, but I'm not hungry. I'll see you at three." The door closed and the slush of slippers grew faint.

For the next four hours, the Commander paced his room, a compact space measuring only eight feet by ten. A twin bed hugged the farthest corner with a gray wool military issue blanket wrapped snug around the single mattress resting upon a metal frame. A military issue chest sat at the end of the bed and a two-door closet with drawers stood to the right of the entrance. Under a single window sat a desk with a laptop and tabletop light.

His training prepared him for situations he'd face as a special operations commander, but he considered London unfamiliar territory. He needed to find out why she came to Korea and learn her identity. With lying skills that matched the toughest detainees, questions were useless. However, a battle of strengths might reveal what words could not.

At 1500 hours, the Commander leaned against Willy and waited for London to step through her apartment door. On the surface, he appeared calm, but inside, his nerves were strung into a tight ball.

London stepped out the door in a Sherwood green Nike Pro body suit made of spandex that matched the color of Willy's paint. A clingy, bur breathable bodysuit exposed her swimmer's shoulders, the deltoids and bicep muscles stretching the fabric. Small, well-rounded breast dipped into a delicate but chiseled waistline. He glanced at his hands and thought they might fit around her waist. Each step exposed a runner's thighs and calves, long, lean, and strong enough to carry her miles without growing weary.

Standing in front of him in ankle high sneakers, London stood around one hundred and sixty-four inches, several inches shorter than himself. A ponytail held her blonde hair out of her face, giving the strands freedom to bounce with each step. Covered, he couldn't check for scars. Scars were a part of a soldier's life, and the first recognizable sign of a violent criminal.

With hands clasped behind her back, London looked at him with a sunny expression that added a golden hue to her blue eyes. The previous signs of exhaustion were gone. Long, dark lashes blinked twice before she placed an open palm against his abdomen. "Let's do this," then turning, she jumped into Willy's passenger seat.

They pulled in front of an arched aircraft maintenance shed inside Cheondo-ro Army Base.

London had visited other times, but she'd never been to the gym. She followed the Commander inside. They passed a locker room, stairway, and office. Soldiers, doing reps, stopped and stared. Despite two large fans attached to the near barren walls, the heat inside suffocated her.

No air conditioning. Good, the heat will keep me

limber. A heavy sweat would awaken London's instincts.

Not a facility for the pampered, with fancy exercise equipment or televisions tuned to sports. The high walls, white overhead, were a dingy gray below. Polished to a shine, the cement floor still showed dark stains from airplane oil. An over-sized South Korean flag hung from the wall, its red and blue swirls supposedly gave stability to the positive and opposing cosmic forces. London touched the Commander's hand. When his head jerked in her direction, she pointed to the flag. "What's the meaning of the bars?"

An easy smile crossed the Commander's lips. "The *kwae trigrams* are *yin* and *yang.* Broken lines are dark and cold. Like *yin.* Unbroken bars are bright and hot. Like *yang.*" He placed an intimate hand on her back, stepping in closer. His touch made London weak, causing her arm to drop.

"Three solid bars are the celestial body. Heaven. Six broken bars, earth. In opposite corners, sun and moon, or fire and water. It is a simple flag with deep meaning."

"Balance. I get it." London turned. Their faces were close enough to touch. She felt his warm breath, and didn't move despite the nausea. She liked his nearness and feared it at the same time. Sensing the questioning eyes of those inside the gym, she stepped away.

The Commander's hand slipped from her back and into her hand. The warmth tickled her skin. Led toward the ring, two men approached. "Hey, Commander, looking for a sparring partner?"

Another man dropped a barbell. "I'm available."

"Not today." The Commander nodded in London's direction. "I already have one."

Other heads popped up from their workout. One soldier said, "A woman, sir?"

"Not just any woman," the Commander lifted a helmet

from the shelf, placing it on London's head, "this woman. She claims to be the best."

The soldier laughed. London felt the hackles on the back of her neck rose. She looked the scrawny soldier up and down. She knew he didn't match her power. For that matter, she doubted any of them could win in a dual to the death, except maybe the Commander. His stance resembled hers, unconventional. Solid and light, proving his speed. His strength far out measured her own. She'd have to find his weak point to defeat him. About to fight a warrior with Shogun sharpness, this fight terrified her, something she'd not experienced. She hoped her internal tremors stayed in the house.

Second-story windows flooded the room with warm light, yet the floor cooled her feet as she sat on a hardwood bench. Soldiers sat on the floor, leaning back on their hands to watch. Others stretched out. Sweaty bodies filled the air with the pungent gas of bacteria feeding on human fatty acids and proteins.

The Commander tightened the Velcro to his gloves as London leaned in.

"I thought we'd be alone," she told him.

"If you are uncomfortable, we can leave."

She bent to tie her shoelace and studied the soldier who'd reduced her as a mere woman. "No. They won't bother me."

He caught the single twitch of her right thumb. *She is lying.*

With headgear and gloves, London appeared relaxed. Her eyes twinkled. "Remember, you asked for this, so no whining when you get pulverized."

"Pulverized?" The Commander jumped into the ring. Balanced, with both hands in the box, he asked, "Me? Not lost a fight in five years."

London snorted and vaulted over the rubber ropes.

"You've never fought me." In position, signaling him to come closer, she mouthed, "Bring it on."

"Rules?"

"I have one rule."

"I am open," he added.

"No holding. I don't like being held." Then she popped her mouthpiece in and raised her hands into a defensive position.

The Commander contemplated avoiding the thing he most wanted to do but agreed.

23

Answer His Aggression

The Commander stepped in to London, expecting her to answer his aggression with a light opposing defensive move. When she dropped and pivoted, he jumped out of reach. To his surprise, she sprang to her feet, landing in unison with him. "Impress—"

An open palm struck his chest, followed by a crescent kick that missed the side of his face. He ducked before the follow-up blow with her fist landed. The Commander countered her movements. Grabbing her wrist, he spun her, placing her back against him. He felt her elbow thrust before it hit and released her before it landed.

In a clever counter move, London grabbed his free arm. She turned with him, entrapping him in the same move he'd used on her.

To gain the upper hand, he bent forward using the same hold, this time pulling her over his head.

London slammed onto the spring floor. She looked up, amused. "Taking advantage of a woman . . . I didn't think you'd stoop so low."

"You laid the rules. Gender preference not mentioned."

The other men circled the ring, cheering the Commander.

"Come on, Commander. You're holding back. We want to see a real fight."

The Commander's pounding pulse drowned out their egging shouts.

Unprepared for her power and unexpected opposition, the Commander found himself facing a formidable adversary in the spar. London's powerful limbs and quick thinking were clear.

She spun into a stance and narrowly dodged his return kick to her chest. She'd expected his move. Keeping low, she caught his leg on the rise. With his leg caught on her shoulder, she pushed off, dropping him to the canvas. Elbow extended like a pro wrestler she dropped, aiming for his gut.

The Commander rolled, missing London's landing blow, and kicked up to his feet. "Close. Not quick enough," he taunted.

Balanced on her back foot, London got into her box and studied her opponent. *He's toying with me.* With open palm strikes, one after another, she attacked.

The Commander deflected her advances, spurring her to faster and more aggressive moves, the joy on her face mesmerizing. She radiated. His pulse quickened when several of her strikes came close. He enjoyed their proximity as much as she did.

Focused, he didn't notice the whooping and hollering of the men gathered around the ring. A

soldier entered the gym, pushed through the crowd, and hung on the ring ropes as he yelled, "Our Commander's fighting a woman?"

Another yelled, "Why not? She got into the ring."

In an aerial flip, the Commander's right foot aimed for London's shoulder. She dodged left, leaving a vulnerable opening. His other leg caught her in the head. His landing blow, though deliberate, lacked the force he'd use in close combat.

The new spectator taunted his superior officer. "Ah . . . come on, Commander, you're letting her off easy."

London grabbed the Commander's ankle and twisted her body over his leg, flipping him a second time.

With effort, he broke free and rolled out of her hold.

"You weren't expecting that. Were you?" she asked.

He backed off and collected his balance. She'd let him clip her, taking advantage of his aggression. He responded with a cool smirk. "Not happen again." Covered in sweat, he chose each maneuver with care, calculating her next move as they continued to share blow for blow. He heard someone yell, "Knock out. Knock out."

Bent low, he rotated as London spiraled into the air, flipping over him. A kick to his back knocked him toward the canvas, but he rolled a second time onto his feet. "Nice."

"I warned you. I'm good."

"You are good. Not good enough," he mocked. They both held back, learning each other's moves and limits.

Ready to apply more pressure, he moved in, arms and legs swinging. London blocked each blow, proving her defensive skills to be as smart as her offensive. He swept in low to knock her off her feet. When she made a move to flip, he adjusted his body to counteract her movements, catching her in mid-flight and taking her to the canvas. On top of London, the change in her turned in an instant.

Sarah's mind snapped. "Blake?" Unsure how he'd found her, he straddled her chest the way he'd done in the past. "You're dead. I killed you."

Blake smiled. "It's your turn, bitch."

"No! I won't let you. I'm not your puppet anymore." Crazed with fear, she fought for her life.

Her muscles tensed, back arched, her body rising onto her hands. Powerful legs caught him around the chest in a vice grip.

Twinkling eyes turned to angry slits. The person London had suppressed surfaced.

The Commander's ribs compressed to the point of breaking. He fought to stand and worked to fracture her hold.

London spun into a death roll, pinning him to the canvas, giving him seconds to refill his burning lungs.

24

On Her Feet

The Commander rolled, breaking London's hold. Again, on her feet, she readied to attack. Her stance changed. Instead of balancing over her back foot, she centered her body over her front toes. Her hands, palms forward, raised to protect her face as her chin dropped.

Krav Maga. She plans on killing me. Why?

The moment he stood, London's body contracted and sprung. They were no longer sparring. Amazed by her aggression and speed, the Commander fought off her death blows while studying her. *What changed?* Then he remembered. She'd warned him, and he'd forgotten. She didn't like being held.

Distracted, he came close to an elbow. It damned near connected with his jugular. London spun. She landed a kick to his thigh. Injured, the Commander knew he needed to end this match, but still he held back. Her pinpoint pupils showed him her pain. Given the opportunity, he'd kill the one responsible. Left without options, he'd have to stop the hallucinations. He needed more aggression. With deadly speed and accuracy, he defended himself.

She grabbed his arm and did a half pike over his head. He wasn't ready. On his shoulders, she rolled, dropping him a third time. She sat on his midsection, both wrists caught in the crook of her bent knees. Her hand raised for a final blow, a blow intended for his heart. The strike never came.

Recognition burned from deep indigo to a soft bluebell seconds before two soldiers pulled her off, and her eyes turned to the color of ash.

Held between two men, survival became London's goal. She twisted the lower half of her body, striking the inside of one soldier's knee, dislocating it. The sickening pop, followed by a crumpled soldier, howling, didn't stop her. With both arms pinned behind her back, she tightened the muscles of her abdomen, raising her legs over the head of her enemy, and wrapped her thighs around his neck, squeezing.

The Commander knew the soldier needed help. He talked to London, jumping to his feet. "Donee, let him go. You are safe. I will protect you."

When the soldier didn't drop, London lifted her body as if free-falling from a plane, creating more force between her thighs as she rose. Her eyes met the Commander's. She saw Blake pleading with her not to kill him. Hate and fear raged.

"Why should I let you get away?" No longer rational, she screamed, "You hurt me! I begged you . . . You bastard. Let me go. Or I'll make sure you're dead this time."

The soldier's face turned a sickly grayish blue. His hands grappled at her thighs as he dropped to his knees.

The Commander's mind raced. Many times, he'd seen men who'd suffered torturous beatings. Their minds broken. And then he knew. *London has PTSD.*

"Donee. Look at me."

"Commander?"

"Yes. Let him go, Donee. He will not hurt you."

Two other soldiers climbed into the ring.

She rose higher.

The Commander held up a hand. "No! You grab her now, she will snap his neck." The men backed off, while the rest stood at the ring's edge, blank faces staring.

He reached out his hand, using his thumb to wipe away her tears. The Commander continued talking. "Let go, Donee. I promise I will protect you."

London's face softened as the soldier's arms fell to his sides. When he dropped, she ducked and rolled. Her expression moved from a distant awareness into the present. Her eyes darted around the room.

The collapsed soldier coughed, gulping air.

The memory of Blake saying he'd kill her hung around, as real as the man she'd choked. She'd had other episodes, but never this vivid. London scooted away, shielding her eyes.

"Donee." The Commander reached for her.

"No! Don't come near me." *Stay focused. How can I get out of here?* She looked around the gym.

The angry glares of mustangs surrounded her, closing in on her. She stood on shaky legs, clinging to the rigging to stay upright. *Too many. I'll never defeat them.* An ambulance siren's *WEE-ooo-WEE-ooo-WEE-ooo* grew closer. *The military police?*

The slow movements of the Commander snapped her attention back to reality as she screamed, "Stay back! I don't want to hurt you."

He watched the bluebell color of her eyes glisten as he said, "I trust you."

"Don't. Killing's easy, you know. One snap and you'd be dead." She backed away as gurney wheels rolled across the cement, screeching in London's ears. Nails on a chalk-board. *I gotta' get out of here.*

The Commander took another step. "I trust you." His hand reached out for hers. "I need you to trust me."

London leaped over the ring and ran, dodging the hands grabbing at her.

As medics helped the injured men, the Commander rushed after London. Too slow. She'd left by the time he reached the gym entrance, nowhere in sight. Both his feet landed in the jeep, igniting the engine. He peeled out of the parking lot and scoured the base, fearing the worst. An American found on a Korean Army base, alone, was a spy.

Fears pushed aside. He continued his search. Scrutinizing the situation, he planned an escape route, adding hiding places and exploring hot spots along the way, noting the time of day.

At 1700 hours, he had time before the sun set. With a planned route of escape in mind, he parked his jeep back at the gym, withdrew his cell phone from the glove compartment, and set out on foot and made a call. "This is Commander Kim. I am calling to check on . . ."

As he talked, he watched for signs of London, a piece of torn fabric, a strand of hair, anything that might show he'd followed the right path. Nothing.

Again, he marveled at her training. Few men, even those who'd completed special forces training, couldn't match her speed or cunning, making her a deadly adversary. He caught a ride on the way back to the gym.

In Willy, he drove to Cheondochon and the bar. The sun sat low, the mountains dark and jagged, a sleeping dragon in the distance. The peach horizon, covered with blue, swirled with beige and burnt orange, streaked by ominous white-gray clouds, promised rain. Passing the bar, he saw a single light inside the upper apartment and knew she'd made it home.

Relieved, he drove back to base and visited with the injured soldiers. The man London had by the throat struggled to speak, his voice hoarse, but he'd recover. He'd survived a tough lesson, one that might save his life. *You never underestimate the enemy.*

The other would wear a knee brace on desk duty for the next six months.

Unable to sleep, the Commander drove to the Defense Department. Inside, he sat at his desk and ran another search on London. He didn't expect to find any information, so when a screen appeared reading, "Top Security Clearance Needed," the Commander sat back, his chair tilting as he stared at the screen. *Aish* . . .

Several minutes as he shuffled through papers in the drawer until he came across the code. before the Commander sat forward and plugged it in, giving him access to London's file.

Sarah Bennett aka London

United States CIA/Spy

A spy . . . Can't say I'm surprised. He continued reading her file. It listed her skills, ranging from Krav Maga to weapons and survival training.

London is stationed in the Republic of Korea on a special reconnaissance, working for both the US and South Korea. Her assignment is to find and destroy a North Korean super engine.

Engaging with London poses a significant threat of bodily injury or even death. With or without a weapon, she is lethal. Assigned to clandestine missions, or suicide missions, she is known to work alone. If you encounter this agent, be advised to stay clear.

His hat smacked against the monitor. The screen bounced off the partition and righted itself. *American bastards* . . . He yanked open a drawer in search of a cigarette and found none. He hadn't had a puff since throat surgery a few years ago. He slammed the drawer shut and continued reading.

London was born Sarah Bennett on 19 March 1992,

to Darwin Bennett and Darling Nestle Bennett Peterson.

Bennett lived homeless in Gatlinburg, Tennessee, at the age

of fifteen. Betty Jo Parker Green took Bennett in and later died

of cancer, 7 December 2010, leaving Bennett a home

and a meager amount of cash. Abducted by Blake Ritchie in 2009, she

became part of a sex-trafficking incident. Bennett murdered Ritchie

in 2010, by glass impalement, and escaped.

The report continued, listing added talents, such as climbing trees and holding her breath

up to four minutes. He scanned the list, turning it off before he finished.

The Commander buried his face in his hands, elbows propped on the desk. *She survived alone.* His mind pictured the tattered girl he'd seen a few days earlier. *And now, they expect her to destroy the engine alone.*

25

Calm the Fear

London, shut away in her apartment, grabbed the bear from her bed and hid in a corner of her closet. Her knees drawn, she hugged herself, the bear stuffed between her chest and legs to calm the fear that quivered in her belly. Every fiber in her wanted to scream, but she knew from hours spent alone in the basement of Blake's hellhole, no one would save her. To calm herself, she spoke words of comfort. "I am alone. Alone is safe."

She repeated her mantra over and over, rocking back and forth. "I am alone. Alone is safe." Repetition kept her focused on healing.

As her mind settled, so did her heart. A faint cry sprung into her thoughts. "You're squishing me."

Yona. She pulled the toothpick thin stuffed animal out, holding his long skinny arms, and stared at him. The comfort of aloneness turned into ice in scalding tea. She pulled the bear to her chest. "I'm not alone. I have you—"

London felt a butterfly dance in her chest. She'd meant

to say Yona, but the image in her mind hadn't been the bear but the Commander.

***

Commander Kim stepped into Lieutenant General Oh Hanbin's office in a formal suit of military blue with three starbursts on his collar, his hat in hand. "Good morning, Commander Kim. Please," the General's opened palm pointed to a seat, "sit."

The Commander sat, his back erect. "Sir. Thank you for seeing me."

General Hanbin poured two cups of hot tea, passing one to the Commander. "You're here concerning the incident at the gym. Am I right?"

"Sir, yes sir."

"I understand you read Miss Bennett's file, and you know she is here on a specific mission."

"Yes sir."

The General fidgeted in his seat, cleared his throat, and said, "We should demand punishment—"

"Sir, I am here to take full responsibility for the mishap between London and two soldiers. I drove London, I mean Miss Bennett, to base."

"Why should you take the blame?" The General leaned back, crossing his arms. "Foolish, I agree, but you didn't injure those men."

"Still . . ."

The General placed his elbows on the desk, clasped his hands, and looked at the Commander over furrowed brows. "Rest assured, son. Miss Bennett will not face any charges. What happened . . ." He shook his head. "An inconvenience to the Army—"

"An inconvenience, sir?"

"Affirmative. Miss Bennett's purpose in the Republic of Korea takes precedence over the crime."

"The Super Engine, sir?"

"Yes." The General scratched his head and continued. "Never mind, for now, that you've learned top secret information. We need Sarah Bennett, or London, to extinguish a global weapon. That needs to happen without endangering peace between the North and the South."

"What about London, sir?"

"Yes, well . . . I see you have developed feelings for this girl."

"I have, sir."

"I'm sorry, son." The General fidgeted with his desk, opening a drawer and closing it as if searching for something. "The country needs her. Shit. For that matter, the entire world needs her."

The Commander stood, bowed, and turned to leave. Halfway through the door, the General stopped him. "Commander."

Hand on the knob, he turned.

"That could be you in the hospital."

"Sir?"

"Miss Bennett understands one kind of fighting— the fight for survival. You are a superior soldier with a conscience. Miss Bennett is a calculated killer. A spy who gets the job done, unburdened by whoever dies, including herself. She's damaged. A deadly combination, don't you think?"

"Yes sir, deadly. I have seen her fight, and that is why she needs me." He walked through the door and closed it.

* * *

Twenty minutes later, the pounding in London's head didn't stop. To drown out the noise, she used Yona's paws to plug her ears, begging for the banging on the door to end. "Go away!" On hands and knees, she crawled from the secluded closet and walked to the door.

When the door cracked open, the Commander placed an open palm against the thin wood. He'd use force if needed. "It is me."

The door opened. He found London in the shadows, with swollen eyes, red against tan skin. He stepped in, resisting the urge to take her into his arms, and noticed one hand behind her back. *Alcohol? Drugs?* "What are you hiding?"

When she didn't answer, he reached around her, but London backed away. He tried a second time, and she backed against the wall, saying, "It's nothing."

"Then show me?"

"Aren't you afraid?"

The Commander chuckled. "Afraid of you? Do I have a reason?"

"I came close to killing a soldier. I might have, had you not stopped me."

The Commander turned, stepping into a spacious living room. Hat in hand, he turned to her. "I did not stop you. You did." A single colonial style straight-backed chair near the fireplace hardly covered the space available. He strode across the room, his steps echoing in the bare space, and sat.

London followed him, her head low, her back toward the kitchen. "I'm sorry."

The Commander flipped the light switch to a three-legged table with an attached lamp and magazine rack. His hand parted the row of comic books, landing on Ritchie Rich. *My lady is a minimalist.*

London's complexion had paled in the light. Concern for her propelled him out of the chair. Unable to stop himself, he reached out to embrace her. London backed away.

"You shouldn't touch me."

"Why?"

"I might ..."

He stepped in, his hand on her waist, and pulled her against him. Her recoil didn't carry weight as she remained within his hold.

Stiff, she said, "I'm not who you think I am. You should leave."

His hand dropped to his side as he stepped around her, propping himself against the kitchen bar, his hands resting on the Formica. "Tell me. Who are you?"

London lowered her gaze. But he'd seen the tears. "I killed him."

"Good. He cannot hurt anyone else. We put 'him' behind us."

Her eyes raised, though her head remained low. She seemed hell bent on convincing him of her evilness. "No! You don't understand. I *meant* to kill him. Premeditated murder makes me a killer."

The Commander pushed off the bar, placing a finger under her chin. "I am relieved."

Her head cocked to one side as she gave him a sideways glare.

"I am! He needed to die."

Eyes clouded over with moisture, allowing a single tear to spill, left dangling from the rim of her lip, caressed away by the Commander's thumb. His voice lowered, softened by emotion. "Whatever happened, that's the past. This," he cupped both cheeks in his palms. "What is between you and me? This is safe."

With crimson cheeks, her eyes settled on his lower lip. He watched as her pink tongue moistened her cracked lips. Slow and timid, she raised onto her toes. Their faces centimeters apart, her lips feverish and wet when they pressed against his.

Exposed, she ran, Yona dangling behind her. He heard the lock click seconds after the bedroom door closed.

The briefest of kisses, the trail of her lips against his, expanded the light blooming within the Commander. Her porcelains broken. Now the only thing standing between them carried the threat of death. He needed a plan to stop the mission.

26

Remembering the Kiss Love You

For the first night since London entered Blake's chilling horror house, she'd slept without dreaming. For years she'd hidden her identity, never getting close to people, not even Joe. She climbed out of bed, stretched, and stepped into a clean pair of jeans and pulled on a white shirt. Remembering the kiss, she felt her cheeks grow hot. *What's happening to me? I'm happy alone, well . . . at least contented. I don't need another man's damage.*

Despite the negative dialogue, London enjoyed being with the Commander. She'd gotten used to having him around and felt safe in his presence. *Safe . . .* An old feeling renewed, and one she didn't expect. Still, she had to let him go. She'd sworn a duty to her country, and that duty didn't leave time for relationships. Once she delivered her report to Joe, a matter of days would pass before the powers above her expected a completion to her mission.

Prepared to meet her maker, she rushed out the door to deliver the latest information.

Joe held a phone to his ear when London entered the office. She sat, her legs propped on the desk as she waited. She could tell he spoke to the head of the Central Intelligence Agency by the formality of his speech. Heavier, with a hint of fear. *For me? No. He might say so, but Joe takes care of Joe.*

Though he sounded calm and humble, his eyes told a different story. His pupils were in tight circles, his free hand balled in a fist as he glared at her. "Yes, sir. I am aware, sir. It is a sensitive mi—" his mouth snapping closed. Silence.

London heard the frustration behind every word. "Yes, sir! I will, sir. Yes, sir. Thank you, sir."

When the call ended, Joe studied her. His lips narrowed into a fine slit. "What's with you? You have embarrassed the United States government."

Still stretched out, her hands resting in her lap, London said, "It was an unfortunate incident—"

"An unfortunate incident?" Joe stood. Hands pressed on top of the desk. He leaned in closer and banged a fist into the wood. "Is that what you think this is? You might have killed that soldier."

"But I didn't." Her stomach churned. Shame had ridden her since she left the gym, but she couldn't break her guarded emotions, not even with Joe.

"You dislocated a soldier's knee. He'll be out of commission for months."

He held me! I warned them . . . Never mind. "I'm here to report my last mission. Do you want to receive my report or continue to berate me over something behind us?"

He pulled a handkerchief from his pocket and wiped his forehead before re-stuffing it. "Fine, give me your report."

London pulled a long cylinder from her ruck and slid out a map, which provided the times and dates of her entry into the tunnel. Using the calculations she'd prepared that morning, she used the map to provide a detailed layout of her plans. She pointed at the location where she exited.

"This is the factory. They named their new Super Engine, BAHRAN. The nearly completed product is inside here." The map included the data she'd memorized on both the missiles and the engine. "If my determinations are correct, North Korea will have completed it within months."

Joe scanned the file. "Doctor Vahid Nazari. You're sure it's him?"

"Positive." She flipped through the papers and found the data on RIG. "RIG, or Rashidi Industrial Group, is located east of Tehran in the satellite city, Pardis."

"Pardis Technology Park?" Joe asked.

"Same area. Doctor Nazari is RIG's leading theoretical physicist and in 2000 began his work on BAHRAN with North Korea."

Joe rubbed the stubble on his upper lip. "So, you're saying that even if we demolish the information, we won't eliminate the threat?"

"That's what I'm saying. It's just a matter of time before they build a new engine. I need to go to Iran and visit Doctor Nazari."

"Fine." He rolled the map and slipped it back inside the cylinder. "I'll call the chief. In the meantime, put together a list of what you'll need."

London stood.

As she turned to leave, Joe stopped her. "London."

"Yep."

"We need you back alive."

"Of course you do. I'm the only one crazy enough to face a million of Kim's army."

Joe grimaced. "Come on, you know what I mean . . . Our country needs you alive. You're no good to us dead."

"So," she corrected him, "you need me alive, for now . . ." and left the room without giving him an opportunity for more rhetoric.

She climbed the steps to her apartment and found the Commander leaning against the door. She struggled to draw a breath, trembling inside at the sight of him. Then everything settled. The calm be brought with him, centered her.

"Interested in a movie?"

She unlocked the door and stepped into the apartment. He followed. Turning, she exposed the long line of her slender neck as she grinned. "I'd love a movie. Do you have one picked out, or do I get to choose?"

"Love's Brief Surrender," he answered.

"Love's Brief Surrender?" London hung her ruck on the hook behind the door. "Didn't that come out in the 90s? I never took you as the gushy movie type. Wouldn't you prefer an action flick, or maybe a thriller?"

"I heard girls like chick flicks."

London shrugged, peeling off her shirt as she walked into the living room, exposing a black sports bra. "Fine." *Time for him to see the real me.* She twisted to see him. His eyes were wide, but he never wavered as she continued walking. "Let's go, but I'll need to change. Give me a second."

The door left cracked, she glanced through the gap. He'd seen the scars. She had wanted him to see them. To unmask herself felt compulsory. Time for him to learn the truth.

He stood by the window, fiddling with his cap.

Confused by his response, she closed the bedroom door.

If the Commander had read her file, which at least she believed he had, he'd expect a few scars, but she doubted he'd expect the level of body art Blake had carved into her. Blake had enjoyed cutting. She'd known it thrilled him. His arousal had pulsated with desire.

He'd inflicted the welted scars as punishment for her

crimes. She hadn't looked in a mirror since she'd escaped. She couldn't. The shame she carried inside was enough. She didn't need to see the scarlet letter.

He never cut her face. Her breasts. Preserving them for pleasure. Her abdomen, a soft cushion to lay his head.

Blake's dramatic routine still gave her cold chills. He'd always started at her neck, pretending to suck out the blood from her carotid artery. *"Mmm . . . Yummy."* Then he'd inhale, trailing the point in the middle of her breasts to the spot between her legs, releasing a breath and rolling over to lie in her scent. To enhance his urges, he'd run his knife across her bare breast and say, *"Tempting, but we can't damage the goods, now, can we?"*

The other scars came later. Gifts from the American government for her service. Two stabbings, a gunshot, and a slice across her breast from a serrated knife, along with a few minor cuts she thought of as mere scratches.

She peeked out the door again to find the Commander as she'd left him. *Why hasn't he left?*

* * *

The Commander stood at the window, hiding his anger after seeing the scars that riddled London's back and upper arms. He wanted to kill the responsible party, but she'd taken care of that herself long ago.

Until now, she'd hidden the truth. *What changed? Does she trust me?*

As much as he regretted sparring with her, he knew it had brought them here, to London's vulnerability. Wanting to save both sides of her, both the woman he knew and the teenage version of her, this path they'd traveled needed to happen.

London opened the door in a pair of jeans tucked into cowboy boots and a fresh cotton shirt. Her shoulder length hair hung loose. Both casual and stunning. The

Commander preferred women with natural beauty, their flaws exposed, uncluttered. London's flaws could not be found in her features. They remained hidden deep inside, but he'd expose them one by one.

He turned from the window and strolled across the room. His long arms encircled her against him. She shuddered but stayed.

* * *

Frozen in place, she felt the vibration inside as she fought off the terror. She wanted this as much as him, allowing his warmth to seep in. Trust still held at bay, she told herself to imagine the impossible. Wrapped in his arms, his heart beating against hers, a wild symphony of war took place. Half ready to run, the other half not letting go.

27

Enlarged Portrait

Under the hum of city lights, London stood next to the Commander at the Mega Coex in Gangnam. An enlarged portrait of Brok Borg and Tove Hjort, two Norse actors, hung above the theater entrance. London's gut swirled. She jerked around when the Commander's hand covered hers. "Popcorn?"

"Popcorn and a box of peanut M&M's," she answered, uncomfortable with speaking for no reason. *Why am I here?* The people crowding around the concession stand put her on edge. She studied each person to watch their body language, expecting one of them to pull a knife.

I need to go.

The sultry night held temperatures that climbed into triple digits. London preferred the heat. If she had to fight, the high temperature made this evening ideal.

Tonight was different. The only fight she faced she'd hidden close. The sweltering heat raised her core temperature, but an internal fire ignited by the man next to her, grew hotter. They'd entered the theater to watch a memorialized love on screen. A love that ends in death.

London wanted to die. She expected to die. Death ended her, or so she thought, until . . .

The promise in the Commander's eyes pledged a new beginning. A tomorrow without the pain she'd grown accustomed to. His gaze an oath to a future she longed to discover.

He squeezed her hand. "Peanut M&M's it is." He took out his wallet, handing the concession worker cash. "A combo of popcorn, drinks, and peanut M&M's."

The server glanced at London. "What to drink?"

"Water."

Then turned to the Commander. "You?"

"Water works."

Once served by the teenager behind the concessions, London followed the Commander.

"Here?"

London had visited a theater once right before her dad passed. A single seat lowered when she'd sat. Enough space between her and a friend. Their bodies never touched. Here, a red leather love seat offered more intimacy.

London hesitated.

The Commander nudged her. "This spot okay with you?"

"Uh . . . Sure." She stepped into the aisle, sitting on the outer edge of the seat, wiping sweaty palms against her jeans before accepting popcorn or candy. The leather squeaked when the Commander sat. His thigh pressed against hers. She wiggled to decrease his touch. It didn't work. Instead, she focused on the popcorn, shoving large handfuls into her mouth, and glued her eyes to the screen.

Like the jumbotron at a basketball game, their image appeared. Her cheeks were chipmunk full of popcorn, while the groomed Commander flashed a captivating smile and pointed at the screen. Underneath, the caption read, DON'T FORGET TO BUY SNACKS! She bit her lip as a bead of perspiration rolled the length of her nose and into her mouth, mingling with the salty popcorn.

Love's Brief Surrender began with the profile of a woman standing at the mouth of Storfjord, in Alesund, Norway. Straight blond strands of hair lifted in the shoreline breeze, the unfinished hull of a longboat in the distance. The scene, warm and bright in the evening sun, scanned tighter on the setting. The woman, arms loose at her sides, a single tear caressing the length of her cheek, watched the longboat set aflame.

The haunting music. The fire. The melancholy woman alone on the shore, and the Commander at her side who'd one day become like the woman on the screen . . .

London stood. "I'm going to the bathroom."

The Commander's soft smile etched at her pain.

Outside, she leaned against the wall. She took in deep gulps of air. *A mistake.*

Sensing someone approaching behind and expecting to find the Commander or maybe an enemy, she balanced her core and cleared her mind.

When she turned, a young girl approached.

The girl had long black hair. Maybe sixteen. She stood around one hundred and sixty-two centimeters and smelled of popcorn and soda.

"*Noona*, are you okay?"

London backed away. Sick of the pain that tightened her belly, a clinging to a fantasy the Commander promised. A dream to stop hurting and being hurt. She nodded, "I'm fine." Once through the doors, she ran from the theater. Out in the heat and the rain, her mind cleared. *What am I doing? I've got to leave. I can't do this.*

London felt her body pulled into familiar arms even as one foot hung suspended off the curb. The Commander's unshakeable grip calmed the panic inside, though it could not shatter the formidable wall she'd erected. "Do not leave, Donee."

She felt faint. *I need to get away. I can't breathe.*

"Stay with me."

Dizzy, London fought for release, screaming, "We can never work!"

He squeezed tighter.

"Let go!" she demanded. "We don't belong together."

He held on. "I am where you belong."

Unable to break his hold without harming him, she stopped fighting. "You're wrong."

London enjoyed the warmth, his hands sliding along her arms. Her back straightened against his chest. He'd made her vulnerable while the downpour cooled the heat threatening her sanity. In the soaking rain, London knew she should break free but didn't. His voice, a bubbling ripple in a freshwater spring, held her immobilized.

"I need you."

London collapsed against him. "Don't. It's no good." Her fingers gripped his hands, wanting to hold on forever, his skin slick from the rain. "Can't you see I'm empty?"

"Not empty, Donee." His voice softened, sounding less desperate. "I will shield you."

"I'm afraid," she whispered.

"Me too, but I'm here." His words both calmed and alarmed her. "Let me be your dome. No longer will you stand in the rain."

She peeled his fingers from her arms, running, dodging cars in the street. After placing a narrow step between her and an oncoming delivery truck, she hailed a taxi amid a steady flow of light traffic.

When she turned, the Commander remained curbside, the rain, now a soft drizzle, couldn't hide his pain.

* * *

Nine hours later, she stood before the unlit door of the brick red Sacred Heart Cathedral in Turkey, a sanctum point, to make the change needed to enter Iran.

Knocking, Bishop Pius Sahaya Bhavsar opened the door and greeted her. With palms pressed in prayer, the priest said, "Namaste. Please come in, my dear child. I have prepared all that you asked."

"Namaste, Excellency Pius. Please, before I leave for Iran, I need to confess."

"Yes, my child." The bishop placed a hand on the back of London's shoulder and guided her to the confessional, two dark wooden booths shaped to match the exterior of the church. Inside the one on the left, London held a ruby rosary between her index finger and thumb. She spoke before he got seated. "Your Excellency, I have sinned."

The door from the booth next to her clicked close, a loud noise in the silent church. "Tell me your sins."

"A man confessed his love to me."

"How can joyous news be a sin, my child?"

Trembling, London answered. "Death will separate us." Her fingers moved from one rosary bead to the next in frantic prayer.

The bishop, who provided her a haven during her missions in the east, understood London's purpose in Turkey. She could hear him fidgeting with the pages of his Bible, the only book he'd need in a confessional booth. He coughed. "Will this death happen by your hands?"

"Yes," she answered, her voice small.

His heavy breath did little to ease her pain. The sound of his *alb*, a long, white vestment he wore daily, crumpling as it gathered let her know he just now took a seat. "Do you love him?"

"Love?" London rolled the word around before looking at the barrier between her and the bishop, her face riddled with emotion. "I trust him."

"Then you must tell him your secrets."

Hunched over, she kneeled on a step and pressed the side of her face against the latticed opening between them. "I want to. But the way he looks at me. It's as if I'm special. What if it changes?"

"You must discover the true destiny of your connection. God has laid out a plan. Open your heart to the Lord's truth."

She released a cynical burst of laughter that echoed in the church, giving her something more to seek penitence. "Destiny brought us together? God's timing is off by ten years."

The bishop reprimanded London while comforting her. "The Lord's timing is never off. Prayer is the answer. Through God, find your path. This man's death will not bring you peace."

"It isn't the Commander who will die, Your Excellency. It's me."

"My dear child. Pray. The Lord will grant you a safe journey home. Bow upon your knees and say four Hail Mary's and three Our Father's."

London bowed her head and felt warmth in the cool confined confessional as the bishop continued. "God is a merciful father who loves you, as he loves me. Faith is the answer, my child."

The bishop's door opened and closed.

"Hail Mary, Full of Grace, The Lord is with thee. Blessed are thou among women, and blessed is the fruit of thy womb, Jesus. Holy Mary, Mother of God, pray for us sinners now, and at the hour of our death. Hail Mary . . . "

* * *

The next morning, she leaned against the marble balcony of a small palace, next to a wellspring, south of the church in the northwestern corner of Constantinople. From where she stood, she could see Bosporus River that unites the Sea of Marmara to the Black Sea. The palm trees swayed to a sorrowful song below as the smell of jasmine filled the air. Distant, continuous honking signaled a traffic jam. No longer the London of America, she wore a long black wig covered by a wisteria-colored scarf, called a *rusari*. A three-quarter length white manteau, embroidered in colorful flowers, covered her baggy black pants that gathered at her ankles. The cardigan-like-coat hid her western figure. Painted nails, contacts, and open-toed sandals finished her new look.

When London stepped off a Turkish plane in Tehran, the temperatures were stifling. She slipped on a simple white-gold wedding band and gave her passport to the Customs and Border Protection Officer; it read Giti Marduk from Razavi Khorasan, a 24-year-old college student. The officer, a sharp-faced, rail thin man, looked at London and asked, "What brings you to Tehran?"

"I've applied to study photography at the University. I'm here for a campus visit." She handed him her camera bag, which he searched through before placing it on the conveyor. Not a complete lie. Days ago, after learning of Doctor Nazari's part in the North Korea Super Engine, London applied at the university on the hap-chance of a check.

The officer took one last look at her passport, passed it back. His face broke into a smile as he greeted her, *"Bah Bah,"* before signaling her to move forward.

"Merci khoda hafez." Thanking him, she asked him to save her. A customary greeting for the Persians.

"Ghorbunet beram." Hearing the man's vow to die for her well-being made London uncomfortable. Such a loyal nation to family and country. But if he learned her identity, he'd slit her throat.

28

Greeted the Driver

Outside the airport, London leaned through the open window of a green taxi and greeted the driver, "*Salaam*. Edge Home Stay, in Malhipalpur." She held out two, one-hundred-thousand *rials*. "I'll pay twenty thousand *toman*?"

The driver's full beard and downward sloping eyes gave him a friendly smile. "Three."

London pulled out a third *rial* from her handbag, which the man accepted. Along the ten-minute drive, the cabbie asked her many questions. Prepared for the chatty cabbie in the land known for extreme traffic noise, London answered his questions and then listened as he told her stories of his life. Part of the Persian Taarof system of ritual politeness. In Iran, men didn't speak to women, but Persians indulged in open dialog while in a cab. As they traveled through the city, she smelled combinations of saffron, sumac, and rosewater.

When he pulled up to the curb, he thrust the *rials* in her direction. "You do not have to pay me."

"Of course." She insisted. "I must. The drive too fast but delightful." Her exposed eyes conveyed her sincerity, even as she lied.

"I'm sorry. If I had paid closer attention, I would have arrived in less time. I have failed to deliver. Here. Take your money."

Her hands gestured toward the cash without touching it. "No. You must keep it."

"I can't."

"Yes, you must. I insist." London stepped out of the cab, grateful to get away once the driver accepted the rial.

Inside the *Baloot* hotel, she handed the cashier a fake copy of Giti's national identification card, and the lady handed her a room key.

The second-floor room was spacious, the floor covered in Emadi stone. Against the blue and white accent wall with a honeycomb pattern, sat a king-size bed. An ottoman sat in front of a window that ran the length of the room along with one other chair.

The service maids had pulled aside the dark blue curtains to allow the easterly sun to brighten the room.

London closed them.

Slumped in the only chair available, she ate the meal she'd gotten from the lobby restaurant before coming up to her room. Stew over rice with flat bread, the local news providing the weather as she ate, while preparing to visit Doctor Nazari. She used her last pinch of bread to absorb the remaining stew and set the bowl to the side before grabbing her overnight bag and emptying it.

She removed an extensive set of polymer make-up brushes, pulled off the fluffy bristles and emptied the contents hidden inside before assembling her revolver.

The sun set before seven that evening, so she left an hour earlier. In black leggings covered with a linen manteaux, she pulled a dark *hijab* over her blonde hair, and left wisps of a dark wig framing her face.

Outside, the yellow cab she'd ordered sat next to the curb. London paid him four hundred thousand *rails* and climbed into the back seat. The drive to Junapur Village took forty minutes. Fortunately, this cabbie didn't talk nonstop. Once in Junapur, the cabbie pulled over at a chicken and mutton store. "I will wait."

"Thank you, but I won't need a return ride."

"A woman alone at night isn't safe."

He's right.

"By waiting at the curb," he continued. "I can watch over you."

"*Mersi.* Allah watches over me."

When the cab driver pulled away, London stood at the store entrance and watched until he turned north, back toward downtown. She turned south toward Radhey Mohan Drive, hoping to avoid unwanted attention as she walked through the neighborhood, waiting for the night-fall to cloak Doctor Nazari's house in darkness.

A short-legged cat with a mushed face and wide-set round eyes circled her feet. Unable to resist, she reached out a hand and stroked the matted fur. A part of her wished she could take the long-haired yellow tabby home. She scratched under his chin. "Sorry. You'd just end up on the streets of South Korea."

She noticed a bowl of food with spilled kibbles around the sides. "At least you're getting fed."

London crept through yards, using the bushes and houses as cover until she reached the scientist's home.

She'd studied the blueprints of Doctor Nazari's house before leaving South Korea. The family's high-end but outdated security system, a Saroush-7, had an over-reli-ance on motion sensors and cloud-based monitoring. The over-sensitive sensors to pets and other movements were often overlooked due to the frequency and struggles to detect movement in extreme heat. The temperatures were predicted to reach a heat index of fifty degrees Celsius with high humidity, making it feel ten degrees hotter.

Bright lights lit the large first-floor window of the grand drawing room, letting her know they were home. Lights glowed in the kitchen, rear, and upstairs bedroom.

The seven-thousand-square-foot house had a grand front entrance that faced east, shaded by evergreens on a two-and-a-half-acre plot. Orange blossoms infused their scent with the fruity undertone of jasmine riding the air waves up from a sizeable garden that bordered a stream. The dangling branches of a weeping willow draped over the water, its leaves dipping and swirling with the current. She imagined Whooper swans landing on the stream during their winter migratory flight each December.

On other visits to the country, she'd enjoyed the villages that sat on the edge of a harsh desert with their imposing mountains circling the arid plateau.

Hidden in the shadows, she noticed a guard, one of two on duty, walking past the backyard pool. The other guard was most likely inside minding surveillance. The cameras and guards weren't her only threat. Staff members moved around inside the house, and any of them might step into her path.

Twice before, a mission surprised her. Both times ended a life, and she'd escaped alive. A mistake here might end her chances of completing her current mission, in North Korea.

She needed a win.

Once the guard turned the far corner, she removed the manteaux, stuffed it inside a wicker ottoman on the back deck, and climbed through a bathroom window.

The kitchen, to her left, carried the sounds of staff members preparing the evening meal.

London's mouth watered. *Lamb.* How long had it

been since her last meal? She couldn't remember. Had she eaten after confessing?

To the right of her, a man of Arabic descent sat behind five screens in a small room with no windows, measuring six feet by six feet. When she pressed the plastic revolver against his neck, he stiffened. Careful with her pronunciation, she asked him for a favor, in Persian, *"mitunam yek zahmat behetun bedam?"*

The man spoke softly. "Yes. Favor. Ask and I shall help?"

She pressed the pistol more firmly as she engaged the trigger and lowered the hammer. His back straightened. The slightest pressure against the point of the gun warned her of the guard's intentions to attack.

"A deadly choice. I wouldn't make it. I'd hate for you to cause an accidental discharge." She confessed to the dastardly deeds she was about to commit and her woe at inflicting them. *"Mote'assefam vali chāre'i nist."*

By confessing she had dust on her head, Iran's version of burying her head in the sand for what she'd planned, satisfied his natural instincts to fight.

"I have a German Sig flattened against your spine. Any movement from you and the family I will save, but you, my friend, will die with a single whistle. *Sooti nadi!*" She warned him.

His index finger dropped away from the panic button under the table, and both hands rose above his head.

He yelled, "Niki. Pari. I am taking a break. Don't disturb me."

"Good. May your breath be warm," London thanked him.

Hunched over, he asked, "What do you want? Who are you?"

"I'm the Sandman." London struck him behind the ear with the revolver handle. "Lights out."

With one guard incapacitated, she slipped outside and rounded the corner to the north side of the house as the grounds guard came around the northwestern edge. To avert conflict, London stepped into the heavy brush of an evergreen bush. Thick branches and stabbing stems bruised her skin, but the fibers of her bodysuit held together. Breath steady, London prepared to attack.

A cat drew the guard's attention when it stepped out of the foliage, its back rubbing against the needle-shaped leaves, purring loud enough London could hear. The guard picked up the white feline. "The little misses have been looking for you, Eskander."

London didn't own a pet. Her chaotic life left her little time or freedom for anything beyond basic needs. At this moment, she'd have taken her four-legged lifesaver home and pampered him had the guard not carried him away. Persian felines hang around local shops in Tehran like part of the scenery. Shopkeepers set out bowls of food near rear entrances as if encouraging the behavior. She'd read once that Mohammad, the Muslim prophet, kept cats as pets. Though dogs are frowned upon, the cat continues to thrive.

The guard ruffled the cat's head, his cooing voice fading.

London stepped out of the bush, removing two tiny stems that poked through her suit. She climbed a palm tree, swinging from a branch to the balcony off the master bedroom.

With her back against the brick deck, she peered in, finding the room empty. A light on in one of the four bedrooms had her guard up. *A maid.* She checked the time. *Should be finishing daily chores soon.*

She'd find the family on the main floor. Persian people prioritized family over everything but God and considered their *batin*, or private time, as a period to relax without the restraints of their *zaher*, or public identities.

An unlocked exterior sliding door invited her in. She slipped into the enormous room, larger than her apartment, and admired the traditional floral rug covering the floor. Two cornflower blue plates on the mantel above a fireplace against the far wall. They'd strung ornate pillows, blue and purple, atop the king-sized bed.

Rubber soles made a clomping sound against the porcelain tiles at the far end of the house as London creeped into the hallway.

She took each step with caution, her black and gold Persian shoes silent against the stairway. At the bottom, she turned left. She could hear the Nazari family to her right when one daughter laughed.

The house, more modern than the other Persian homes she'd entered, still had decorative stained-glass windows above each door and window. The glossy marbled floors and displayed pottery reminded her of a visit she'd made to the National Art Gallery in Washington, D.C., before she'd been forced to drop out of school.

From her position, London could see Doctor Nazari. The thin doctor had short steel gray hair.

He smiled at his daughter, who sat at his feet. A smile that had large white teeth and kind eyes. He didn't appear to be a mass murderer, but appearances are often the last clue.

She found Doctor Nazari's office near the front of the house, out of sight from where the family gathered.

She crossed to the study and entered the room lit by a single monitor. In this room, heavy curtains covered the windows. A Bedouin-Amman rug, intricately patterned and made of pure wool, cushioned the sound of her shoes. In the room's center, she sat in front of the screen at a Kingstown Admiralty Executive Desk.

The screen brightened when her hand covered the mouse as she opened an incognito desktop. After turning off the auto tracking systems, she clicked on the document's file and discovered the machine remained connected to the RIG server. She opened the icon resembling an envelope and brought up Nazari's email and sent a message:

To: JDaily@CIA.gov
Subject: Central Intelligence Committee #14685199
Case: #14685199
Ready
L

An agent remotely linked the two systems, collected data, and secured control. Fortunately, RIG had failed to protect their work with two-factor or multifactor authentication. Next time the scientists at RIG opened a program, the deployed data wiper would destroy critical infrastructure with irreversible data loss on BAHRAN.

London could hear the family's random mumblings several rooms over as the virus uploaded. Behind the desk, a full bookshelf displayed alphabetically ordered scientific texts from worldwide authors.

An original copy of *The Red Badge of Courage* by Stephen Crane lay oriented horizontally next to an image of Nazari standing next to Ayatollah Ali Khamenei.

London's dad had also kept a copy of the American Civil War novel, and she was familiar with the story.

Fear and courage in battle. Dr. Nazari should be afraid.

She picked up Crane's book and turned to page sixty-four and read, *He suddenly lost concern for himself, and forgot to look at a menacing fate. He became not a man but a member. He felt that something of which he was a part—a regiment, an army, a cause, or a country—was in a crisis. He was welded into a common personality which was dominated by a single desire.*

As she tucked the book into her ruck, the bar continued

to scroll across the screen.

Three hours after entering the doctor's home, London stepped out of a taxi and re-entered the airport, checked in at a food service kiosk, and ordered a falafel sandwich.

After scarfing her food and going through security, she stood in line to board her plane. She showed the gate agent her boarding pass prior to stepping on the ramp. As she walked the ramp, she heard a whistle blow three times in the distance.

She boarded the plane, sat, and waited, despite the Iranian military's search of the airport for her.

Two Sepah Pasdaran, Islamic Revolutionary Guard Corps, in blue uniforms held a Fajr 224 submachine gun pointed at the passengers' faces, their fingers on the trigger as they entered the plane. The one in front held a photo in his hand.

London assumed a picture captured on one of Nazari's hidden cameras was clasped between his gloved fingers. The IRGC members alternated between image and passenger, systematically verifying each occupant. When he stopped in front of London, he smiled. Rooted to the seat, her heart thumped louder than the roar of the ocean. His eyes chilled her.

He signaled for her to stand.

She reached into the pocket of her manteaux and slid her finger into the trigger guard of her plastic revolver. Useless against them, but it would take care of herself.

A IRGC member pushed her aside while aiming the Fajr at the man by the window, prompting her to back away and watch the scene unfold from behind the gun's barrel.

The officer signaled the man to stand and said, "We have an eyewitness placing you near Junapur Village tonight. You are under arrest for the attempted assassination of an Iranian scientist."

The man's jaw tensed, and his nostrils flared, but he

stood. "You're mistaken, officer. I'm a Turkish salesman. I came to Iran to promote Kuru Kahveci Mehmet Efendi coffee to the purchasing manager at 777 Industries."

London noticed the man did no "tutting" after speaking, a prominent Turkish exclamation for "no."

He held up his hands, both submachine guns remained pointed at his chest. "Let me show you my card." His hand lowered with a slow, yet large, swoop to say, 'just a moment' as he reached slow and easy into his breast pocket and produced a business card. "You can call Rahimi. He's the purchasing director."

Turkey? I'm not falling for it. From the looks of it, neither is the Sepah Pasdaran.

London guessed him to be a Mossad spy from Israel. The Israelis she'd encountered used that two-fingered symbol. His actions were so deep-rooted, he hadn't noticed his mistake.

The Iranian military must have suspected him of being the person behind Doctor Nazari's break-in. Too bad for him the guard she knocked unconscious had awakened.

29

CIA Cover

Joe sat behind his plain double-pedestal metal desk. His office, no larger than a bank cubicle, as he poured over Claire's orders for the Whiskey River Saloon. The saloon operated on a tight budget, something Claire ignored. He struggled to focus, his mind turning to London.

Assigned to London even before her first mission, he'd been with her since. Regularly, she gave him headaches, but she always finished the job.

He hadn't wanted this assignment, or any assignment attached to London. Nor did he want a relationship with Claire, but he stayed for London. To protect her.

He supposed he'd fallen for her the first time they'd met. An unruly twenty-year-old, dangerous, and exquisite, full of anger and hate. Her hips had danced back and forth when she walked, and she had a way of exposing her long neck without making it obvious. A natural sex appeal that lured him.

Then there was Claire. Claire hated London. He

couldn't blame her, not really. London ignored orders, all orders, and Claire hated her for it. Claire considered the bar her assignment, and London was the help.

London considered herself an independent contractor, and in her mind, Claire was along for the ride. *Geesh!*

The door opened, and Joe heard Claire shouting, "You can't go in there!"

The officer that stepped into Joe's office in uniform, taller than the average Asian male. Trim. Muscular. Both pretty and masculine. Joe figured he must be the man Claire had been complaining about. Why else show up at the saloon and barge into his office?

Slamming the door in Claire's face, the officer stood in front of Joe's desk. "I'm Commander Kim, with the Republic of Korea's Marine Corps. London and I . . . friends."

"Friends? Please . . ." Joe signaled the Commander to sit. "What can I do for you? I assure you, if you're having trouble with London, I'm not the man to ask for help."

The Commander sat. "No, sir. Trouble? No. London, I handle."

The Commander offered his hand, which Joe accepted. *Great. He doesn't speak fluent English, and my Korean sucks.*

"Joe Parks." The Commander's powerfully muscled hands were like a vice grip. Joe suggested coffee. The offer was rejected. After hiding his hands under the table, he rubbed away the pain. "So, the gym?" Joe spoke louder than this stranger.

"No gym."

"You're not here about the incident at Cheondo-ro Military Base?"

"No, sir. Fault mine. I apologize for London."

Joe wiped his forehead's balding head with a handker-chief. "She didn't, uh . . . apologize?" He sat back, crossing his arms. "That's London. So . . ."

"Here because of mission."

Joe unfolded his arms, feeling the clammy sweat of his palms, and sat forward. Gathering the papers on his desk, he bundled them together, smacking the table as they joined in a neat pile, his face deadpan as he asked, "Mission? To what mission are you referring?"

"Super Engine."

Joe coughed. *How could he know? London would never reveal her purpose in Korea.*

"I'm here. Replace London. My men are better equipped. Two days in and out. Take her off assignment."

Joe asked, "What is your relationship with London?"

The officer didn't answer.

The two of them together . . . Joe glared at the officer.

London had never shown interest in him. Nevertheless, he'd always believed they'd be together; a type of marriage agreement . . . Till death did they part. "If you're interested in London, you should have learned she doesn't back off from a job. More than that, she's good. Don't underestimate her. The woman's a rattlesnake. Deadly with one bite."

"I have five men ready. London one woman."

"One woman who can handle five men," Joe added.

"Yes, but twenty? Thirty?"

This officer made Joe nervous, and he wasn't the nervous type. On the outside, the officer appeared kind. He had a twinkle of gentleness to his eyes, but underneath the exterior, he wasn't a man you'd wish to tangle. Somehow, London had become ensnared. "You say that you and London are friends?"

"Yes, sir."

Joe crossed his arms over his desk and leaned forward. "First, London doesn't have any friends. She doesn't trust people. Further, if you knew her, you'd understand she'd never allow such a dismissal of a mission, if there was one." Joe studied the officer. "I would reassess your situation, Commander. For now, it may feel as if London cares for you. I've been with her for eight years, and I can say with certainty, London cares about one thing. Revenge. Especially against men who exploit a woman's vulnerability."

"Thanks for advice."

Joe consulted his watch, then looked up. "If you don't believe me, ask London. She should arrive back from Iran any—"

"London? In Iran?" He stood. "Why?"

Joe enjoyed the officer's surprise and wiped his forehead again, telling himself the perspiration damping the cloth came from the fluorescent light overhead. "Didn't she tell you?" He sat back. "Surprising, since the two of you are so close. Then again, London is secretive. Keep a close eye, soldier. She may disappear in the middle of the night. Once she does, you'll never see her again."

Joe watched the officer back away from the table one step as he placed the cap on his head, body rigid. "My General will call." The Commander turned to leave.

Joe followed him through the short hallway and past the kitchen, feeling as though he'd won. When he turned, he found Claire huddled in the corner next to his office.

His anger boiled. London had chosen this man to bond with, having never bonded with him. He slammed the hall door shut, turned, and slipped on a pepperoni. "Damn it!" He threw the slice of salami at Claire. "Were you listening?"

Claire stood straighter and brushed back her hair. "I would never!" and turned in a huff. The bell jingled, signaling the Commander had left.

Joe walked back into his office, pounding his fist against the wall. London would be back soon. He'd learn the truth then.

* * *

London stepped off the plane in her typical cotton shirt and jeans after discarding the traditional Persian clothing and makeup in Turkey. Without a bag, she entered the airport, ready to wash away the desert sand. The Incheon International Airport reminded her of a modern version of the Starship Enterprise, with glass windows on the walls, ceiling and even around the shuttle service that ran through the middle of the lobby.

"London."

She stopped mid-step. *The Commander? How?* Turning toward the sound, she found him leaning against a glass wall that overlooked the lower terminal. "Why are you here?"

The Commander stepped away from the wall. "Pick you up."

"How'd you know I'd be here?"

"Joe."

"Joe? He told you I was at the airport?"

He stepped up to her, his hand removing the dark sunglasses from her forehead. His flirtatious smile did nothing to ease her tension. When he slipped the glasses over his eyes, she repressed the idea of cuffing him on the jaw and gave him her version of a Pan Am smile, fake from cheek to cheek.

"Why the silence?" he asked.

London grabbed for the glasses and missed. "Why'd he share my information with you?"

He shrugged. "Have to ask Joe." He switched to his native language. "I thought you might want a ride home, so I came. Happy to see me?" He slipped an arm around her waist and gave her cheek a peck.

London stepped away, both horrified and excited. "I don't need a ride." She set off at a brisk pace toward the escalator. Airport congestion forced her onto the metal escalator, navigating fellow travelers. At the bottom, she looked back. The Commander hadn't followed. Not that she cared, she told herself, but she casually glanced over her shoulder.

A person she'd skirted on the steps pushed her out of the way, provoked, she guessed, from her standing on the landing. She let it go, finding the Commander's back to her, paying for what she guessed was cold brew. Behind the coffee stand were open steps from the second floor.

Hungry. Her stomach grumbling. She ignored the fast-food stand displaying bowls of fresh fruit and water, heading straight for the exit door. Once outside, a refreshing autumn breeze blew through her loose hair.

The Commander passed her, paying no attention to the line of taxicabs parked along the front entrance as he crossed the street into the parking lot. London followed, poking along, hesitant yet eager. When she stepped up to Willy, she climbed in. She noticed the Commander never looked to see if she followed.

Cocky bastard. He must think I'd follow him into a nuclear mushroom.

Inside the jeep, he twisted the lid on a water bottle and offered her a drink. "Can you hang glide?"

"Hang glide? I've been skydiving."

"I would like to take you. We could swim in the lake below the mountain."

He leaned in closer as he spoke. Close enough his eyes became dark swirls, scary and mesmerizing. She fought the urge to squirm. To jump. To stay her nerves and settle her empty stomach, she took a drink. "Swim? Sounds cold."

The engine revved. "Sounds like fun." He leaned back against his seat, one hand on the steering wheel. "Water is cold. Sun warm."

At ninety-seven kilometers on the 130 Expressway from Incheon to Seoul, London draped her arms over her head. For the briefest second, she wished she had the scarf she'd worn in Iran. "When?"

London watched as the Commander's military cut, longer on top, blew in the wind. She studied his profile. Her sunglasses covered his long lashes and part of his thick brows. Wide cheekbones tapered to a smooth jawline, prickled with fresh whiskers on his chin and upper lip, adding to his handsome features. When he swallowed, his pronounced Adam's apple bobbed. A thick cord of pumping blood ran the length of his neck. Her hand lifted, and with a feather's touch, she felt his blood pulse before jerking away, embarrassed.

The Commander clutched her falling hand and held it. "How is next Saturday? Can you get off work?"

Delayed dates could only mean he was going on a mission. Her head snapped in his direction. "Are you leaving?"

"Worried?" he asked. The corners of the Commander's eyes crinkled as he removed the glasses and handed them back to her.

"No! Just surprised. Where're you going? How long?"

"Only a day or two. Not going far. A tsunami hit Oryukdo Island off the coast of Busan. Cadaver dogs will assist my team while we search for survivors and recover the dead."

London wanted to ask him to stay. Their time together grew shorter by day. She wondered if it was worry she felt or selfishness. "When will you be back?"

"Soon."

Lifting her hand, he kissed her palm, leaving tendrils of electricity raging up her arm and into her belly where it stirred. Staring at his plump, rose-colored lips, she remembered their one brief kiss. She wanted more. Much more. Like the actress in Love's Brief Surrender, she wanted it all. The perfect love. Only perfect love can't survive.

Shifting her gaze to the road ahead, she said, "Sounds safe enough."

"Your whereabouts . . . Care to share?"

The Commander detected her posture change. Seconds before, she'd radiated with jittery emotion. Now her hand was icy and stiff, holding the sunglasses millimeters from her face. Frozen, she pretended to relax before firmly setting the glasses on her nose.

"I went to see a friend."

"A friend?" he asked.

"Yep." Her lips smacked together. "He had information I wanted."

30

Toying with the Idea of Survival

Sticky notes covered the map on top of London's countertop. She downed a bottle of water as if she were standing at a bar having a shot of tequila, and studied the notes she'd made alongside the map. Her last mission's success rested on the back of concentration, but toying with the idea of survival kept popping into London's head. *If I make it to the trees . . .*

A knock at the door disrupted her thoughts. She shoved the map into the drawer and slammed it shut. *Back early?* The thought surprised and excited her. She rushed to answer the door.

Joe stood there, drenched from the rain and looking unhappy. London stepped aside for him to enter. "Something wrong?"

He entered with a hunched back that made him look older than his years. His gait teetered to the right. *It couldn't be . . . He's never drunk.* "You've been drinking?"

Slurred words sputtered from his mouth. "Do you

care?" His hands hit the counter with a thud, and loose sticky notes folded beneath his fingers.

London didn't move, her eyes fixated on the man leaning against the laminate. She couldn't comfort him. They had joked around and gotten to know each other over the years, but she never felt close to her handler. Ordered to work as a team, she'd remained unattached.

Joe straightened. Turned. One hand held firm against the counter for balance. "Sarah, do you ever wonder what life away from all this might look like? A glimpse, maybe."

Until London met the Commander, she hadn't considered a life outside the one she lived. Now ... dreams of a future faded with each morning.

When she closed the exterior door, he continued. "Earlier, a man stopped to see me. Are you in love with him, Sarah? He has feelings for you. Seems to believe you have returned those sentiments."

London let out a breath. "You're drunk."

"I asked you a question?" His hand clenched the bundle of notes, his eyes two slits in dark red sockets.

"I don't understand the question."

"Love?" He slammed a fist on the counter. "You don't understand love, Sarah?"

"Calm down, Joe." She walked over to the counter, gathering her notes. "I don't. Do you?"

His face softened. "I do."

London assumed the moisture in his eyes was tears.

With an unsteady step, he walked over to the single chair and plopped into it. "When that man came to my office ..." He hung his head low as he brushed the rain from his forehead. "I hated him. I feared him, too. I mean ... we got a job to do, and this man is messing with our plans." He frowned at her. "Do you know why he came?"

London's breath stuck, forcing a choking sound to escape. "The Commander?"

Joe smiled a sickly-looking grin. A slight laugh escaped his lips. "The Commander. Is that what you call him?" His hands ran the length of his thighs, wiping the moisture from his head onto his jeans.

"Yes, the Commander. He asked to take your place." Joe locked his eyes with hers. "I hate him. Want to know why I hate him?"

"No, I don't." London moved to the kitchen, pulled another water from the fridge, and opened the cap. She pulled the map from the drawer, smoothing the edges. "Why?"

"He loves you. That bastard loves you. It was that moment..." Joe's voice cracked. His hunched body slumped deeper as he spoke, his head raised. "I love you, Sarah."

London's head snapped up from the map. Love hadn't been what she'd noticed the first time they'd met. Lust had burned in his eyes since the beginning. Maybe now, he confused lust with love. His desire to touch her made her cringe.

Joe banged the arm of the chair. "I'm the coward that's in love with you, and I'm also the one who's assigned jobs that might get you killed. All these years I've watched you leave on one mission after another and not once did I stop you. But this guy..." He moaned. "I'm the coward. He..." his voice trailed. "He's willing to die to protect you."

Face buried in his hands; London watched his shoulders jerk. She thought through ideas to comfort him but couldn't come up with one. "What about Claire?" It was a foolish question. She knew he didn't love Claire.

Joe's eyes, stung chili red from tears and alcohol, searched her face. "Damn it! I'm in love with you! Not Claire."

"Sorry."

"Shit. When have you ever been sorry?" He pulled out a hanky and wiped the snot from his nose. "You know, I've always hoped you'd love me back."

"That's why she hates me," London added. "Claire."

Joe laughed. "I guess she does. I hear women sense these things when they're in love." He got out of the chair and walked to her. "I've been thinking . . . What if we let the Commander go—"

"No!" London slammed the bottled water against the wall.

"We could go away. Start over." He stepped around the cabinet, reaching for her.

"No!"

The gap between them closed. "Sarah."

"Don't call me Sarah. I'm not her." Angry and crowded by his closeness, she pushed past him.

Joe's arm shot out, pulling her against him. He choked as he spoke. "You don't have to do this."

London turned her shoulder into him and twisted out of his hold. Free, she swung, catching Joe by surprise as an open palm connected with his face, slapping him with enough force he lost balance. He tottered across the room and fell into the entrance hall. Her words hung low in a menacing tone. "Go away Joe. Touch me again, and I'll kill you." She stepped over his legs, crossing to her bedroom.

"Wait."

As he clambered to a standing position, the click of her lock broke the hostility in the room.

The sound of heavy breathing warned her he stood on the other side. Neither spoke. When she sat on the bed, the springs squeaked. "Sarah—"

"I'm not Sarah. Go away. If you help him . . ." Hysteria caught her words. Gasping for air, unable to take in a proper breath as she shouted, "Joe . . . Help me stop him! I'll die either way. If you love me, stop him."

"Okay, Sarah. If that's what you want, I'll stop him." He turned to leave but didn't. "London?"

"What?"

"Until he showed up, it never occurred to me . . . I mean, we always talked about the possibility, but never once did I believe you might die. Now, I'm scared. Swear you'll come back. Promise me."

Yona clutched to her chest, London whispered, "Yeah. Sure, Joe. I'll come back."

When the front door closed, London pulled Yona to her face before stretching out on the bed and cried till she fell asleep, not waking until past noon the next day.

When morning came, she went over the details of the previous evening. She'd been angry at Joe for suggesting the Commander take over her mission, and even angrier that the Commander suggested the idea. Hollow, yet oddly full, she screamed, "What is wrong with me? I don't care!"

But she did.

"Fight it out, boys."

Love. Caring. Someone to share this empty life. These were the last things she wanted.

"I am alone. Alone is safe." She rambled her mantra as bath water splashed beneath the faucet. A neck and back ache forced her upright. She twisted at the waist, satisfied with the loud pops that rippled up her backbone.

After a long bath, she concentrated on the mission, going over each minor detail. Step by step, she searched for a way to survive, but survival remained unlikely. Sure, she'd gotten away once, but she didn't destroy millions of dollars' worth of weaponry. Once her mission was complete, death was imminent, even if she escaped the initial wave of soldiers. North Korean officials were tenacious. They'd hunt her. One day, they'd find her. A quick death trumped torture.

To keep from missing the Commander, London worked

long hours at the bar, handing beer to drunken soldiers. By midnight, her cool smile didn't deter their advances.

Private Nelson was the only drunk who worried her. He always came in around ten and stayed till the bar closed, sitting at the same corner table the Commander and his team sat, watching her. London thought the private had something planned. She hoped he'd wait. In a few days, she'd be gone, and they could avoid the unpleasantry.

When she climbed the steps to her apartment at three A.M. the night she expected the Commander to return, she heard Nelson's drunken breaths following her. Rather than wait, she turned. "You need something, soldier?"

"Yes. You."

"I'm taken."

Stepping up, he asked, "By that Asian?"

"Yeah, by that Asian." Unintimidated, she didn't move, smirking inside but unsure whether her words weren't true.

Nelson took another step. "Don't you want a man that can satisfy you?"

"You?" she shouted. "Go home Nelson, I don't need satisfying."

"Ain't a woman that doesn't need a real man to share her bed."

London descended two steps from the top landing, coming face to face with Tony. "Do you think you are man enough to satisfy me, Private?"

Nelson wrapped an arm around her waist and pulled her in, his lips pressing the blood from hers.

London didn't move, nor did she stop him, remaining impassive as the kiss lingered. When Nelson let go, his smile was smug, at least until he saw London's bland expression. When her smile turned venomous, the light in her eyes changed from bright and mocking to menacing. "Before I kill you, I suggest you run."

Private Nelson backed up a step. His face paled in the overhead light. "You're not serious?"

London took another step toward him. "Forewarned . . ." With a hand to his shoulder, she swung around his back, knocking Nelson off balance as he tripped backwards. With one arm around his throat, she pressed a knife against his larynx. The other arm braced his head as she whispered, "You aren't good enough. I need a man who's faster than me and more confident. That Asian is both."

As her grip tightened, Nelson begged, "Okay. Okay. I'll leave you alone. Don't . . . Please don't—"

"Kill you?" she asked.

"Yes. Please don't kill me."

London slid off his trunk, placing a hand on his shoulder as she took one step up, then another. Twisting at the waist, she looked at him. "Nobody likes a bully. Now get lost."

Eager to get away, Nelson missed the last three steps and fell, scurrying to his feet and running. London watched, leaning over the rail, her smile cramping her jaws. When the private disappeared, she started back up the steps. "Another one got away. Oh well, next time."

31

Wash Away the Filth

To wash away the filth of the private's touch, London slid into a hot bath. Underwater, each noise seemed to expand, surrounding everything in an eerie, liquid echo. Peaceful sounds, like those made by aquarists when they cleaned the glass, or rocks sinking and clanging against the bottom, the swish of a fin, and the suction created by an eel slinking into its hole.

Like an octopus changing colors, she pretended to dive into a hidden hole, modifying her skin to appear flat and porcelain white. In the imagined cooler water, her heart rate slowed. She grew sleepy. As her diaphragm fatigued, she blew out small bubbles of air that rose to the surface, reminding her of crocodilian breaths.

The urge to breathe grew steady, like the banging that rang in her head. Her meditation broken, she sat up. Forced out of the tub, she grabbed a towel that had hung unused since she moved in.

He's back.

Wet prints against the wood floor puddled as London ran to the door. She skidded the last few feet, bumping her toe. Elated and yet terrified to find the Commander, she cracked the door.

"Give me a sec and come in."

The door slammed shut as she ran to the bedroom, praying she didn't nosedive.

A quick brush of her hair, the wet, slick strands making her self-conscious. *I look boyish now.*

She pulled on her clothes, stepping from the bedroom unaware the dripping water exposed hardened nipples. In a handful of strides, she covered the room. In front of him, his greeting smile warming her, she said, "I've missed you."

The Commander pulled her against him, kissing away a droplet from her temple. "Sounds like an invitation."

He removed the towel from her hand and led her to the only chair. "First," he stepped in closer.

London waited for his kiss as one of his legs pressed against her thigh. Her body gave way as she toppled backward into the chair.

"We need to dry your hair." Gently, he dried the dripping tendrils.

London reached for the terry cloth, irritated by the change in mood. "I can do it."

She yearned to drink his toxic wine and feared him touching the slime she couldn't wash away. She stood. "I . . ." she tugged at the towel and gave up when she couldn't yank it from his grasp. "A week has never seemed so long."

She stretched the hem of her shirt, aware of the thin cotton pressed around her nipples, igniting their sensitivity. "Are you thirsty?"

The Commander's hand glazed hers and knew he followed. "I am. Not for what's in your fridge. How long since you've eaten?"

She peeked out between the cabinet and counter. "Uh, it's three-thirty in the morning. Isn't it early to eat?"

He leaned against the bar, glancing at the map she'd left. After Joe's disturbing visit, she'd forgotten to put it away. She shoved it into the drawer, the edge sticking out of the corner, and checked his response.

The Commander appeared unconcerned, but London knew better. He never missed even the smallest details around him.

He reached across the counter, taking her hand in his, stroking it with his thumb, though it wasn't her hand that felt each stroke.

"I haven't eaten, but I don't mind sleeping instead," he nodded toward her bedroom. "That is, if you have room for a tired soldier on your bed." His smile, erotic, as two dark eyes studied her reaction.

Though she'd dreamed of this moment and moved her lips to answer, "yes," she grabbed the towel out of his hand and ran for the exit, yanking open the front door. "I'm starving, and this town never sleeps. Let's go out."

His stride, powerful, yet smooth and unhurried, the surrounding space in his control, he took the towel and, with nothing to prove and everything to enforce, entered her bedroom.

"Wait. I . . ." London stuttered. "I thought we'd eat."

When he stepped out, he held the colorful manteau she'd bought in Turkey. Like an idiot, she'd had it mailed to a post office box she kept in Seoul under an alias.

"Put this on." He held the manteau out for her to slip into. "It is chilly tonight."

Instantly aware of the cool air, her nipples tingled against the slight breeze of the open door as if the wind had been his hand. "Ah, yes. Excellent idea." She moved against him as she covered her scantily clothed body and exited the apartment.

They drove to an all-night Japanese restaurant. Curious to learn the foods he preferred, she asked the Commander to order.

He ordered *Tempura Donburi* as he explained the dish to London. "Tempura means battered, and don means rice bowl. Makes an enjoyable late-night meal." He handed the menus back to the server. She took them and stepped away from the table.

The server returned with two bowls, placing a bowl in front of London. "What's in it?"

The Commander pinched a prawn between his chopsticks. "Fried prawns and vegetables. The dressing is a sweet soy sauce. Try it."

London took a bite, enjoying the crunch. "It's good." The food wasn't heavy, so it wouldn't make her feel bloated. "Last year, I ate *Peixinhos da Horta in Portugal.* The vegetables are breaded like Japan's green beans."

The heavy load of the Commander's weary eyes watched her.

London carried the guilt of keeping him out when he needed sleep and regretted not inviting him into her bed. *Why come see me before resting?*

Despite his lack of sleep, the Commander shared stories about the tsunami response clean-up as they dined. "All-in-all, we retrieved 184 bodies."

"Any survivors?"

"A few. Those able to evade the water's reach. We found a fifteen-month-old girl perched on top of the H Avenue Hotel on Gwangalli Beach. She got wrapped in a used tire."

"She survived?"

He nodded. "The little *tung tung* was one of the lucky ones. The tire protected her from debris. By the time I got up to her, she'd fallen asleep."

"*Tung tung*?"

"Round."

"Oh." She laughed, watching the Commander hold out his hands, rounded like the toddler's body. "A chunker."

His laugh, like the sun warmed him from inside, pleased London. More relaxed than she'd ever seen him, she watched him eat. Elbows on the table, he leaned forward in an obvious state of exhaustion. Though his eyes remained heavy, they had a happy shine to them.

London smiled in response. "What about her parents?"

"I prefer to think they survived."

They talked as they ate, and London felt her nervous jitters relax. The Commander eased her fight-or-flight instincts.

Around four, he drove back to the apartment and pulled to the curve. "I'll pick you up tomorrow around eleven."

"You're leaving?" London brushed her hair behind her ear.

The Commander leaned over the hand brake; his brows raised as he rested an elbow on the armrest. "Did you want me to come in?"

The heat that rose into her face must have darkened the freckles that dotted her nose and cheeks. Unable to respond, she stepped out of the vehicle and ran up the steps. At her door, she took a last look.

Relaxed at the wheel, one arm resting on the back of the passenger seat, he casually waved before driving off.

Once inside, London leaned against the door, her heart racing. She sank to the floor, her knees too weak to keep her upright. *Am I afraid?* She sat there, one arm covering her eyes while the other clutched her chest. "Do I want him?" *No. No. No! I can't.*

She rolled onto her knees and stood. In the bedroom, she flattened herself against the mattress. Yona pressed against her face.

A loud beep, followed by another, brought her face

out of the soft stuffing of Yona's round belly. Searching, London found a box on the bed with a pink ribbon. The beeping continued as she ripped it open. Inside, she found a pink iPhone. The lit screen read *Honey bear.*

She dropped the box, kicking it across the floor. The phone started beeping again. Off the bed, she used Yona's long, thin arms and thick pads to retrieve it as if the stuffed toy were some sort of bomb barrier. When the cellphone stopped ringing the second time, a message appeared.

The Commander? Slide what green button?

She'd only used a burner flip phone.

Her mind raced back to an early mission in Syria. She'd hidden near an ISIS hideout. Seconds after a guard passed, the flip phone rang.

She hid, breaking the phone and burying it in a pile of food waste.

When the guard stepped around the corner, her knife jabbed his jugular, slicing down to his clavicle. His oxygen cut off, silenced his screams.

Since then, she hadn't carried a phone. Death didn't make her tremble, but surprises . . . made survival ratings dwindle.

As the incessant ringing continued, she placed a finger on the green button and slid it to the right.

The Commander said, "Hello."

"You put this phone in my room?"

"I did. To call you."

Irritated, London contemplated smashing it against the wood floor. "Luck with that one."

"There's a switch on the left side." He sounded amused. "Do you see it?"

London lowered the phone from her ear and looked. Yelling, she said, "I see it." Embarrassed, she lifted the receiver to her ear. "It's there."

"Good. Flip the bar up. With the sound off, no one

will hear incoming calls."

"Ha! Pointless, since I won't carry it."

"I hope you will." The gentle pleading in his voice urged her to do as he asked, though she knew she wouldn't.

Joe's warning hummed in her mind. Phones reveal locations. *Of course, dummy. That's why he wants you to carry it.*

"London." The Commander's tone questioning.

To make him happy, a lie slipped through London's lips. "I'll carry it."

His breath in the phone told her he'd held it waiting for her to reply. "Good."

London listened to him breathe, counting each exhale. *He's tired.*

A long pause before he next spoke. "I'll see you later."

"Eleven, tomorrow. Yes. I'll be ready." A fumbling tongue kept her from asking him to sleep at her apartment. "Goodnight."

Another pause. "Sleep well."

The hesitation in his reply told London he wanted the same thing. When the phone clicked silent, the desire to call him back overwhelmed her, but she didn't.

32

Today was Different

At ten till eleven, London sat on the top step waiting, giddy with excitement after a sleepless night. She hadn't wanted a man to touch her since Blake. Last night, that had changed. Today, she needed more.

Earlier in the morning, she let Joe know she had completed her preparations, but chose not to disclose when she'd chosen to depart.

Tomorrow was it. D-Day. Today would be her goodbye. A going away present. She'd barely slept. Giddiness kept her tossing while crippling anxiety screamed inside her brain to stop the impending doom of messing everything up. Thoughts of leaving the man she'd grown to trust sent a jolt through her, driving her forward.

You can do this. Hell, you've done it a million times. Clients lined up. Okay, I was poppin' pills and chugging back . . . high-balls.

A cold sweat beaded on her forehead as she released a dizzying laugh. She rode on the edge of panic, trying to slow her frantic heartbeat. A star rolled between her fingers making fine, stinging punctures as it passed along her hand.

When the Commander pulled up in Willy, she ran down the steps, jumping into the passenger seat. "Morning. I watched you drive up. It's a beautiful day." *Shut up, dumb ass.*

The Commander paused a moment, a smile spreading across his face. *My lady likes me.* He leaned across the middle dash and planted a light kiss on her lips. Without backing away, he said, "*Achim*," the Korean word for good morning rumbling off his throat. Then kissed her again. This kiss, not as brief as the first, flared nerve endings long veiled. His lips, warm as the sun at high noon, eased away the early hour chill. When he rolled back into his seat, goosebumps rose on her arms.

Calmer, London leaned back in the seat. *Wish he'd kissed me earlier. Could of used it.* Sunglasses on, she asked, "Where we going?"

"A surprise."

"I hate surprises."

"This one you will like."

As the route he drove became obvious, London knew they were headed to the base. She squirmed in her seat. "I'm not sure you should bring me back here. My last visit didn't go well."

He covered her hand with his. Blood rushed back into her fingertips. "Don't worry. This time, I know the person beside me."

She laughed. "You know me?"

"Not then. Now. You many hidden secrets, but I cracked code." He pointed a fist at her head. "It took a bomb."

An explosion of fingers made her laugh harder.

When his hand landed back on hers, his expression changed. "I may have been hasty. I regret testing you."

"Test me? I guess if we're going to be honest, I tested you, too."

"Me? Why?"

"To see if I could kill you."

The Commander's head shot a quick glance in her direction. "You wanted to kill me?"

"No! But if I needed to, you know, just in case . . . In case . . ." she turned her gaze away from him. She tried seeing herself delivering the lethal strike. *Skills there. Doing it? Not sure.* "In my work, I'm never sure . . ."

"And what did you learn?" he asked.

"Probably. Yeah. I might, but I also learned that you might kill me, too."

Surprised by her straightforward answer, he asked, "And you are happy with that?"

"Of course. Aren't you?"

His head nodded as he tossed around the idea. "I guess I am, since we are still together."

"Exactly."

London wanted to place his hand against her cheek, to take in his sea grass and gun powder scent.

At the heliport, a helicopter sat whirling on a circular helipad. As they approached the bird, they ducked low, a powerful wind pushing them back. Yelling, a junior pilot jumped out. "It's ready, sir." He attempted to bow, despite his already angled body.

The Commander slapped a hand on the man's shoulder. A silent thank you. Then jumped into the pilot seat. London stood there, staring up at him. "You fly?"

"Jump in." When she didn't move, he added, "You are safe with me."

She'd told Bishop Pius she trusted him. The leap. Trusting anyone. Let alone a man. Huge. She was ready to have faith in one. Him.

Without hesitation, London ran around the helicopter and did as he asked. She strapped her seatbelt as he checked the controls. The younger pilot handed her a helmet and stepped away. Once strapped, she heard the Commander yell over the noise, "Hang on."

With the ground cleared, the helicopter tipped on one skid and lifted them into the air. The rotor disk tilted forward. They lost a little altitude, but the Commander kept the stick advancing. As he picked up speed, London braced for a 'blowback,' but the nose stayed steady.

With his sleeves rolled back, London enjoyed the thick chords of muscle on the Commander's forearm as he cycled between them flying forward and banking left or right. She'd flown in planes from every country without fear of flying. Helicopters had large glass panels, Multi-Function Displays, that made the earth below appear in your face, which was a bit unnerving.

Hope he's as confident with the hang glider.

It took them fifteen minutes to reach *Naejansan* mountain, with its rocky dragon back mountaintops, and another fifteen to navigate the trees to a flat cliff side, landing around one-hundred yards from a hang glider, near the cliff edge.

The controls off, the blades wound down. The Commander jumped out, crossing around front, and helping London out. His eyes were wide with enthusiasm, his cheeks rosy, as if he'd spent the last half hour skiing. He looked happy. Relaxed. Stress free.

So, this is him off duty. London wondered who she might have become without the CIA. She couldn't quite picture it.

Together, they ran across the hillside, peeking over the edge of a waterfall.

Let's dive off a cliff. Sure. Why not? Dying together. Exactly what I had in mind.

A pristine lake had formed at the base, the water's overflow carried away as it wound across the lush field. Six deer stood grazing on apple-green grass. Across the water, evergreens grew as tall as the trees back home. In the distance, the birdsongs sang. "It's gorgeous."

He slid his hand in hers. "You wanted to swim."

"No," she reminded him. "You suggested we went swimming. I said it's too cold."

The Commander squeezed her hand. "You win."

He moved the glider an inch, his level of perfectionism matching hers.

"Ready?"

London took another peek over the edge. "Are you sure we can do this? I mean, both of us and only one glider."

He ruffled her hair. "Shall we find out?"

"No, I'm not . . ." She grabbed his arm. "This is a first."

He'd read her file, knew the ways the CIA had trained her, but couldn't resist teasing. Innocence crossed her features. "Can I believe a woman who grunts over boulders and climbs thirty feet of granite, hand over hand?"

"Hey! I've lived this long making careful choices. Choices I could control. I can't control this. Wind and air."

His arm slid behind her waist as he pulled her in close. "I can." He'd chosen hang gliding to build trust. In the air, everything in the past faded. Up here, she only had him.

"How? Are you a bird?"

He pulled her in closer, a mischievous grin on his face. "I have security clearance."

33

Brink of Destruction

The twenty-foot aluminum alloy tandem hang glider sat tied a few feet from the brink of destruction.

I'd rather spar throwing knives than get attached to that thing and jump off.

The Commander walked to a nearby trunk filled with equipment and removed a harness made of rope and nylon webbing along with two parachutes. He handed the first parachute to London. Then lifted two nylon sacks that once unfolded were a close resemblance to a sleeping bag.

While she put on her parachute, the Commander attached the pod harness to what he called the airframe. A steady breeze blew from behind. "Look." He pointed upward. "The higher the sun climbs, the more it burns away the cool air. It is a perfect day for gliding."

As they slipped the nylon straps over their shoulders, London asked, "Did you draw a map of where we'll fly?"

Plans are good.

His right hand nose-dived into his left palm. "Afraid I

will make a mis-turn and we will collide into a granite wall?"

Uh, yeah! "It can happen?" she huffed as she cinched her strap extra tight.

He double checked her work. "Let us be free and ride the wind without a map. The birds and clouds will be our guide. Safest way."

"Sure. That instills my confidence. 'Let's let the wind take control,'" she mocked him. "And birds ... Are they homing pigeons?" London took a step backward, her upper body twisting as if she were ready to make a dash for the helicopter.

"Do not panic. This is not a first for me. You see, I am standing."

He stepped in closer, pressing his warm hands against her cheeks. Their eyes locked. Her faith waned. An internal battle waged war inside.

He moved in closer. "Each other. The birds and clouds. This is all we need."

"How can a bunch of birds and clouds guide you?" she asked.

"Simple." He took her hand and led her to the glider, raising the wings above their heads while keeping it tilted toward the wind. "For every sixteen feet we fly, we will drop a foot."

"Good. It will be a brief flight." *Longer would be better. More time before we die!*

He poked her side with his finger, and she buckled from his touch. "That is why we follow the birds and stay with the clouds. Wait and see, when the birds soar without flapping their wings, we will catch a Pegasus and rise, giving us more flight time."

"I'd rather ride the Pegasus than trust a few strands of rope and webbing."

"Next time." He clipped on her harness and then snapped himself in as well. "Relax and let me do the work.

When I turn, lean with me. Outside of that, enjoy the ride."

His soft voice, controlled. Patient. Comforting.

"Trust the wings. They are not an umbrella that opens, dropping you to the earth. They carry you, like an albatross, soaring and gliding. Then it lands light. Easy."

London forced a step backward. "The gooney birds. Have you ever watched an albatross land?"

He reclaimed their forward step. "Okay. Think of a Boeing 777. Ready?"

"Yeah, let's fly."

London's heart pounded as they raced along the short slope. That uncertain time as a soldier runs into battle, legs heavy with the weight of death, but you can't stop the momentum. The last step off, a slide into nothingness, plunging several meters. She gripped his shoulders until her fingers went numb to reassure herself, she wasn't alone. She was safe. With him.

When the wings caught a lift of temperate air, they soared, and London's stomach lurched into her throat.

Prone, with the wind whisking past her body, a forceful howl like the sound of her windbreaker tied to a stick, bellowed in her ears. The chill air turned cooler, clinging to her exposed skin. Lacking warmth, she struggled to pull herself closer to the Commander, but the cables restrained her.

The Commander shouted over the wind, "If you are chilly, slip your feet into the pouch and zip up." He bent his knees, releasing the aluminum base with one hand while zipping the thin cloth cocooning him. "What do you think?"

"The drop messed with me."

"Did not think you feared anything other than people."

London snatched the bar, studying the scenery. "I don't!" she said, sounding suddenly unsure.

The back of the Commander's head beneath her, she

felt guilty for lying. He'd seen through her lies and though he'd doubted her, the moment for her vulnerability had arrived. She wondered how that might feel, then shook her head to dislodge the questions.

A gust of warm wind whipped her hair into the corners of her mouth and eyes. She brushed at them uselessly and said, "I mean, I've never thought about fear, at least not until you came along. Now, I'm paralyzed by it. I'm most afraid of losing you." She buried her face in the pod harness.

The Commander turned sideways. His prone torso was parallel to the bar. They circled sharply to the left.

Compelled to look up, London didn't expect his light peck.

"You will not lose me. We are tied together."

Terrified the transition in his position might cause them to plunge groundward, London clasped the alloy bar, waiting for the sudden drop.

When they didn't crash, she opened her eyes to a forest of pine trees that transformed into rocky cliffs, with treetops morphing into narrow protrusions. The kind of mountains goats loved to climb. An inaccessible terrain. As they passed over the trees, they changed again into fluffy brush picks with tiny bristles.

She tried to remember if she'd flossed her teeth that morning.

Nearing the next group of clouds, they'd slipped several hundred meters, passing over the *Shinheungsa* temple. A massive bronze statue of Buddha rested at the entrance.

They drew closer.

The day before her dad had left for Iraq he'd taken her to Dollywood. This flight reminded her of the Mystery Mine roller coaster as the Commander created the illusion they'd strike the building, or worse, the statue.

"History says this temple is the oldest wooden Zen temple in the world. Years ago, we would have flown over a hundred monks training in *Sunmudo*, the Korean Buddhist martial arts. The monks would train with an assortment of weapons, from swords to throwing stars."

Ka-Bar knives, shuriken and the Indian Katar, close combat weapons, were London's choice, but she didn't share. "What is it today?"

"Just place of quiet reflection."

London observed prayer flags waving from the entrance and wished they'd land to look around. The notion of a fearless life returned. Here, in the clouds with him, it seemed possible.

As they grew closer to a group of genus clouds, the glider shuddered. The Commander entered the thermal, and yelled, "Turn!"

London turned left with him and screamed when the nose lifted. She compared the speed to riding in a power-boat at seventy miles per hour, then hitting a wave. The lift felt like a gut punch. She shrieked, "W-o-o-o-w!"

They circled the thermal and within moments, they'd ascended over six hundred meters. Weightless, London's belly churned and rolled when she glanced at the ground. The detailed landscape had lost all definition and become colorful splotches of undefined land.

Again, their personal roller coaster brought uncertainty as a granite peak appeared ahead. She held her breath and closed her eyes, feeling as one with the Commander, shifting with him, her movements in tune to his. When her eyes opened, she witnessed the right wing glide centimeters past the cliff face.

He'd brought her here for this moment. Her life in his hands. Her heart rate slowed the way it did when she faced danger, her body and mind becoming one with the wind. One with the glider. One with the man.

The clouds dusted the wings, chilling the air. They rode the thermal for seconds, but it seemed as if minutes passed before the Commander glided out and continued their flight.

When they dropped low enough, London removed her camera, no longer afraid of freeing her hands. She zoomed in to snap a picture of a Spotted Nutcracker flying below. A juvenile, without the rich shades of dark brown feathers seen in adult plumage, when the nutcracker's teardrop spots reached maximum coverage.

After two hours of flight, they forked left, turning into the wind and landing smooth as a honeybee. A firm land underneath her feet left London shaky, the way she'd been the first time she dismounted a horse after a two-hour ride. She leaned against her pilot, feeling light-headed. As her arms encircled him, she noticed the hard muscle underneath his jumpsuit. The thumping of his heartbeat against her palms soothed and thrilled her.

"Are you okay?"

The effects didn't last, but London lingered. "Fine. Maybe just a little weak."

The Commander swiveled in his gear and drew her closer. "We can stay here until you're steady."

She stayed, the touch of him stronger than her urge to draw back.

When he stepped away, she accepted his hand, their fingers interweaving. She shuffled across the grass at his side.

"Okay now?" he asked.

No. "Yes," she lied. Nothing would make any of this okay. Once they said goodbye, life would go on. A goodbye without regret seemed all she could offer.

As they strolled toward the lake, London stooped to pick a handful of bell-shaped flowers, protected by white, wooly hairs. She'd often used the stems to prevent sepsis or shock after an injury.

The Commander bent, crouching like a dragon,

touching the wine-red petals. "A Grandmother's Flower."

"What?"

"We call the Pulsatilla *koreana*, the Grand-mother's Flower."

"Why?" London asked.

"It is an old tale about a woman who visits her daugh-ters. The oldest turns her away, so she hikes through the mountains to her youngest daughter's house but never arrives. Legend says that a gigantic bird settled on a branch overlooking the fallen woman. When the bird flew off, the Pulsatilla remained."

London's hand sank. "The petals are the grandmother's wings. How sad."

He squeezed her free hand. "A fairy tale, written so adult children felt guilty for rejecting their parents. Not wings. Grandmothers bowed back."

"Did your grandmother's back stoop?"

He laughed. "No. My grandmother's back remained strong. She practiced yoga until she died at ninety-two."

London's head snapped upward when a vulture flew overhead.

"The old woman I lived with in the mountains taught me vultures will regurgitate if you get too close."

The Commander laughed again. "Is this firsthand knowledge?"

"I doubt it. She believed everything her husband told her. In her defense, they will projectile vomit if you scare them."

When London saw a blanket spread out near the water with a basket on top, she released the Commander's hand and ran over. Settled next to the basket, she opened the lid. Inside, she found raw pea snaps, apple slices, almonds, black olives, carrots and seaweed rice rolls. "You did this?"

"I did. You like it?" The Commander passed London a Benito tray.

"That depends on what you have to drink."

He slipped a hand inside and withdrew two bottles of Cherokee Red.

London squealed, hugging him around the neck. "You get me." The Ronnie Milsap song she'd always sang in the mountains came back to her. She stood, holding out her arms as she twirled the way she'd done at Clingman's dome. As she spun, she sang a verse, "Smoky Mountain rain . . ." humming, she dropped to the blanket. "Really? How did you know?"

"Let us say I am resourceful. I scanned the internet for popular Cherokee soft drinks and took a chance."

Accepting a bottle, London twisted the cap, gulping half the soda in one swig, savoring the long-forgotten flavor. Wiping her mouth with the back of her sleeve, she gave the Commander a goofy grin. "It's been years since I drank a Red."

The Commander opened his own bottle and took a sip, his lips puckering from the flavor.

London giggled. "You don't like it?"

He took another swallow, shook his head, and handed her the drink. "I am not a fan." He pulled out a bottle of water, opened the cap, and drank deeply. "Tell me, did you live with Lady Green long?"

"I guess we lived together a few years. She loved to walk the woods around the campground, digging up sassafras roots and such."

London scanned the mountains and pictured the woman who'd become like a mother. "She caught me stealing food from picnic tables." She reflected a moment before continuing, her mind many kilometers from where they'd landed.

"I knew how to hunt. Duda taught me. When Lady Green caught me, I'd been living downtown, hiding in sleazy holes that would wash you away in the rain."

She took another swallow, relishing the calories as she dredged up old memories of hunger. "The bears were less scary, so I took my chances in the hills hiding in trees." London laughed.

"You found a way to survive."

"Well, yeah. I was starving, and the picnic tables offered an easy meal. Like Yogi Bear, I lifted me a few *pic-a-nic* baskets."

She stretched out her legs and leaned back on her hands, crossing her feet. "The old lady never said a word, but she watched me, stern like. Pure meanness. I guess she pitied me."

The Commander listened as London described her time in the forest. She made funny facial expressions to imitate the old woman he knew she'd loved. He brushed the tangled strands of hair from her face and felt her hesitation. Though he wanted more, he waited. Her satin eyes wide open with fear steadied his need. To earn a gazelle's trust required patience.

"Did you go back?" he asked.

"No! I stayed away and foraged for my food."

Turning sideways, the Commander spread out and laid his head on London's lap. "Tell me more."

London's heart did a triple beat, but she didn't move. The way those dark eyes watched her took her breath. Shaken by her response, she questioned her plan and reminded herself that this moment, and the next, she wanted. Longed for. Letting the doubt slip away, she concentrated, trying to remember things she'd spent years struggling to forget, like how to seduce a man. The visions came back. Ugly contortions of shameless sex, thrilling the defiled minds of wicked men.

When her words faltered, the Commander started to move. London laid a trembling hand on his chest and continued in a thick voice. "Sometimes, I'd see her watching me, standing beside a yellow buckeye. When I'd look up, she'd step behind the tree. Other times, I'd discover a dead rabbit near camp."

"Did you ever talk?"

"Naw. Not until that winter. When I ran from home, I'd only gathered stuff a young runaway thought of. I think I had four throw blankets and a pair of long Johns. When you're hanging from a tree in twenty-two-degree temperatures, you can't stay warm." She shivered, reliving the freezing cold. "I slept little that night. My teeth chattered like a set of false choppers gone mad. I'm sure you've experienced those kinds of nights." London investigated the surrounding treetops, remembering how she buried her head under the blankets, wishing to be safe and to sleep by the fire.

"The bears were sleeping, you know. They didn't scare me. Those damned flying squirrels . . . They'd climb in next to me to get warm. One morning, I found one stretched along my calf. Just a baby, but it scared the hell out of me. The temperatures were the best thing about that night. The cold slowed the squirrels' reflexes." She raised her hand. "I'm not afraid of squirrels, but when you detect one curled against you . . . Well, anyone . . ."

The Commander rolled to his back. "Is that when you and the lady started living together? When winter came?"

"Yeah." She smiled. Her eyes cast away as if watching an old movie. "That last night on my own, a blizzard . . . The temperature must have dropped to five degrees. My toes, my fingertips, and the tip of my nose were numb. I thought I'd be dead by morning, so I curled inside my bundle and waited. That's when I heard her."

London's hand tenderly brushed the Commander's cheek as if one snowflake had landed there. "I heard 'Hey, you. Come on down here.' I peeked over my hammock, thinking I heard a ghost. There stood that strange old lady.

No longer cold, I thought I'd seen an angel come to take me home."

London chuckled. "Except for her size, she could have passed for Bigfoot. She wore enough layers to keep a hairless cat warm. I didn't want to get out from under my blankets. But there she stood, next to a roaring hot fire. A pot of steaming food boiled a cloud at her feet. If that hadn't lured me down from my lair, the pair of wool socks dangling from her hand did."

London bent her knee to the side, tugging at a brown sock. "Bombas. Hot or cold, it's the only kind I wear."

The Commander watched the rise and fall of her small breast and ignored the socks.

"We drank a cup of instant hot cocoa, and I followed her home. True story. I guess that's the beginning and end. I hunted. She cooked." London's eyes got starry. "Man, she'd rival any Michelin star chef. She'd cook up a pot of beans, fried morels rolled in batter and collard greens cooked with bacon ... What a meal."

As the Commander raised onto his elbow, his wide glazed pupils and flared nostrils scared London. She shifted her gaze to his hair, his jaw, his hands. They belonged to the man she trusted, the man she longed to touch. Believing in him, she readied herself. When his lips covered hers, she didn't fight the passion but softened her response, inviting him. His kiss proved tender, unlike the tongue-shoving idiots of her past days.

His hand on her neck, he pulled her into him as he lowered them both to the blanket, his body half covering hers.

London shuddered, unsure if fear or desire had taken hold, but she didn't want him to stop. Instead, she rolled, placing him beneath her, and got to her knees. Her hands slid along his sides as his shirt rolled up his chest. Bending over, she licked a line between taut muscles, watching his eyes darken. She released the buckle on his belt and felt his need pressing against her fingertips.

The Commander stopped London's panicked aggression as she teased his erection by rolling her over and placing a hand to her chin. Her pain. The tormented expression she wore, the way a dead soldier wore a coat of blood, he questioned if today was right. "You are pale." He kissed the tip of her nose, and the tension in her body eased. "Not sure you are ready." He pulled her beside him, quieting her fears, as he held her close.

Raging with anxiety, London raised her chin, her eyes meeting his, and said, "I'm ready." Pupils widening in half fear, half need, as she whispered, "I trust you."

Covering her face in tiny kisses, his lips a velvet touch against hers, sending waves of desire through her as he spoke. "Then let us go slow and make it memorable.

34

A Race

Their naked bodies hidden by the ripples of water they'd made entering the lake, London pressed against him, allowing the water to swirl against their skin. "I never knew . . . We . . . I wouldn't have waited. I regret that now."

The Commander raised her chin, kissing the tip of her nose and pressing his forehead against hers. "No regrets. Today begins our lifetime."

She pushed away, splashing him. "Race you to the other side."

"Did I ever tell you I trained with the Underwater Demolition Teams?" he asked her.

London pressed her body against the Commanders. Her fingers walked up his chest, resting on his collarbone. "Really." She bit her lower lip, her eyes raising to his. "I out-swam bears in Abrams Creek."

"What are you not telling me, London? I doubt Phelps could out-swim a bear."

She kissed a trail up his neck. "The bear stopped to

blow bubbles."

With the truth out, London dove into the water, getting an early lead.

The Commander dove in after, passing her to the halfway point. Treading water, he gave her a chance to catch up.

London slipped underwater a few strokes behind him.

A minute passed. Then another. "Is this how you win races?" He backstroked toward the far side, waiting for her to surface. When she didn't come up for air after three minutes, he stopped. Trained to handle dangerous combat situations, the Commander couldn't quell the rising anxiety brewing inside. To control the uneasy fear that crept in, he regulated his breathing.

"London."

Another half minute passed. Jaw clenched, his body full of adrenaline, the Commander dove, his hands searching the murky water. *Nothing.*

Four minutes. He yelled again. "London." Mouth dry, he dove again.

A row of tiny bubbles rising from the depths near shore caught his eye as he rose to the surface.

Bubbles . . . She's playing with me.

Her CIA record flashed before his eyes. . . . *trained to hold her breath up to four minutes.*

London emerged from the water, inhaling a deep breath, silver strands running the length of her body in thin streams. She reminded him of a teenager toying with his vulnerability, innocent and wholesome.

She brushed the hair from her face. "I win." She watched as he swiped at an invisible bug, but she'd seen the tick in his right eye. She giggled to herself. *My hero has a weakness. Me.*

"You cheated." He dove underwater, surfacing close to shore.

London stretched out, balancing on her elbows, allowing the gentle waves created by the Commander's long strokes to wash over her. The waves licked at her breast. She admired the breadth of his shoulders, his powerful forearms.

Prone, walking on his hands the way he'd been on the glider, he moved up the length of her until only his torso remained submerged. "Cheats never win."

"Then why am I on shore?"

He pulled her underneath him, her body pressed up against his. "Now, which one is submerged?"

The light in London's eyes died, and she rolled onto her stomach, escaping his hold.

The Commander changed course to avoid the dangerous tug of isolation she relied so heavily upon. "Tell me more about the mountains." He slid in close, propped up on elbows.

Raised, puffy lesions ranging between five to fifteen centimeters crisscrossed London's back. When she sat upright, he noticed two scars on her chest. Sunken, elongated lines told him the wounds had healed poorly. Another scar, beveled and irregular, protruded like a second navel between her eleventh and twelfth rib. *A bullet wound.* A shot to the intercostal space told him she may have lost a kidney.

"Tell me more about life with the old lady."

London pulled a blade of grass and chewed on the end. "She died. What more is there to tell?"

"What happened?" He rolled over and stretched out an arm to stroke her hair.

"Cancer. When I got home . . ." She paused, turning her head from him. "I mean . . . I found her delirious. She called me *Mohe.* That was her daughter's name. She asked why I took so long. A week later . . . She's dead." London brushed an eye with a swipe of her palm. "I stayed on, selling my photos to different magazines. Then, you know, life goes on . . ."

The Commander knew. He'd experienced the same after losing his dad. "Were you happy in the mountains?"

London stood, walking over to a boulder, where she stretched her back against the hot rock.

"Happy picking berries with Miss Green. Once I cut a cave inside a blackberry patch and crawled in on my belly to watch the bears eat. When she found me—whoa . . . I guess I scared her. I must have been seventeen by then. She chased me with a twitch, threatening me."

London felt her face burn. She'd acted like a scared child, running back to the cabin.

"Looking back, I suppose the bear smelled me among the berries, but he was too busy eating to care." To form the bear's muzzle and lips, she formed her hands the way one made shadow animals. "He'd stick out his thin lips, the way a baby puckers for a bottle, and wrapped them over the plumpest berries. They must've tasted good. He had black berry juice dripping off his lips. I swear he slurped it back in."

"Other than the backside of a camera, how did you get by?"

"Moonshine. Could use a shot of Ole Smoky right now."

"I thought you did not drink?"

"Not since." She shook out her hair and stretched her legs, extending her toes like she'd do in the mountains. "Back then, I'd soak in the water at Mill Creek and knock back a pint of white whisky all day while crunchin' on moonshine pickles."

Standing, the Commander's naked body, though blemished from battle, London thought him a scenic landscape of symmetry.

"We will go there together." He held out his hand. "I

can get time off—"

"I can't." London glanced at the cliff side where the helicopter must still sit. "Don't ruin this moment, Commander." She ignored his hand and stood, sweeping up her jeans and pulling them on in a rush.

The Commander reached out to stop her. "Donee . . ."

London placed a hand to his chest, flirtatiously fluttering her lashes. Her deep blue eyes pleading, she said, "Memorable. Remember?" She smiled. "Let's keep it that way."

The long hike back to the helicopter remained solemn and quiet until they neared their lift-off site. The *whop, whop, whop* of blades spinning along with the noise of the turbine engine that resembled the sound of a jet plane guiding them through the woods.

When they arrived, the chopper sat ready for lift-off.

Namgi was busy loading the glider as Joowon turned, saluting the Commander. "Sir," he yelled over the loud whoosh of the blades, "the bird's ready."

The Commander slapped Joowon on the shoulder, nodding his thanks. Ducking low, the wind blowing dust and leaves around his feet, he helped London into the helicopter and went around to climb into the pilot's seat.

An hour later, London stepped out of the jeep just off the bar entrance.

The Commander jumped out of the vehicle. He came around and stopped her, her foot on the bottom tread of the stairway. "Donee, I need to talk with you about—"

"Tomorrow." She told him. "Talk to me tomorrow. Right now, I'm tired." She kissed his cheek and climbed the steps. Up top, she waved goodnight and entered.

With a hand on the windshield, the Commander propelled himself into the driver's seat when his phone beeped. He read the message as the engine ignited.

* * *

Back at base, the unit was briefed on an emergency mission. "The Flying Tigers need . . ."

As the General continued with their orders, the Commander feared London might leave on her own mission soon. He hoped he'd return in time to stop her.

" . . . your team has the skills needed for this mission. Should be in and out in a day."

At nineteen hundred hours, the Commander's team loaded into a helicopter and flew off for Yemen to the port city of Hodeida. Though the Commander prepared his team for the work ahead, his mind struggled to stay focused. He wondered if the order came down as a distraction. What part had London played on the call?

35

Her Final Mission

The next morning before dawn, disclosing nothing to Joe, London stuffed Yona into her bag and left. She'd never taken off without informing him, but this time . . . her last mission, London wanted to leave without goodbyes. She needed space to grieve. Not death. She cared nothing for whether she lived or died. This misery, an anguish that nauseated her insides, grieved the Commander. She hadn't understood until now. The end, a death of sorts, left behind an undefeatable agony.

Yesterday, London had averted the Commander's questions. She'd suspected he had wanted to ask her to abandon the mission and let him go in her place. To discuss her looming death as if it were debatable. Unacceptable. Did he think she'd live without him? *Crazy.* She'd never consider it. If they must die, let the first death be hers.

The road stretched ahead. Each footfall far heavier than the last. The weight of leaving him drained her mental reserves, weakening her legs. They felt heavy, like weighted lead. In the end, logic triumphed, eradicating the emotion that compromised the mission.

The whine of a passing engine made her pause as she hoped to find the Commander in Willy, driving up to hijack her. She imagined him whisking her off to a remote hideaway, where they'd live out their ordinary days the way normal people did. Married, raising children, and watching their offspring in a school play, or perhaps winning a pageant.

Irrational, since she hadn't told him of her departure. She kept walking.

When the 7-Eleven appeared, she crossed the lot and entered the store. After purchasing two coffees, one hot and the other icy, she dumped the cold into the trash when, upon exiting, she didn't find Willy parked at the gas pump. The urge to pull out and rush back to him, stronger.

Overnight, the temperature had plunged to fifty-nine degrees. The hot coffee warmed her frosty fingers. River conditions would make her swim north uncomfortable.

Expectations of frigid water took her mind off both the mission and the Commander, reflecting instead on Kodiak, Alaska, a training exercise with Navy Seals in early November. Each morning, they'd pull on their wetsuits, get doused with a hose and take the plunge.

The memory was still vivid. Despite many years bathing in the snow-fed waters of the Smokies, London had gasped as she plunged into the Pacific. To stay afloat, she had tread water, her arms banging against small chunks of ice. To regulate the gasping, she held her breath for periods and practiced short bouts of breathing until the evenness of the rising and falling of her chest steadied.

The instructor had thankfully thrown a lifeline before hypothermia induced confusion and drowsiness consumed her.

"Grab hold. I'll pull you out."

London had commanded her frozen fingers to grasp the cord. Willing herself to endure, then, as she often did, to fight the pain. Once they'd hauled her into the boat, the uncontrollable shivering seemed endless as she watched other trainees struggle to stay buoyant. Seconds before they sank, one by one, the seals extracted them.

Now, searching back, each hardship she'd experienced had proven invaluable. Those practices had sustained her life numerous times. She wondered if they'd save her this time.

It took over two hours to reach the Punch Bowl near the North Korea border and another ten to reach the church. She had questions for Father Wadesworth Halverson. During the walk she sensed someone following. She'd first sensed their presence at the 7-Eleven. Though she hadn't looked, she figured there were two people a half kilometer back.

When she reached Wadsworth's rectory, he stood outside as if he expected her. His eyes turned to the stars. As she approached through the yard, he said, "*Hei, hei.* Come in and join me for breakfast."

"Thank you, Father. I'm starving."

"Vownderful. This will be our first meal together."

London suspected their last. "My timing has never been this perfect."

She followed Father Wadesworth into his private quarters, a rich room with dark wood bookshelves lining one wall, a room with simple, yet elegant furniture made of walnut with white cushions. Next to the window that covered the far wall, a two-person table, round with a glass top, sat laden with food. "Blueberries. Yum. Father, have you been reading my mind?"

"Yow like blueberries?"

"They're my favorite fruit." *How did he know I'd be here?*

They ate smoked salmon, boiled eggs, and radish slices

with sour milk porridge, washed down with hot cocoa, leaving a chocolate milk smile on London's face.

When they finished breakfast, London felt sluggish. "Father, can I ask you for a favor?"

"Anything, my child."

She handed the priest an envelope. "Will you make sure Commander Kim gets this letter? Claire will know where to find him." She knew better than to give it to Joe. He'd never give the Commander the satisfaction of reading her last words. Claire would find the act satisfying. "It's . . ." She pushed the official-looking envelope into his hand. "I left the church a little too. It isn't much."

Father Wadesworth clutched her letter with a bony hand, nodding his consent.

She sat on top of her hands, squirming, her eyes downcast. "Another question?"

"Yes."

"When we go to Heaven, do we see the people we know . . . I mean, someday?"

"That's a tough question—"

"If you can't answer, I—"

"Now hold on. I didn't say I couldn't answer yow, only that yow ask a hard question." The priest rose from his chair, walked to the bookshelf, and pulled a compact Bible from a tableside drawer. He crossed to the couch, patting the seat next to him.

The priest took a lengthy breath, eyes heavenward, as if seeking guidance. With the release of air, he turned to London. He opened the Catholic Bible to 1 Thessalonians chapter four. "Paul says," he pointed to verse fourteen, "if we believe Jesus died and rose, so too vill God, through Jesus, bring with him those who have fallen asleep." He shut the Bible, handing it to London, and took her hand in his. "We understand that sleep refers to death. We must believe Jesus vill rise with those who sleep in faith."

Tears blurring her vision, London asked, "Will I make it?"

"Do yow have faith?"

London buried her face in her hands and cried, "I've killed. So many ..."

A comforting, warm hand patted her shoulder. "You are in love?"

She looked up, surprised by his comment. "Love?"

The priest crossed a knee. "In more than a dozen visits, we've never spoken of death. Now, yow want to find out if two people can meet again during our spiritual life, and yow deny love?"

Her lips trembled as tears trickled. "Will we? Meet again ..."

Father Wadesworth handed her a second tissue as he answered. "The faithless must fear the wrath of God, not the faithful. If yow believe, yow vill meet again in Heaven."

"Won't God punish me? I mean, for the killin'?"

"I believe Solomon, the son of David, can answer this best."

He opened a worn leatherback Bible from the coffee table.

London scooted next to him, her eyes on the Word. They read together.

There is ... A time for every affair under the heavens.
A time to give birth, and a time to die;
A time to plant, and a time to uproot the plant.
A time to kill, and a time to heal;
A time to tear down, and a time to build.
A time to weep, and a time to laugh;
A time to mourn, and a time to dance.

"This is yowr time tow laugh and heal. Dance, London. Dance until death seeks yow. Then die without longing.

Embrace love. Those who mourn you vill then dance in your memory."

He patted her knee. "Live without fear. God hears your sorrow. He understands the sacrifice you've made for man and country."

The priest left the room. London wept over the future she'd never have with the Commander. On her knees, her throat burned from unresolved grief. When her sorrow had spent, she stood, tucking the tiny Bible inside her rucksack, and walked into the night.

Near Yoke Ridge, a tribute site for fallen soldiers during the Battle of the Punchbowl, two men stepped out in front of London. One was the man she'd tied to a pole months back. The other she recognized from pictures. *The Serpent.*

"My brother tells me you tied him to a pole." Black and purple serpent scales covered the length of his arms and up his neck.

London smiled. "He was weak. Cried like a baby. Shoulda' seen him. Pee'd all over himself."

The Serpent turned to his man. "She's the one? You sure? Not a big thing, is she?"

The man didn't look frightened like he had back then. He punched one fist into the palm of his other hand. "It's her, Boss. Let's kill her."

Colored contact lenses gave the Serpent's eyes a dragon's glare.

Cheap trick.

He stared at London, his body relaxed, one hand dangling a light machine gun known for its high rate of fire, the M249 Saw. "Most expect to die in my presence. You don't look scared."

"Listen, Serpent. You've got me fair and square. I'm defenseless and you're holding a powerful weapon. Hardly a situation in my favor, but as it sits, you've the upper hand. Since you need a weapon to take me down, it seems I frighten you."

The Serpent laughed. "I like you, lady. You got some balls." He grabbed his crotch with his free hand. "I didn't come here to kill you. I wanted to meet the woman who weakened one of my men."

His goon took a step back, no longer tense with need for revenge. "Boss. That bitch caught me drunk."

Those dragon eyes never left London's as the Saw raised shoulder height.

"I swear. I'm sober. Give me a chance. I'll kill her."

"You see, lady, without fear I have no power." The *whooping* of bullets firing rapidly ripped through the man's body too fast for him to crumple until London heard the *clank* of the weapon cycling. "I rely upon power. Now that we have settled this between us two, I forgive you."

Without glancing at the dead man, London said, "He needed to die."

When the Saw rose a second time, London held her ground, planning how she'd kill him before the gun fired.

The Serpent studied her quizzically. "You really aren't afraid of me?"

"Not in the least," she said.

"Hmmm ... Respect." The gun lowered. "Let's not meet again. Next time, my respect will die with you."

"Or, you." London walked past him as she continued on her designated path never looking back.

At midnight, she stood riverside. She removed her hoodie and jeans, tucking them in her ruck, then pulled on a Helix thermal cold water wet suit. A balaclava covered her head and neck. Before slipping into a set of fins and stepping into the Imjin River, she smeared on reflecting face paint.

Her rebreather in place, she submerged, feeling the engulfing chill.

* * *

Claire entered the saloon to find Father Halverson making a cup of coffee. "Father, what brings you here?"

Claire tied on an apron as Father Halverson sipped the black coffee. She watched as he pulled a paper from his pocket and pushed it across the counter. "London asked me tow deliver this. She said you'd know who the note vas intended."

Claire took it with shaky hands, held it for several moments before placing it into her apron pocket.

36

Hear the Cell Ringing

The Commander arrived home two days later. After climbing the U-shaped staircase to London's apartment, he pounded on the door, certain of the reason behind her absence. He'd called several times during his mission without an answer.

He heard the ringing of her phone.

As he knocked, the back of his neck prickled, warning him of a presence approaching from behind. He rotated. Snagging the wrist of the intruder, he wrenched their arm, forcing them to twist until their back was to him.

Claire carried a folded note in her raised hand. Rigid with fear, she didn't cower as the Commander extracted the note. "I didn't read it." Her breathy words came too fast. "I wanted to. But I didn't."

The Commander noticed the sweat dripping down Claire's neck and released her, crumpling the note as she stepped down, spinning to face him.

"Aren't you going to read it?" she asked.

When he didn't respond, Claire rubbed her aching arm. "Fine. I'll take off." She stepped down two steps before turning back. "You know, she left without saying a word to me and Joe. All these years we've been together . . ." She studied her hands as if she expected a letter to appear. "I never hated London. Just that she was always so cocky, like she had control of everything. I suppose maybe I wanted some of that control, so Joe would notice me instead."

Without speaking, the Commander watched Claire trudge down the remaining steps. Though he sensed her pain, he cared nothing for her suffering.

Alone, the Commander sat on the top step and unfolded the single sheet, his hands shaking.

It read, *I'm full. Goodbye.*

* * *

Joe's office door burst open.

A madman in uniform, the Commander bellowed, "How long she is gone?"

Joe rolled his chair from the office desk absently and ran his fingers across his slick scalp. "This is between London and the United States government. I'm not at liberty—"

"Tell me!" The Commander vaulted over the desk and slammed Joe against the wall, holding him with an arm pressed against his neck.

"I . . . don't know." He sputtered. "She snuck out."

The Commander increased the pressure on Joe's windpipe.

"Okay." Joe's voice choking out the words.

The Commander's hold slackened.

"Father Halverson showed up yesterday morning. Until then, I didn't notice London had disappeared. She must have departed sometime after dusk, two nights back."

"Route, she take?" The Commander released his hold.

Gasping, Joe said, "The . . . Imjin. She'll swim . . . up

the river. I swear . . . That's all she shared."

The Commander turned and shuffled through the paperwork on top of Joe's desk. A coiled map with London's handwriting lay on top of a filing cabinet. He seized it.

Coughing, Joe screamed, "Hey. That's government property!"

The Commander shifted his stance, punching Joe, knocking him to the floor. His words clipped and rich with rage, he said, "You sent her to die alone."

Crumpled on the floor, Joe choked out, "It's her job." He used the wall to stand, blood dripping onto his white starched shirt, and took a step toward his enemy. Tears gathered as he spoke. "I let her go because I detested her for choosing you."

The Commander struck him a second time and bolted outside to his jeep. Shaken and enraged enough to kill, he cleared the passenger seat and landed behind the wheel. The engine revved to life, and the tires squealed. Fear settled deep inside the marine, a fear he'd have to wrestle to save London.

The drive to base gave him time to regain his composure, but the fear stuck to him like swamp water. When he entered General Hanbin's office, the secretary greeted him.

"Commander Kim. Is the General expecting you?"

"No, but I must speak with him."

The secretary picked up the receiver and dialed. "I'm sorry to disturb you General, but Commander Kim is here, and it seems"—her eyes locked with the Commander's,—"urgent, sir."

When she placed the receiver back on the landline, she signaled for the Commander to enter. "He'll see you."

The Commander passed the secretary's desk and entered the General's office, his hat clasped between his palms, knuckles white, and bowed.

The General stood as he entered. "Please, come in. What's so urgent?"

Back stiff, the Commander said, "Sir. I would like approval to cross the demilitarization line and safeguard the victory of London's mission."

"I see." The General sat, his poker face revealing nothing.

"She fled to North Korea two days ago. I have glimpsed her map, and I am confident that if we leave soon, we will arrive in time to guarantee the job is completed."

The General leaned back, clasping his hands while he studied the Commander. Several seconds passed before he spoke. "London is a proficient American spy who accepted this mission while understanding the risk. Are you confident what you're seeking isn't to rescue the woman?"

"With respect sir, London is one person ordered to complete an impossible mission, without backup. You say she is skilled; my team is also proficient. Granting your approval will ensure the mission's success and offer her a fighting chance."

The General adjusted his position with one hand placed on his armchair. "Are you saying this Miss Bennett, err . . . your London, is ill suited to the task?"

The Commander lowered his head, squeezing the hat between sweaty palms. "No, sir."

"Why should I risk five outstanding men for one?"

The Commander bowed in respect to his leader, holding his position longer than necessary. "Please, sir, she will die if we don't go."

"Sit." Placing both arms on the desk, the General leaned forward as he opened his cell, then jabbed a single number. "I'll speak with General Turner."

"Thank you, sir." An unfamiliar tension twisted in the Commander's gut, but he remained dutiful.

The General relaxed, the air about him jovial, making it apparent the person on the other end of the line was a friend. "Hey, Harley. We missed you Friday night."

Quietfilledthespaciousroom,astheCommanderwaited.

General Hanbin laughed and said, "One of my men wishes to evaluate the Army's backup plan to rescue the spy your country sent to North Korea." A pause. "From what I've gathered, she left two, maybe three, days ago."

Each space of silence was short-lived. "I grasp it's a top-secret mission, but what can you tell me? Mhm . . . Mhm . . ."

The hush gave him reason to squirm, but the Commander held himself rigid, counting the ticking of a wall clock.

"Okay. Thanks. See you next Friday."

The General closed his phone and leaned back in his chair, his stoney eyes on the Commander. Scratching the edge of his nose, he said, "You're moving with or without my approval?"

"Sir?"

"If you did leave without my approval, that would be insubordination?"

"Yes, sir."

The General rose, frowning as he drew a cigarette out of a box and twiddled it between his fingers. His expression soured, though his attitude remained professional. "General Turner confirmed what we'd already speculated." He lit the cigarette and continued.

"London entered a seaside tunnel a couple of months back. Her original mission was to map the underground rooms and search for the super engine their leader claimed he had in development. The tunnel ended up larger than expected, over fifteen miles long, exiting close to the *Suipcheon* stream. Her current mission is to destroy the weapon. I'm sorry, soldier." He placed both palms flat on the desk, cigarette smoke rising from between two fingers. "The United States Army will not be sending a reconnaissance mission. General Turner claims the girl has a death wish and doesn't want to be rescued."

"Sir. Will you give my team permission?"

Nausea swept over the Commander as he waited on his superior. Many times, his team had flown into dangerous gunfire to rescue fellow soldiers. Beforehand, like any battle, he'd faced fear. Fear kept a soldier alive. Drove his men to move faster. Stronger. Authority over fear had provided them with emotional detachment.

This was different. He felt shaken and weak. Life without London wasn't an option. Resolved, he sat straighter, allowing his lungs to expand, and drawing off the energy rush that came with it.

Inhaling on a cigarette stub, the General crushed the butt in the ashtray, then turned to the window. He exhaled before he spoke, releasing a gray haze. "I'll tell you what I can do. I can turn a blind eye. If you go, you and your team will move alone. There will be no recovery. We can't risk another war."

The Commander bowed again, straightened, and planted his cap on his head. He left without the General turning away from the window. Outside the General's office, he called his first in command. "Gather the men and meet me at the weapons storage unit."

37

A Clenched Jaw

The Commander pulled up to an old rusty Quonset hut, once the living quarters of American soldiers during the Korean War. A stack of metal bed frames still sat against the far wall. His squad had claimed it for planning purposes early in the team's development.

Lieutenant Hyuk greeted him outside the shed. The lieutenant stood with his feet apart and hands on hips. Bulky muscles and a clenched jaw made him appear menacing.

Once the jeep was parked, Hyuk approached the Commander's vehicle. "Commander."

"Lieutenant."

"A word, sir."

The Commander stepped out of the jeep and followed the Lieutenant until they were out of earshot of the other men just inside the metal structure.

"Sir. Out of respect, London's disappearance has nothing to do with the Korean military. It is not our duty to preserve and protect an American spy. Nor do I agree with risking our men to save a *migukin* Yankee."

The Commander remained quiet as the Lieutenant spoke, understanding why Hyuk hated Americans.

"You know the truth." Hyuk continued. "America weakened our country against the North during the *Pueblo* kidnapping. When our students protested the negotiations, those American bastards fired on my grandmother. Because of them, she lost the use of her left arm."

The American government had denied the killing of some protestors, but Hyuk, like his grandmother, told a different version of the story.

During these negotiations, a spy from North Korea tried to assassinate the South Korean president, called the Blue House Incident, angering the citizens further, causing more hatred toward anyone from the States.

The Lieutenant continued. "London knew the risk. She accepted the mission." Arm thrust out toward America, he continued. "For her country, not ours! If they need a combat search and rescue, let the Americans accept the risk of war, not us."

The Commander placed a hand on his military brother's shoulder, and the Lieutenant stood at ease. "I understand your pain, but London is not one of the American soldiers who shot your grandmother." He patted Hyuk's shoulder. "Stay. I will go alone."

He walked past the Lieutenant and faced the rest of his men, who saluted him as he entered the hut.

"As you were."

The four men relaxed.

Private Wonho opened a metal chair and sat, leaning forward over his knees. "Sir. Do you have a plan?"

"A map, a river, and a tunnel." The Commander unfolded the map and joined the rest of his team around a rickety wooden table left by previous occupants. He placed a rock on each corner of the map. The team listened as the Commander pointed to the town *Geonsol-ri*. "My understanding is London swam up the *Suipcheon* stream and entered the North somewhere upriver."

Private Namgi's finger followed the three-and-a-half-kilometer stream. "Spots of low water will make the route tricky."

"Yes, but it's a clean route that takes her under the DMZ line. It appears she watched the weather forecast and planned her departure with the rain," the Commander added.

Captain Wonsul made a circle around the watch tower. "If she's swimming upriver, the tunnel must be near the Eoeunsan Tower."

"I suspect you're right, Captain." The Commander opened a bottle of water and swallowed a mouthful. "London has a two-day lead. My guess is she left before dawn on Sunday." Setting the bottle to the side, he leaned with both hands on the table, wobbling the uneven legs. "I caught a brief glimpse of a map London had strewn out on the kitchen counter. She'd circled this church." He let his finger slide across the map to *Haean* Catholic Church. "I suspect she will visit with the priest before entering the north."

"A Christian spy? Wow!"

The Commander gave Private Wonho a stern eye. Wonho backed away, his hands in the air. "Hey, I'm a Christian too."

Wonho's attention turned to the map as the Commander continued with his plan.

"If I am right, I can reach the tower before she enters the tunnel. I will scout the area from here." He pointed to the tower. "With any luck, the hidden weapon's location will be within eyesight."

Wonsul slapped a hand against the wood, nearly toppling the Commander's drink. "Let's do this."

The Commander grabbed the map, catching his drink and the corner of the table in time to prevent a leg from collapsing. "Hold on, soldier." He righted the table before looking each man in the eye. "London is on a suicide mission. This time, I go alone. If you follow, there's a chance you will not come home."

Corporal Joowon took a step forward, and said, "Sir, if you don't mind, sir, your family is our family," saluting his commander.

Lieutenant Hyuk unfolded his arms and stepped up to the table. "We serve the Republic of Korea. If war breaks out from this invasion, *our* people will suffer. We cannot value one life over an entire country."

The Commander studied his men, his face grim as he continued. "Hyuk is right." The Commander's eyes locked with the lieutenants as he spoke. "I ask none of you to follow. If you chose to cross the demilitarization line, the choice is yours alone."

He'd shared everything with these men. Their successes had awarded him respect among his peers. He understood this mission endangered their lives. Fear had left him questioning his command before each mission, yet he trusted the five men before him. In return, if needed, he'd sacrifice his life for them . . . A straightforward choice.

Captain Wonsul stepped up, followed by Namgi and Wonho, their arms around each other's shoulders. "We're in."

"This is a mistake." Hyuk stabbed his finger on a stable corner of the table, the vein in his neck throbbing as he spoke. He turned on the Commander. "Saving this girl won't bring back your parents, Commander. Your whole life you've been picking up strays, believing you can make amends for their deaths. It wasn't your fault they died, and now this new stray chose to leave. She accepted the consequences the moment she entered the North."

Captain Wonsul raised a fist, but the Commander placed a hand over his, lowering it.

"It is possible," the Commander admitted. "London might be another pet project to ease my guilt, but when I put together this team, I took a risk on each of you."

He turned to Namgi, who stiffened. "You nearly got yourself locked in the brig for going AWOL. Wonsul couldn't hit a bullseye from five feet away."

The Commander walked over to Joowon. "You wanted out of the ROK, and Wonho," who stood next to Joowon, "choked during his first training mission, exposing the team to explosives."

Hyuk glared at something beyond the team when the Commander said, "I found you, Lieutenant, fighting in a back alley, and turned you into a soldier. Now, because of the risks I have taken, the best in the ROK stands in front of me."

The Lieutenant hung his head, shaking it back and forth. "She isn't part of the team."

"Not a team member, Hyuk. A part of me. I will not leave her behind."

With Hyuk standing on the outskirts, the remaining men strategized their plans. It took just under an hour to finalize their mission. Phoning the General, the Commander said, "Goodbye, sir."

"Good luck, Commander. You and the boys come home safe."

"Yes, sir."

* * *

Low water meant risk of exposure, but London preferred this longer route up the Imjin River over cutting through the fence and risk being seen by those guarding the demilitarization line. She entered North Korea, fighting the current, deep as the depth allowed.

Closer to the surface, boats passed.

London practiced holding her breath as she attached remotely detonated specially designed seal bombs to the boat's hulls. Originally made to keep marine mammals away from fishing nets, London used the bombs as a distraction. She could ignite them from shore, producing a shockwave that traveled for long distances. The loud noise would, if needed, draw attention away from her.

Upstream, she swam several kilometers before easing out of the water. On land, she hid among a thicket of Japanese spicebushes, repacking her rebreather, changing her clothes, and munching on a handful of granola, nuts, and shiny, black spice berries. The mittens-shaped leaves hid her from the passing captains who fished in the Imjin.

The boats had more than a dozen lit helmets sweeping the dark the way airport lights swept the runway.

Lying low, she found two grubs curled inside a dead log. Twisting off their heads and squeezing out the fecal matter, she ate them, washing the almond flavor away with warm water.

An hour passed before she crawled through the underbrush toward the back entrance of the cave a half mile away.

She'd reached the unmanned opening using the momentary distraction of guards changing their posts to enter the tunnel moments before factory workers began their workday. As she attempted to sleep, her mind racing through options, the factory hummed with activity.

Industrial presses pounded metal into shape. The hiss of air compressors refilling was as loud as a radial saw slicing logs into timber.

London believed the factory produced more than the engine she'd came to destroy. Covid had changed the Kim family's demand for weaponry. Their people were starving while the Father of Korea, Kim Jong Un, placed emphasis on suicide drones, early warning aircraft, and other unmanned systems.

To sleep, London pictured the freshwater fish she'd swum with, counting them like sheep. Under the polluted waters of the Imjin, surrounded by a primordial forest, decimated by logging, the *Lenok* swam in large numbers.

Unable to sleep, she drifted to thoughts of the old lady, remembering the days that led to her death. Her mind a mess. Once delirium set in, memories of the past became the present, back to the time her daughter and husband still lived.

When she wasn't delirious, she slept, waking to eat, but eating little. In the evenings, she'd call for Sarah. They'd spend the nights together lying side by side as the old woman reminisced about her daughter's childhood, days with her husband, the three of them loving each other and life.

Before she died, she spoke of death for the first time, speaking as if dying were a simple matter, the way one bought milk at the store.

"I'm leaving soon."

"Where to?"

"To Jesus. He's here, waiting for me. I didn't know they had collard greens and morel mushrooms in Heaven. I will eat well."

"Did Jesus tell you that?"

"Yes. Well, no." She seemed to have a moment of clarity. *"Not the way you talk to me. He casts images."* She stared past Sarah, her eyes fixed on the silvery shimmer of the moonlight that widened across the tiny room through the window. *"An image,"* her bony hand stretched toward the light. *"I could have touched it. My daughter. She's there, too. So is my husband. They're waiting for me."*

"You see them?"

"Oh, yes. My husband is young and handsome. You

think he will recognize me?"

"He will. He must. You're as beautiful as the day of your wedding."

"Don't be silly, Sarah. I have walrus wrinkle, and my skin's as thin as a Man-of-War jellyfish."

The old woman was silent a moment. When she next spoke, her voice had softened. "I'm not afraid to die. It's just hard to leave you."

Sarah struggled to keep from crying.

"I remember the first day you came to the campground. You were so skinny. If you hadn't stolen that food, I'd have stolen it for you. You're a wonderful child, Sarah, resourceful and loveable. Promise me you won't forget that?"

Sarah laid snuggled up against her, the tears now silently soaking her pillow. "I promise."

"I will miss this, Sarah. You and me. Together. But I'm ready."

The soft purr of breathing followed.

The next day, the old woman didn't eat, and when awake, she didn't speak. On her last day, she stirred in bed, more alert and energetic than Sarah had seen her in months, asking for a bowl of pureed peaches.

London sat on the bedside feeding her the way a mother fed an infant, scooping the dripped puree from the sides of her mouth. The crinkled face that reminded London of railroad tracks softened as she studied Sarah's face, as if she knew death was coming and wanted to remember.

Placing a crooked finger against Sarah's cheek, she said, "You did well." Through the night, her body, still warm, was lifeless, with Sarah asleep at her side.

Locked in Blake's horror house, London remembered the nights she'd cried for the old lady, wishing she could go home.

Home?

From the moment her dad died, home had become a foreign word until she moved into the mountainside cabin. Their relationship had never become one of laughter and joyous family time. They'd both suffered painful losses and no longer felt joy, but the muted walks in the woods, sitting near a warm fire, and reading a comic book in the dim light as the old lady sewed, had been peaceful, even loving.

Stunned by this revelation, London forgot counting the fish. *I loved her* . . . Deliberating this emotion. Love. The comfort behind such a word when spoken brought forth the Commander's image. London knew then that she loved him. She loved him in an unmeasurable way. Beyond that of the old lady, and greater than her father. This was a love she'd die to protect, and strong enough to make life worthy.

He had become . . . *Home.*

* * *

The Commander and his team crossed the river at Peace Dam and continued onward toward North Korea. The highway twisted, turning northeast onto a two-lane road. From *Cheonmi-ri*, they took a narrow gravel street that zigzagged into the mountains. When it curved southeast, they parked and started out on foot, hiking three kilometers over rough, mountainous terrain. Their goal, Eoeunsan Tower, but first they had to get past the border fence.

The danger would increase once they passed through into North Korean territory. Farmers, or the Worker Peasant Red Militia, walked through the woods more than anyone, carrying AK 47s, light machine guns and RPOs. Exempt from military duty, the farmers trained each month, a Korean National Guard of sorts. Except these men saw through the trees. They noticed the unnoticeable. And the Commander's team needed to remain unseen.

Tackling the open hillside of Eoeunsan Tower might leave them more vulnerable, so the plan to take out the men inside and head northeast became their toughest challenge ahead.

38

Desperate Men Behave Outside the Law

Entering the southern side of the Military Demarcation Line, the men kept their rifles ready and stayed low and on the lookout for any patrol teams from the North. The law forbade North Korean soldiers from crossing the MDL line, but desperate men behaved outside the law, even in suppressed societies. Meeting up with a team unaware sealed your fate. The soldiers were smaller but tough, most training from early childhood.

When Corporal Joowon spotted a Korean hare, called a *santokki*, a while back, the Commander ordered him to kill it. The spotted bunny now hung from the corporal's back. "We'll use it to distract the soldiers if we need to."

"How?" the corporal asked.

Private Namgi swatted at the endless bugs swarming around them and gave the younger soldier a gentle shove. "A landmine." Namgi chuckled. "We'll follow a deer path and toss the rabbit on a mine. The soldiers will investigate, giving us a chance to get away."

"What if the Korean People's Army are following the deer path?" Joowon asked.

Captain Wonsul shushed him. "We're not following the deer tracks, but if needed, the landmine might work."

Using hand signals, the team quietly squatted in the dense brush. The Commander pulled out a map and pointed to the spot they'd pass under the fence. With the coordinates marked, they got up and kept walking, stepping in their leader's footprints toward the designated latitude and longitude.

The moon, a waxing crescent, was brighter than the Commander wanted as they approached the fence. Calculating the moon's cycle, he knew London had left on a new moon, crossing the border in complete darkness. Thinking back, the last time she'd disappeared had been a full moon, giving her four days to arrive with a new moon to shield her in the dark.

Twenty meters from the fence, the Commander signaled for his men to stop. Pointing toward a bunker to their right, thirty meters from where they stood, he said, "Rest. We cross in two hours."

They munched on spam and kimchi in the dark, drinking water from canteens. The Commander noticed that each of his men appeared on edge, staring into the woods. Most likely performing a mental roadmap of what lay ahead.

He stepped away from the small group, giving them more time to prepare mentally as he moved to the edge of the forest and surveyed the fence line. American soldiers from the 2nd infantry were inside hidden bunkers, while others patrolled the line. Without a sanctioned mission, the soldiers would shoot before asking questions. He needed to study their routine. With spotlights every twenty feet on the chain-link fence, it was the Commander's job to keep his team alive.

Checking his watch, he estimated the next guard change was thirty minutes away. The North should change in unison, giving the Commander and his crew time to cross. This wasn't the first time his team had entered North Korea using this method, but each time carried the threat of being their last.

An hour later, the Commander crawled toward the fence and felt the earth trembling under his belly. *An explosion.* He wondered where.

Under extreme threat, like London, living now carried the risk of dying. To survive, they both needed to complete their missions. The upheaval from the explosion had given him an opportunity to sneak in and cut the wire. He used a voltmeter to test the fence's electrical current.

The dry ground prevented a complete circuit. Using rubber clamps attached by wires, he routed the flow of electricity around a space two-and-a-half feet wide by the same height. With the current rerouted, he made four cuts in the wire and slid across the sand, leaving a trail wide enough to spot in the light. From this point, ten feet between each beam, the shadowed line remained visible.

Through both cattle fences, his men followed one by one. Namgi came last, removing the clamps and swishing the sand. They'd timed their movements five minutes apart, their lives risked on an estimation, which was little more than a guess. The cut in the fence may go unnoticed for up to ten hours or be seen within minutes. He hoped for the former, giving them time to reach London and leave the area.

39

An Empty Factory

Lights out, the darkness held the same eerie quiet London experienced the last time she'd walked through these tunnels. With the factory empty, she descended the shelves. Her toe slipped, the raw wood scraping her shin bloody on her way down.

Ouch! That f-ing hurts.

A broom stick propped against the corner helped her stand, but not before she smacked her head against a metal trash can.

The noise echoed.

She drew back a foot, glaring at the can. "I ought to . . ."

Braced in an offensive position, she waited. No one came.

The super engine and the computers that controlled it sat near the closet. She worked fast, aware that someone could enter the factory at any moment. She had zero camouflage under the light of glowing monitors in the stark darkness.

The satellite-enabled laptop she pulled from her ruck brightened the workspace even more.

Let there be light.

She infected the computers with the same virus she'd used in Iran.

London checked the time. The Great Leader cut the electricity at ten to hide energy shortages through the night. She'd need to rely upon each computer's internal battery to complete the download before they died.

While the green downloading light clicked across the screen, she removed a plate from the super engine, revealing its delicate heart. She looked inside with a penlight held between her teeth.

Her needs analyzed, she withdrew a hollow metal sphere from her ruck, along with a rubber belt and two rollers, laying them aside.

A walk around the factory provided the missing items needed to complete a revised Van de Graaff Generator. Once completed, it could direct an x-ray beam, using ionization of air around the globe, capable of damaging the electrical circuits inside the super engine beyond repair.

The long and tedious assembly of the two-foot ESD left her fingers raw. A wide gash on her index bled. She glued the wound closed and lifted the generator onto a conveyor belt before pulling on a KN95 surgical mask.

A factory loader nearby would have made moving the engine easier, but the noise would attract attention. Instead, she found broken jacks in a parts closet. She scattered the pieces to repair four and placed them under each corner of the super engine on a cement platform, jacking it higher. After removing a section of the rollers from the loader, she placed them under the raised engine and lowered the jacks. The heavy engine moved into place below the generator.

When the ESD accumulated a positive charge, it released an x-ray beam. The high voltage pulse released an acrid plastic smoke and surged into the super engine, destroying the circuitry.

An insignificant amount of C4 was connected to a wireless hand-held remote and placed inside the belly of the machine.

London turned her attention back to the computers.

With one percent remaining, a man holding a cellphone entered the factory. The screen's blue light gave her away.

He flipped on a high-powered military grade flashlight and directed it toward her.

The screen line turned green as the frightened worker backed out of the room yelling, "Intruder!"

Success.

The upload bar at 100%, London grabbed her rucksack and ran out of the back entrance, twisting her ankle as she landed. She ran uphill limping, determined to reach the trees and prepared to die.

Four guards sprinted in her direction, slowed by the steep hillside and rocky terrain. When the nearest soldier got close, she threw a shuriken like a frisbee, dropping him to his knees. The star-shaped weapon sank into his jugular. A second dug into another soldier's shoulder. It didn't stop him.

A third man grabbed London from behind. He spun her. A fourth clipped her in the jaw with the butt of a rifle. London buckled.

She never felt a soldier's bayonet slicing open one of her biceps but felt the slippery blood running the length of her arm. Focused on stabilizing her warbled mind, she didn't notice when a rifle butt slammed into her abdomen, but the pain jolted her back to the fight.

She landed a kick to the soldier's groin and rolled to a stand as a bayonet stabbed beside her. Withdrawing the knife from her boot, she spun. The knife sliced open the thigh of the soldier next to her. He dropped. Blood pulsated from his femoral artery, spraying her in the eyes.

Adrenaline coagulated the blood on her arm. She never felt pain or fear in the heat of a battle.

Two more soldiers were closing in. London backed away, keeping her eyes on each opponent, focusing on the olive green of their uniforms rather than their faces.

Everything slowed. London homed in on her abilities. She held a short Indian dagger, a double-edged blade intended for stabbing and thrusting, sweeping it broadside as the soldiers neared. The other hand held a rock.

When a female soldier raised her rifle, London threw the rock, catching her between the eyes. The last soldier ran at her, bowling them onto the ground. With seconds to defend herself, she flipped him, landing on his back. With both hands, she jabbed the knife into his brain at the base of his skull. His body went limp.

Ignoring the swollen ankle, London ran. Shots fired her direction from far below, missing their target in the dim moonlight. Bullets sounded like grenade launchers as they whisked past her ear. In the forest, hidden in the shadows of low branches, she climbed a tall Lacebark elm tree and felt the first burning under her ribs.

Rifles pointed. Soldiers crested the hill. They searched the forest floor, none of them suspecting she'd have time to climb. Braced, unmoving, she stood between two branches.

London remained motionless until she could no longer see their lights.

Chirping birds, squirrels bouncing between branches, and a wild boar rutting in the dirt, told London she'd lost the soldiers for now. She turned. Her heel landed on a short, dead limb. It broke under her weight.

Smacking hardwood, the image of her right forearm's radius and ulna bones snapping flashed through her mind. The ten-foot fall landed her draped over a thick branch. Her damaged arm gripped the limb as she used her abdominal muscles to lift herself into a straddled position.

She recalled the training she'd received at Sherman Kent School for Intelligence Analysis. Her commanding officer repeated daily a mantra he swore by. "Survival demands unconquerable effort."

London thought of the Commander. Heavy laden with suppressed tears, her vision blurred.

With her back against the trunk, legs dangling, and one arm hanging uselessly, she waited. Waited for him to come, sure he wouldn't make it in time. She'd doubted his promise to protect her and prayed he'd find a way. She steadied her breaths and calculated the pain. *It's a ten. No . . . A six.* She shrugged it off. *I can get through it.*

She pulled a chunk of bark off the tree and clenched it between her teeth.

The remote . . .

She felt inside her pockets, finding the remote. She kissed it and pushed the button.

The explosion, though small compared to other bombs she'd set off, shook the tree. Screaming and rapid sounds of confusion followed the collapse of mountain and cement sending a cloud of dirt and smoke in the air.

London lowered her chest, clutching the tree limb while lifting the dangling arm into place.

One, two, three . . . she pulled.

Her teeth burrowed farther into the wood chunk as an internal bellow filled her skull. Silent tears flowed down her cheeks.

You're close, Commander. I feel you.

She took slow, deliberate breaths, rising into a sitting position, wondering if her life was worth saving.

40

Empty Eyes

The Commander focused ahead, watching for trip wires and landmines. The Worker and Peasants' Red Militia governed the region. The Red Militia were farmers clad in threadbare uniforms. A red star displayed proudly on their helmets beneath a miner's lamp. Thin to the point of emaciation, their empty eyes held little that clung to life or hope. The farther north he and his men crept in search of London, the more potential for an encounter with the enemy.

Signing to his team, the Commander made a wide arc with his fingers after pointing to his eyes, indicating to search out the enemy. After scanning the hilltops, he pointed west toward Eoeunsan Tower, making a circle around his finger and then directed his thumb downward to instruct them to circle the hillside and come in from behind.

It took over three hours of tediously slow progress to climb the mountainside to a point beneath the tower. Serving as a lookout, Wonsul remained behind a rock on the slope, using binoculars to track the enemy movements inside. Their attention directed north, toward the presumed explosion point, making them easy targets.

Once beneath the wooden structure, the Commander raised his rifle, melding as a single entity as he climbed the steps. The creak of wood made him freeze, finger on the trigger, hoping he wouldn't have to shoot.

On the landing, the Commander heard the scratchy call of a starling and flattened himself against the wall. Shifting his rifle, he pulled a knife from his belt.

The door swung open, and a soldier stepped out.

The Commander placed a knife at the enemy's jugular and whistled to his men. With his hostage leading, they stepped inside, blood dripping from the man's throat as the Commander said, "You move, he is dead."

He looked right to find a rifle trained on his head.

A Red Militia, shallow and drawn, smiled. His finger rested on the trigger as Hyuk and Namgi stepped in behind him.

After shoving his hostage, the Commander ducked beneath the gun barrel and swept his leg to knock the farmer off his feet, sinking the knife into the man's chest as he fell. He rose into a handstand, kicking another in the face.

From behind, a soldier slammed his foot into the Commander's kidney. The force knocked him through the door and against the widow's walk railing. One side of the wooden plank broke free.

The Commander fell through the opening, grabbing the post on his way over.

The attacking soldier struck the Commander's fingers with the butt of his rifle, causing him to lose his grip. As he dangled by one arm, dodging the man's feet, Hyuk picked the soldier up from behind and tossed him over the rail.

"You need a hand?"

The Commander reached out, clasping Hyuk's hand, and heaved himself back on to the decking.

Upright, he yanked the Lieutenant in close for a quick, manly hug, slapping him on the back with a fist and releasing his hold. "Glad you're here, *hyung*."

"You better be. I just saved your ass."

Hyuk finished off the man left lying on the floor inside with a knife, slicing his carotid artery, a *whoosh* escaping. With four dead, Hyuk signaled Wonsul to join them while the Commander located the tunnel.

From their higher advantage, he spotted the tunnel entrance through binoculars. The primary entrance faced the Southeast. Nearest to them, on the southern side, the ground had collapsed. No doubt the bomb detonated by London.

With the area under heavy guard, some soldiers were busy cleaning debris from the explosion.

Hyuk joined the Commander on the far side of the lookout.

The Commander pointed to a pile of land and rubble a kilometer or more from where they stood. "Hole. Size of a semi-trailer below the trees."

They watched soldiers searching near the river, an obvious escape route, while others guarded the woods. A third set scoured the tall grass below the tower, headed their direction.

"We will go around and come in from behind. If she is in the trees, we will find her. Ridge and forest cover is heavy. Shame we lack London's gift for tree climbing."

"Huh?" Hyuk asked.

The Commander winked at Hyuk. "You will see." The Commander clapped Hyuk on the back. They left the tower, careful to remain unseen. "We have approximately two hours until someone comes to check on the tower, another half day before they have us in their sites. Stay alert and keep down."

They dropped behind the hillside into the valley below, searching for a route to take them behind London's suspected hiding place.

* * *

Weak from two days without food or water other than a few drops of condensation, London slouched on the branch. She'd slept only minutes at a time, fearful of rolling out of the tree. Even if she'd allowed herself more sleep, the growing pain in her abdomen kept her awake.

Her head pressed against the tree trunk as she scanned the woods. She listened for the man who'd promised to save her. It was foolish. Stealth in the woods, the Commander would come soundlessly.

Idiot. He can't find you. Dehydrated, she'd started talking to herself in the first and third person, her mind too dull for lucid thought. *A death sentence. Do you want him to die?*

In a hoarse whisper, she squeaked, "No! He can't die." London's teeth chattered in the early autumn chill. To stay warm, she cradled her broken arm, hugging herself.

North Korean soldiers had scanned the woods for more than a day when she overheard a lieutenant instructing his men. "You three guard the woods. The rest pull out."

When cold, hunger, and thirst lured her thoughts into the darkness, London wanted the Kim's Army to find her. Death seemed the better choice. Even torture eventually ended misery. *How much, God? I can't hold out.*

Thoughts of suicide . . . Rolling off the branch ended things. The snap of a twig or the clunk of a rock transported her wayward mind to the present, but no one came.

Dozing, she dreamed of the Commander sitting below the waterfall, the spray splashing his legs.

" . . . *we communicate by whistling and bird calls.*"

"Teach me."

"Can you whistle?"

London puckered her lips and blew but sounded like a tea pot right before the boil.

Laughing, the Commander showed her how to cave her tongue behind her bottom teeth and say 'oo.' "Soft. Without forcing the air between your lips."

She tried, but the wind didn't whistle.

His hand touched her cheek, his kiss exploring her mouth with interest, releasing her too soon. "Why d'you kiss me?"

"To moisten your lips. More fun than instruction."

She leaned in for another kiss. Their lips lingered. When he released her, she tried again.

She pursed her lips and a soft whistle blew. London bounced. "I did it."

"Now, close your eyes. Listen to the birds." As each sang, he'd tell her about the breed. "That rattling call, like a bugle, is the crane. Hyuk rattles like the crane."

"The Lieutenant chose a crane? Odd, since the crane resembles Wonsul, who's not only tall but thin."

"He likes cranes, Wonsul chose the loon. They have a haunting yodel. He raised his hands to show her.

London shivered. "Reminds me of a coyote. What about Wonho? I bet he chose the swan."

The Commander's eyes narrowed, as if jealous of the handsome ladies' man. "Wonho chose the starling—"

"Figures," London splashed the water, "the starling is a handsome bird." She gave him a cheeky grin.

"Swan his first choice, but they are mute. They hiss, and threatened, they snort."

When the eerie cry of a child filled the sky, the Commander stopped talking and listened.

Watching him, London asked, "Is that your bird?"

"Listen," he whispered, pointing skyward. "The call

of the Chinese sparrowhawk draws attention. A person wonders if it is the call of a child, or the lyrical scream of a predator . . ."

"Talk to him." London urged.

Lifting his chest, the Commander called and got an answer. His eyes twinkled when he leaned in close. "He caught a rabbit but does not wish to share."

London gave him a shove. "You goof."

Her broken arm slipped across her leg, dangling over the side, the pain pulling her from the dream. "Commander? Did you call to me?" The forest, like all of life, recognized the smell of impending death and grew silent. The unheard waves of suffering wove through the trees.

A child cried in the distance. "Is that you?" A second cry. "Did you find a rabbit? I'm so hungry." She licked dry lips and whistled.

Soundless. She tried again, believing her imagination would bring him to her.

Still nothing.

On the third attempt, her call was weak, but true. This time, the harsh trill of the starling answered. She sat upright before taking a deep breath and returned a whistle. It trilled, answered by a sparrowhawk.

Overjoyed, she kept whistling, but no answering response came.

The whoosh of a rope draped over a branch, startling her. Unsure if she felt relief or panic, she waited for the Korean soldiers. The creaking sounds of a braided rope, taut from the weight of a climber, took London's breath away. *They've found me.*

The Commander swung from an overhead branch, lowering himself in front of London. "Next time, try not tell the enemy we are here," and kissed her.

Wonsul appeared, handing her a canteen. "You try to wake the dead?"

Death vanished from the forest as life buzzed around them. Birds took flight. Squirrels jumped from branch to branch. London heard a deer, its slow quiet steps moving against the underbrush. She couldn't move, shaken and relieved, her eyes never left the Commander.

"How?"

He twisted open the canteen lid and raised it to her lips. "Sip slow."

London lifted the container higher to drink in gulps.

"Slow." He lowered the canteen. "Anything broken?"

"My arm." What passed for a smile mushroomed across dry, cracked lips. She took the canteen and drank deeply. When the Commander lowered it a second time, she said, "My bag is up there," nodding her head upward.

Wonsul climbed and grabbed the bag, lowering it to Hyuk.

The Commander pointed to a belt, strapped to an adjoining branch. "You set your arm?"

"No choice." London winced when he touched the swollen limb, hugging it to her chest.

"Good girl. I wrap, then get us out of here. Okay?"

Wonsul handed the Commander a roll of cloth and tape.

"Why'd you come?" she asked.

The Commander used a second cloth to make a sling. "Is not obvious?"

"What's obvious is you could have been killed."

He brushed loose strands from her face, wiping away dirt smudges on her forehead. "I had to . . ." His voice caught. "Prove I am better soldier than you spy."

London smirked, her face pale. "I'm still alive. That says something." She gave him a silly smirk. She'd never been this sleepy and felt so good.

The Commander's posture stiffened as he lowered his head and met her eyes. "You are not alone, Donee. My team, we will get you out of this tree. Home safe."

Dizzy and weak, his words waned in and out. "You two come alone?" She dropped her head back against the bark to rest, then jerked forward. "Are you injured?"

"One question at a time. Entire team is here. No injuries. We followed your map. You are tree climber. Up seemed reasonable. Now, you tell me. You hurt anywhere besides your arm and jaw?"

"A minor cut, a scratch, nothing to worry over. It stopped bleeding two days ago. And a sprained ankle, but it doesn't hurt."

Noticing the rip in her right sleeve, he tore open the material. Dried blood covered the area. Wetting a cloth, he washed the crusted scab to find the wound oozing with puss. After applying antiseptic, he wrapped the arm, amazed London wasn't feverish. "Anything else?"

London's eye twitched as she licked her lips. "Nothing. I got away lucky, didn't I?"

She's lying... When he couldn't find any obvious wounds, he nodded to Wonsul. "Okay. We are ready." He explained each move to London. "Wonsul will tie you to my back—"

"No!" She hadn't peed in two days. Between a full bladder and the pain in her abdomen, London knew she'd pee the moment she moved. "I ..." She stifled a cry. "I ..." She turned her head. "Can't you lower me by rope?"

The black and blue bruising on her jaw angered the Commander. To quell his anger, he relaxed his shoulders, taking in a lengthy breath, releasing it through his mouth. Calm, he answered, "Strapping you to my back will be quicker and reduces the risks."

"Still, I ... have to ... you know, jeez ..." Frustrated, she blurted, "I have to pee."

Methodically, the Commander double checked her arm before shaping a rope into a harness. "Then pee."

"I can't!"

He fitted the rope over her shoulders, long, dark lashes hiding his eyes. "I ever tell you about Japan's rescue mission? Tsunami struck the coast in 2011 after a 9.0 earthquake. My team helps. Recorded waves reached around thirty-six meters, and stretching inland over sixty-five nautical miles." He used a carabiner, pulling the looped rope under one of London's legs, adjusting it to support her bottom. "Wonho joined the team two weeks earlier. New recruits struggle." His eyes widened as he recounted the story.

London heard Wonsul laugh.

"We were standing on top of a building, when building collapse under him . . . Wonho, how far did he fall?"

"Four meters, sir."

The Commander pulled the crotch rope, running the shoulder rope underneath. "He broke his fibula. When bones snap, skin pops. We all heard it." Pulling the shoulder straps tight behind her head, he attached a second carabiner. "I rappelled to the ground and used this same rope procedure to anchor him to my back."

He grabbed the branch above, lifting himself before turning his back to her.

Wonsul attached the carabiner to the safety gear.

London asked, "What happened?"

"We had worked over eighteen hours without eating, sleeping, or relieving ourselves."

"Wonho peed on you?"

"If that were the case, the smell not so rank." He twisted, attached to the ropes manned by Namgi, Joowon and Wonsul on the ground. "Do not tell Wonho, but I prefer your bodily excrement to his."

London gasped, "You mean he . . .?"

"He did." Positioning her legs around his waist, the Commander told her what would happen next.

An internal rip seared her insides as her bottom rolled off the limb. Intent on freeing the team, she didn't flinch. Instead, she clung to his neck with one arm and buried her head against his back. Teeth clenched as a traffic jam of nerves reawakened and the dam spilled, covering his extremities.

41

Lines that Bound Them

London's body limp, the Commander removed the repelling lines after signaling Lieutenant Hyuk to scout ahead.

Though worried about any unseen wounds, he fought the urge to check. Security remained his top priority. For now, whatever injuries she'd sustained needed to wait. Ready, they set out.

Hyuk came running as they left the tree. "They're closing in, sir."

Looking to the south, the Commander said, "Head north. They will expect us to travel south. We will circle around."

The lieutenant took the lead with Namgi in the rear, Commander and London center.

Namgi asked, "What's our exit strategy, sir?"

"Exit through the Tunnel of Aggression."

"The Tunnel of Aggression? I hear it's heavily guarded, sir."

"Ten years ago, my battalion found a narrow northern

passageway." The Commander hefted London on his back. "Top secret. There were two battalions, roughly four hundred men, guarding the entrance. It will be difficult, but our best chance. The tunnel is tight. Dark. Caution is the key."

Granite cliffs with trails just wide enough for the human body, tree roots that spread like octopus tentacles, and loose rock made their progress slow. They'd crossed ten miles before London regained consciousness. Both she and the Commander were dry, but the ammonia stench lingered, furthering her humiliation. "Let me down and I'll walk."

Worried she hadn't told him everything, he said, "In two kilometers, we will rest. Once you eat, I want to examine you. If everything looks fine, you can walk."

Climbing higher into the mountains, they traveled with an autumn breeze blowing through the rustling leaves. The scent of earth, animals, and plants filled their lungs, clean air unpolluted by the stench of the modern world. The Commander imagined a home in the field below, a boy and a girl running through tall grass while both he and London hung their laundry on the clothesline or plowed the garden. He shook his head and chided himself for being distracted.

With another four and a half meters from the hardened artillery site, the Commander instructed the team to rest. He heard London groan when Hyuk lifted her off his back. Her complexion was as pale as the white tiger. He offered a drink. "You hungry?"

* * *

Both hungry and thirsty—and suspecting an internal bleed—London pushed the container away, afraid the water might release fecal matter into her abdominal cavity. "I'm fine."

Wonho used London's solar cylinder to make nettle tea, while Joowon wrapped her in mylar. He pulled the rabbit from his pack. "Meat?"

London laughed and fought the need to buckle. "You found the sparrowhawk's rabbit?"

The Commander's quizzical gaze made her laugh harder. She covered her face, concealing the pain laughing brought on. "Before you found me . . . I must have been delusional. We were back at the waterfall."

"The hawk brought rabbit across the D-line and dropped him at Joowon's feet."

Had the mylar warmed London, or was it the Commander's smile? She watched him instruct Joowon to skin the rabbit. *He must be hungry.* She moved to stand, hoping to find edible plants along the trail. Electric shock pain, white hot, burned her insides.

She pretended to drink nettle tea, curled inside the mylar, and watched the small team. The men rested. Some propped against a tree while others stretched out on the hard ground, rifles at their sides, safeties off. The scene reminded her of a pride of lions. Fully relaxed, yet ever vigilant . . . Alpha soldiers. Ever aware that even the largest lions can be taken down.

Could she bond with these men? A warmth spread, her heart pounding, not from pain.

I'm not alone.

She choked, nearly swallowing the tea.

The men sprung to their feet, rifles pointed, scanning the trees in case anyone nearby heard her sputtered coughing.

Under the protection of "the pride," she filled her lungs with cool moist air, relaxing the muscle spasms.

When no immediate danger came, Joowon settled next to the fire and quartered the rabbit into pieces and stuffed the cylinder. While they waited, they snacked on roasted Japanese sweet potatoes. The skins pulled from the starchy root with ease, exposing its creamy white flesh. The sweet flavor released, the caramel scent wafted around her. For the first time in over a day, her mouth grew moist.

Cooked, the rabbit fell from the bone as a droplet of fat rolled down the Commander's fingers onto the ground. London imagined a fox sniffing the dried juice and wanted to be the furry creature.

As they ate, overlooking a worn path below, a group of seven kids carrying weighted sacks walked along the mountainous trail. The last ragged boy made her eyes damp. Ready to snatch him and free him from tyranny, London whispered, "He can't be over three."

"Shhh ..." the Commander warned. When they passed, he explained. "Children begin training at five."

"That boy is five?" London blurted.

"Tiny, but willing to die for his leader. The average DRPK citizen is shorter. Weighs less. They are starving. Low caste children."

London had seen lots of kids hiking in the woods while scouting the land. Never one this tiny. "He couldn't be older ..." she trailed off, ready to follow. Someone needed to protect them from mountain lions or tigers. The painful swelling put an end to thoughts of defending the children. The pain kept worsening. She suspected she'd pass away before nightfall without medical intervention and regretted the men risking their lives for the walking dead.

They had several miles of travel to reach the Punch Bowl, where the Battle of Bloody Ridge took place during the Korean War.

Will time run out?

Her stomach emptied on the pine needle trail.

The Commander kneeled beside her. "Tell me where you hurt."

London jerked away. "I'm fine." She pulled herself onto her knees when the men started packing their gear.

"If I'm to die this day, I die my way. On my own two feet."

"You are a stubborn woman, London. I am also stubborn and will not let you die."

The men gathered their backpacks and got back into formation, guarding London.

* * *

The Commander shadowed her, watching her faltering steps buckle underneath her, the slump of her shoulders worsening. A leader, he'd never felt weak, but capable. In this moment the warrior felt powerless. When she lost her balance, his hand snaked around her waist, hugging her against him.

Each time, she pushed away. "I'm fine. Really. I'm fine." Her tenacious independence placed his men in greater danger. He hoped one day she'd trust him and become part of a team of two.

They trekked near a logging site, staying far enough away to remain hidden until a pile of discarded logs offered them a way through the camp. Between the piles, a group of women from a nearby village sold wares to the workers. An elderly woman carried a baby strapped to her bent back, while two young boys stood near their mother around a cart full of medical supplies. The Commander suspected she'd bought them from China. Gauze pads, disinfectants, and bandages were in great demand throughout the North.

"These women are called grasshoppers," the Commander whispered. "The great famine forced them to buy food on the black market, no longer relying on government rations."

"Is it legal?" London asked.

A massive tree fell too close to where the women squatted, but they didn't move. Desperate, they accepted the risks to both them and their children.

"Most soldiers turn heads but if caught ... That is

why called grasshoppers." He slipped easily in and out of his broken English. "They move around. Avoid capture." Like the boy, these women were small, fragile-looking, but tough. Each had a beauty about them despite their many sacrifices for a leader they revered as their god.

Back in the woods, a deer path followed a river out of the mountains into the danger zone, the final point seven meters from the fence. The Commander knew they'd removed most of the mines in this area years earlier.

* * *

The tunnel, when they reached it, had a large opening, like the ones London had explored. The team studied the soldiers. Three guards stood near the northern entrance, while others sat on benches near bunkers. Heavy artillery placed carelessly were piled under simple tents. London estimated over a hundred soldiers walking around, making the total number much higher.

"They must be afraid."

"Not afraid, Donee. Ready."

When did he start calling me Donee? She thought back but couldn't remember. As she struggled to collect her memories, she heard his voice over and over, *Donee.* She liked it. With him, she wasn't a spy, or a broken girl. She belonged to him. The name Donee allowed her escape from the past and present.

42

The Shivering

London's skin, dehydrated and dry, felt clammy and cool in thirty-six degrees Celsius. Her extremities were chilled. The shivering intensified as the pain and bloating of her belly became intolerable. Her gut had enlarged to the size of a new melon.

When they first arrived in the danger zone, thirty meters from the secret entrance, they took a break while analyzing their escape route.

London vomited a second time. Saliva mixed with blood and acidic bile burned her throat. To hide the upchuck from the Commander, she swished leaves with her boot and inhaled a rattled breath. She couldn't let on. He'd insist on carrying her, a potential death sentence for the entire team.

The group bent low, moving behind concealing shrubs, edging forward, flattened against the wet soil. Unable to keep pace, London slowed, fearing for the men's lives. An unaccustomed emotion, but one she couldn't shake as the fever increased.

When an enemy soldier came close, the Commander left the line. The ground beneath her vibrated as the foliage shuddered. Then silence. The threat had passed.

The peace of having the Commander at her side helped as she slid further from the present.

"Donee?"

"I'm okay." Her voice was weak. She inched ahead, fighting the urge to sleep. Heavy lids and blurred vision slowed her progress.

Ten meters from the secret entrance, the Commander signaled his team to stop.

Between them and their exit, another enemy waited, and London, in a state of near delirium, veered left toward him.

The Commander motioned to Wonsul, who slinked over.

Hoisting her by the shoulders, the Commander hauled her into a seated position behind a bush.

Wonsul pulled a penlight, sweeping the shielded light back and forth, testing her eyes.

The Commander whispered, "Donee, look at me."

She didn't. Instead, her eyes darted, as if she were searching for him. "I'm freezing. Need the pain to . . . Head pounding."

Wonsul asked, "Do you ache anywhere else?"

"Mmmm . . . Dizzzzy."

Wonsul withdrew a mylar blanket. "Help me. She's in shock."

The Commander opened a canteen and wet London's lips. In her thirst, she swallowed and sputtered as the water rose back up, full of bile and dark blood.

"Shit, sir. I mean, she's hemorrhaging, sir. Help get this blanket under her."

The Commander opened the blanket camo side out to avoid being spotted as Wonsol eased London backward.

She moaned, and the Commander stifled the noise with a gentle but firm hand to her mouth.

She fought him, her weakness evident as she swatted, vague movements as though she swiped at a lazy fly.

He leaned forward and whispered, "Shhh . . . We leave this place. Safe soon."

When Wonsul cut through her suit, exposing her abdomen, London's swollen and tender belly had a bruise five inches long, shaped like the butt of a rifle. "Could be kidney damage, or maybe her spleen."

The team members listened, silent, as Wonsul searched for other wounds, each aware their position might become apparent but knew London's extended abdomen hinted at certain death.

If the Commander moved her, she might cry out, exposing his team, but he lacked a safe alternative, so he signaled the men to move out. The choice was straightforward since delaying offered each member zero chance of survival.

"Donee."

London moaned again.

"Donee, I need to carry you."

"Can I . . . make . . . it?"

"Yes." The Commander dampened the fear that rattled him. "We go home now. You, me, and the boys. Do you hear? Donee?"

Hunched over, the Commander balanced himself as Hyuk strapped London to his back and secured her with the harness she still wore. His friend's reassuring hand on his shoulder providing an extra bit of strength to his resolve.

He hesitated for a split second before striking out. Deep fear gripped him as he led his men toward the opening.

The team sprinted the last three meters, rifles pointed, ready for an attack.

* * *

Hyuk watched the Commander as he tended to the woman who threatened the team. He was angry the officer he respected, his friend and leader, had risked it all to save her. And yet, their superior fought past his tangible fear and shaky hands and continued to lead. Hyuk's respect amplified even as his anger grew.

As the last man entered the tunnel, bullets ricocheted off the granite.

Ignoring injuries, the men, forming a single line in the narrow passageway, pressed through the tunnel using penlights to prevent them toppling over one another in the pitch black. The path closed in around them. The sharp-edged rocks tore at their skin and cammies, forcing them to maneuver sideways through the tight spots.

Low ceilings forced Hyuk to stoop. He helped as the Commander made a makeshift stretcher by inverting the sleeves of two jackets over two hiking poles. The delay narrowed their chances as they lifted London onto the stretcher before continuing.

At the main access point, the voices of North Korean soldiers echoed. Far off, but close enough. They'd have to rush to the exit. The threat to tourists made the passing more dangerous as they cleared the tunnel.

Bullets pinged off the sandy limestone floor around them. Namgi and Joowon were on his right. Hyuk watched as blood splotched Namgi's ear and then struck Joowon's backpack. He hoped the Kevlar slowed its trajectory. Joowon stumbled from the bullet's bite as he cursed a battle cry.

Blood poured from Namgi's nicked ear. Joowon grabbed hold of the young commando and forced him forward, both men breathing heavy.

Pushing harder, the team covered the meter into South Korea, exiting the tunnel into a group of foreigners here to experience bits and pieces of the Korean War.

Hyuk yelled, "Get out!"

The tourists didn't move, some of them pulling out cameras as if witnessing a reenactment.

Lieutenant Hyuk shouldered London's legs and shot his rifle straight up. "Now!"

High-pitched screams made it impossible to ascertain the threat from behind.

Hyuk pushed the guide, who scrambled to get the tourists moving, some bumping into the Commander.

* * *

Behind him, rifles drawn and cocked, made a metallic thwack. The distinctive click of the hammer told the Commander his team rotated; their rifles pointed into the inky darkness.

Wonsul dashed ahead, toward the tourism building yelling, "We need an ambulance! Call 119."

Inside the museum, the Commander snatched an employee's cellphone and punched in the emergency number. "This is Commander Kim Daeju, with the ROKMC. We need an ambulance at the Tunnel of Aggression tourism building. Hurry! The patient is a Caucasian female, twenty-eight years old with a possible bleed in her abdomen. She is unresponsive. I repeat, the patient is unresponsive."

London lay stretched on the floor, feet elevated, covered by the mylar blanket, her breathing shallow.

"I'm here, Donee. The ambulance is coming. Hang on. You are going to be fine."

The team forced everyone out as the Commander lay next to London, pressing himself against her cool body.

"I love you, Donee. Stay with me."

43

Disengaged in Both Mind and Body

The EMTs rolled London into Asan Medical Center and rushed her into emergency care, leaving the Commander waiting. He hadn't known deep loneliness since his father stepped out in front of a cabbage delivery truck. He remembered the depth of silence despite the noise, seated outside the emergency room in this hospital at fifteen.

After his mom died, the Commander's dad started drinking. He'd come home each evening, unable to remain upright or communicate coherently. The Commander hated him. As a boy, he'd perched on the roof outside his bedroom window and waited for his dad, frightened, until he'd see him stumbling up the alley steps. The night he didn't show, the boy learned his father had stepped off the curb, into the path of an oncoming vehicle.

Then, as now, he sat with his arms stretched out on his knees and hands clasped, head bent low. This time, like then, he faced the dark hours of waiting and the distress of whether London would perish.

He remembered the day he observed London wielding control over the flirtatiously aggressive soldier months back. He'd been a vacant shell prior to that day, going through life for his country and team, without plans or dreams. Now, he dreamed of a family, a home, a world of love and laughter. His head rested on the tips of his thumbs, discouraged by the possibility of losing the woman who might complete those dreams.

Disengaged in both mind and body, he waited for the nurse to call his name. He didn't hear the child's cries across the room or the nurses calling out names, the emergency room door opening and closing, the squeal of gurney wheels, or the old man sneezing.

All he heard were his prayers, asking God to save her.

"Commander Kim?"

Jerking upright, the Commander looked at the doctor walking his direction.

"Are you Commander Kim?"

At the sound of his name, he jumped to his feet like a rookie soldier responding to an angry drill instructor. Instinctive and trembling. "Yes sir! Is London okay?"

"She's stable, but her injuries are serious." The doctor offered the Commander his hand. "I'm Doctor Yang. I understand you're the guardian of London . . ." he checked his records. "Do you have a last name for London, Commander?"

"Kim," he answered, his voice calm.

"Married?"

"No."

The doctor's brows rose as his lips moved to speak. Shaking his head, he asked, "Are you the guardian of London Kim, Commander?"

"I am."

The doctor studied the soldier, like he wanted to ask a question but lost the chance when a child ran past, brushing against his leg, the child's mother in pursuit.

"Kyong, come back here."

The Commander caught the child by the collar and held him until his mother snatched him.

Doctor Yang grinned at the child before turning his attention back to the Commander. "Miss Kim's minor issues are a double fracture to her left arm and two deep cuts. One cut is on her left biceps"—the doctor swept a hand across his upper arm—"and the other across her thigh, along with multiple abrasions, a sprained ankle, and several broken ribs. With time, the ribs will heal. The arm will require metal plates. Doctor Gwan is stitching her wounds. We've ran test on another potential risk, but the results may take a couple of days. I'll get back with you on that one."

The Commander's legs weakened as he listened to the doctor's calm tone go through London's injuries.

"Our chief concern is an internal bleed. I understand Miss Kim fell when a lower tree branch broke."

"Yes." The Commander answered in a matter-of-fact tone.

"During the fall . . ." the doctor's eyes shifted from the chart to the Commander, "it appears Miss Kim's spleen ripped. We also suspect bruising of the kidney. It says in the chart you found Miss Kim at eleven-hundred hours yesterday afternoon and the two of you walked for six hours before the ambulance arrived."

"I carried London several kilometers. Then she walked until the last meter."

The doctor scratched his head. "Commander, the injury to Miss Kim's organs appeared to have happened three days ago. Can you explain this? This woman's injuries resemble a wounded soldier's in a war zone."

"I can," the Commander answered, still appearing calm while his insides bounced around as if inside a pinball machine. "Three days ago, London climbed a tree, stepping on an unstable branch and fell. I found her yesterday at eleven-hundred hours. Before lowering her the rest of the way to the ground, I investigated both the injuries to her left arm, and the one on her thigh, treated them and inquired on any further damage, to which London assured me there were none."

"You did a superb job setting the arm, Commander."

"London set her arm." The Commander continued explaining as the doctor's eyes widened. His jaw opened to speak and snapped closed again. "It was not until we entered . . ." He changed the course of his words. "Until we were near the museum, that London exhibited signs of extreme weakness and passed out."

The doctor's brows rose, closing the gap between his eyes. In a deeper voice, he said, "The injury incurred from the fall produced a slow bleed in her spleen. Miss Kim would have experienced extreme pain and bloating almost immediately. Your story doesn't match the injuries, nor could she have remained upright for six hours."

"Five and a half hours, sir."

"Five-, six hours, it doesn't matter. After two hours, if she were still standing, she would have held an arm to her abdomen, hunched over and likely crying in pain, and you're telling me she never complained?"

"Yes. London never complained until the end. She vomited twice. The last time, moments before she became unconscious."

Again, the doctor's hand moved through his hair. "We're talking superhuman strength here, Commander. It's a tough story to believe."

"Believe it." The Commander narrowed his gaze. "London is unlike most women."

"She must be. Let's hope that strength gets her through the operation." The doctor closed his chart. "Miss Kim will enter surgery once they've prepped a room. The surgeon will make a small incision into her lower abdomen where we will remove the spleen and check the kidney for any tears or bleeds. Unless there are further complications, the surgery should take two to four hours."

"Danger level?" The Commander asked.

"A splenectomy is a relatively safe procedure, but Miss Kim has lost an impressive amount of blood, and we can't say to what extent this incident has damaged her other organs. As with any surgery, blood clots and secondary infections are a risk. The greatest threat lies in whether Miss Kim will awaken." He held the chart between both hands and gave a slight nod of his head. Then he left. He disappeared around the corner as quickly as he had arrived.

The Commander sat, clasping his cap between shaky fingers.

A large-screen TV hung suspended from the ceiling above the waiting room. On screen, the newscaster announced, "According to the latest report, China released additional information on the death toll for the village of Wuhan China. These new numbers report that fifty percent of Wuhan's infected citizens have died from Covid-19. Three cases were reported today in Namhan, in Seoul, and none in the north or south."

The Commander's mind rolling over questions, didn't hear the rest. *How could I miss the signs? Why? What if . . . No! She will survive. I refuse to let her die.*

He didn't see Lieutenant Hyuk approach, but the sturdy hand on his shoulder felt comforting.

"*Hyung,* how bad is it?"

"They are taking her to surgery."

"London's strong. She'll be fine." Hyuk sat.

"Any gunfire?" the Commander asked.

"We sprayed the tunnel, but there were no return shots fired."

The Commander nodded. "Thanks for coming." His head drooped. "The rest of the team?"

"They're coming in now."

Minutes later, the five team members were seated around the Commander, sitting erect, their heads pressed against the wall as if it were a pillow, staring upward toward the colorful squares of pastel stars along the upper floor balcony, while the Commander sat legs apart, elbows on knees, head down.

Together, they waited.

Namgi had dried blood on his uniform but refused medical care.

Four hours and twenty-five minutes lapsed before Doctor Yang came back. The Commander, alerted this time by the clank of swinging doors, approached the doctor, who eyed the men suspiciously. The Commander glanced back at his men as they stood. They, too, appeared to have passed through a war zone.

"Commander."

The Commander approached the doctor. "The surgery?"

"Time is our predictor. They're closing the incision now. As for the surgery, we removed the spleen and examined Miss Kim's kidney. The kidney has a minor bruise that should heal in a few weeks. The next seventy-two hours are critical. Every hour she survives is in her favor. If she gets through, I'd say she will recover without incident."

"Thank you, *Uisa.*"

Doctor Yang cupped a hand on the Commander's bicep. "Don't get your hopes up yet. She has a long recovery ahead."

"Hope? Facts dictate decisions. Not hope."

"Well then, let the facts guide us." Doctor Yang shook the Commander's hand. "Once Miss Kim is moved to the intensive care unit, a nurse will come for you." He checked his chart. "I understand she'll be taken to one of our VIP rooms?"

The Commander pulled out his wallet. "I will take care of the charges."

Pointing toward the front desk, the doctor said, "The receptionist can help you." The doctor stood there a second longer, his head tilted in contemplation, then straightened.

When the Commander turned toward his men, Lieutenant Hyuk walked over to him. "You haven't eaten a solid meal in two days. Go eat. I'll let the receptionist know where they can find you."

The Commander folded his wallet, stuffing it into a back pocket. "You guys go ahead. I will eat later."

He walked over to the receptionist and asked, "Where do I pay my bill?"

The receptionist pointed toward the billing department. "Follow this hall and it's the first room on the left."

Hyuk stepped up next to him. "When they move Miss Kim to her room, will you let us know? We'll be in the cafeteria."

"I told you—"

"Yes. I hear just fine. Listen, Commander, if you don't eat, London will use the double-edged knife she's keeping hidden in her boot on me. So do me a favor and at least get a cup of coffee."

On the edge of his seat, the Commander sipped black coffee, bitter to the point of undrinkable, his ear tilted toward the steps leading to the waiting room.

Hyuk ordered him rice with kimchi soup, but the Commander didn't eat. "Commander." Hyuk slapped a hand on the table.

The Commander's glance was brief, but dark, heated eyes sent a brutal message.

Hyuk's chair screeched against the floor. "Whoa," his husky hand snatching the chair back as it tipped over backwards and covered his heart with his free hand. "I thought you'd come across the table."

"Maybe we'd better leave him to himself." Joowon stood, picking up their dinner trays.

Wonho got up, picked up his own tray, and followed Joowon. Wonsul went next, then Namgi.

The Lieutenant stayed behind but remained silent.

The Commander scooted in his chair, crossing his arms on the table and staring at the soup. "I'm sor—"

"Don't talk, eat."

Lifting the spoon, cabbage spilling over the sides, the Commander took a bite. One bite followed another. The two shared their meal in silence, their thoughts active despite the noise of the cafeteria.

"Commander Kim, please come to the receptionist's desk. Commander Kim . . ."

Taking three platforms at a time, the Commander rushed up the stairs. Behind a desk the color of butterscotch, a middle-aged woman stood wearing a black suit, with dyed hair and gray roots. "Are you here for Kim London?"

"Yes."

The woman handed him a slip of paper, which he crumpled in his hand.

"Miss Kim has been moved to room 521, on the top floor. To get there . . ."

Passing two elevators, the Commander turned left at the end of the hall, rushed through double doors, and entered a single elevator, punching in the code.

44

Wringing His Hands

Joe was wringing his hands while Claire continued banging around in the kitchen, preparing the evening's vegetable soup, unaware London may be dead. "Where is she?"

Claire's head popped around the edge of the door. "Who?"

"Who?" Joe asked.

"If you mean London," Claire stepped into his office, the ladle dripping onto his floor, "she'll get here. She always does."

Joe checked the time. "It's been eight days. She should have been back two days ago."

Claire scowled. "So? She died. That's what she wanted." A loud crash brought her back around. Everything on Joe's desk, from the files he always kept in a rack to his clock, was scattered about on the floor.

He stood, his face red as soup broth. "What the hell is wrong with you, Claire? London's our responsibility."

Claire swung the ladle around in lazy circles, dripping

droplets on the wall and floor. "Only reason you're upset is because you never got with her. That girl doesn't like you. If she is alive, she'll be with that commander. You can bet a gallon of my soup on that one."

Joe's fist bunched. "Shut up, Claire. You make me sick with your jealousy. I'm in love with her." He dropped into the chair. "Even if she doesn't care. I love her."

"Well, now ... Most likely, you're in love with a dead woman."

Joe threw his phone, barely missing Claire as she screamed, "You're crazy!" The phone landed on the wood flooring and skidded into the dining area.

With Claire back in the kitchen, Joe picked up a map off the wooden planks, caring nothing for the other contents, and studied London's route on the map.

Had the recent rainfall been enough to allow her safe passage into North Korea? If not, could she swim the Suipcheon stream, in low water, surrounded by fishing boats, their crew armed to kill? He knew the chances were slim, even for London.

His mind shifted back to the day he'd begged her to leave with him. Banging a fist on the desk. "I shouldn't have gotten drunk." He crinkled the map. "That damned Asian. He's turned me into a lunatic."

He wiped the snot from his nose and pulled open the top drawer. From inside, he pulled out a picture of London, the one he'd taken the day they arrived in this godforsaken country. Even then, the expression she'd given him as the camera clicked was hard and unhappy.

She had always been angry, yet he'd thought her beautiful, though too sinewy and thin the day they'd met. Even so, she'd lived up to the CIA's expectations after they'd found that boy dead. London had killed him ruthlessly and hadn't let emotions get between her and the job since. She could kill quicker than the best and escape before they fell dead.

Angry at himself and the commander who threatened the life they'd built together, he slammed the frame against the far wall, shattering the glass.

She's gone.

He walked over to the broken frame, staring at it from above, then stooped to retrieve it between shaky fingers. Glossy eyes blurred his vision as he wiped away the shards of glass.

***

After the explosion in North Korea, General Yoo placed the four Tunnels of Aggression on high alert and checked recent video surveillance for any unknown intrusion.

The General received a call from the Haean Tunnel's Field Commander informing him the spy had escaped, something about a forgotten entrance.

Hours later, General Yoo sat next to the fireplace at his residence, a steaming cup of tea on the end table, and the Rodong newspaper in his hands when the phone rang. His wife entered from the kitchen and lifted the receiver, handing it to him. Without speaking, she left as quietly as she'd entered.

"Hello."

"General Yoo, this es the Director of RIG, Vahid Nuri."

"Ah yes, Director."

"I es afraid I have bada news." The Persian director's speech, slow and drawn. "Di esuper engine has been destroyed, along with di software. We have identeefied de esailant, but unfortunately too late. Eet es not the first time Giti Murdok has traveled inside Iran, but we believe she es an American spy, and suspected to be in South Korea."

After hanging up, General Yoo made a direct call to the Great Leader, his fingers struggling to dial. Yoo's leader wasn't the kind of man to accept the news of an escaped spy calmly. His life could be in danger. Keeping the information, meant certain death.

"The assailant entered Iran with a fake passport under the name Giti Marduk."

The Great Leader asked, "What do we know about this spy?"

"Not much, Respected Comrade. We have a picture, but the invader is in disguise. Your men have provided details on a Joe Park, an American bastard. Park works for the United States CIA and is running a bar called Whiskey River Saloon. I've instructed two soldiers to tap his phones and follow him. He may lead us to Marduk."

"Find this spy and bring her to me."

"Yes sir."

* * *

Back at the Whiskey River, Joe sat at the bar drinking a bloody Mary, waiting for news. When the phone rang, he jumped, spilling his drink. He yanked a towel off the roll, tossing it on the liquid and then answered the call.

"Joe Park?"

Stiff, as if the commanding official stood in the room, Joe answered. "Park speaking." He heard the shake in his voice.

"This is Davis."

"Yes. Yes. Tell me. Have you heard . . . the mission? Is London alive?"

"We received confirmation that an explosion occurred inside the location reported by your agent."

"London?"

"Presumed dead."

Joe collapsed in his seat.

"North Korea's leader announced minutes ago the bomber died soon after the explosion. The Director of the KPA General Political Bureau, General Yoo, is responsible for the kill."

Joe whimpered as he cradled his head in his hands. "Her body?"

"I'm sorry, Park. Director Haskell denied any responsibility for the bombing, claiming London was a rogue agent. London understood her mission and accepted her fate. The CIA is grateful for her service—"

"Dying for her country and marked as a traitor is hardly a victory worth celebrating!"

"It's a victory when you consider Sarah Bennett . . . uh, London, gave her life to save millions. She's a hero, even if the world doesn't hear of her feats."

A hero, Joe thought to himself. *There will be no medal for London, only a firing squad in a public execution.*

* * *

North of Joe, in Pyongyang, North Korea, Private Sun sat at a small table in a dismal room, a single light overhead. General Yoo stood over him as he listened in on the conversation between Park and Davis. Sun covered the receiver and reported. "Her name is Bennett, Sarah Bennett." He continued to listen. "The Americans believe she is dead."

General Yoo slammed the tip of his cane next to the power boosting equipment. "Search the hospitals. I want her found."

"Yes, General."

Commander Yoo sent a message to the Great Leader's spies in the South, instructing them.

* * *

Behind his desk at the Chosun Ilbo, Captain Hwang pulled out his flip phone and read, American spy. Name: Sarah Bennett, aka London. Escaped. Injured. Kill.

Hwang turned off his computer and requested leave. Outside the multi-storied building, he looked up at the statue of Admiral Yin Shun Sin. He admired the admiral's leadership. Each day, he left the daily newspaper and bowed. The leader represented what he believed to be every Joseon citizen's dream. Reunification.

When he straightened, he made a promise to his hero. "The Great Leader will lead us to a victorious reunification, and the world will fear the *Joseon Dynasty*."

Upon entering the Asan Medical Center, his fourth stop, Captain Hwang approached the receptionist. His voice, smooth. Pleasant. "I'm looking for Sarah Bennett."

"Are you related?"

"Yes. She's a cousin. My father called from the States. She's been hospitalized, but he didn't know where. Could you help me? Sarah is like a sister."

"I'm so sorry. Let me check." The receptionist studied patient records; her head tilted forward, exposing her gray roots. "I—"

A boyish man, thin with enormous eyes and narrow cheeks, walked over. He wore a black suit, tie, and pink Fila sneakers. "I'm afraid we can't give out that information."

Gray roots stood and bowed toward her superior. "I'm sorry. It's that . . . they're family."

"Still," the tall stiff man nodded apologetically, "it's against our policy."

"Yes." The North Korean studied the two behind the counter. His thoughts twisted. Images of their throats slit made him smile. "Yes. Privacy."

"Thank you. I'm glad you understand."

Captain Hwang moved away from the entrance, observing the lobby. Five men in dirty military uniforms, rugged and sleep deprived, sat together. After ordering a coffee, he sat in a wing-shaped chair and watched. Patience, his best attribute. The captain, confident he'd found the location of Sarah Bennett, needed only to wait. Soon, he'd find and kill the woman who weakened the Great Leader.

45

Invincible

The Commander stepped up to room 521, weak in the legs. Joe had once called London invincible, but his warrior woman lay unconscious, intubated, her skin ashen. Except for the rise and fall of her chest, forced by a machine, she appeared lifeless.

His hands curled into fists. If Joe walked up to him now, he wouldn't walk away alive.

The Commander inhaled, long and slow, releasing it before stepping inside. Near the bed, he rolled a stool to her side, pulling it in underneath him before placing a hand over London's as he sat.

"Do you dream of night we met?" He spoke to her in broken English. "Moment your edgy seawater eyes look at me, I become addict. I study your fear hidden like a riddle. Learn more." Trembling, he stroked her slender fingers, hoping his touch might wake her, and dropped his voice to a whisper. "No riddle, Donee." He leaned closer. "I find balance. You and me." He laid his forehead against her hand. "Love. *Saranghae.*"

* * *

Over the next three days, Captain Hwang followed the five soldiers around Seoul. When they spoke, he tried to place himself strategically to eavesdrop. Their commanding officer never showed up. On return to the hospital, he got a job in the cafeteria and watched.

In a matter of days, the coronavirus caused mayhem, filling the hospital with patients. The medical facility's normal flow disrupted by doctors and nurses racing from patient to patient.

* * *

London was off the ventilator when her fever spiked to one hundred and three. With a positive Covid test, they covered her bed with an oxygen tent.

A low-grade fever compounded by a cough and sore throat, the Commander slept in a corner chair.

London's wheezing woke him. Pushing the call button, he yelled, "Nurse!"

Short gasps of air caused the veins in London's neck to thicken as her lungs struggled to take in oxygen.

"Nurse!" Leaning against the tent he said, "The doctor coming, Donee."

The nurse ran through the door, her face covered with a mask and wearing gloves. She checked London and ran back out. Seconds later, she returned, followed by a pale-skinned doctor, with dark bags under his eyes.

The Commander stepped away from the bed as they checked her vitals, his own chest rising and falling with London's. His sporadic breaths making him dizzy. He'd heard rumors of patients dying from Covid. Unsure whether London's broken body could handle this new enemy, he pulled out his phone and dialed Darling Peterson. He'd gotten the number the night he'd researched London's past.

He stepped into the hall. Guilt hung over him. London might be furious when she came to, but if she didn't survive, Mrs. Peterson had a right to know her daughter might die.

The phone rang four times before a tentative voice answered, "Hello."

"Mrs. Darling Bennett Peterson?"

"Yes. Who is this?"

Walking through double doors, seeing the sunrise for the first time in days, the Commander answered in his best English, "I'm Commander Kim Daeju, a friend of your daughter."

"My daughter?" Darling's voice went hushed as she apparently covered her mouth to whisper. "How do you know my daughter?"

"We, ah . . . work together, ma'am."

"Why are you calling me? I haven't spoken with Sarah for . . ." she trailed off and stopped.

"Sarah is in the hospital, ma'am. I thought you should know."

"The hospital? Where are you? Is this some kind of sick joke?"

The Commander heard a deeper voice in the background and assumed it was Darling's husband.

"No joke, ma'am. I brought Sarah here last week. She had surgery. Remove her spleen—"

Darling gasped, "She didn't sell her organs? Did she?"

"No, ma'am." The Commander tempered his anger. "Sarah has contracted Covid-19. We're at Asan Medical Center in Seoul, South Korea."

Darling cried out and muffled the phone. When she came back, her voice sounded shrill. "We're coming. Tell Sarah I'm coming."

"Ma'am—" She hung up.

Walking back into London's room, they had once again intubated her to a machine. The loud sucking and swishing noise forcing her lungs to rise and fall.

The doctor looked up from his chart and said, "Commander Kim, one of Miss London's lungs collapsed." He shook his head. "I'm sorry. We're doing everything we can, but for now, it's . . . well, Miss Kim must fight to live."

As he'd done for hours every day since they entered the hospital, the Commander sat on the stool and held London's hand, talking to her, encouraging her to live. "You're strong, Donee. Keep fighting." He didn't mention the phone call with Darling Peterson, nor her mom flying to Korea.

That could wait.

Late the next day, the Commander heard a woman's piercing scream and recognized Mrs. Peterson's shrill voice. How she'd flown into Korea and entered the isolated VIP floor of Asan Hospital amazed him, but if Mrs. Peterson was anything like her daughter, the Commander knew better than to be surprised. He stepped out of the room.

Darling stopped, staring at him. "You . . . Where's my daughter. I want to see Sarah now!"

The nurse, all five-foot-one of her, stepped in front of a five-nine Amazon warrior. "Ma'am, you can't go in there."

Darling rushed past the nurse, her husband, Wing Commander Peterson, trailing behind. At the door to London's room, Darling shoved the Commander with gloved hands, as if headed to the Queen's court, and entered.

A doctor shouted, "Call a guard."

"There is no carp in carp-shaped bread." The Commander watched Mrs. Peterson, his tone humorous and light. London was more like her mother than he'd expected. Both strong women with a determination to fight their way to victory.

Without a mask, Darling stepped up to her daughter's bedside and whimpered, "Sarah. Baby. It's Mom, I'm here sweetheart. Mommy will take care of you." Darling crumpled over her daughter, a complete turnaround from the woman who first entered. "I'm sorry, Sarah. I'm so, so sorry."

When a guard arrived, the Commander took a seat. He listened as the guard spoke with the attending doctor and Mr. Peterson. Peterson had papers from General Turner, authorized by General Hanbin. Seconds later, the guard left.

Red with anger, the doctor crossed his arms as he stared at Mrs. Peterson, defenseless against a prima donna.

Wing Commander Peterson walked back into the room and placed a hand on his wife's shoulder, nodding when she looked up.

"You promised she'd be safe. You said the CIA wouldn't let anything happen to Sarah. Look at her! My baby is dying." Darling stood, clinging to her husband's coat. "Call Doctor Marshall. Tell him to get a bed ready. We're taking Sarah home."

"Darling, Asan Medical Center is an excellent facility with the best doctors in South Korea. I'm sure—"

"No!" She got closer and whispered, "They don't like us. These people don't care if she lives or dies. They hate Americans."

The Commander crossed the room and stood at London's bedside, making himself apparent for the first time since London's mother arrived. "London not leaving."

Darling's hand rose to her chest as she took in a sharp breath. "How dare you!"

"London belongs with me. She stays."

Her jaw hanging, Darling looked from the Commander to her husband, and back again. "Do something. How dare he talk to me that way." Her eyes bulged as she stomped around the bed and slapped the Commander. Wincing, she ran to the bathroom and washed her hands, yelling as she did so. "Her name is Sarah. *Filthy foreigner.* Sarah Bennett. I am Sarah's mother, and I," emphasizing I, "will say where and who takes care of her."

The Commander remained at London's bedside, and rose to his full height, despite his weariness. "I'm sorry, ma'am. I cannot allow her to be moved. London safer here."

Still aghast, Darling screamed at her husband, "Why aren't you doing something? Have him arrested, or . . . anything. He can't talk to me that way."

The Wing Commander asked, "What would you have me do, Darling? Arrest him? I don't have the authority. We're guests here." When Darling didn't quit screaming, he left the room, asking the nurse to send Doctor Lee to the room of Sarah Bennett. When the nurse raised her brows in question, he added, "London."

"Oh. Miss Kim. Yes, I'll get the doctor."

The doctor entered, his hand outstretched. "Hello. I'm Doctor Lee, the Chief Medical Officer of Asan Medical Center."

The Commander shook his hand, stepping back as Doctor Lee addressed the nurse.

"Wing Commander Peterson tells me there's a problem in Miss Kim's c —"

"Her name is Bennett. Sarah Bennett," Darling interrupted.

"Yes. Thank you, ma'am." Turning to the Commander, Doctor Lee asked, "Are you and Miss Bennett married?"

"No, sir. Engaged."

The Commander turned to Mr. Peterson and bowed. "I hope you will accept me."

Wing Commander Peterson turned away, swallowing. His large Adam's Apple a bobbing point, pressing against his neck. "Now isn't the time to make permanent plans."

Darling jumped in. "Of course we won't accept him. He isn't American. Look at him, he's ... weak. A pretty boy." Then she turned to the doctor and explained. "Sarah needs a strong *American* soldier to control her wild temper. He"—she pointed at the Commander—"could never handle her."

The medical officer cleared his throat. "Yes." He stepped away from Mrs. Peterson. "Commander, who is Miss Bennett's guardian?"

"I am, sir."

Glaring at the Commander, Darling brushed past her husband. "Doctor Lee, my name is Darling Peterson, and this is my husband, Wing Commander Peterson, from the United States Air Force. We are personal friends with the four-star Commanding General Paul Martin of the United States Army Specific, and my husband works directly with the United States Department of Defense. I am on a first-name basis with Hillary Clinton's personal assistant, and friends with the wife of business tycoon ..."

The Commander understood why London mentioned her mother often forgot she was on the ground. Humored, he watched Doctor Lee struggle with patience as the doctor's hands gripped his stethoscope and listened as Mrs. Peterson rattled off names.

Doctor Lee said, "Mrs. Peterson, how can I help you?"

Her chin elevated, Darling said, "My husband, the Wing Commander and I, wish to make plans to move Sarah back to the States."

Doctor Lee turned to Commander Kim. "Commander, are you okay with this?"

The Commander shook his head as he spoke. "No, sir."

Darling screamed, "I am her mother! Why are you asking that ... weak, pathetic man? He doesn't know what my child needs."

Doctor Lee took in a breath. "The Commander is a

respected leader in the ROKMC, with several medals. I assure you; our soldiers are not weak."

Darling stepped backward, looking the Commander up and down. Her lip curled, "Poppycock. That model is no leader." Then she straightened, staring at the doctor as if he were a servant. "I'll speak to the board," and stormed out of the room.

The doctor bowed to the Commander and the Wing Commander. "Excuse me. I have other patients."

The Wing Commander smiled. It was a weak smile given apologetically. "Yes."

With the medical officer and Darling gone, Wing Commander Peterson crossed his arms and turned to the Commander. "I think it's best, son, if you let Sarah go. My wife is a stubborn woman. I'm afraid she'll keep shouting until I overstep your authority here. I'd sooner not humiliate you."

Commander Kim sat on the stool next to London, allowing her stepdad to think he was handling the situation. Relaxed, his feet placed firm against the congoleum, the Commander said, "Sir, I respect your position of authority, but here in Korea, the law is on my side. London stays with me."

Wing Commander Peterson shoved his hands into the pockets of tailored slacks and strode out of the room.

46

Reading His Body Language

While serving the table next to the five soldiers, Captain Hwang handed a lady banana milk and got lucky when the big one answered a call. From a distance, he watched the Lieutenant, reading his body language. Confident the soldier spoke with a higher official, Hwang stepped in closer.

A tall woman stood in the lobby, screaming at the hospital receptionist, demanding to speak to the board president. "I am Sarah's mother and the wife of Wing Commander Peterson, of the United States—"

Captain Hwang listened in as gray roots cut off the American bitch. "Yes, ma'am."

Her broken English poor. "I try, ma'am."

The receptionist redialed and spoke with who Hwang assumed to be the board president's secretary before replacing the receiver. The woman's eyes shifted from the phone to Mrs. Peterson. "Our director, she will speak, ma'am."

"Finally." The haughty lady crossed her arms, one hand wrapped around the strap of her purse, scanning the room.

Hwang left the cafeteria, pulled a black suit jacket on, and found a spot at the coffee bar.

* * *

Darling studied a handsome man in a black suit, short and thin, who sat at the coffee bar. Next to him, a mother wept with a child on each side. Five men sat together. One busily cleaning his nails with a knife blade. Two others rested with arms crossed and eyes closed. The next man read a magazine, while the last one watched her, his back against the wall.

Impatient, Darling Peterson bought a coffee, got comfortable in a wing backed chair, and tapped her foot against the floor tile. A short, slender woman entered in a lab coat, her hair pulled into a bun.

Darling stood.

"Mrs. Peterson?" the president asked.

"I am. And you are?"

"Doctor Baek, the Board President of Asan Medical Center."

Doctor Baek, a middle-aged woman without a wrinkle and only the roots of her hair tinged in gray, held out a hand. "How may I help you?"

"As you must be aware, my daughter is in critical condition on the fifth floor. I insist you make plans to fly her back to the States. Covid restrictions will soon make it difficult for a return flight, and Sarah's health will improve under the care of our family physician. Doctor Palin is widely regarded for his exceptional reputation among his peers."

***

Captain Hwang stepped off his stool and pretended to be reading the local paper lying on an unused tabletop.

"Are you referring to Miss Kim?"

"Yes. No! You see, her name is Sarah. Sarah Bennett, that's with two t's."

Hwang's rustling of pages added to the noise, going unnoticed as he moved in closer.

"Our records show your daughter's name is London Kim. As you requested, my staff has investigated this matter. The hospital lacks the authority to decide where or when Miss Kim . . . er, Miss Bennett leaves without the consent of her guardian."

***

"Exactly!" Darling yelled. Embarrassed that others might hear, she took a deep breath and exhaled, her eyes darting to see who may have overheard. The well-groomed man in a suit and oxfords glanced up at her and smiled.

She smiled back, straightening her blouse as she turned back to the president. She lowered her voice. "You see, I am Sarah's mother. She's my daughter."

"Yes."

The president pulled a phone from her pocket and clicked on a text before continuing. "To settle this matter, I placed a call to General Hanbin, Commander Kim's superior officer, and our country's military leader. The general is aware of the situation and has ordered a travel ban for Miss Bennett."

She held the phone up for Mrs. Peterson. "It seems our government has reason to question your daughter once she recovers. He has placed Commander Kim in charge."

Wing Commander Peterson entered the lobby and approached Darling from behind. When he placed a hand on her wrist, she jerked, then relaxed. "Thank God." She turned back to the president. "This is my husband, Wing Commander Peterson."

Peterson shook the president's hand before turning to his wife. "I'm sorry, Darling. I spoke with General Turner, and he says she stays. The United States will not cause an international crisis."

Darling scowled and stalked off. In passing, she smiled at the well-dressed man as she left the lobby.

* * *

Commander Kim, at London's bedside, answered his phone as Darling entered.

"Commander, London's position . . ."

A siren in the background made it difficult to hear. "Please repeat."

Hyuk spoke slower, without raising the volume. "Mrs. Peterson has compromised London's safety."

The Commander ended the call and stood to face Mrs. Peterson. His stool crashed to the floor when he stood. "London is in danger—"

Darling bristled. "Of course she's in danger. She's surrounded by a bunch of foreigners who don't respect a mother's need to protect her child."

Commander Kim drew in a deep breath and focused on each word as he spoke. "A North Korean assassin overheard your conversation with the hospital president. My men have been watching him. Short, in a black suit. Did you see him?"

Darling's eyes widened. "I . . . He . . . Coffee . . ." She placed trembling fingers to her lips. "He's an assassin?"

"You confirmed London's stay and her floor." The stool forcibly rolled against London's bed.

"He'll attack tonight." The Commander pointed as the stool made a soft clang when metal struck metal. "Stay here and watch London. My men and I will prepare."

The Commander walked out, leaving the door open.

Silent as a gentle wind's whistle, Darling said, "Her name is Sarah."

She lifted the stool and sat next to her daughter, noticing how slender her hands were. She reached out to take it and then withdrew. In a small and frail voice, she whispered, "I'm sorry I haven't been . . ." She hiccupped. "You deserved more from a mother. When your father died . . ." Her hands trembled as she spoke. "I'm sorry. You won't believe me, but I kept track of you. Honestly, I did. Even while you lived with Old Lady Green."

* * *

London's eyes fluttered open to narrow slits to find her mom next to her. She was gray around the temples but still beautiful. A beauty queen with long limbs and thick blonde hair that hung in deep curls along her regal neck. Too tired to keep them open, she shut her eyes and listened as she drifted in and out of consciousness.

Darling's chin quivered as she spoke. "Right before . . . You know . . . What we need not talk about," the older woman sniffled, wiping her nose with a tissue. "I gave the old lady money for taking care of you. I'd met your stepdad by then." She stopped for a second and added. "He's a kind man, Sarah." She paused, pressing her cheek against London's forehead, inhaling. Her natural perfume, lilies of the valley. Spring-like, floral, and fresh.

"I know. Kevin wasn't. I let you down. I wish I could take it back. If what's happened between us, we fixed . . ." Her words came in waves, taking her time before speaking. "You have two brothers. They're seventeen. Twins. Their names are Kyle and Sam." Blotting her eyes didn't help stop the tears. "We haven't told them about you . . . but we will. Soon. I promise. Once you're out of here, you'll meet them. We'll be a family, Sarah."

Darling reached for London's hand a second time, pulling it to her lips. "Sarah, please tell me that man will save you." She hiccupped again. "I'm scared." No longer able to hold back, Darling emptied her lungs of air, filling them with fear and regret.

* * *

The Commander stood in the doorway, listening. He walked over, placing a hand on Darling's shoulder. "London trusts me. I hope you will too."

Darling glanced at the Commander, then stood. Her arms wrapped around his broad shoulders as she buried her face against his chest. "I'm sorry. I'm a foolish woman whose lofty pride prevents her feet from touching the ground."

The Commander chuckled, touching London's arm. "That is what London said too."

Darling lifted her head. "Sarah said that?"

"Not in the same words—"

"What words did she use?"

"I don't remember . . ."

"Please, tell me. I doubted if Sarah ever thought of me. I'm interested in what she said."

"Hmmm . . . She mentioned your pants being on fire and forgetting you are on the ground."

Darling laughed and wiped her eyes. "She said that?"

"She did."

Darling offered the Commander the stool and stepped out of his way. She crossed to the other side of the bed. "She always was a smarty-pants. When she was little, she'd bite me when I tried to hold her." The light returned to Darling's eyes as she recalled Sarah as a child. "She'd roll her pudgy hand in my hair, as if my hair were her security blanket. Then, if I made her mad, she'd give it a yank."

Giggling, she turned toward London. "You never

wanted me once your dad came home. I admit jealousy got the best of me. When he came around, you were cheerful and loving. When he left, you turned into a little tyrant. You were always a daddy's girl. Oh, how Darwin loved you." She sniffed. "It seems silly now. All little girls love their daddy. I guess I just wanted to see you smile . . . for me."

Darling rubbed the hair from London's cheek and turned to the Commander. "What do you want me to do?"

He stood. "Sit here. Don't leave her side, no matter what happens. You must trust me. When dark . . ." he told Darling what to expect.

Trembling in fear, she promised to follow his orders.

47

Readied Himself for Battle

Next to London, the Commander readied himself for battle. Eyes lowered, head bent, and one hand on hers, he meditated to ease mind and body. He would act as he'd always done, though he regretted the soldier would die.

A flicker of movement tore him from his trance-like state.

London's index finger twitched as Doctor Yang entered. London's chart between his hands, he said, "I'm sorry to disturb you, Commander. The lab results I spoke with you about have confirmed my suspicion. I thought you might want to read the results."

Standing, the Commander took the chart, flipping through the report. A word in bold letters jumped off the sheet, knocking the Commander back onto his seat.

"Is the b . . ."

The Commander's head snapped, his finger to his lips. "Shhh . . ." He pointed to London and covered an ear with his free hand. He withdrew from her bedside, signaling the doctor to follow, and stepped into the hall. Out of earshot, the Commander explained. "London is waking. For now, surviving is enough. This"—he pointed to the chart—"she is not ready."

"Of course. I understand. My first concern was the bleeding, but that has passed. For now, the baby is stable. Is it yours?"

"Yes."

"The mother. Will she wish to keep the child?"

Eyes glistening, Daeju watched London through the glass door. "London is a day-by-day girl. Tomorrow does not make promises in her world."

Doctor Yang took the chart. "It's a conversation you need to have soon. If she doesn't want the baby—"

"She will," the Commander interjected. "I know she will."

Alone, the Commander leaned against the wall, wearing a grin that bruised his jaw muscles.

A baby.

The shock subsided. He re-entered the room. The doctor stood over London, flashing a penlight in and out of her eyes. "Miss Kim, can you hear me?"

London didn't respond.

He curled back the covers and exposed her left foot, clicked his ink pen, and poked the center. Nothing. He ran the pen over the center of London's foot. It rippled.

The Commander chuckled as he said, "She's ticklish."

The doctor tried again, and the foot rippled in response. "An excellent sign."

Darling entered with a cup of coffee. "What sign?"

"Miss Kim—"

"Bennett," Darling added respectfully.

The doctor glanced at the Commander and spotted an approving nod. "Miss Bennett is responding to stimuli."

Hesitantly, Darling asked, "What does that mean?"

"I can't say it's an absolute, but it seems Miss Bennett is coming out of her coma."

Darling rushed to the bed, her palms cupping London's cheeks. "Sarah, it's Mom. Can you hear me?"

London's eyes darted under her lids as if she were dreaming. When she started fighting the intubation tube, Doctor Yang gave her a sedative.

Darling shrieked, "What happened?"

"I'm not sure." The doctor called for a nurse and checked London's vitals. "It's best if we don't excite her. She needs time. Not all healing is visible."

The Commander laid a hand on London's forehead and found it damp but cool. He leaned in and whispered, "It's okay. I'm here."

London's tension lessened. He felt a slight squeeze.

A nurse entered. "Did you need something, Doctor?"

The open door revealed a man in a black hoodie. As he strode past, his muscles flexed when his eyes landed on London.

Absorbing the rising panic inside, the Commander's expression remained professional. *He'll be back once night falls.* He filtered the voices of the incessant hospital staff, attuned to the click of the enemy's shoes striking the tiled floor. Another half second passed before he nudged the nurse aside, and unseen, pursued the assailant.

When the assassin stepped into the elevator, the Commander called Hyuk. "He got off on the sixth floor. Find him."

The nurse remained at the door, observing the Commander when Doctor Yang called to her. "Nurse, I need you. The patient's airway . . ."

Doctor Yang removed the endotracheal tube. The suction cup sucked out old saliva and deflated the small cuff connected to the ETT. "Miss Kim, I'm going to remove this tube. Take a deep breath and cough." London coughed, and the doctor eased the tube from her throat.

Several throaty coughs erupted. "You're doing fine, Miss Kim."

When the Commander came back, his phone rang. "Did you find him?"

The Lieutenant answered, "Sorry Commander. He got away."

As the Commander rehashed his plan, London slept, the shades drawn, oblivious of the assassin.

Darling remained at London's bedside, under a single dim lamp over the bed, sharing memories of London's father, Darwin Bennett.

* * *

Jolted by London's earlier reaction, it hadn't occurred to Darling that her presence could upset Sarah.

Hesitant to touch her child, Darling asked an endless barrage of unanswered questions. "Do you love him, Sarah? Do you trust him?"

Darling wondered how the charming soldier could save her child. "I want to trust him, but he's so damned easy spoken, a respectable gentleman. Heroes aren't gentle." She glanced over at the sleeping Commander. He sat in the dark of the far corner, arms crossed, feet flat against the floor. "I confess, he has a scrumptious, Herculean physique, but has he ever killed anyone, Sarah? If he can't kill . . ."

Fear stiffening her weary body, Darling peered over her shoulder and pleaded with the Commander. *Please . . . wake up. How in the world will you save my child?*

48

Jump

The world slowed around Darling, each tick of the clock a potential alarm sounding, her nerves spiking. Sleep evaded her despite the gnawing exhaustion that caused her eyelids to droop. To suppress the fear eroding her sanity, she skimmed Mary Kay Andrews's novel, *Summer Rental*, unable to absorb a single word.

At midnight, a nurse entered. Darling noticed the Commander didn't move, his chest rising and falling at an even pace. She watched as the nurse took London's vitals.

The nurse glanced at Darling and smiled. London's breathing had remained steady since noon. "Sounds good."

The hours passed without incident. Morning would rise, with only the Commander getting a night's sleep. Darling's doubts increased as panic defied logic. Desperate, she released the hospital bed's brakes, ready to escape with her daughter, her rattled mind absent of the IV bag and beeping monitor.

Thoughts died, forgotten when her peripheral vision

caught the nearness of an unknown presence. Her weary back straightened. Frozen with her hands on the bedrail, she stared into twin pools of vile darkness. Evil studied her, questioning her pleading silence.

Clad in black, the light caught a glint of death in a gloved hand. Darling screamed a soundless warning, "Knife!"

The deadly blade rose, amplifying Darling's hysteria.

An arm circled the killer's neck from behind. The assailant twisted to break the hold, but death's grip held. He fought for air, thrusting the knife downward, ready to take life even as he succumbed.

* * *

The descending arm twisted, the blade striking the metal bed frame in a blur of emotion. The loud clang of metal against metal echoed in the sterile room. The Commander spun the attacker as the assassin drew a second blade.

Jumping back, the Commander avoided the long-curved metal, pulling a combat dagger from behind his back while his right forearm blocked the lethal strike.

In one move, the Commander disarmed the assailant. Wielding both knives, his movements smooth as a rising cobra and the precision of a black mamba, he diced the enemy. Blood erupted from the assassin's chest, thighs, and abdomen.

* * *

The fight lasted only seconds. The silence of death mirrored the pounding in Darling's chest, the memory of what she'd witnessed forever etched in her mind.

Fear drove Darling as she scooted across the floor from the Commander. Engorged veins stood out on his neck and arms. His uniform soaked red, his eyes never showed death's touch, but terror filled her belly.

The soundless fight had drawn no attention. Two

killers, one standing. Pulling the phone from his shirt, the Commander tapped with a bloody finger. "It's done."

Seconds later, two doctors and three nurses piled through the door. One doctor dropped to his knees seeking a pulse, while the other attended to Darling.

London's monitor alarm sounded, showing her heart rate at one hundred and twenty beats per minute and rising.

* * *

Sarah lay naked under the shadow of her attacker. Blake had forced her upon a piss-poor mattress inside her torture chamber. Her abductor held a fistful of her hair in his hand as his knees indented the mattress and pulled her into place. Above, his penis stood, a mountainous erection between a furry scrotum. Chill drool dripped into her eyes like a leaky faucet. "Do it, bitch. Lick 'em."

* * *

Outside the hospital, sirens wailed. The smell of blood made Darling dizzy. She squeezed the bedrail at London's side, screaming irrationally. "What's . . . Is she . . . Don't let her . . . Sarah . . . Mommy's here, baby."

A nurse pulled Darling from the bedside. "Your daughter will be fine. We need to give Doctor Yang space. He'll administer Miss Kim a sedative."

London thrashed against the bed. Three nurses attempted to hold her, but she was too strong.

* * *

Sarah's heart raced as she inched her hand across the mattress, pulling a glass dildo from under a crinkled blanket. It had taken weeks to break the nearly indestructible sex toy. Blake enjoyed rough sex, and considered the pain euphoric, both giving and receiving. Today, he intended to receive, but Sarah had other plans. With her fingers over the jagged tip, she guided the broken point to his anus.

Today would be Blake's final ecstasy, a crucifixion.

His pleasure driven sigh a grotesque boom in Sarah's ears, becoming the squelch of an emergency broadcast system, raising the hairs on the back of her neck. With a shaky hand, she hesitated. This isn't me. I didn't kill that squirrel in my bed. Can I kill him?

* * *

Unable to stand back as nurses floundered against London's strength, the Commander firmly eased two of them out of his way. He whispered as he grasped her wrist, "Easy, Donee. They cannot hurt you. You are no longer alone."

* * *

A bizarre curiosity consumed Sarah as she studied Blake's face. His arousal glowed through dilated eyes as pre-cum dribbled from his erection. Ready to end her captivity, Sarah shoved the glass deep inside and impaled him, inhaling a metallic scent that smelled of a rusty fence as blood spilled.

* * *

London's strength nearly matched the Commander's. Her veins popped, eyes moving rapidly under closed lids, her body fighting an unseen demon.

"He is gone, Donee. We killed him."

* * *

Blake's gratification turned to wild anger. "I'll kill you, you stupid whore."

Sarah felt his hands clasp her neck, a vise that threatened her life. As she struggled to breathe, his spittle dripped onto her cheek. Filled with fear of him and what she'd done, she watched his azure eyes turn crimson. His retina bulged as he choked her. His hands tightened. Fear of death stirred Blake's anger. "You're dead, you fucking cunt."

Lungs on fire, Sarah's agitation calmed as thoughts of her demise echoed in her brain. At first, she wanted to die. Dead, Blake could never own her.

No longer paralyzed by her actions, Sarah fought, determined to end his reign over women, and twisted the jagged-edged dildo deeper as she choked, "You first."

Blake's rage turned to terror. Red eyes faded to a glassy haze. His face chalky white. He fell face first into the prison he'd trapped her within.

Weakened, Sarah didn't move. She gasped, her lungs compressed by his body. His limp penis lay across her neck. She felt vomit press against her esophagus, forcing her to push him away. She rolled to her side and emptied her stomach.

On shaky legs, she barely took the four steps needed before collapsing against the pedestal sink in her claustrophobic bathroom. Sarah splashed water to cleanse her face, the sink now red with his blood.

* * *

A Risperdal-induced calm allowed the nurses to roll London into the body bag as policemen lined the hallway. Hands shaking, Darling shoved her way to London's bedside, fighting when they zipped the bag closed, her screams frantic. "No. She can't be dead. Get away from her."

Shoved to the side, Darling saw the Commander watching. *What?* Darling screamed. *Why are you waiting?*

When the police arrived, the doctor wheeled London from the room.

Darling clung to the gurney, screaming incoherently as they rolled into the elevator.

Trailing, the Commander followed, fighting emotions

that left him weak and overwhelmed.

He did not make eye contact with the second executioner as they passed side by side, but knew he was there. The assassin watched London's corpse pass. Behind him, a second gurney carrying the dead soldier rolled into a separate elevator. Both headed for the morgue.

49

Inside a Secret Room

The Commander hid London inside a secret room in the morgue. When the special effects artist—also known for her works for top-tier events in film arrived—he gave her close-up shots of London's face and wounds.

After studying the images, the artist set up a make up case on a gurney. Her canvas, a woman who died that morning in a car accident. The artist recreated London's wounds out of trauma makeup, using softer colors, since the bruises had faded.

For the abrasions and incision, she used a reddish-pink foundation and outlined the jagged wound with a black eyeliner pencil. Inside the pencil line, she applied a blood-red pigment, then used a small brush to soften her work. For a more convincing image, she varied the blend for a realistic effect and highlighted the outside edges.

Highlights added depth, giving the wounds a raised appearance. Since the wounds weren't recent, she moved London's discarded bandages to the dead woman, applying them to the fake wounds after the doctor stitched in a false incision.

The final touch, the face and hair. In the end, the dead resembled London close enough to fool anyone in dim light.

That night, the Commander stood behind a one-way mirror, waiting for the assassin.

Just after midnight, wearing a doctor's coat, face mask, and gloves the assassin slipped into the morgue. His fingers drifted across the cooler as he searched for London's marker, pausing at the unit labeled Sarah Bennett. His fingers lingered on the card before sliding out the tray.

The toe tag checked. He removed the sheet.

His knife grazed the curve of her breast. With disturbing tenderness, he fondled her as if she were his lover, caressing himself in the shadows. His erection softened as he wrenched the sheet over the body with an icy indifference, zipped his pants and closed the mortuary door, leaving, unaware the Commander watched.

Behind the glass, the Commander's fists clenched, resisting the urge to kill the assassin. Logic stilled his rage. One dead assassin led to more. They'd hunt London, intent on killing. The hatchet man needed to believe London had died, gratifying Kim Jong Un's vengeance.

His thoughts of revenge tamed, the Commander reminded himself that he controlled the unwary killer.

For the next months, with London and her baby hidden, the guerrilla plagued the Commander's daily activities, saving him the work of tracking the North Korean's movements. They found devices in Commander Kim's wardrobe, inside his room, in Willy, his cell phone and even at his desk, an impenetrable fortress. The Commander left the devices intact, faking ignorance. This unwanted spectator prevented him from telephoning London, from visiting her, or from any missions that might provide information to the North. His thoughts, consumed with memories of London and curiosity about his child, they couldn't decipher. They were his own.

He lived pretending London had been a task he'd completed with efficiency. To continue this ruse, he issued General Hanbin full access to his accounts, and the General settled London's bills.

* * *

Outside London's private hospital room, under the pseudonym Kim, she watched a squirrel climb a tree. As he jumped from tree to tree, the smaller branches with brick-red leaves dipped with each landing.

She'd been at Mutsu General Hospital in Japan for three months. At least, that's what Doctor Tanaka told her the day she awakened.

She cradled her belly with both hands while sitting in a rocker by the window and rocked her fetus, telling the child stories of the children playing at Kanaya Park.

Doctor Tanaka entered, trailed by a young Japanese woman carrying her breakfast. The food tray placed on the over-bed table, the girl scurried out with tiny steps, her hands clasped at her waist.

With arms crossed, the doctor leaned against the window seal. He stood around one hundred and seventy-two centimeters with peppered gray hair, a thin man with a friendly smile and deep grooves in his cheeks. "Tomorrow's your release date."

The tingling in her hands and feet, that the doctors claimed was phantom pain, shot sudden daggers that opened fire on her limbs. To quiet the daggers, she pressed an open palm against her calf and asked, "Where will I go? I don't know anyone?"

Squatting, Doctor Tanaka raised London's leg, rubbing his hands against her skin. "You're not alone. I'm here if you need me. In the meantime, until you regain your memory, the monks at a Buddhist temple in Osorezan have agreed to house you."

"Who's been paying our bills?" A question she'd asked many times without an answer. Beads of sweat dotted London's temple. Another symptom of PTSD. She'd been told of recent trauma, a trauma she couldn't remember but the effects she lived with daily. Flashbacks of a man, blood, and a knife haunted her. London feared the unshakeable man inside her mind could be the baby's father.

Sometimes, she saw an old woman's face lined with silver hair; a sewing needle neatly placed in her collar. Each time she materialized, London drew the blankets closer, chilly, and sad.

"One day, you'll remember. Until then," the doctor's lips curled under, in an awkward and comforting closed-mouth smile, "rest at ease. You are not alone."

"Who's with me?" London stopped rocking. "Is it the person who pays my bills? Tell me."

"All in time. So, for now, focus on healing and brace yourself." He pointed to her belly. "That one will soon impose itself on you. Grab a pen. Your future is an unwritten book. Scribble away."

A hand towel dabbed at the perspiration on her upper lip as she spoke in a cynical tone. "Face an unknown future with a baby and a handful of Buddhist monks? Doesn't sound promising."

Her legs ached despite the hands quelling the fire. "Will I be a worthy mother, Doctor? My stomach protests when I imagine raising a child. It frightens me. What if my parents never wanted me, or worse, what if they abandoned me? Why aren't they here?"

"I can't answer those questions, but someday, you will. Whoever they prove to be, you love your baby. That's the first step to motherhood."

She returned to cradling her child with her arm snug around her belly and rocking while reaching for a tissue.

The doctor left her staring out the window.

I'm strong. I can do this. She looked at her swollen belly. *We can do this.* She promised her baby she'd overcome the broken fragments of her mind and win. "It's you and me, kid. We're safe."

Packed and ready to leave the hospital, London climbed into the back seat of a Nissan Cedric, strapping herself in.

"I have one last thing before you go." The doctor handed London a double-edged Cossack dagger with a hilt and sheath made of ivory. "This was with your things when you arrived. For obvious reasons, the staff chose to keep it in the safe. The handle is worn." He withdrew his hands. "It must be important."

London pulled the blade from the sheath, noticing the silver filigree, and resheathed it. Unsure why, she pressed the dagger horizontally under the belt of her maternity dress and said goodbye to Doctor Tanaka.

"You have my number. Call if you need me. You're not alone, Donee."

Where have I heard that before?

Surrounded by trees, with a steep slope on the driver's side, London sat in Doctor Tanaka's car, driven by a young intern, taking in the scenery that spurred memories of a past she couldn't remember. She felt peaceful, as if the mountains, cliff sides, and trees were home. A silly thought but encouraging.

The active mountain was laden with a heavy snow cap and ringed by a cloud of mist where ice and rock merged. It stretched toward her, a mirrored replica painted in colors of indigo and pink, as white sands lined the shore of a crisp autumn lake.

The road veered into a realm of silica sand and sulfuric

rocks shaped by volcanic activity. Shades of asparagus and orange marmalade enshrouded the craggy rocks, statues against a mountainside.

She breathed in the sulfur-laced air, a rotten egg taste assailing her nostrils.

At the temple gates, the intern said, "Tiny hot springs bubble up, spewing sulfur from the ground. It's beautiful once you get past the smell." He parked, inhaling a deep breath, and releasing the air.

London opened the door and got out followed by the driver. His hand stretched toward the scenery. "You turn the corner and step into an oasis."

"Is this where I'll be staying?"

"As long as you need," he answered. "Stay or leave when you're ready."

"Ready to remember?"

He shrugged. "Or to let go."

"If I remember?" she asked. "What if I don't want to go back?"

"Then, I suppose you still have need."

"So, I can stay?"

"If you wish."

"And my baby?"

The intern nodded. "And your baby."

50

Prayers for the Children

London's days settled into quiet rhythm, adopting the temple life. Rising at five, they prayed from six to six-thirty. When the prayer finished, she joined them for the fire ceremony.

In the ritual hall, Abbot Shinkojo tossed thin wooden tablets into the roaring fire. Each tablet engraved with prayers for children who'd died in utero or postnatal. Flames licked the ceiling as Shinkojo recited the names of the lost.

As the tablets burned, the monks chanted to the beat of drums, revitalizing their minds and purifying their spirits. In the early morning hours, the monks' chanting sank into London's being, their voices rising and falling with the rhythmic drums. Surrounded by grief, heat, and harmony, something inside softened. Despite mourning for the lost souls, she knew . . . peace.

London looked monk-like as she walked through the graveyard in below-freezing temperatures. Wrapped in a white kimono under a brown robe, she wore a bright yellow shawl draped over her shoulders. The layers hid her growing belly.

She and Shinkojo walked side by side, keeping a steady pace, passing piles of stone pebbles with sitting statues. He enlightened her on Japanese death rituals, pointing toward the steep red bridge she'd crossed upon arrival. "The River Styx divides the living from the dead."

"I'd rather be lifted to Heaven, but go ahead." London picked up a pebble and placed it on top of a stack. "Tell me why the children didn't cross the bridge?"

"Not that simple. You see, all are judged in the afterlife, but a lost child's time is short." He picked up a rock along the riverbed. "These are the souls of those children."

London placed a few more pebbles in a stack. *Too innocent for hell if you ask me. What happens if I dam the water?* She smirked at the thought, then smiled. *Instant Heaven.*

"Datsue-ba, taught the children to pile pebbles to reach paradise. The hag knocks the pebbles over, stealing the child's clothing. To save their souls, bodhisattva Jizo hides stones inside his robe, piling them on the bank. This is the way children may attain new life."

He held a pebble gently between his fingers. "The angel shelters them on the beach, as do the monks of Bodaj-ji Temple."

"How can a mountain and a river control the souls of humans, Shinkojo? They are lifeless."

"Is a silent volcano still active?" he asked. "Do rivers move rocks and trees? My people believe life is in everything."

London threw out her arms. "Can a volcano erupt without a powerful God to give it heat, or a river flow without rain from Heaven?"

Shinkojo clasped his hands in prayer. They stood near

a bubbling hot spring for warmth, accustomed to the sulfuric smell. Pink and blue pinwheels tucked into a pile of rocks spun in the winter breeze.

London blocked the wind with a hat she'd weaved together with rice and straw as she turned toward the statue of the goddess Kannon. The god held a child in each arm.

Abbot Shinkojo had spoken of the statue when she'd first arrived, revealing the sculpture's power to keep expectant mothers safe.

London placed a protective hand on her swollen belly. "I'd rather not place the fate of my child in the power of a stone statue."

When the walk ended, she returned to her room and readied herself for the day's chores.

Most days, she swept the halls, but today, she helped prepare the meal. She learned to cook *shojin-ryori*, a vegan meal of miso soup, tempura squash, lotus root, *shiso* leaves, and sake. Guided by the "rule of five:" the colors white, green, red, yellow, and black. The seasoning of each dish differed from the others. The monks believed the body was balanced with the sweet, sour, bitter, salty and *umami*. In winter, they ate roots to warm the body.

She enjoyed cooking, having never done it, at least as far back as she could remember. Maybe she'd been a chef, but she didn't think so. Still, she wanted to cook more often. Wielding a knife as she chopped felt right. *Did I work with knives?* She didn't know the answer, but the truth grew nearer.

After dinner, she bathed in a tub made of Japanese Cyprus. The monks taught her the process of purifying and healing with the lingering scent of fresh pine, smoky and sweet, with unique earthy undertones of spices and flowers. The Cyprus wood symbolized sorrow and mourning, but to London, it was pacifying and inviting, plus the warm sulfur water alleviated the swelling in her joints.

During the silent evenings, carrying a rice lamp, she walked down the long hall to her room wearing a pair of wooden flip flops and toed socks. Her feet slipped as she walked, making each step a loud thumping boom.

Elevated by two rows of wooden teeth, she couldn't control her strides the way she did in boots or moccasins, making her sound clumsy and childlike next to the soundless footsteps of the monks. Often, she pictured an older man in the shoes. He wore his black hair long, pulled back from his face, a bow in his hand. He had a familiar face, one she recognized without fear.

The image of him wearing the clogs caused her to giggle.

After closing the thin, elaborately painted wooden doors to her room, she sat in a square stone-lined pit next to a kettle of boiling water. A sweet bun, filled with red bean paste, rested next to the hearth on a lacquerware platform.

As the scent of lilac swirled around her, she sat in lotus position on the hardwood floor, rocking back and forth and drinking hot tea, talking to the child inside.

A month prior, during one of her lengthy walks alone, the name Sodam Isolde had come to her. She didn't understand why the names were significant, but she liked the way it sounded. Now, six months pregnant, Sodam became active in the evening hours, kicking her mommy into sleeplessness.

Exhausted, London stretched out her sheeted comforter over a *tatami*, or floor mat, and covered herself from the night's bitter cold.

Restless, eyes closed, she counted her breathing. Something felt different tonight. Most nights, the silence of the mountains lulled her to sleep the way the hum of an echo could be sustained for thousands of years. The stillness broke. The wind outside her door made her more aware of the change. The creak of wood reinforcing her unease. London tensed.

She placed her hand on the hilt of the knife, hidden under the mat. She lay unmoving. Waiting. Calm. The door cracked and a dark figure stepped through. Soundless as a snake's slither, they crossed the floor, stopping and kneeling at her bedside.

In a single slash, London sliced the intruder's hamstring. On his back, incapacitated, she circled to her feet, dropped on his chest, and raised the blade for the kill. The moon glowed silver through the open door. That's when she saw him, the man she knew to be Sodam's father. His expression was full of pain as two black almond eyes pleaded with her.

Fear and instinct took over as her blade sank into his chest just as he whispered, "Donee, it's me, Daeju."

Without hesitation, the knife pierced the skin, cut through bone, and entered his heart. Recognition came with the thrust of death. Memories flooded back like lava through her mind. "Daeju?"

With perception came reality, as the moon's silver glow grew dull in those whisky-colored eyes.

"Daeju. Daeju!" She pressed a hand to his heart, the other cupping his face as she kissed him.

"Don't leave me." Screaming, London ripped off her gown, pressing it against the wound as blood covered his chest and spilled onto the floor.

Underneath her hand, his pulse slowed until it beat no more.

"Nooo!" she screamed. She laid his limp hand upon her belly. "Your daughter, Sodam, she has the hiccups. Can you feel her?"

Too late. The Commander's final breath went unheard.

Ready to die at his side, London pulled the blade from

his chest. Held high between both hands, Sodam's faint hiccup slammed into her consciousness as she hurled the knife across the room.

She'd killed the only man she'd trusted. The only man she loved, bringing to fulfillment an early prediction. Frenzied screaming for help brought no one to her aid. Collapsing against his chest, she clung to his lifeless body.

"I killed him."

51

The Beat of Drums

London woke to the beat of drums, the steady chant of the monks, and the stark light of a winter sun. She awakened not to a blood-covered body, but a tear-soaked pillow. Alone with her baby.

And she remembered.

52

Slumped in a Chair

Slumped in a chair, several empty beer cans were stacked on the end table, along with an open bag of sweet potato chips. Poor food and inactivity had rounded the Commander's face and belly. Black hair hung in his eyes, and stubble covered his jaw. "It is time," he told Hyuk. "My spirit is gone. I am no good to the country if I cannot fight."

"Take a desk job." Hyuk picked up the trash off the floor. "Get a hobby, anything to get out of this apartment."

He threw open the curtains and watched the Commander flinch when light poured in.

"I have tried to stop them, *Hyung*. I cannot. They have beaten me. If I kill even one man, they will know London lives. I need your help."

"My help? I don't like the way this conversation is going. If you are here with us, they won't look further. The way to protect her is by staying where you belong."

"I belong with her. With my child. I am less a man without them. No good to you or the people."

"Even if you retire, you can't go to her. What is there to gain by leaving the men who trust you to lead them?"

The Commander stood, placed a hand on Hyuk's shoulder and said, "You will lead them, *Hyung*. I have led them long enough. Now, I need your help to be with London. By ending this life, I can live another."

Hyuk slapped his arm away. "I won't do it. This, right here." He beat a fist against his chest. "Your men. This uniform. That is your family. I won't let you throw it away for her and her child."

"My child, Hyuk. She is *my* child. This," he pointed around the room, "was my family. Not anymore. London and I constructed a bridge between our souls. It is time I cross that bridge and claim what is mine."

Hyuk threw the trash can across the room, spilling its contents. "She's nothing but trouble." He punched the door and made a fist-sized indent in it. "I warned you. Why didn't you listen?"

The Commander lifted his chin, the first defiance Hyuk had seen from him in months.

"You are wrong."

For sixteen months, Hyuk had watched the Commander change as he worked to divert Kim Jong Un away from London. In the past weeks, depression had lined his friend's eyes. Defeated and heartbroken, he sunk into the chair. "How do you want to do this?"

The Commander opened a bottle of soju and poured a shot of the clear rice wine, downing it in one gulp. "Suicide. It is the only way."

"Now you're talking *michin*, Commander. Crazy talk. Dying won't fix anything."

Crazy might have made all these months separated from London bearable. "You are wrong. Dying fixes everything. You cannot follow a dead body."

"Nor can a dead body live."

"That is your part in the story. You will help me. With a little pig blood and a spent bullet, you will convince the team I am dead. If the team believes your story, so will the enemy. They will return home and leave me and London alone to raise our daughter in peace."

* * *

Days later, Daeju sat at the small table inside his room, a pen in hand, wearing his formal uniform. His hand shook as he wrote.

Being a civilian has forced me to face my life. I am haunted by the lives I have taken.

I have no regrets; it was an honor to serve my country. Forgive me. Without London, I no longer have a reason to live.

Commander Kim Daeju

Standing before a mirror, he pulled his army issue gun from its holster and fired a single round.

The smell of charcoal smoke from the blast permeated the walls of the small apartment building.

Commander Hyuk ran down the hall when he heard the shot and busted the door lock as he forced his way in. The Commander had slumped to the floor. Hyuk dropped to his knees and cradled his leader, his sobs raking his chest as he grieved his loss.

The two had shared a distinguished career together, fighting side by side for their country. One woman had divided them. Hyuk felt weak. The Commander's faked suicide finalized the end of their friendship, the end of an era, and an end to an outstanding soldier.

He refused entry to anyone besides Doctor Yang who had agreed to help. Together, they lifted the Commander's body and rolled him out on a stretcher. Three days later, they held a funeral, with General Hanbin officiating.

Commander Hyuk followed the hearse, his team

behind him, carrying a picture of Commander Kim with a gold star and a ribbon tied to the frame. The gold star was the highest medal a soldier could earn for outstanding military service.

Countless soldiers stood at attention in the rain to pay their respects.

* * *

Park Ji Jin watched through binoculars on a nearby roof. A Bluetooth earpiece connected to a bug on the General's podium. He listened.

"Commander Kim Daeju served the Republic of Korea for twelve years, completing over one hundred missions without losing a single man. In the past year, many of you trained under him, learning the skills he wielded in the field. In the years Commander Kim and I served this country, he never lost his edge, his self-control, or his dignity. He was a noble man, a one of a kind. The nation mourns the loss on this day as we say goodbye to a hero. We will miss him."

* * *

That night, Joe watched Commander Hyuk, Lieutenant Wonsul, Captain Namgi, Private Wonho, and Private 1st Class Joowon as they saluted their leader with a clambake from the rooftop. A picture of the Commander and London taped to the back of the Whiskey River Saloon as the fire burned, their beers raised in a toast.

"To Commander Kim and London. May their lives reunite, and their spirits pass over together."

Joe had emptied the apartment of London's things for its new tenant, a man this time, one unswayed by a heroic South Korean. Banning any non-American soldiers from his saloon, he'd made sure the Koreans couldn't influence his team again, blaming them for London's death.

He believed the Commander weakened her, making her vulnerable to mistakes. A mistake that prevented her from coming home. Home to him.

Lugging a bag of London's personal items, he walked down the steps, missing the girl who'd livened his life. London owned little but an old hand-stitched quilt, a picture of her father, a few comic books, and a handful of goodwill outfits. Bagged, he set them out on the curb and entered the saloon.

* * *

Walking to Willy, Commander Hyuk saw the bag and picked it up, tossing it into the back of the jeep.

* * *

Two days later, Park Ji Jin stood in the graveyard, looking at a burial stone.

He contacted his commanding officer, preparing to return home. Nineteen months had passed since the Great Leader sent him to kill Sarah Bennett. When she died, he'd continued gathering intelligence on the Commander in case her death was a hoax.

Now, with the Commander gone, his task was complete.

53

The Historic District of Rye

The last of today's customer's paid London for Nora Roberts' latest novel and exited the bookstore.

London followed her to the door, encouraging the woman to leave a review next time she visited. She locked the door to Shropshire Books in the historic district of Rye, East Sussex, England.

Soon after moving to Rye, she'd bought the store. The sale of a few meager books per day augmented her savings, most of which she'd spent setting up a home and starting the business. It allowed her to keep Sodam at her side during her early years. Advertisements for comic books were her means to reach the Commander, hoping to lead him there.

Of the few things she'd revealed of herself, were her love of comic books, and a desire to live in England, near the ocean.

She turned to close and lock the door, catching the evening sun on a glass showcase with a column base.

Inside the glass The Red Badge of Courage rested on a bookstand.

Sodam lifted chubby arms as London turned to scoop her up and strapped her into the bike trailer before straddling her classic Dutch bicycle. "It's Wednesday, Sodam. What would you like Mommy to get you at the market?"

"Owange."

"An orange? Let's hope Miss Amelia has some." London peddled down the cobblestone road, heading west to Strand Quay along the River Rother.

When she first moved to England, she'd ridden all over Ipswich to reconnect with her father's past, the memories he'd shared of the area. Darwin Bennett had been stationed at the RAF Lakenheath Air Force Base an hour from town.

Needing a more secluded location, London settled in Rye just before giving birth to Sodam.

Multiple sailboats were tied off along the quay. The two rode past the multiple shops lining Strand Quay until they reached the farmer's market.

Amelia, an older woman in her early sixties, worked a garden each year, earning money on the side to pay for her family's annual Mediterranean vacation. She and her husband owned the farm behind London's property.

London and Sodam often walked across the field to visit the Border Collie puppies they raised.

She found Amelia's booth near the river. Underneath the pop-up canopy lined with fresh fruits. Amelia smiled as London parked the bike against the guardrail. "Hello. Sodam ordered me to pedal faster on the way over. We're out of fruit again."

Sodam's hand reached through the zipper opening of her bike trailer. "Gwape."

Amelia grabbed her pudgy fingers. "You want a grape? Hmm . . . let me see."

"Gwape. Gwape." Sodam squealed.

Amelia pulled a plump grape and dropped it into Sodam's hand. Little fingers encircled the fruit and disappeared inside the tent. "What can I get you today, Donee?"

London picked up an orange, rolling it around in her hand. The fruit, both plump and round, was the size of a softball. "I wasn't expecting to find oranges. How much?"

Amelia brushed her short, gray-flecked hair off her face before adjusting her glasses. She smiled pleasantly as she answered. "For you and Sodam, sixty-five pence."

"Sixty for a dozen," London bartered.

Amelia picked up a bag and shook it open. "I picked them fresh this morning. You've been over to my place often enough to know I grow the juiciest oranges. I'll tell you what, since we're neighborly, I will sell a dozen to you for sixty-three pence each, but that is the best I can do."

London opened Sodam's tent and adjusted the crocheted baby blanket. She had crocheted more blankets for last year's fundraiser than any other mother. "I heard the church is running another fundraiser for cancer kids."

The older woman blushed.

"I thought I'd join the bike ride. Readers are always eager to support my ride."

Amelia had been the president of St. Mary's Catholic Church fundraising program for over twenty years. "Yes, umm . . . Sixty-two pence and only because of your wonderful contributions to our fundraiser ... I can't do any better than that." Amelia bagged twelve of the biggest oranges and handed them over.

London took the fruit and tucked it inside a saddlebag. With the money exchanged, she kicked the kickstand and struck off for home. "Thanks, Amelia. Sodam and I may be over later to feed the puppies."

Amelia yelled as London rode off, "Next week I'll have fresh strawberries. When you come over, I'll give you a handful."

London yelled back, "Cheerio."

London and Sodam pulled up to an attached Victorian mid-terraced home on Tillingham Avenue.

With nothing to her name except a knife and a baby, she'd bought the home for the cast-iron fireplace, pine floors and the garden that opened onto a field of sheep overlooking the River Rother using her savings from ten years of killing. It didn't feel right but she had a child to raise, and it was on a dead-end road, close to her store.

When they entered the front door, Sodam pointed to the painting above the fireplace. "Appa."

"Do you see *Appa*, Sodam?"

Again, the child pointed to the picture and said, "*Appa.*"

London looked up at the painting she'd commissioned soon after buying the house. The photo had been taken at the lake, after their flight in the mountains. Each day she'd waited for his arrival the same way she'd hung on to the sound of that stupid bell at the Whiskey River. Listening. Confident he would come to them.

"*Appa* loves Sodam. Blow him a kiss." Sodam's chubby palm laid against her lips as she made a tiny smack and blew the kiss up to the painting.

"Can you help *Omma* take these oranges to the kitchen?"

Sodam grabbed the bottom of London's dress, forcing London to follow her unstable legs as they swung wide with each step, her round head bobbing, arms flung wide.

With the oranges placed in a bowl on the table, London scooped a bucket of grain from the bin by the back door. "Want to feed the sheep?"

Sodam's eyes lit up. "Seep. Feed seep."

In the backyard, all colors of tulips lined the privacy fence, with a stone path leading to the rear gate. Before they stepped off the patio, Mary Moore, their neighbor, stuck her head over the fence.

"I've been expecting you." Her eyes shifted to Sodam. "I have a couple of carrots for the sheep, Sodam. Do you want to feed them?"

London walked to the fence and held Sodam up so she could take the carrots. Sodam tried to take both carrots in one hand. When they dropped to the ground, she squirmed in London's arms until she set her down.

"Thanks, Mary. Oliver still at work?"

"You know Oliver. He's a bit of a workaholic. He comes home, eats, and sits in front of the telly. Knackered, he is. Hasn't looked at me a day since our first anniversary. After twenty-seven years, I don't expect things will change."

"Yes. Well, I'm sure he loves you. He still comes home."

"Absobloodylutely. Bout time you found yourself a chap. Father for the little one . . ."

"Now, Mary Moore, don't you dare try to go set me up. I told you; Sodam has a father."

"Yes, dear. I believe you. Just think a wee one should have a live father, rather 'an just o painting a one."

London laughed. "I guess Sodam and I should get to feeding the sheep." She pulled an old carrot from Sodam's mouth. "Before she eats the goods."

The "woolly's" were waiting when the gate opened. Sodam held the carrot out for the Shropshire sheep when one of them yanked it out of her hand.

The raspy sound of an engine out front prickled London's nerves. She grabbed Sodam under the arms and quietly closed the gate. Back inside, she placed Sodam under the stairwell.

Since birth London had been placing Sodam under the stairs anytime she heard noise warning of potential danger. The little girl thought of the room as her playroom, since London had filled it with her favorite toys, toys she only played with inside. *Stay quiet, little one.*

Grabbing her knives from the crochet basket, she pressed herself against the wall and looked out the front window. Residents rarely drove anywhere in this riverside town, making the randomness of a vehicle outside her front door unlikely.

A polished blue jeep sat parked out front. London's heart skipped as a man inside jumped out. He wore ripped white jeans with a blue and white awning-striped shirt, a blue cap, and sunglasses.

"Daeju?"

She backed away from the window, barely speaking loud enough to hear herself. "Sodam. It's *Appa*." Her heart lurched as she watched him through the sheer curtains. "Appa is here, Sodam. He's here!"

The Commander walked toward the house, upright and proud, with that cocky gait that still screamed leader.

London pulled their daughter from the hiding place and whispered excitedly, "*Appa's* home."

Sodam pointed to the large painting. "*Appa*."

London set her daughter on the floor and straightened the black and white plaid dress Sodam wore. She brushed back her black hair, pulling it off her face with a daffodil pin. Squatting in front of the child, she noticed slobber dribbling down her chin.

London grabbed a tissue from a box on the end table and quickly wiped the dribble away. "The picture is a painting. Appa is outside this door. He's waiting to meet you. Make sure you smile for Appa."

She kissed Sodam's forehead. "Okay?"

Sodam's head bobbed like a buoy, as a smile took shape and then disappeared, her eyes wide with uncertainty. Her brown orbs resembled her father's, but like London, she had freckles that dotted her cheeks and nose, standing out against her darker skin.

London felt tears forming in her eyes as she hurried

their daughter over to the door and opened it. Daeju's dark figure filled the doorway.

One day, when the danger passed, London had known he'd come, but the wait . . .

Sodam shyly stood, clinging to Yona, whose raggedy body hung limp, limbs dangling onto the floor. When her mom gave her a gentle shove from behind, Sodam took a step forward and looked up, her eyes wide, hesitation written on her little girl face.

London noticed Daeju's hair was longer than he'd worn back then. Stubble sprinkled his chin and upper lip, but his eyes . . . They were just as she remembered. Honest. Penetrating.

* * *

Daeju watched his daughter's chubby legs step toward him, wearing an eager smile that exposed her four pearly teeth, and then faltered and stopped. Plump baby lips stared at him questionably.

Unable to wait, he squatted at her feet. "My little *Aegiya*." He held out his arms, clutching his cap in one hand. "*Appa* is home."

Wide eyes stayed fixed on him, one arm around Yona's skinny neck, choking the life out of the stuffed animal. "*Appaji?*"

The Commander recognized the raspberry scent of London as she bent low next to her child. He'd waited too long.

"Say hello to *Appa*."

Sodam raised out her arms and the Commander scooped her up.

* * *

London stood next to them, tears stinging her eyes. "I named her Sodam. After your mother."

She felt a familiar tingle when the Commander stepped into her, sliding an arm around her waist and pulling her close. His touch no longer frightened her. The memory of his love filled the quiet of her nights with comfort and peace. She'd cried, not tears of pain, but the joy of surviving.

"She is perfect." Daeju winked and lowered his head, their lips connecting with a promise of more.

London wiped away his tear with her thumb and grinned. "We've missed you."

Daeju had taught her that life was a ripple in the water. Sometimes it tickled and other times it knocked you over, but it was all right to stand up again and ask for help. Now, she could stand in front of a mirror and never feel shame or a longing for death. Life had become precious.

Epilogue

Seven months later, in the smoky mountains of Tennessee, Wing Commander Peterson entered his home carrying a five-by-seven envelope addressed to Darling Peterson. "Darling, you got something in the mail."

Darling stood in the kitchen, a flower apron tied around her waist, the aged Barbie of the twenty-first century. Placing a wooden spoon on a tray, she closed the skillet lid, sealing off the zesty scent of lemon and rosemary before turning. "Who from?"

He handed her the envelope, giving her a peck on the cheek and shrugged. "There isn't a return address."

Darling opened the seal, pulling out a picture of Sarah, the Commander, and a toddler in front of a picket fence, tall golden grass behind them. Pressing the picture to her chest, she took in a deep breath to hold back the tears.

Her husband set his briefcase on the dining table and walked over. "What's wrong?"

Finding her voice, she whispered, "Sarah's alive." Passing the picture to her husband, she grabbed her purse and then snapped the photo out of his hands.

"Where are you going?"

Bouncing around the room, she spoke in her most sophisticated voice, "I'm going to Neiman Marcus. I'm a grandmother now. I can't possibly show off my first grandchild without one of Jay Strongwater's floral frames. I'd be a joke at the officer's club."

The Wing Commander stayed her hand on the front doorknob. "You can't." Taking the photo from her, he walked into the kitchen, turning on a gas burner.

Alarmed, Darling shrilled, "What are you doing?"

Holding the picture over the flame, he said, "We have to burn it."

Darling grabbed the picture, thrusting the flames under the faucet. "No, you can't."

"We have too." The Wing Commander knew the North continued to look for Sarah. A spy spotted near their home soon after they returned from Korea, and another two months back made him cautious. He'd read reports from General Hanbin and knew they'd flown Sarah to Japan and lost track from there. Later, he'd read a second report that Commander Kim had supposedly taken his life a week after retiring from service. "If you keep this picture, you'll get them killed."

Dropping the photo, the water pouring over the three faces; the emulsion separated. Defeated, Darling asked, "Do you think we'll ever see them again?"

Shutting off the water, he pulled the picture from the sink and dried it with a towel. The faces smudging. "We got a picture." Holding it over the flames, the edge caught on fire. "If we got one, there will be more."

"My daughter has offered me hope."

Wing Commander Peterson hugged his wife. "Maybe one day, a visit."

Bonus Chapter from

Moonlight
&
Murder

Anna Michelle Page

Chapter One

The warning call of a lone wolf howled in the distance as Indy, a big red quarter horse trembled, his ears rapidly swiveling front to back. Conservation Officer Juliette Gardiner snubbed up on the reins to steady the prancing horse as her hand pressed against the butt of her rifle. The musty smell of overturned grass hung in the air.

Bear.

The charging bear crashed through the trees, its head low with intent to kill.

Juliette yanked the Remington 870 from the saddle scabbard, aimed, and fired. *Missed.*

The 12-gauge shotgun went wide when Indy bolted sideways, slamming her arm against a tree. She heard the snap of bones and felt the heaviness of her arm. No pain.

On average, it takes three seconds from the moment a bear charges until it is too late. Fortunately, this bear gave her five. With two seconds to drop the charging bear, she slammed her rifle down against her chaps, recycled the chamber, and aimed.

In the grizzly's final lunge forward, Wolf came from somewhere behind, clamping down on the bear's neck. The big bear rolled, stood, and shook off Wolf's hold. The gray wolf attacked a second time.

Juliette, rifle aimed, held Indy between taunt thighs and waited for an opening, even as her mule danced nervously in the brush behind her, pulling against the saddle horn.

The bear swiped a giant paw, tossing Wolf to the side like water in a bucket, shook his massive head, and huffed.

Juliette fired.

The bear dropped with a thud, the bullet buried between his eyes. Juliette felt dizzy climbing off the horse, flinging the reins over a small branch. Indy snorted, his eyes wide, ears forward. With the bear dead, her pack mule, Hee-haw, calmed. Indy dropped his head and munched on bits of grass poking between dry leaves.

The quiet of the forest felt unsettling after the attack.

Wolf stood and shook off the blow, trotting over to her. She'd found the pup two years earlier while investigating the killing of an entire pack of wolves. Wolf, the only survivor of four pups, huddled in the back corner of the den, frightened and hungry.

As part of the ICOA, the Idaho Conservation Officers Association, she'd hired on to manage the wolf population, wolf conservation, and the legal hunting of wolves.

Injured, but unsure how badly, Juliette pressed her back against the tree and lowered herself to the ground. Wolf lay beside her and placed his muzzle against her face, expecting kisses.

"You're late," she whispered, "but also right on time."

She tried to raise her left arm and felt the heaviness of her hand. With her right hand she gently raised the dangling and useless arm against her chest, leaning back slightly to help hold it in place, and scratched Wolf behind the ears.

Juliette thought she might pass out from the torrent of pain, which threatened to overwhelm her. And maybe she did. She didn't know.

When she next opened her eyes, the bear still lay dead,

and Indy and Heehaw hadn't wandered away. Wolf's head rested on her outstretched legs.

Beads of cold sweat dripped down Juliette's forehead. Her mind struggled to grasp the impact that had taken place within seconds. Her first bear attack and kill, and her first injury on the job.

She stood, careful to keep the broken arm in place, pulled a row of duct tape and two leather repair straps from her saddlebags, soaking the leather with water from her canteen. Then she took a long drink before gathering four thin branches from the forest floor around her to form a makeshift splint. Once protected, she taped the arm in place to keep it elevated.

On her feet and standing over the bear, she could tell the creature had seen better years. She rolled back its lips to find worn and stained canines, rounded by too many years grazing on plants. Its cinnamon-colored coat was shaggy, and its legs looked long from lack of belly fat. The meat would be worthless, tough and wild tasting, but she could still harvest the fur.

Later.

Mounting jolted her arm. She screamed, dropping low over Indy's neck to let the wave of pain pass. How long she lay there, she didn't know, but the morning had turned with the sun high overhead.

Between the unusual heat of the day and the incapacitated agony of a broken arm, a cold sweat took hold, making her shiver. With each labored breath, she felt her entire reality shift. The once-familiar sensation of warmth and strength was now replaced by a chilling uncertainty. Could she make it the last five miles home?

* * *

Doctor Dutton Bae drove down US95 from the University of British Columbia, in Kelowna, to Bonners Ferry, Idaho.

He'd driven over five hours, his silver Porsche Cayman not the best vehicle over the harsh mountain highway. Ten miles from town, according to his GPS, the right front tire popped. He fought the right pull of the steering wheel as he gradually released the gas pedal and his vehicle slowed to a stop.

Once fully stopped, he drove another five feet to a gravel drive and pulled in, parking the Porsche alongside the road, got out, and opened the trunk for the spare tire and jack. He pulled out the tire, then remembered he'd loaned the jack to a friend. *Perfect timing.*

Surrounded by evergreens with only a narrow driveway to guide him, he walked about a mile, hoping to find a house with somebody home. The calming sound of wind blowing through pines, mixed with the rustling leaves of white oaks and the cool spring air, made the walk enjoyable. When he stepped out of the trees next to an open field, sweat dotted his brow. A horse whinnied somewhere behind him. Ahead, another horse, returned the call, drawing his attention to a treehouse-looking structure. That and the screaming pigs.

Dutton approached the ten-foot chain-link entrance to the three interconnected stilted structures, intimidated by the extreme measures to keep people out. Two pigs stood just inside, their heads swinging back and forth, their mouths chewing with no obvious food to eat, both intermittently screaming a high-pitched squeal.

He tried the gate, worried someone inside had been injured.

Locked.

An instinct and the hint of sweat mingled with leather drew his attention to the field that ran alongside the drive. A big red horse stepped out of the trees with a person slumped across its back. A yellow horse with a black mane and tail followed. That horse had oversized, jackrabbit ears. The animal looked like a horse-sized burro.

Both horses plodded toward him as if returning home, while two pastured horses pranced up and down the fence line, as if welcoming home barn mates.

When the lead horse came to a stop a few feet from the ground-building that Dutton assumed was a barn, his head rolled back toward the saddle.

Dutton ran over. When a large dog nudged his elbow, he stroked its bushy head while assessing the situation.

"Is this your person?" The dog's chartreuse eyes pierced him in a fixed stare, almost menacing, but Dutton felt no real threat from the dog.

When the woman's body started slipping from the saddle, he pulled her into his arms, cradling her within his hold. "Okay. What now?" he asked the dog. "A blown tire and an unconscious woman."

With few choices, he carried her to the gate. Slight in stature, she had short, dark hair parted to the side with a streak of pearl aqua in her tousled bangs. She moaned in his arms, her first sign of regaining consciousness. Reins still tight in her hand, she kept the horse plodding along at his side.

The squealing pigs made his head pound as he searched the rocks with his foot for a key. "Don't stand there squealing at me. Help me get in."

The locked gate swung open, startling Dutton, who stepped in before it closed. Pigs' snouts, round and moist, sniffed the woman, a familiarity that eased his mind entering the gated home. The pigs were too close as Dutton struggled to take the first step, fighting them off. "I get it. You want me to help her."

The pigs quieted, their round piggy eyes watching him.

The odd dog, big and lanky, took the lead. With more important concerns, Dutton pushed aside his desire to know where he'd seen one like it before. Not much of a wilderness man, he'd spent his youth in the city roller-blading at the skate park, competing in Hapkido, a type of martial arts, and reading medical books.

"Back off so I can."

The pigs stayed on Dutton's heels, quiet except for the click of their hooves on the metal steps. Dutton glanced at the woman. "This sounds crazy, but I think the pigs understand me."

The first building, no bigger than the bedroom at his rental house, had a plank of live edge wood, painted with fairy flowers and polished to a shine, hanging overhead. *Sherlock Helm.*

When no one answered his knocking, he tried the handle. The door opened into a compact living room with a retro 50s kitchen with an ice cream style bar to his left. He stepped in and slammed the door behind him with his foot, leaving the noisy squealers and the hairy beast on the wrap-around porch.

He laid the woman on the couch and checked her pulse and respiration. She had a goose egg on her forehead. He palpated the knot, but couldn't rule out a concussion. He left the arm for later. *Good for now.*

When the pigs squealed even louder and the dog's claws against the door gave him pause, he let them in. The dog plopped on the wood floor, panting, his tongue hanging out the side of his mouth. The pigs dropped their round rumps, watching his every move.

Dutton searched her pockets. No phone and his still inside the Porsche. He needed to call 911 or find a vehicle.

"Eh . . . She rode in on a horse. I'm in the right place since there's a picture on the mantel with her in it." He turned to the pigs. "Will I find a car in those buildings below?"

The bigger pig of the two, pinky clean, grunted.

Dutton laughed. "Did you answer me?"

The pig grunted again.

Dutton ran a hand through his hair. *I'm losing my mind and following the advice of a pig.*

Closing the door behind him, leaving the animals inside, he made his way back down the steps. The gate was locked, with no visible means of opening it. Instead, he walked through the yard and entered a side door into the garage. Inside, he found a jeep with the keys still in the ignition.

Next to the oversized garage door, he found a red button on the wall and pushed. Before the door had fully opened, the big red horse greeted him with a head nod as he and Big Ears came walking through, continuing past.

Curious, Dutton followed them into an attached barn, scattering chickens as the four-hoofed animals entered their stalls and started grazing on hay.

Big Red stood in his stall, muzzle thrust inside a feed tub, bridle on, while Big Ears remained tied to the saddle horn. The horse's stank, a rank smell that reminded Dutton of the family's dog after he swam in the murky pond. Guiltily, with thoughts of leaving them there, he unhooked the lead line and disconnected the rope from the horn. Then he unbuckled every buckle on the bridle until it came off in pieces.

Soaked with perspiration, he untucked his shirt, flapping the shirttails.

With the horses free to graze, Dutton left them standing, though burdened with a saddle and canvas bags, and returned to the jeep, started the engine, and drove it from the barn. He parked the jeep near the entrance and went back up for the woman.

He let the dog lead him down the steps. At the bottom of the steps, the pink pig crossed in front of him, partially hidden by the dog, and the gate once again opened.

Stepping through, Dutton walked over to the open

jeep and set the woman onto the seat. She cried out when he withdrew his hands. Once he had her safely belted, he climbed into the driver's side and drove toward Boundary Community Hospital.

As the wheels rolled onto the pavement, the woman's head lolled his direction. Two bottle green slits opened wide and peered up at him. She jumped in her seat and cried out as her back pressed against the door, hand gripping the handle.

Dutton flashed his palm urging her to stop. "I'm a doctor. You fell off your horse. I believe you've broken your arm, though I can't say for sure without examining it, and maybe—"

"You're a doctor and you *think* I broke my arm? Why should I trust you?"

Unable to come up with a logical reason, he remembered the pigs. "Because your pigs trusted me."

"My pigs?" Her hand dropped from the handle. "What makes you think Oink and Squeal trusted you?"

"They let me in." He braked, pressing his hand on the horn as an elk crossed the road. "I carried you to the gate after you fell off the horse. One second, it's locked, and the next, it swings open. I can't explain it, but the pigs were squealing, and then the gate opened. It had to be them."

She noticeably relaxed, propping her back against the seat. When she looked at him again, she smiled, the corners of her eyes crinkling with what appeared to be delight.

"You believe me?" he asked.

"Sure."

He thought her smile hypnotic. "Good. Because I'm not sure I believe it myself. Did your pigs actually let me through the gate?"

"Sure enough. Otherwise, you wouldn't have gotten in." Her eyes shot open wide enough to pop out of the sockets. "What about Wolf?"

"What wolf?" Dutton kept his eyes on the road, more concerned about getting her to the hospital than paying attention to what she said.

"My wolf? He just let you carry me?"

"Oh. You mean the dog." He glanced at her. "He's big. What kind is he?"

"A wolf."

Dutton's mind raced as he retraced his steps to figure out how he got himself into this mess. *Ah, the Porsche.*

"Never heard of that breed."

"It isn't a breed. Wolf isn't a dog. He's a wolf."

Dutton swerved into the left lane before jerking back over. "That dog was a wolf?"

"No. That wolf is a wolf."

"*Jesus Murphy!* He didn't act like a wild animal."

Juliette placed a hand on her forehead as she tried to sit upright. "I think I fell off of Indy a couple of times on the way back. Passed out or something. I feel dizzy."

"Indy? Is that what you call Big Red?"

The pain kept Juliette from saying something hateful at her horse being called Big Red. "Yeah."

"Lie back and take it easy," he told her. "Bonners Ferry isn't more than a *kitty-corner* from here according to the map. Would you know the way to the hospital?"

One eye open, Juliette looked out the window. "Keep going straight and turn right on Comanche Street, then another right on Kaniksu. The hospital is on the left."

When they pulled to the emergency entrance, Dutton got out, entered the building, and returned with a wheelchair. Juliette seated, he pushed her through the open door and up to the check-in window. "I'm Doctor Dutton Bae. I have a patient with a fractured arm and a possible concussion. Is a room available?"

The middle-aged woman with an unfriendly scowl glanced up at Dutton. "Hold your britches, doctor. I need a name first."

"Her name?" Dutton studied the woman's face as if the injured party's name would come to him.

Juliette leaned forward, saving him from announcing he didn't know her name. "Juliette Gardiner."

"And you? Any ID, doctor?"

Dutton opened his wallet, handing her his driver's license.

"You work for this hospital?" she asked.

"Yes."

"You an emergency doctor?" She handed him back his license with a doubtful expression.

"Family medicine."

"Are you Miss Gardiner's physician?"

"No."

Juliette leaned forward a second time. "Yes. He is my family doctor."

Dutton's brows furrowed, his eyes cast on Juliette as the lady behind the counter entered his name in Juliette's record. "If you and Miss Gardiner will have a seat, I will call you once a room is available. One of our emergency doctors will tend to her." She hadn't bothered to find Dutton in the system.

A forty-nine-minute wait irritated Dutton. A patient care technician drew up Juliette's paperwork, and Dutton wheeled her into room 104, helping her onto the bed.

The door opened, and a woman entered, blowing a loose strand of hair from her face. She looked tired, judging by the circles under her eyes. "Jules, what happened?"

"I got rushed by a grizzly."

"A grizzly? When are you going to stay out of the woods? Get married. Have a couple of kids."

Without waiting for a response, the doctor turned to Dutton. "Hi. I'm Doctor Susan Tenny. You with her?"

"No. Well, yes. It's a long story."

Susan lifted the blanket off Juliette. "Let's have a look at that injury. This is quite a splint job." She turned to Dutton, smiling instantly. "Is this your handiwork?"

"Impressive, isn't it?" Dutton teased.

"Quite."

Juliette narrowed her eyes at Dutton. "I did it."

"I figured as much. Impressive for a conservation officer. A complicated task, considering you had only one hand." She took out a penlight from her pocket and flashed it across Juliette's eyes. "Tell me. How did you survive a grizzly attack with only nonthreatening injuries?"

"Indy, my horse, got scared when the grizzly attacked. He slammed into a tree. My arm broke. The bear is dead, and I'm here."

"Well, that wouldn't have been my first guess. So you killed the bear, even with one arm broken?"

"That or die, so yeah, I killed him."

"And when did this happen?"

Juliette didn't know the answer. There were gaps in her memory. "Maybe today. Maybe yesterday. We were five miles from home. I think I passed out a couple of times, but I'm not sure. Last thing I remember is shooting the bear. That is until I ended up in the jeep with him at the steering wheel."

"And you are?" The doctor directed her question to Dutton.

"A complete stranger with a flat tire. My name is Dutton Bae. I moved here from British Columbia after accepting a temporary residency at the clinic."

"Doctor Bae?" Susan asked. "I heard about you. I see you're listed as Miss Gardiner's family physician. Welcome. I imagine we'll run into each other occasionally."

Eyes blurry from the headache, Juliette thought Susan had tried to hide a smile as she looked down at the chart. When she raised her head, it was gone.

"Okay, Jules. Time to remove this tape and makeshift splint to see what we're dealing with."

A fiery pain seared inside Juliette's arm as Susan pulled the tape away and lifted the arm away from her chest.

Both the radius and ulna had snapped.

Juliette remembered seeing the visual image as the bones snapped seconds before she fired the rifle. Crying now, she never noticed when a nurse entered and inserted an IV, never heard Dutton and Doctor Susan discuss the severity, never noticed being rushed into the operating room. The pain consumed her.

Acknowledgements

I'd like to thank my wonderful writing friends and family who encouraged me during the writing of *Alone*. Vivienne, Dan, Helen, Darlene, and my lovely family for supporting me. Without you, *Alone* would have ended up another story buried on my hard drive.

I'd also like to thank my editor, Sarah Hendess and cover artist, Michelle Argyle Park.